BRETT DEVLIN EASTON

SEALs of Honor, Books 11–13

Dale Mayer

SEALS OF HONOR, BOOKS 11–13
Beverly Dale Mayer
Valley Publishing Ltd.

ISBN-13: 978-1-773360-61-4
Print Edition

Books in This Series:

Mason: SEALs of Honor, Book 1

Hawk: SEALs of Honor, Book 2

Dane: SEALs of Honor, Book 3

Swede: SEALs of Honor, Book 4

Shadow: SEALs of Honor, Book 5

Cooper: SEALs of Honor, Book 6

Markus: SEALs of Honor, Book 7

Evan: SEALs of Honor, Book 8

Mason's Wish: SEALs of Honor, Book 9

Chase: SEALs of Honor, Book 10

Brett: SEALs of Honor, Book 11

Devlin: SEALs of Honor, Book 12

Easton: SEALs of Honor, Book 13

Ryder: SEALs of Honor, Book 14

Macklin: SEALs of Honor, Book 15

Corey: SEALs of Honor, Book 16

Warrick: SEALs of Honor, Book 17

Tanner: SEALs of Honor, Book 18

Jackson: SEALs of Honor, Book 19

Kanen: SEALs of Honor, Book 20

Nelson: SEALs of Honor, Book 21

Taylor: SEALs of Honor, Book 22

Colton: SEALs of Honor, Book 23

About This Boxed Set

Brett

High seas terror and international intrigue all wrapped up in homegrown problems of the loved-and-lost-and-found-again variety…

Rescuing hostages trapped on a yacht in the middle of the open ocean is a routine mission for an elite SEAL like Brett. But when one of the hostages turns out to be his ex-girlfriend and her kids, the same-old, same-old takes a turn for the discombobulating. Particularly because she's single again…

As a way to heal, Ceci walked away from Brett years ago, straight into another intense relationship. Now she's a widow raising two kids. Her plan to stay single and safe from heartbreak feels a million miles away when she comes face-to-face with her rescuer—the man she's never been able to forget. Unfortunately, "safe" is no longer in the cards anymore…in life or love.

Devlin

Cupid apparently has a soft spot for SEALs and he's lined his sights up on Devlin next. He's not looking for romance, but he finds the right woman in the worst possible place.

As part of a military unit helping train Afghan soldiers, Devlin is learning how to use the latest combat drones. After a murder is committed on the base, suspicion falls on the drone's drop-dead-gorgeous designer. Devlin can't stop himself from running to her rescue. Following their return Stateside, another employee in the same company turns up dead. Once again, all evidence points to the designer.

Bristol had no choice but to take her latest drone models to war-torn Afghanistan, given how behind schedule she is in her work and because her boss is pressuring her. The last thing she expected was disaster to strike and, for all the world, *she* looks like the one to blame. When the bodies pile up and her research goes unfathomably missing along with her best friend, she's determined to find out what's going on, damn the danger.

Devlin has made it his mission to keep her safe while she seems to be doing everything in her power to make his job— and resisting her—impossible.

Easton

Trips to Canada's wilderness for joint military training are something Easton always looks forward to. Meeting the lovely photographer contracted to capture the base and trainees for new marketing materials adds a whole new twist to a straight-forward routine…a twist with both a light and dark undertone.

Summer tends to get lost in her art so she's been called ditzy, absent-minded, and a host of less flattering names. She doesn't let any of it bother her. Her passionate nature has a rewarding creative outlet, and she adores traveling for her work. Unfortunately, her undistracted concentration means she isn't always taking care of herself the way she should. So, when she's attacked, Easton is the one who realizes she's unwittingly stumbled into a dangerous situation and she needs his help to stay safe.

The escalation of violence has Easton holding Summer close enough to kiss, close enough to shatter her ability to focus on a single other thing…

Sign up to be notified of all Dale's releases here!

https://geni.us/DaleNews

BRETT

SEALs of Honor, Book 11

Dale Mayer

CHAPTER 1

BRETT CHAPMAN BROKE through the surface of the water. He reached out a hand and touched the sleek side of the yacht. Moving silently through the dark night, the water lapping around his body, he made his way to the lower deck ladder of one of the world's ultra-yachts. Unfortunately, the Million Dollar Baby was in trouble. Big trouble.

The yacht had been taken by pirates, the passengers and crew held as hostages. The captain had managed to send out a distress call before they were boarded. Brett's unit had been called up soon after. He knew several of the guests. His mother had married into a wealthy and boisterous Greek family eighteen years ago. His life had never been the same. It had just been the two of them before, and now it seemed like there were hundreds of family members in his life. As they'd accepted his mom and him, she in turn had adopted all of them.

According to the intel several of his extended family were onboard.

With any luck his mother hadn't heard the news yet. Or there would be hell to pay.

Brett had shipped out within hours of the distress call. The unknown at this point in time was who was behind the pirates – if anyone. This area of the ocean along the African coastline had seen much turmoil lately with similar attacks.

It had calmed down somewhat in the last few months, but the captain had no business bringing the yacht into this area given the recent dangers.

He scaled the ladder onto the lower deck. This was one of the biggest models he'd ever seen. The deck offered a large park-like setting that opened to the ocean. He presumed there was some kind of security measure that closed off this area during a storm.

Security lights shone low on the walls of the deck. It was deserted too. Next on his list to search was the engine room. So far he hadn't seen anyone – crew – or pirate. He took several minutes to reach his destination. There he quickly scoped out the gleaming room to realize it would take an engineer to handle this state of the art system, and none of the pirates were likely to be as technologically advanced as that – he hoped. With any luck the maintenance crew was still alive and capable of dealing with any issues in the yacht.

Using the blueprints he'd memorized, Brett moved quickly through the decks. As he cleared each floor he updated his team. He was set to meet Chase in four minutes, one deck up. As he arrived on the third floor he realized these smaller rooms were likely the crew's living quarters. He did a quick sweep through the bedrooms. The first three were empty and as he approached the fourth he heard a sound that made his heart freeze.

A child's cries of distress.

He went to open the door but found it locked from the inside. He tapped once and then tapped two more times. The door cracked opened and a terrified woman's face peered out. He brushed her backwards and slipped into the room out of sight. And he choked back a shocked gasp.

Two little children were wrapped around the woman's

legs. He knew of them, but hadn't met either yet. And he knew exactly how old they were. The boy, Jimmy, was four and the girl, Jennifer, was almost two.

Their mother, Ceci, was on the outside edge of that huge extended family his mother had married into. And the only woman he'd ever loved.

In his night gear he knew she couldn't recognize him. And she had to be terrified of his weapons.

He held a finger up to his mouth and whispered, "It's okay, Ceci. It's me, Brett. You need to remain here with the children, and stay as quiet as you can be."

She gasped in shock then her face lit up in relief and joy.

He squatted down to the boy and said in a low voice, "Jimmy, you have to be very, very quiet until I come back here and help you, and your mom, and sister off the boat, okay?"

The little boy sniffled, his eyes huge, lower lip trembling. But he straightened up and nodded. Good. At a single rap on the door, Brett moved quickly and without another word, he slipped into the hallway where Chase waited for him. As they moved away Chase said, "Twelve hostiles are on the top floor above us. All hostages are with them."

"Weapons?"

"Machine guns and grenades, a few handguns. Nothing major."

Brett snorted. It said much about the type of work they did that those weapons weren't considered major.

Still, that was good news. He really didn't like facing rocket launchers. All criminals appeared to have access to the latest and greatest. In close quarters like this, it was a recipe for disaster. Then again so were grenades.

In silence, he went to the main stairwell and slowly crept

up one landing. When this went down it would happen fast. They needed to take out as many hostiles as they could to narrow the odds before the others found out they were onboard. Stealth was paramount.

Too many men with guns and happy trigger fingers.

And too many innocent people to get hurt.

Under the cover of darkness, they moved steadily through the ship. Just as they were reaching the next floor gunfire erupted at the other end.

They raced to the aft of the ship and the sound of returned fire. As they approached, a group of passengers raced down the staircase toward them screaming.

"Take them off the yacht," Chase yelled to Brett.

With a quick glance between them, the gunfire now heavy and hard, they split up. Chase went up to help while Brett kept moving the passengers down to the rescue boats.

As soon as he delivered them into the crew's hands, they took over, leaving Brett free to race back down to where he'd found Ceci and the kids.

He knocked on the door hard and called, "Ceci, it's me, open up."

A gunshot fired through the door barely missing his head.

"Shit." He didn't have time for this. Moving back, he reached out from the side and gave a powerhouse kick, popping the door open. Bullets whistled through the open doorway. But he was already on the ground and lining up for the shot. The gunman stood in front of Ceci. She huddled behind him, the babies in her arms. There was the shot... He took it, dropping the gunmen to the floor, a bullet through the forehead. Brett jumped to his feet. "Ceci, let's go now."

He grabbed Jimmy in his arms, and ushered Ceci with Jennifer clutched in hers out the door, then he raced them down to the boats.

The gunfire ceased.

The silence ominous after so much noise.

He knew that could be good or really bad. Transferring the kids to the open arms of the crew, he gave Ceci a hard glance, noted the panic and fear in her eyes and said, "You'll be safe here."

At least he hoped so.

He raced back upstairs. Just as he was about to creep up over the last stairs he caught sight of a hostile hiding under a corner of one of the rowboats, a gun lining up towards Mason's head.

Brett never even hesitated. He pulled the trigger. The pirate collapsed.

Mason turned, weapon in hand, instantly lining up on the new threat, saw Brett, saw the gunman, then gave a quick nod.

Brett snuck over to where Mason stood. "Are we in the clear?"

Mason whispered back, "Not yet. Waiting for Hawk."

Chase frowned. That wasn't good. That meant... He slipped back into his hiding place. It wasn't a long wait. Two pirates marched Hawk into the center of the deck, semi-automatic rifles prodding him forward.

The pirates started yelling at the SEALs.

Chase didn't understand the words – the language being one he wasn't familiar with. But the gist of the meaning wasn't hard to understand. They could all go to hell, and if they didn't do it fast enough they were going to shoot Hawk.

That wasn't going to happen. Brett ran through the

blueprints in his mind and realized from the level below there were stairs that came up on the far side of the pirates. That's how they'd marched Hawk up. And if he could get there fast enough it was how he'd get the drop on them. He quickly slipped down the stairs, crossed the deck, and snuck up that way. From his new vantage point, he could see his unit were all holding weapons trained on the hostiles. These guys didn't care. They planned to shoot Hawk and go down in a hail of fire figuring their own lives were already forfeited.

Brett lined up a shot, waiting for them to give him an opportunity. The second man lowered his arm just a fraction – but it was enough. Hawk was out of the line of fire. Shots rang and the first man dropped. Brett shot the second one.

At the sound of gunfire behind him Hawk turned and said, "Thanks."

Brett grinned. "Anytime."

They did a full sweep of all the decks but didn't flush out anymore gunmen. On that note all of the hostages were released back onto the yacht and the dead gunmen taken over to the boats. As far as he was concerned the gunmen could go into the water for the sharks. Thankfully it wasn't his decision.

His concern was for Ceci. He headed down to the rescue boats to find her. One of the men said, "She won't go back on the yacht. And so far, she's refused to be checked over." Brett walked across to sit down beside her and the kids. Both kids had their faces burrowed against her, and her arms were locked around them. He sat down beside her and gently rubbed her shoulder.

"Ceci, are you okay?"

She nodded, her gaze huge, wordless.

"It's going to be okay. We got them all."

"Good," she whispered, glancing down at Jimmy who'd lifted his head to stare up at Brett.

Jimmy opened his mouth and said, "Did you kill them? Did you kill the bad men?"

Brett nodded. "All the bad men are gone. They can't hurt you anymore." Jimmy didn't need to know the details – just needed to know the bogeymen were never coming back.

To Ceci he said, "Why don't you want to return to the yacht?"

"I do not want to go back on there – or on any like it – ever again." She shuddered. "You don't know what it was like. The threats they made." Her arms squeezed the two young children, clutching them close to her.

Brett looked down at the little boy. "Did they hurt the kids?"

Jimmy's bottom lip trembled. "He pushed me."

Brett reached out and touched the little boy's cheek gently. "The bogeymen won't hurt you anymore."

The little boy nodded his head. "My name's Jimmy."

Brett smiled and held out his hand. "And I'm Brett. I knew your mom a few years ago."

Jimmy brightened. "You're one of the good guys?"

The little girl beside him pulled her head out from against her mom's shoulders to stare up at him. "Hi." As soon as the word was out of her mouth she shoved her thumb in.

Brett's heart melted. "Yes, I'm definitely one of the good guys. No more bad guys here now." He crouched lower brushing a blonde ringlet back off her face. "Hi to you too."

Her thumb popped out, and she gave him a toothy grin as she tried to stand up on her mom's knee. Ceci hugged her tight.

"How did you come to be on the yacht?" Brett asked.

"We were supposed to come for just a few days to get away." She waved her arm aimlessly in the air. "To have a break. A holiday."

"Do you know all of these people?"

"No," she said with a note of defeat in her voice. "But Jason Turner was coming. And he was allowed to bring a friend so he asked me to come."

That made sense. Jason Turner was part of Ceci's extended family and therefore part of Brett's. He also thought Jason might've been Jimmy Senior's best friend. Only Jimmy had been killed in Iraq several years ago. As he looked down at the little girl, he realized he probably never had a chance to even see his own daughter.

"They're beautiful," he said to Ceci. "Jimmy would be very proud of you and of them."

Ceci's eyes filled with tears, her lower lip trembled in a movement all too similar to her children. "Oh, I don't think so," she whispered. "I put them in danger. How is that anything to be proud of?"

"This is not your fault," he said. "I don't know why it was sailing in these waters or how it came to the attention of the pirates, but yachts scream money and the pirates are desperate. However, it's over. You can all go home and get back to your normal lives."

She smiled mistily up at him and said, "Thanks to you."

He straightened and looked back toward the huge yacht. "Not just me. I come as part of a team."

"Thank your team for me, will you?"

He hopped onto the yacht, turned back and waved. "I will. You take care of those kids and yourself."

The zodiac in which she was sitting slowly pulled away and headed toward shore. Onboard was one injured passenger and Ceci with her kids. As he watched the churning wake streak out across the water he had to wonder if he would ever see Ceci again.

CHAPTER 2

"MOMMY, WHEN CAN I go outside?"

"Not right now. We'll go later." As if. Ceci stood staring down at her son, wondering what had happened to her life. Getting away from the yacht had seemed like such a life-changing event. Until everyone realized her passport and those of her children were missing along with her purse. Hence her current residence at the US Embassy in Somalia until her new paperwork arrived. That was where the crew from the rescue ship had brought her. The injured passenger from the yacht had been taken to the hospital.

She was stuck here for the foreseeable future until the damn paperwork could be taken care of. Who knew such delays could occur? Jason had called several times checking up on her. He'd been considerate and pushy in a back and forth way. As if he'd had expectations and having missed out was angling for more. It was only through the phone calls that she'd realized how badly she'd misread the situation. She was *not* interested. Not like that. Not with him.

Jimmy started crying.

"I promise we'll go out in a few minutes." But she'd said that over and over.

So often he no longer believed her. Then again, she wasn't a good liar. And even worse at saying no. Look at Jason, he still didn't get it. It wasn't fair of her to not want to be with Jason because of pirates, but it was the last thing she wanted to be reminded of. Then again she hadn't encouraged him to think they were heading in that direction. She liked him fine – but as a friend. She winced. He'd be upset at that phrase.

She'd married a soldier fully prepared for him to go to war and maybe not come home one day. It was only when she lost Jimmy that she realized she hadn't been prepared at all. She hadn't faced the reality of what life without him meant. The emotional devastation not only for herself but also for the kids. The financial responsibilities were a separate reality check altogether.

The pirates had just brought it all back again. Even worse, it had placed her children in danger. And somehow Jason was to blame. In her head, she knew that was wrong. It made no sense. He'd been trying to help her out, hoping to give her a bit of a break. And she'd been so excited hanging out on the yacht. Why the hell had she assumed they'd have a lovely week away without a romantic entanglement? She'd been desperate for a bit of fun. When the opportunity had presented itself she'd jumped at the chance. She was such an idiot.

Now she found it hard to even step outside these very nice accommodations to walk around the supposedly safe property. She didn't want to be here. Her kids didn't want to be here.

Even worse it was getting harder to keep these fears hidden. All the well-meaning family was crowding in on her mental space asking why she wasn't out enjoying the experience. Pretty soon she was going to have to admit she was terrified to go outside. And yet she was in the US Embassy – as safe as she could get.

Why was it she couldn't have the opposite reaction? Shouldn't she be going out and enjoying every day knowing she'd been given a second chance? But it had happened so fast, so out of the blue that she found herself looking for the boogeyman around every corner.

And then there was Brett.

Seeing him had brought up a ton of other conflicting emotions from before Jimmy. They'd been an item once. Years ago. She'd broken off their relationship, dating several other men before meeting Jimmy. The man she'd ended up marrying.

But she'd loved Brett first.

She sat down in the living room, the kids at her feet playing with Lego blocks, wondering how her life had gone so wrong. Brett also represented trauma in her past. Yet it didn't feel that way now. She'd regretted breaking up with him soon after. There'd been desperation in her actions when she'd hooked up with Jimmy. As if afraid life was passing her by and all the good guys were gone. Foolish – she wasn't even thirty yet.

When she'd met Jimmy her life had changed, and she'd known that was exactly what she wanted. But as she looked back it wasn't that she'd wanted Jimmy as much as she'd wanted to settle down.

Now look at her.

She was a widow with two kids, and Brett looked to be the same as he always was. Actually, better. There was a dangerous edge to him now that was damn sexy. And he'd packed a punch before. Too bad. She'd lost her bikini body after having kids. She never regretted having them, but at times it was hard to see herself as a sexy woman and not just a mother.

She leaned back against the couch and closed her eyes. She just wanted to sleep. To have the world go away. Instead, the phone rang. An insistent chime she couldn't ignore.

She wasn't going to answer it. But it rang and it rang and it rang.

"Mom, the phone," Jimmy said as he leaned against her knee and stared up at her. Even she could see the worry in his eyes. She reached down and pulled him into her arms and hugged him close. "I know, baby. It's probably just another reporter. I don't want anything more to do with them."

That had been her excuse every time.

"Reporters yucky," he said. He let her squeeze him for another quick second before he squirmed out of her arms and slid down to the floor back to his Legos.

If only her life was that easy.

She sat down on the floor to help him build a truck.

A hard knock on her door interrupted the idyllic haven she'd formed. The harsh sound sent shock waves through her system. The children immediately started crying. A response to her fearful reaction more than at the visitor.

"It's okay, guys. It's snack time."

Immediately the tears dried up and the kids raced to the door. She'd ordered food to their room for every meal after the first day. The kids knew the system well.

She felt a little bit guilty because she knew she hadn't ordered anything. But if it stopped them from being afraid then she was all for the little white lies of life.

She peered through the peephole. And froze. It was Brett.

Shocked, her forehead dropped against the door.

"Open the door, Ceci." His tone was calm, quiet, and determined.

Shit. He'd never let her walk away from this. She opened the door. "Wow, what you doing here?"

"How long did you think you were going to be able to hide?" he asked her, his gaze carefully assessing her.

She frowned at him. Not sure exactly how he'd found out, she said cautiously, "I'm not hiding at all."

"My mother phoned." That's all he said. He leaned against the door jamb and crossed his arms over his chest, apparently unconcerned at the turmoil in her heart.

"Your mother?" Damn that woman. She was the most caring, loving, interfering woman Ceci had ever met. But she was also determined to manipulate the family, extended as well, as far as she could reach. She didn't understand boundaries. Hell, she blasted through every one she came to as if they weren't there. Especially if it was for *your* own good. "I'm sure it must have been nice to talk to her."

Brett walked in. She glared at him. "You could wait until you are invited."

"And that would be when hell froze over." He stopped and stared at the pile of Legos on the floor then back at the two little kids wrapped around her legs. She watched as he immediately sat cross-legged on the floor and in a calm and quiet voice said, "Hi guys, remember me? Of course, I'm not wearing my night gear right now, but I'm the man that carried you to the boat."

Jimmy's face brightened up cautiously. Jennifer's thumb immediately went into her mouth.

"I'm one of the good guys, remember?" Brett said with an easy smile.

Jennifer smiled at him. The thumb came out and she

toddled closer, her arms out. He scooped her up and gave her a quick hug. Then he perched her on one knee. Not to be outdone Jimmy raced over and sat down on the other.

Ceci watched in amazement at the easy acceptance of the stranger in their midst.

Brett smiled at him. "I came to see if you guys were doing okay?"

"We want to go outside," Jimmy said in a teary voice, having no idea he just broke a dam wide open.

"That's a great idea. I'm sure your mother has shown you the playground in the backyard. Maybe we can go down there." He raised that gaze and pinned her in place.

Immediately she crossed her arms over her chest and started chewing on her bottom lip. And here she'd been hoping to keep things quiet a little bit longer.

Jennifer shook her head. "Mommy says no."

Brett uncrossed his legs and stood up with both of the kids still in his arms. They both squealed and clutched at him.

"Well I think we can fix that right now," he said laughing. But there was a note of steel in his voice and she…

Ceci didn't dare raise her gaze. She couldn't.

"Ceci, let's grab shoes and coats and get these kids out to the playground."

Both kids squealed and tried to squirm out of his arms. He set them down and they ran for shoes and coats.

Ceci shook her head in a quiet desperation and said, "No, not today. We're not going outside today."

"Or any day?" Brett stood in front of her, and she realized she hadn't fooled him one bit. Brett was bound and determined to force her outside. Damn his mother anyway.

Completely overruling her, he had the children dressed

and standing at the front door in minutes. When she protested, he placed a finger across her lips and shoved her arms into a vest. He opened the apartment door, pulled out a pair of slip on shoes and dropped them in front of her.

"Put them on." He stood implacable in front of her. No threat, but absolutely determined she was going to do as he willed.

Trembling she stepped into the footwear and stood before them. He wasn't going to carry her out.

And there was no way she was going outside any other way.

BRETT HAD NO idea what was going on inside her head, but it was obvious she'd become terrified of the outside world. And that had to stop now. It wasn't healthy. For her or the kids. She obviously hadn't recovered from the hijacking.

"We're doing this for the kids," he said, watching the stiffness leave her slight frame. "They need fresh air. They can't stay cooped up inside all the time regardless of what you want."

She wasn't really fighting going out, but she wasn't exactly giving her okay either. He pushed her out into the hallway, dragged out the stroller he'd found in the closet and set Jennifer in to buckle her up. Tucking his arm through Ceci's, he walked the family toward the park.

Whether she wanted to or not they were going outside.

Beside him, Ceci walked like a robot, not looking around but staring straight ahead. She didn't pull her arm away from him, but neither did she actively hold his.

Whether she hated him or not wasn't the issue right now. She needed to get out of this prison she'd created for herself.

"Any word on when you'll get your passports?"

She shook her head. "No," she muttered. "I never thought I'd be in an embassy for a week."

At least she was talking to him. "It won't be much longer."

"Then why haven't we gotten them yet?" she asked. "Jason and the others made it back to the US safe and sound."

"You left your documentation on the ship. Did anyone try to find them?"

"The pirates took my purse. No idea where they put it." She shook her head. "This is just a comedy of errors." She turned to glare at him. "And there's nothing funny about it."

"There's something odd in the paperwork for the children," he said. "I checked with some of the people I know in the embassy. It's what they are trying to fix."

"That's the same line of garbage I got when trying to get death benefits after Jimmy died." She shrugged. "I think governments just like to make things difficult."

"You left the country without anything to prove the children were yours."

"It never occurred to me. They said I didn't need anything but our passports. I *had* those."

"Is Jimmy listed as the father on the birth certificates?"

"He's listed on the registration papers I sent in. I never did get copies of their birth certificates, so I don't know." She shrugged. "Who knew something simple could turn out to be so difficult."

"It's not that they are doubting that the children are yours or that you're an American citizen because they can prove that part, but they need to have a paper trail. They are expediting the paperwork to get that accomplished."

She snorted. "Expediting, right. I've been here a week already, remember?"

"Part of the reason for the delay is the national holiday. Two of them. One in each country. Not everyone lives on your time."

"I just want to go home," she muttered.

"It's only a few more days."

"Says you."

He glanced over at her and saw she was once again chewing on her bottom lip. He reached up and smoothed his finger across it. "Stop," he scolded gently. "You'll hurt yourself."

She gave him a shuttered look and walked over to the bench at the back corner of the grounds. They were still in the secure compound. For all intents and purposes they were on US soil here. She was safe.

"You could look at the bright side. Realize you are safe and sound and this just shows government bureaucracy at its best."

"I know." She watched the kids scream for joy in the sandbox. "That makes me feel even worse. I don't feel safe here. I feel like something else is going to happen, and it could be even worse. Although I escaped the pirate nightmare in my head it's still not over because I'm not home."

"Sure, but this is an adventure."

She shot him a fulminating look.

He grinned. "How many holidays have you taken since the kids were born?"

She snorted. "The yacht was to be the first one."

"Then make the most of this. It could be years before you get a chance to go overseas again."

"Sitting in the US Embassy, stuck for all intents and

purposes until pencil pushers get my paperwork in order, is not my idea of a holiday," she snapped.

"Look, I get it. You're pissed off, frustrated and probably still dealing with fear from the pirates. But this isn't so bad," he said with a grin. "You're not in any danger, your passports will be ready in a day or two. So, think about the kids and do something fun for them."

At her glare and thick silence, he realized he shouldn't have opened his mouth. But he'd never been one to hold back. "Look, I'm sorry. I understand this isn't easy and I've done a ton of traveling so maybe it's easier for me, but why aren't you enjoying the time you have here?"

"Because I'm scared," she whispered. She bowed her head. "And what does that say about me?" She gave a painful laugh. "The whole time I was married to Jimmy I wanted to travel. I wanted to go see the world. Then as soon as I get the opportunity to do just that it's without Jimmy and all hell breaks loose. It was one of the big issues between us. Then I lost him. And now all I can think about is that I must've made his life miserable and it was over something I knew nothing about. Traveling is not what everyone says it is. I just want to go home."

"You feel guilty?" He reached over and laced her fingers through his. "Jimmy is gone. You can't change that. And I doubt he would've blamed you."

She stared down at their fingers and then squeezed his tight. "Have you ever made a decision in the heat of the moment, and all you do is look back and regret it?"

There was an odd silence. Then in a hoarse voice he said, "Absolutely."

CHAPTER 3

S HE STUDIED HIM intently. "What decision do you regret?"

He stayed silent, a small smile playing on the corner of his lips. "You first."

Why hadn't she kept her mouth shut? She shook her head, and muttered, "I can't tell you. At least not yet."

"That's okay," he said. "We're all entitled to our secrets."

A gentle silence ensued between them. As if the chasm had been approached, and a bridge had been built, but neither had made it to the other end. Ceci tilted her head to the sun and let the warm rays soothe her tattered soul. It was stupid that one incident a week ago should still ravage her peace of mind so badly. But it brought old traumas to the surface. Ones she thought she'd dealt with. Was this post-traumatic stress? Surely one incident shouldn't ruin her life.

"It's as if I'm still in danger."

His other hand reached over and covered hers. She glanced down to see her fingers gripping his hand so tightly her knuckles were white. Immediately she tried to loosen them. With his hand holding one of hers she stretched out the fingers of the other.

"Is that because you didn't see the gunmen after they were killed? To know they couldn't come after you again?" Brett asked quietly. "Or because you didn't stay on the yacht as everyone else did to pick up the pieces of their lives? Everyone has to find closure in their own way. What is it going to take for you?"

"If I knew that, I would have done it," she snapped irritably. "Sorry. I didn't mean that to sound as short tempered as it did." She could sense Brett's gaze on her face.

"You acknowledge that the danger is over. That you're away from the ship. Away from the gunmen…and yet, still hiding away inside."

"You think I don't know that?" she cried. "It's like a fine edge of sandpaper is rubbing along my nerves. As if there is something secret going on around me…but no one will tell me." She shrugged. "I know it sounds stupid. Why do you think I'm so irritable? So angry? I keep telling myself to stop it. To grow up. Stop being such a fool. And yet I can't. Instinct is screaming at me to run." She leaned back against the bench and closed her eyes, her arms now crossed over her chest. "It makes no sense, but I can't ignore it."

"I'm not going to argue with instinct," he said. "In my business, it's huge. It's what keeps us alive."

"Sure, but you're one of those over the top macho men in the military. You're trained to do and be everything." She gave a self-mocking laugh. "Me, I'm nothing. I'm a mom of two beautiful little kids. That's it." She refused to open her eyes even as she felt Brett shift beside her. She knew he was looking at her. Searching for something to say. She could sense the intensity of his gaze as it wandered across her face.

"Do you really feel that way?"

She bit her lip. "I hate that I do." Her eyes flew open as she stared into his huge, warm eyes. He'd always been so accepting of her faults. She, on the other hand, never had any kind of tolerance for them. "Do you hear me? Do you hear the whiny brat inside? It's not who I am. It's not who I want to be. But right now, it's like I'm stuck in this space. I don't recognize who I am." She waved her hand toward the children. "It's so hard to try to keep it contained, so I don't affect them with my foolishness."

"Let's go back to this instinct thing. Let's examine that a little more closely."

That prompted a choked laugh from her. "Fine. What's to examine? I feel like I'm in danger and I don't know why." She glared at him, daring him to laugh at her.

"Right now? At this very moment? While I'm sitting here beside you?"

"No…" she said slowly. "But it's there in the background."

He sat back. "When did that feeling start?"

"As soon as I arrived here." She looked around the high walled garden. "The place is secure, but I always know outside of that wall it's a very non-secure world."

"Is that where this coming from?"

"I don't know." She waved her hand back to the building. "The first day it seemed normal, people were talking to me, there were several conversations as we dealt with the paperwork. I was given the small apartment to stay in with the kids. Everything seemed happy, normal. At the time I was still in a state of shock. I slept every chance I could. We slept, ate, slept and ate again. Anytime I ventured out, it seemed like there were eyes everywhere. There was never anyone obvious, nothing wrong that I could see…so I stayed inside."

"Okay, I'll accept that. There has been a lot of strife with the embassy. I doubt I can get answers, but I know people who can. Discussions going on that don't concern you can affect the atmosphere. If they heard about an imminent attack and are preparing for it, I don't imagine in this case they'd explain it to you."

She looked at him. "Why not?"

"Because in their mind it would have nothing to do with you. The attack would be on the embassy itself. You would be collateral damage although they'd do their best to keep you safe," he said. "US embassies have been attacked before. There's no guarantee this one's safe at this time, but there's no reason to believe otherwise. I would prefer to have you home, but until we get your passports in order this is the best place for you."

"Great," she said under her breath.

He laughed. "I'm not trying to scare you, but given your sense of something being off, I'm trying to help you understand how safe you really are here." He looked around the garden. "I have no idea what's going on with the locals, but there's always strife. Still, if there's going to be an attack then the embassy makes a sensible target," he admitted. "But it's not likely."

She hopped to her feet. "On that note I think I'll go back inside. Unless it's not safe."

"It's as safe outside as it is inside," he said. "This area is under surveillance and there's heavy security that you cannot even begin to see."

She let out a heavy sigh. "I'm being foolish, aren't I?"

"There's nothing foolish about it." He stood up and walked over to Jimmy and squatted down beside him. "How about we go for a walk around the grounds? Your mom needs to move a little bit."

Jimmy ran toward her, and sandy fingers and all, she picked him up, laughed and gave him a great big swirling hug. She placed him down on the ground as Jennifer toddled toward her.

"It's really nice outside, Mommy," Jimmy said.

They happily wandered the many pathways of the lawn and the gardens. A slow meandering stroll rather than a walk to let the children go their pace. And it did feel good to be outside.

"Thank you."

She felt that assessing gaze but she refused to look at him. "You're welcome."

BRETT DIDN'T KNOW what to think. He didn't want to downplay her fears. Many times in his life his instincts had saved him. Who was he to criticize her right now? Time would tell if her instincts were true or not.

He could make a few inquiries and see if there was anything going on in the embassy, not that anybody would feel free to talk to him about it. As they strolled toward the back entrance she froze.

He grabbed her arm. In a low voice, he said, "What's the matter?"

She pointed up to the top floor of the building. "I just thought I saw somebody in our apartment."

His gaze traveled to the window she pointed out. "Are you sure that yours?"

She nodded. "We look down on this playground all the time."

"Cleaning service?"

"There hasn't been one yet," she said softly.

"Then let's go find out."

After a moment of silence as they walked toward the

back door she realized she was gripping his hand hard.

She murmured for his ears only, "I'm afraid I'm really losing it."

"Don't think that. We don't know anything yet. We'll go check it out."

"And then what?"

"We'll deal with that when we know more."

She sighed. "You're always so logical."

"It's who I am."

Back in the small apartment, Brett entered first and gave a quick check over then opened the door for Ceci and the kids. She walked around and shrugged. "Everything seems to be in order."

At the window, he studied the garden below. She had pointed out the correct window. But if there had been anybody here they were long gone now.

He turned his attention to the room. There was no sign there had been an unwanted visitor.

Jimmy had already plopped down in the middle of the heap of Lego blocks seemingly unconcerned.

Brett gave another quick glance around the small area and said, "What are you doing about food?"

"There is a dining room downstairs that we're welcome to go to for meals, but I only went there once. I didn't care to go down again so I order up."

"Then I'll go downstairs and see if I can muster up something for the family."

"Hot dogs. I want hot dogs," piped up Jimmy.

With a quick smile at Ceci, Brett walked to the door, calling out, "Be back in a few minutes."

He strode down to the reception area, surprised to find the desk empty. He should've asked Ceci where the dining room was. He carried on down the main hallway looking for someone to ask. Instead he found the empty dining room. He checked his watch. It was almost dinnertime. What was the chance he could get Ceci to come down here and eat?

"Excuse me, can I help you, sir?"

Brett turned to face a man in black pants and a white shirt. His name tag said Martin.

Brett smiled and held out his hand. "I'm here with Ceci and the children. She was looking for dinner."

Martin nodded. "We could send dinner for four to her room."

"That would be good, thanks." Brett glanced around. "There aren't many people here."

"No. We're expecting a group back anytime. They've been at meetings in town all day."

Brett stood for a moment awkwardly wondering if there was something he was supposed to order differently for the kids. "You do understand there are two little children upstairs."

Martin laughed. "Yes indeed. Hot dogs, chicken fingers, and fries coming up."

"Glad to hear that." With a smile at the other man Brett turned and walked toward the reception area. At the last minute he turned and said, "When is the group from the embassy due back?

Martin looked at his watch. "Fifteen minutes ago."

It had to be his line of work that made him so suspicious.

He was also just a guest here. He had been called in because of Ceci's problem by a worried family member. That didn't make his presence official in any way. But now that he was here, he couldn't help feeling some odd vibes. And that just reminded him of Ceci's fears.

He turned back to Martin and asked, "Any chance of a coffee?"

"Absolutely."

They walked back into the dining room and Martin pointed out a coffee bar against the wall Brett hadn't seen when he first walked in. Perfect. Ceci would enjoy a cup.

"Would the little ones want something to drink? Perhaps some milk or juice? Just let me know and we will send it up for them."

Brett immediately snagged two cups to fill. "Actually both would be great."

"I'll make a note of it."

Walking carefully so as not to spill the drinks, Brett made his way slowly back to the elevators. Using his elbow he pushed the button.

The door opened to let out two men, both with dark complexions. They glanced at him, their gazes hard, cold before brushing past.

If not for his quick step back, he'd have ended up wearing the coffee. He frowned, studying the backs of the two men as they walked away. He suspected from the fit of the suit jackets they were packing weapons underneath.

Then again this was a US Embassy. There was conflict all over the world and embassies were often targets. Of course, they were armed.

Not liking the direction of his thoughts, he stepped into the elevator and again using his elbow managed to get the elevator doors to close and start climbing.

As he approached the right floor, he realized his nerves had sharpened, making him even edgier. He wished to God Ceci was back home where she belonged. Who knew it would take so long to get replacement passports? Surely they could've expedited the process. At the door he gave a light kick with his foot and called out, "Ceci, open the door."

It opened quickly, and Ceci smiled around the edge when she saw the coffee.

"Oh my goodness that looks wonderful." She was reaching out eagerly with both hands to take the cup when he heard something erupt several floors below – a sound that made his blood run cold.

He'd heard it too many times in his life to not know what it was. Gunfire.

Shoving the cups into her hands, he ordered, "Stay inside and lock the door."

He bolted for the stairwell.

CHAPTER 4

CECI LEANED AGAINST the closed door, her hands still full with the drinks. The brew sloshed up the sides of the cups her fingers trembled so badly. Clamping down on her raging nerves, she carefully placed the cups down on the coffee table before running back to lock the door.

"Mommy, who was that?" Jimmy asked.

"It was Brett. He forgot something, but he'll be back in a few minutes," she said in a breathless voice. She had to stay as normal as she could for the kids. Almost normal. She stared down at her nails and realized she'd picked off her favorite nail polish. The teenage stress reaction coming to the fore once again. She clenched her fists, wrapped her arms around her chest and collapsed at one end of the couch. She'd heard the same sound Brett had, and it wasn't one she was likely to forget. There had been enough gunfire on the yacht to make her wish to never hear it again.

How the hell could she have gotten into another horrible scenario? Was she just a bad luck magnet?

"Why? What's wrong, Mommy?" Jimmy scrambled up onto the couch to sit beside her, his hands in his lap. He stared at the cups and said, "Can I have some milk?"

Her gaze went from him to the coffee then to the small refrigerator in the room.

"There isn't any. I'll see if there's anything else for you

to drink." She went to the fridge and opened it up. "How about apple juice?"

Jimmy laughed and clapped his hands as he ran to her. Jennifer, not to be outdone toddled behind. Ceci poured two small glasses, gave one to Jimmy and picked up Jennifer in her arms holding it for her. She took several big gulps.

When she was done, she squirmed to be let back down onto the floor, then raced back to the Legos. She could barely click the blocks together, but it kept her happy to be with her brother. It should be naptime for Jennifer but with all the excitement going on she wasn't sure that was a good idea. Jimmy took his glass and wandered back toward the Legos too but wouldn't sit down. "Can we watch TV instead?"

"Sure, if there is anything on. Remember we're not at home anymore."

"Yeah." His voice was sad as he added tearfully, "I want to go home."

"I do too," she said quietly.

She tucked the two babies beside her and gave Jimmy a hug, dropping a kiss on top of his head.

"We will be soon, sweetie. Just trying to get the paperwork fixed." She picked up the remote and started flicking through the channels to see if there was anything appropriate for the kids. There was a show about baby animals so she put that on. Replacing the remote on the coffee table she picked up her cup instead.

Settling back into the corner, she took several sips and sighed. It was already cool.

What a nightmare. From pirates to...whatever this was. She dropped her head back thinking of all the recent craziness in her life. And then there was Brett. Damn, thoughts of that man consumed her. She didn't know what to think about him right now, yet he was a lifeline at this crazy juncture.

He'd always been a very capable man, while she'd always been highly insecure. That hadn't been a good combination for them. She set down the cup and curled up on the side of the couch. She couldn't afford to sleep now, but it felt good just to close her eyes. With Jimmy at her side she realized there was no sound out of Jennifer. She glanced over at her daughter to see her crashed on the couch. Jennifer wasn't going to sleep very well in that position, so Ceci picked her up carefully and laid her in the center of the big bed. Since they arrived they'd been sharing it.

As much as her side of it looked very welcoming, she didn't want to leave Jimmy unsupervised. She walked back to the couch, snagged up Brett's coffee, then snuggled back in the corner. She leaned her head against the pillow and closed her eyes with the animal documentary going on in the background and Jimmy sprawled out beside her.

BRETT RACED DOWN the stairs to the second floor and peered down the hallway. It was empty and quiet. He quickly climbed down to the main floor, hugging the wall as he tried to see what was going on out in the hallway. When he couldn't see enough he slid through the doors and peered around the corner.

The front reception desk was still empty and there was no sign of anyone. He moved toward the dining room and checked out the big room. It too was empty. He frowned. Where was Martin?

Walking quickly across the dining room he headed for

the kitchen where there should have been banging and clanging of pots and pans in meal preparation. The place was silent. In the kitchen he ran to the stove and held his hand over the top. It was cold.

There was nobody here, and there hadn't been for several hours. Still, it didn't have to be something to set off any alarms as the van with the embassy staff had been gone all day.

It was four o'clock. He'd have thought with the approaching dinner hour, somebody would be doing prep work, but maybe not yet. With a suspicious glance at the gleaming stainless steel kitchen he moved to the doors on the other side.

He listened carefully. Nothing. Reaching out, he twisted the knob and pulled the door ever so slightly open. Still quiet. Holding it open enough that he could peer around the corner, he saw a very large boardroom. Also empty. So where the hell was everyone?

He understood the van was late by a good fifteen minutes and that had been ten minutes ago, but this was adding to his suspicions. He walked to the door on the far side and checked behind it.

It was a storeroom of sorts.

The lower floor was in an H shape of hallways. And now he was in the second one. And again it was empty. His stomach sank realizing they were probably into something much more major than anything he had wanted to see. Moving carefully, he went from door to door checking to see where everyone was.

Now back out in front of the reception he realized the place was deserted.

Except he'd heard gunfire. There was a directory and

map on the side wall. He walked over to see what it was he could be missing. There was a downstairs, but it was not for the general public, and there were two more floors above containing conference rooms and apartments. At the computer on the front desk he quickly checked to see if it told him anything about how many people were in the consulate. But he had no way to access the logins.

Frustrated he pulled out his cell phone and quickly sent a message to everyone on his team giving them an update. After pocketing it again he headed for the stairs, but the door to the stairwell was locked. He stared at it. Then pulled out his credit card.

He knew exactly what to do with this.

CHAPTER 5

Ceci woke to the sounds of the phone ringing. She stumbled to her feet and made it to the side table where she answered it. "Hello," she said in a sleepy voice.

"Good afternoon. There was a request for food for you and your family. Would you like to have that down in the dining room or should we bring it up to you?" She glanced around at the kids, one still sleeping on the couch the other on the bed. She didn't really want to have the food just yet but didn't want to put them out. Besides, she couldn't guarantee when Brett would be returning. "Delivery please. And now would be fine thanks."

"What room are you in again?"

She gave him the room number then hung up. In the bathroom she splashed cold water on her face, trying to wake up. Catching the window out of the corner of her eye she realized it was late afternoon. Not quite dinnertime but close. She could only hope Brett returned in time. That he hadn't already brought a chill to her soul. He'd gone to check out the gunshots.

Determined to ignore the fear choking her, she sat down on the couch beside Jimmy and switched the television channels. There wasn't much in the way of news.

She really wanted to check in with her family, but she'd lost her phone on the yacht and hadn't been able to get a new one yet. She'd occasionally gone down and used one of their computers but with the children it was difficult. A tablet would be helpful too.

And she wanted her damn phone. She'd have called Brett already if she had it. Just to check up on him.

Her gaze widened as something struck her.

Out loud she murmured, "Why did they ask for my room number?"

They never had before. Surely they had to know her number to phone her? Worried, she chewed on her fingernails as she hopped to her feet and stood in the middle of the room weighing the options. She studied the room. It was a large suite, and there was a double door closing her off from the other half.

The double doors were locked. Her husband had taught her how to open most locks. She took a kitchen knife and walked back to the door. It didn't take long before she had the lock open. Although, was this really the best idea? She opened them and checked the other half of the suite. It was a duplicate of her own. With the children still sleeping she quickly packed up and transferred all the gear to the new place. Realizing the caller would be arriving any minute, fear set in. Panic lit a fire under her feet as she knew she didn't have much time.

Scooping up the Legos she quickly collected everything into the bag. She moved Jimmy into the center of the new bed and then carefully transferred her daughter in beside him.

With her heart pounding in her throat and choking with fear she raced through the room checking to see if she'd forgotten anything. Indeed she had. She'd forgotten the bathroom. Using the empty garbage can she scooped up everything in the way of toiletries from the bathtub and sink and transferred it to the new bathroom.

As she stood in the doorway she remembered the fridge. Opening it, she took out the last of the juices and few pieces of fruit. In her new room, she took a deep breath and stood with her back to the now locked double doors for a long moment. She collapsed on the new couch. Had she overreacted?

What the hell was Brett going to say when he found her gone?

She walked to the front door and listened. Was anyone outside? With her ear cocked she heard a knock on the old door. Her heart pounding, she shoved her fist into her mouth determined to not make a sound but at the same time she wanted to cry out to Brett she was over here.

When she didn't answer there was a louder knock.

Holding her breath, she waited. If it was Brett surely he'd call out to her? There was a clatter of dishes as if the waiter had brought up her food. Immediately doubt set in. Was it just a food delivery? As soon as she considered there might actually be a meal waiting, that she'd panicked for no reason, hunger set in. If he left the food outside, she'd bring it in here.

The knock came again, this time followed by a loud voice. "Hello, are you in there?"

She refused to answer. She cast a glance back at the children but they slept soundly. And then she heard confirmation that everything in her world had gone wrong. There was a hard split. And the door to their old room opened. With her fist clenched she slid down to the floor, her body trembling. Her terrified gaze locked on the double doors. Would they guess what she'd done?

Within seconds she heard the intruder's footsteps racing down the hallway.

Oh, dear God. She took a chance and opened the door to look outside. The food trolley sat with its multiple food dishes stacked on top. Should she take it? It was for her. She didn't know how long she was going to be holed up here. Would they do a room by room search or would they assume she'd left the building?

She snuck out into the hallway and lifted the lid on one of the food trays. Sure enough that dish was Jimmy's favorite. Hot dogs and fries. There were also several bottles of milk and juice.

She quickly wheeled the cart into her room. She didn't know if the guy would remember he'd left it behind, but she could use the food. Inside the room she could hear Jimmy waking up. She pushed the cart toward him with a big smile.

In a low voice, she said, "We'll eat, if you stay very quiet so that your sister can sleep."

He looked over at his little sister and said in a whisper, "How come she's still asleep, Mommy?"

For the second time in the last hour she froze. Was this a natural sleep? Jimmy was overly tired. She'd napped today too. And the coffee had tasted a little off, but she hadn't really considered that there might have been something in it. Why would she?

She still had the cups so she studied the residue on the bottom. She held the cup to her nose and sniffed. Was there an odd odor? Or was she just exhausted? Besides, if she'd been drugged shouldn't she have slept a lot longer? Then again how long had she been out? And why would the children be sleepy? They'd only had apple juice that had been delivered earlier that afternoon.

BRETT CREPT DOWN the wide staircase that wound down to a hallway. This level was full of more meeting rooms. And again the place appeared deserted. So where the hell was everyone?

The hallway split into two sides. He slipped down the right side. Somewhere in here should be an exit leading to the garage underneath. After opening the first door he came to a large room. It appeared to be more empty offices. He moved down to the next door. This one opened to show a small office area, but the desk was empty and there was no paperwork on top. Also there were no computers. He continued his search until he was back at the stairwell facing the opposite direction.

The first door was a fire exit and showed metal stairs, likely leading to the garage below.

He made it down two flights before all the lights went out. It took a few minutes for his eyes to adjust to the darkness. He could hear a woman crying. Was she alone? Then he heard a harsh voice. He could just make out the words.

"Who else is here?" raged the voice, followed by a heavy thud.

Again the woman cried out.

Brett's gut clenched tight. The asshole was beating her. How many men was he up against?

He eased back into his hiding position as the door beside him burst open. Taking the stairs two at a time, a man raced up.

And Brett saw the automatic rifle. He dove for the man's feet and pulled. He went down hard with a loud exclamation. Brett snagged up the gun and spun it so it pointed at him.

"Who the hell are you?"

The man stared at him in surprise, then some language Brett didn't understand exploded from his mouth.

Brett hit him hard in the gut. "English. Speak English."

Instead the man spat at him.

That made it easy. The fight was short and sweet. With the man now dead on the floor, Brett grabbed him by the foot and dragged the asshole down the last few steps and tucked him around the corner out of sight.

Now armed, and with proof there was an attack on the embassy, he quickly updated the rest of his unit. They were in town as the unit was due to fly home tomorrow. It had been the call from his mother that had sent him racing to the consulate.

And what he'd found was ten times worse than what he'd expected.

CHAPTER 6

CECI COAXED JIMMY to eat a little bit more. Eyeing the extra food, she considered how to pack it up to take with them if she had to run. Anyone traveling with children knew they ate constantly. And she had very little in the way of snacks. Or luggage for that matter.

Damn she wanted to go home. While Jimmy worked on finishing the last of his hot dog, his head and shoulders drooped with fatigue again. She sorted through their personal belongings now in a mess on the bed.

She didn't have much to pack. She'd been given a large carryall that looked more like a beach bag to her, but it had a zipper on the top and lots of pockets on the outside. She quickly packed up their few pieces of clothing and the toiletries she'd collected.

"Are we leaving again?" Jimmy asked, his mouth full of fries, his gaze wide with uncertainty.

"Don't talk with your mouth full," she said automatically. She didn't answer his question because she didn't know how. If there was an attack at the embassy someone would find her eventually. It was a question of whose side they'd be on.

When she was done, Jennifer was still tucked up in the middle of the bed sound asleep, and Jimmy still worked on his food. She walked over to the window and stared outside.

The place was empty. She still had no passports, and if she couldn't stay here where was she going to go?

Plus…where was Brett? If anyone could help her it was him. Since he raced off and told her to stay inside, she hadn't seen or heard a sound. It'd break her heart if anything happened to him. It was hard to keep down the waves of stress that rolled through her. Packed and ready to run, yet she had nowhere to go. She could continue to move from room to room but what good would that do. It wasn't like she could stay hidden forever. And soon enough she wouldn't be able to keep the kids quiet either.

As she stared out the window again, she studied the gardens outside the gate. She couldn't see much but everything appeared normal. With night not far off, it was getting dark, adding to her fear. There would be no sleep for her tonight.

She was sure that was gunshots she'd heard earlier.

Only there'd been nothing since. Neither had there been an announcement saying everything was well. Just this distressing silence. She sat down on the couch and turned on the TV, hoping for a distraction only to quickly realize anybody outside could hear the TV and would know they were there.

"Finished, Mommy." Jimmy hopped off the chair and ran to the bathroom to wash his hands. When he came running back, he clambered up on the couch and sat on her lap. She pondered how to keep the children quiet so as not to draw attention to them.

At four and almost two that was impossible. With Jimmy in her arms she got up. Her little girl was still out. She doubted she'd sleep through the night but it had happened before. She knew the children were picking up on her fears, but it was almost impossible to change that given the situation.

Placing Jimmy on the bed with a book she quickly cleaned and washed up a few dishes. She was careful to be quiet and make as little sound as she could. Even so, it seemed like everything she did was super loud and anyone outside of the suite would hear her. When she was done, the room looked normal. She could hear someone down the hallway, the footsteps hard, fast, and determined.

She raised a trembling hand to her temple and slowly massaged it. Inside, her breath caught in her throat. There was no place to hide. Should she have grabbed the kids and run? But where to?

When the footsteps came closer, she let out a hard gasp and wrapped her arms around her chest, too scared to breathe. Jimmy couldn't be seen from the doorway as he was tucked up in the pillows. The only thing visible was her bag. She scooted off the bed, raced over and snagged it, tucking it up against the side of the wall out of sight. Whoever came in would have to walk all the way to the end to see them on the bed.

Ceci looked around for a weapon. There had to be something. The lamp was a flimsy looking thing. Not quite the club she was looking for.

But there were chairs. Making a fast decision she grabbed the one Jimmy had been sitting on and pulled it around the side of the wall with her. Her collection was starting to grow. She'd prefer a single chair leg, but maybe if she smashed it over somebody's head she'd end up with one.

As she studied her hiding spot she realized just how insane this really was. She was in one of the safest places in the world, and here she was trying to find weapons. She ran her hands over her face and gave her cheeks a light scrubbing.

Dear God, maybe she did need help.

WITH ONE OF the enemy down, a weapon back in his hand and messages back and forth to his unit, Brett felt a whole lot better about his position. Not great yet because he had no idea what was going on, but it was obvious the embassy was under attack. Likely from within. His biggest concern right now was getting Ceci and the children out. But he had no way to do that at this point. He leaned back against the wall wishing he could hear the conversation on the other side. The voices rose and fell but were too indistinct now to understand the conversation. The woman who had been crying was silent.

He felt his phone vibrate in his pocket. Checking the message quickly he held it so the light on the screen didn't shine in the window.

Two vehicles had been mobilized. His team was coming. They'd contacted the local government. As yet they had no word of backup from the military. Besides, if a coup was happening the local military were the last people they wanted to call on.

Footsteps came closer outside the double doors. He shifted deeper into the shadow to where he'd stashed the other man. The doors pushed open.

"We have to make sure we have completely evacuated the building," a woman said.

"We're pulling a team together," responded a man. "As far as we know most of them are down here. The woman and her children are still in their room."

"Most is not good enough. We need to make sure all are. And the woman needs to be taken care of. Do what you want with the children."

"Understood." They walked slowly up the stairs leaving Brett stunned at the casual dismissal of Ceci and the kids. He needed to know more of their plans but his heart was already panicking at the thought of not getting to her in time.

If the people who'd passed him in all likelihood were planning a floor by floor search. He needed to get Ceci out fast. As they went up the second landing he stood and twisted so he could hear more.

"We're waiting on the military to bring a unit in here. We'll set up offices on the main floor."

"The US isn't going to stand for this, you know that."

"I'm counting on it." The feminine voice rose in anger. "Like we need any of their shit now. There's no reason for them to have the embassy here. They should've been kicked out a long time ago."

"There hasn't been time. We've only been in government a couple of months."

Brett melted back against the wall, his mind spinning. He pulled out his cell phone and quickly texted Mason. *The military are in on it. New government no longer wanting US Embassy on their soil.*

He pocketed his phone and made his way to the double doors to the garage. On the other side of them silence descended. Shit. He opened one a crack. At least there was no light shining through. To the right he heard a couple of loud voices followed by raucous laughter that raised the hairs on his forearm. Not a sound he liked to hear at any time.

There were several vehicles parked in front of him. Staying low he slipped through the double doors and raced to the side of one then down toward the back, then stopped and listened.

Peering around the doorway, he spied a large truck. He headed toward the men's loud laughter. As he came around he saw an unconscious woman on the ground, her clothes being ripped off as two men laughed at her. This, he could fix. He came up behind the first man and got him in a choke hold before quickly snapping his neck. He let him drop to the ground as the second turned, saw him and reached for his weapon. Brett kicked the gun out of his hand then drove his right fist into the man's jaw.

The man's head snapped backwards and he dropped to the ground.

Assholes.

The first man was dead, the second unconscious. Brett reached down and checked the woman's pulse. It was strong. She was alive, and as he couldn't see any visible injuries, he assumed she'd been knocked out or fainted. He swooped her up into his arms and immediately disappeared amongst the vehicles. He had to find a safe place to stash her while he figured out what was going on down here and who else he was up against.

There was an exit sign up ahead. He raced toward it to see the doors were propped open. So not a good sign. He backed up and spied a pickup with a flat tire. He carefully lowered his cargo into the pickup bed. Hopefully no one would look for her here. He ducked down behind the vehicle and retraced his steps to the stairwell he'd come down and headed to the far side. Ahead he could see three still figures on the floor. When he reached them he saw two men in suits both had bullet holes in the head and the third was Martin from the dining room. In his case, the bullet hole was in his temple.

Shit. He quickly updated Mason. Now to collect Ceci

and get the hell out of here.

He was hoping to find a service elevator. Not everyone would know about that. He raced up the stairs to the first landing, passed it and headed up. On the top floor, he realized he still had yet to hear or see anyone.

The hallway was empty too.

That was at least a good sign. He strode to her door where he gave a short knock.

And got no answer in return. But the door slowly swung open, the lock broken.

CHAPTER 7

S HIT. WHAT SHOULD she do? The sound of those footsteps stabbed her in the gut as panic threatened to empty her stomach.

Then she heard the harsh whisper. Was that her name? She raced to the front door and held her ear against the cold wood. On the other side she heard a low male voice call out, "Ceci?"

Brett? Should she take the chance? If she made the wrong decision it could have fatal consequences.

"Ceci, it's Brett. Open up."

With her throat threatening to close on her, she unlocked the door and peered through the crack. "Oh my God, it is you."

Brett spun at the sound of her voice. His confusion turning to relief. She motioned him inside. "Hurry, hurry."

"What happened? Why are you in this room and not that one?"

"I was afraid we weren't safe over there." With a glance down the hallway in both directions he slipped inside the room and closed and locked the door.

"Did someone come here?"

She held a finger to her lips and motioned to the sleeping children in the bed. He immediately nodded.

She gave him a quick rundown of the events including

her race to move into this room. "I did hear somebody arrive with the trolley and go into the room. He left and so far no one else has come by." She shuddered. "But I'm terrified someone will at any moment."

She walked into the center of the room and turned to face him. "Tell me what's going on?"

"I don't have all the details," he said. "But there's an attack on the embassy. I found three dead men in the bottom garage level and one woman who's unconscious but alive." He walked over to the window where he peered through the curtains. "Before getting shot one of the men told me there'd been a meeting off the embassy grounds and that the staff were fifteen minutes late getting back." He looked at his watch. "Make that an hour late now." He turned to look at her, his face grim.

She had her hand clasped over her mouth to still the shriek trying to sneak past. "Oh my God, did you say three men are dead?"

He raced toward her, wrapping her tight in his arms. "It's okay, we will get out of this."

She shook her head. "How can this be happening again?"

He rubbed her arms up and down. "I have no idea. I don't understand the government's history here. I've never been to this embassy before. However, it is and that's what we have to deal with. I don't know how many men are involved. In fact, there's not a whole lot I can tell you at this moment."

With her eyes locked on his, she whispered, "What are we going to do?"

He gave her a gentle smile. "We're going to wait. My team's en route. I believe a military operation is responsible for taking out the embassy personnel. I don't know if the vehicle that was supposed to return with the staff has been hijacked, if those people have been killed or if they are being held hostage somewhere. There are so many unknowns. The only thing we do know is that we have to stay safe."

She went to the bed to where Jimmy slept – book in hand.

Behind her Brett asked, "How long have they been asleep?"

Her shoulders rose and fell. "Jennifer's been out for a while. Jimmy slept earlier, then woke up to eat and fell asleep again." She admitted, "I was starting to worry something was wrong."

Brett studied their pales faces.

"Is this not normal behavior for them?"

She twisted so she could see his face. "It's hard to say. This is not a normal situation. There has been a lot of poor nights' sleep, lots of stress and fear. Obviously they are tired."

Brett looked around the room. "Are there any leftovers?"

She pointed to the fridge. "I stuck everything in there."

She watched in confusion as Brett walked to the fridge, bent down and opened it, pulled out one of the plates. He ripped off a chunk of hot dog left on Jimmy's plate. He put it in his mouth but didn't chew. She didn't understand what he was doing until he opened the garbage and spat it back out. Then he took the plate and upended it into the garbage and proceeded to do the same with every other dish she'd placed in the fridge. As she watched her own dinner hit the garbage she felt sick. She'd planned to take some of that.

"What are you doing?" she asked in a harsh whisper when he sniffed the apple juice the kids had drunk from earlier. He made a face and dumped everything down the sink. "We might need that."

He raised his gaze to hers, a cold sharp look in his eyes. He stroked a gentle finger across Jimmy's cheek. Then he looked at her and said, "The food was drugged."

HE WATCHED HER disbelief as she stared at him for a long time before she pivoted to stare at the bed. She reached out to touch her children as if making sure they were safe. She'd been worried that something was wrong…

When she turned back to him this time the shock had faded and anger had spiked to take its place. Brett was glad to see the anger. Fear incapacitated. Anger at least gave her some tools to work with. In this case she *should* be angry. Somebody had drugged her children.

"Are you sure?" she asked in a hard voice.

He nodded. "Yes, I recognized the smell."

She gazed at the garbage can. He knew she was going to blame herself for not having recognized the drugs.

"I've had some training in this matter," he said quietly. "You couldn't have known."

She closed her eyes and just sat there. Not defeated, just blank as if not knowing what to do next. He placed a hand on her shoulder, gave a gentle squeeze. "They will pay for this."

Her gaze flew open. "I need to get them out of here and to safety."

"And for that we have to stay hidden. I don't know how many terrorists are here but so far I've taken out two of the five I've seen and left a third unconscious."

"That leaves two more." She stood up and walked toward the front door as if to leave. She wasn't thinking straight. "And maybe the man who delivered the cart of food. I don't understand why they'd drug the children."

"Make it easier to finish them off later? To keep them quiet? Maybe they didn't want to have to kill them?" There were other just as bad reasons, but he had no plans to bring those up. She had enough to worry about.

Tears came to her eyes to mix with the fire.

"There could be any number of men here we don't know about." He caught her by the arm and turned her around to give her a hard shake. "Don't do anything stupid. We have to be smart about this."

Her eyes snapped at him. "They hurt my children."

"We have to make sure they don't do anything worse than this."

She spun around and cried, "Why? Why are they doing this?"

"As far as I can tell there's been a recent coup in this government, but it's unstable, so either someone is trying to take over or the new government doesn't want the US here any longer."

"So they just kill everyone? Don't they realize there will be a price to pay?"

"Often people don't think past a moment in time. They like to think they are a superpower and can handle the US."

She snorted. "Like that's going to happen."

She sat down on the end of the bed and looked up at him, most of the anger drained from her stiff frame. Now there was just sadness. "Three dead men," she whispered. "Those poor families."

"Three that I saw, so far." He knew she had to be comparing her loss to this situation. "And yes, I killed two of the enemy. But there are still two who passed me heading up the stairs."

Fire spit from her eyes again as she asked, "Why did you not kill them?"

This lady was bloodthirsty. He liked it. "Because I needed to hear what they were saying. That's how I found out the military was involved."

She winced. "Sorry. I'm not really that vengeful."

"You have every right. They drugged your children."

She turned to look back at the two sleeping babes. "On the other hand this is a perfect time for them to be sound asleep. This is not the kind of trauma they need. Not after the pirates."

"Best if we can get them to safety while they sleep. Set you up in a hotel somewhere safe and sound."

She raised her eyebrows. "And of course you have a way to make that happen?"

"Maybe. Maybe not." He stared off at the window wondering about the chances of exiting safely through the garage.

"If we could get down to the garage level," he said, "I could hotwire a vehicle and drive us out of here."

She waved her hand at him. "There's going to be security at the exit," she said. "Especially now."

"That's a definite possibility. But the only other option is to go back out to the garden and over the fence."

"In order to do that we have to make sure we aren't seen. And find a way over the fence."

He nodded.

She frowned. "And is the top of that fence electric?"

"Most likely."

She shook her head wildly. "Then we can't take that chance."

"I can short it out," he said. "That's no problem. The issue is going to be getting to a place where we can't be seen in order to scale it. As soon as they realize that some of their men are dead there's going to be hell to pay."

She gave a clipped nod.

"Exactly. It's the same issue as trying to get down to the garage." She took a shaky breath and stood up. "Let's go. I'm already packed."

He gave her an approving smile. "If I carry Jimmy can you get Jennifer?"

"Yes but better if we could take the stroller as well. It will hold two of them in a pinch."

He considered that. "I'll strap it to my back."

She got up and used the washroom, then quickly loaded up the last few things she had for the children into the one bag. With the bag strapped crosswise over her shoulder she bent down and scooped up Jennifer.

Turning around to check Brett's progress, she gasped in shock. He had the stroller on his back and the weapon over his shoulder. Her heart pounded at the sight of it. He'd had it when he'd entered the room but she'd been so focused on everything else, she hadn't noticed.

He held out the kids' boots and coats. "Maybe dress them first?"

She looked outside at the darkening sky and agreed. They quickly dressed the sleeping children. When they were done, she picked up Jennifer and he had Jimmy. She took a deep breath at the front door and turned to look at him. "There's really no other way is there?"

"I'm so sorry." He shook his head. "We could wait here until my unit arrives, but we can't guarantee someone else won't find us first."

"But the city out there is a jungle too, will we be any safer?"

He gave her a slow, quiet smile. "Sweetheart, out there – that is *my* jungle. We'll be fine."

And she believed him.

CHAPTER 8

S HE REALLY HAD no choice. She had to do whatever she could to save her children. She just wished she understood how this world worked. At least she wasn't alone anymore. Brett at her side made all the difference. She followed him down the hallway going in the opposite direction they had taken before.

She wanted to ask him why.

She wanted to ask if he really knew what he was doing.

Instead, she stayed quiet and followed his lead. When he pushed open the door to a large storage room she really wondered what he was up to. But then he pointed out a double door elevator, and she realized this was the service elevator entrance.

If they wanted to stay out of the public eye this was their best chance.

After he pushed the button, he moved her back gently behind him, the rifle tilted up under her son's body, ready. When the doors opened to show an empty interior she let out a heavy sigh of relief.

Still keeping an eye out in case anybody followed them, he motioned at her to enter. He then stepped in beside her and pushed the button for the garage level. She buried her face against her daughter's sleeping neck and sent up a silent prayer for someone to watch over them. She'd found little enough faith to call on lately. She'd been raised without religion, but right now she could use some help from above.

"Stay inside until I check it out," he whispered. He gave her a hard look to make sure she understood his request.

She nodded. She had no intention of going out there until he said it was all clear. He checked to the left, then the right before motioning for her to come out and follow him.

"Is this where you were earlier?"

He shook his head. "No. On the other side."

Too bad. She hadn't been able to forget there was a woman lying in the back of a pickup. If the other guys found her before she managed to get herself to safety then she was dead too. If Ceci had no children she'd bug him to help the woman. But since she did, to save her was a hard call. Maybe he could save all of them.

As they raced down the hallway to the open door she wondered what kind of people were prepared to walk through a building and shoot everyone in sight. Had they no respect for the sanctity of a human life?

He held up his hand to stop her. Then he slipped around the corner to take a look at the cars. She could see several fancy ones, several more police issue looking, and a couple of big SUVs.

At one SUV he tried to open the door. Of course, it was locked. He checked every other vehicle on this side looking for any unlocked. When he came to a truck, his grin flashed. He hopped in, did something under the dashboard, and the next thing she knew the truck revved into life.

Yes! Now that was much better. They might just get out of this hellhole. He came racing back toward her and motioned at her to come. There were no car seats for the children so they laid Jimmy down on the seat between the two of them. She got in and buckled up with Jennifer still in her arms. Brett buckled Jimmy up as best he could. He put the stroller in the back of the truck, then got in and backed the truck up.

He drove through the garage, made a couple of odd turns so she wasn't sure what he was up to until he came to another truck. He put theirs in park and hopped out. Before she knew it, he'd collected the other woman and managed to get her into the back seat where he strapped her in similarly to Jimmy's arrangement. He hopped back into the front of the truck and carefully drove his way to the exit.

They came up to double security gates. There was some kind of computerized box about twenty feet in front of the doors. He pulled up to the side and stopped. He checked something above the windshield and found a card. He slipped the card into the slot and the lights flashed, followed by a loud click and the security gates opened. And just like that he drove out of the garage and onto the busy streets.

He pulled his phone out and tossed it to her. "Find Mason under contacts and send him a message."

She did as he asked. He gave her the exact wording of what to say.

"Good. Now hit send, please."

"Done."

He reached out for the phone and slipped it back into his pocket. She looked around to see traffic moving in all directions. "Now that we are free from that place, where do we go?" she asked. "I still have no passports for us."

"The paperwork is in progress, and we will get it as soon as it's completed. Right now we need a place for you to lie low. The woman in the back seat needs to see a doctor."

She turned to look at the pale, slack face. "We need to

take her to the emergency room."

"I'd love to but it would be a hard story to explain. And right now we don't want to let the world know there's been an attack on the US Embassy."

"But she needs to see a doctor," Ceci protested. "She could be badly hurt."

"That is an entirely different story." He flashed her a big grin, changed lanes and took a right hand corner.

She didn't recognize the area at all, but then she'd only driven straight to the embassy after being taken off the yacht. She sat quietly as he took several more turns and eventually merged onto a highway that seemed to take them further out of town into a flat countryside.

His phone rang. He pulled it out of his pocket and answered it. "Mason. Yes, we're on the highway heading toward Bullard's house." He glanced over at Ceci. "No, she's not hurt. The children are sleeping off a drug, but it wouldn't hurt to have them checked over. I rescued a woman who was in the process of being raped by two of the military men taking over the embassy. She's out cold with a head injury. I didn't dare take her to the hospital. Our ETA is nine minutes."

Ceci's heart damn near stopped when she heard the explanation of what had happened to the poor woman. She turned to look back at her. It did explain the disarray of her clothing. Ceci wanted to cover her up, but she had nothing other than the clothes on her back. How could these men do that to her?

When she finally turned back around and looked over at Brett he seemed to be studying her. "You okay?"

She shrugged and settled back down in her seat. "It's a little difficult to hear what happened to her." She nodded toward the woman in the back seat of the truck.

"*Almost* happened to her," he corrected. "With any luck she will remember little. I killed one of her attackers and knocked the other unconscious."

"Should've killed them all," she said passionately.

"There's a fine line," he admitted. "I can't go killing all the rapists and murderers in the world."

Unable to hold back, she cuddled her daughter close as she stared out the window. "Too bad."

"We agree on that. In the military I've seen a lot of things I don't like. It would be nice if justice moved faster. But it often fails everyone. In those times it's very difficult to do what I do."

She let that slide. "Who is Bullard?"

"He was a SEAL years ago. When it was time to walk away, he finished his medical degree and picked up some special training."

She winced. "He went from smashing bodies to fixing them?"

Brett laughed. "He hadn't quite finished his degree before he signed up for BUD/s training and like most SEALs, ten years was more than enough. Now he's doing what he can to help people."

"Just from a different position?"

"Exactly." They drove in silence for another minute then he took an exit ramp off the highway. Several miles later he turned a corner and drove down a long driveway to a very large house. In front of the property was a high security gate. Brett parked in front of the gate, hopped out and spoke into the security system. He faced the camera and waited.

She held her breath to see if they'd be allowed to enter. Brett must know him well to call on him in these circumstances, she thought. She'd much rather be inside that security gate than outside here waiting for someone to find them.

Ceci heard the strong click of the gate releasing.

"Thanks, Bullard," Brett called out.

Ceci waited as he got back into the truck and started up the engine. When the gates were open wide enough he drove around the circular driveway ahead to the front door. "Stay here," he said. "I need to get this woman into Bullard's clinic."

Clinic? She watched as he gently removed the woman from the back seat, hating to see her body lying so limp and cold. For all she knew the poor woman was dying and they'd been dragging her around town. How bad would that make her feel? Brett climbed the tall wide staircase to the front door. She watched from the window as the door opened automatically to let them into the front hall.

She studied her own daughter's pale face and bit her lip. What kind of animals would do something like this to innocent women and children?

Not knowing how long she was going to be there she leaned her head back, closed her eyes and rocked her daughter gently. A few minutes later, sensing something but not sure what, she opened her eyes and glanced around. There were several very large, black, dangerous looking dogs sitting on either side of the circular staircase at the bottom.

"Well that answers that question." she said softly. "I won't be going outside on my own."

Even as she said that Brett came racing out and took the stairs skipping every second one. When he reached her side of the door, she used the power button and lowered her window instead.

He gave her a big smile and said, "Okay, let's get the children checked over."

She motioned at the four dogs. "Is it safe?"

He turned to the dogs, studied them and made an odd whistle sound that rose really high at the end. The dogs, as if released from some kind of a tight hold, bounced toward him barking excitedly, tails wagging. He gave them a big happy welcome. When they calmed down enough he helped her out of the truck with Jennifer in her arms. He reached inside and gently tugged Jimmy toward them so he could lift him up. With the door closed he led the way up the stairs. She was happy to follow but didn't let him get too far in front. The dogs might know him, but they sure didn't appear to be happy to see her.

"Don't worry about the dogs. They are not dangerous unless you happen to be an intruder. Because you're with me it will be fine."

Under her breath, she whispered, "Sure. Like I'm going to believe that."

BRETT LAUGHED AND motioned at her to move ahead of him into the hallway. He could understand her nervousness. Those four and the generation that had gone before them were well-trained guard dogs. But they were also family pets. Bullard wouldn't allow anything other than that. Brett agreed. Every animal should be allowed to have a good side. Too often guard dogs had their aggressive side groomed to be dominant, and it didn't allow the animal any chance to be the kindhearted soul he was on the inside.

Striding to the large marble foyer he kept an eye on Ceci. Bullard was different. With any luck the two of them would get along. Bullard's man of the house was waiting for him at the edge of the clinic. Only friends were taken this far into the building. He had a different entrance for those he wasn't so comfortable allowing into his home. Brett had been here before as had most of the SEALs. Thankfully they hadn't needed to come for his medical services.

At the door to the clinic he could see the woman from the embassy stretched out on the bed. On the second one a few feet away he laid Jimmy down, tucking him up against the pillow. Motioning at Ceci to lay Jennifer beside him, Brett asked, "How is she?"

"Unconscious," came the terse answer.

That was Bullard.

Brett looked over at Ceci and smiled. She was studying the massive man in front of her with a frown and not a little bit of trepidation on her face.

"He's fine. Bullard has a gruff manner but he's all heart inside."

"Bull," Bullard said in a laconic voice. "I am what I am."

He straightened from examining the woman to study Ceci. As if understanding instinctively the fear that kept her in place, his gaze softened. He reached out a massive hand and said, "Hi, I'm Bullard."

Brett watched as Ceci gently grasped his hand in hers before dropping it quickly.

He walked over and put an arm around her, tucking her up close. "We think both children have been drugged," Brett said. He motioned at the two sleeping children. "They've been asleep too deeply for too long and in the most unnatural way."

Bullard picked up the sheet and covered the woman on the bed before taking a look at the two children. He checked their eyes, nose, throat, and pulse.

He nodded. "We can take blood and run some tests if you'd like but looks like they've been given a heavy dose of sleeping medicine."

He spun to look at the two of them. "The real question here is why."

"No," Ceci said in a determined voice. "The real question is, are the children going to be okay? What if it's not a sleeping drug?" As the last words tumbled from her lips her bottom lip trembled. Immediately she bit down hard.

Bullard nodded. "If I didn't see signs of them rousing I would immediately be looking at pumping their stomachs out," he said. "No child should ever be drugged. I don't care what the reason."

He waved his hand around his clinic and said, "Not unless they're having major surgery or some other dramatic disease." He turned his gaze back to the sleeping children. "But to knock them out for convenience?" He shook his head. "No."

Brett watched as Ceci raised Jimmy's small hand to her lips and kissed it gently. "They didn't do anything," she cried. "We were all just in the wrong place at the wrong time."

Bullard smiled. "I've heard that way too many times in the last thirty odd years." He turned to study Brett. "As has Brett. So many of the world's problems impact innocents who were there at the wrong time."

Just then Jimmy made a cute little snuffling sound, and he brought his hand up to rub his face before rolling over and tucking his knees up to his chest. He settled into a more normal sleep.

Ceci smiled. "That's the first natural movement he's

made in the last couple of hours." She reached over and stroked Jennifer's cheek. "Now if only she'd wake up from this heavy sleep too."

As if on cue Jennifer's mouth opened and a half snort, half snore whispered out.

Ceci turned to Brett with a teary smile on her face. "Looks like she's starting to wake up."

He nodded, a smile on his face, too. "They're beautiful."

He really did want a family of his own. He'd never actually seen the joy, the need or even desire for it before though. But now watching Ceci with hers, he realized he'd missed out. There was much more for him to learn about the family unit than what he'd experienced so far.

As he raised his gaze to Bullard, he caught the knowing look in the older man's eyes.

Brett frowned at him, not sure he liked the twinkle in the man's gaze.

Bullard returned to the woman. Brett walked to the opposite side of the bed and pulled the sheet back to search for her ID. "She had no purse with her and doesn't appear to have anything on her now."

"We'll have to find out who she is. We can snag her fingerprints and run them through the database. If she was at the embassy it shouldn't be too hard."

Brett nodded. "Is the kit still in the same place?"

"Always. When something is in the right place there is no need to change."

Brett went to the full floor-to-ceiling metal cabinets. On the left side he pulled out the fingerprint kit. He stopped and stared at it. Then laughed. "It might still be in the same old cabinet, but it's not the same old kit."

"Hell no," Bullard said agreeably. "If the enemy's technology is going to advance, then I sure as hell need to keep up with it."

Brett ran images of the woman's fingerprints through the database from the handheld scanner. He loved these things. "Is this one hooked up to your computer?"

Bullard looked at the scanner in his hand and said, "Yes." He walked to a large desk with several computers, turned one on then keyed in his password. Walking away, he motioned at the computer and said to Brett, "Use that one."

Brett pulled up a chair, plugged in the fingerprint scanner and started the search. All government personnel had their fingerprints kept on file, so he thought this should be a fairly quick search. And it was. Within minutes he had her name.

"Amanda Goring." Parts of her file were open and available. "She's thirty-seven years old, worked at the embassy for the last two years. Fully trained in weapons but works as a translator. She speaks seven languages."

"Wow, wonder what that must be like," Ceci said rather enviously.

"Confusing as all hell," Bullard said. "I speak just as many and sometimes they all get messed up in my head."

"Lots of things get messed up in your head," Brett said jokingly. "We're always trying to do too much at once."

"Absolutely." On the far wall Bullard pulled open a large cabinet and wheeled out a portable X-ray machine. He pushed it toward the woman.

Brett stood. "Can I help?"

"Yep." Following Bullard's instructions they took several X-rays. When they were done, Bullard returned the machine to the closet and then entered a small room on the other side.

Ceci said, "He really has all this equipment here? Why?"

Brett's hand automatically reached for hers. "Because he needs it. Not every day, not all the time. But when he needs it, it's available."

CHAPTER 9

CECI COULDN'T IMAGINE anyone needing this type of equipment in their own home. She understood this was a clinic, but it was also in an isolated area and the place was empty. So it was no ordinary one. Bullard might be a doctor, but he didn't appear to be a general practitioner as she knew them to be. She also understood there were secrets she was never going to get answers for.

Brett belonged to a world she didn't understand. Her husband, Jimmy, had been part of the military but nothing like this. He'd been a records clerk. That's what he'd liked. When they'd married he'd had no wish to go overseas. That had changed when the babies arrived.

Brett was sent out on missions that were incredibly dangerous.

Now that the children were safely recovering, the relief eased back, leaving her worn out.

"Any update on the embassy?" she asked.

Brett shook his head. "No. Other than the fact that my team arrived to find the place empty. And of course the military are denying any involvement."

"Of course they are."

He gave her a bitter smile.

And she understood he'd seen this before. "I guess there is no chance of getting our passports anytime soon."

He nodded. "We should have them in another two days."

She let out an exaggerated sigh. "For somebody who said there was no update that's a lot of one."

He laughed. "Maybe, but they aren't exactly the answers we were looking for."

"No, but it's a start." She looked around the well-equipped clinic. "This is an amazing room."

Behind her, walking so quietly she never heard him, Bullard said, "Thank you."

She started. "Good Lord, you walk just like Brett does."

He tossed her a smug smile. "It's our training."

She sat down beside the children's bed. She was tired, but she had no idea where they were supposed to spend the night. She didn't think this was the final destination, though she felt safe here. If they were allowed to stay here she would.

They certainly couldn't leave until the children were awake. She studied the unconscious woman. "How badly hurt is she?"

"Couple of cracked ribs, looks like a skull fracture. That's the one that worries me."

"Really?" she said. "There's almost no blood."

He nodded. "That happens sometimes."

"Doesn't she need to go to a hospital then?" She stared around the clinic. "Are you set up for surgery?"

Brett laughed. "There's not much Bullard can't handle here."

"That might be true, but depending on the issue, a hospital might be a better option." He studied Amanda's features. "On the other hand, we don't want the military to know she is still alive."

"In the meantime…"

Bullard nodded. "In the meantime, I'll keep a close eye on her. Swelling on the brain is the issue. If that happens we'll have to do something about it. But hopefully she'll pull through this just fine."

He lifted his gaze to Ceci. "Looks like you need to have a bite to eat, maybe a hot cup of tea then some sleep."

She shrugged. "That's not going to work out so well if the children are just waking up."

He gave a great booming laugh. "Isn't that the truth? How about a cup of coffee instead?"

She nodded gratefully. "That would be wonderful."

Within minutes she was escorted to a lovely little patio on the edge of the inground pool, hot tub, and almost a fantasy backyard. With the darkness settling in, the lights shining, it was stunning. She stood in amazement, not daring to move in case it all disappeared. It was just so much to take in. From behind her Brett said, "Isn't it beautiful?"

She turned to look at him. "I'm not even sure I know words to describe this."

"Bullard has always loved the outdoors. So this combination of civilization and the natural surroundings is the result." Brett nodded toward the lighting. "He worked very hard to make it the way he wanted it."

"Oh my. I wish I had such a thing for myself and the children."

Brett looked at her. "Maybe one day you will. Not everything has to happen today. Some things need time."

She understood that. But she liked his view. And she *really* liked Bullard's place.

Behind her she turned to see the man who'd originally shown them into the clinic holding a large tray out for her. She smiled and accepted the cup of coffee.

"Where would you like to eat?"

Not seeing a table, she looked around. "What are the options?"

Brett stepped in. "We'll sit over on the patio by the pools, Dave."

Dave nodded and with a smile said, "Good choice." And he melted into the background.

"Patio?" She studied the beautiful scene in front of her but couldn't see what he was talking about.

Brett held out his arm, she slipped her hand through and he led her down a few stairs to the left.

"This is just like old times," she said with a smile.

An awkward pause hiccupped their camaraderie, but then they entered a beautiful stamped concrete patio that was completely surrounded by water. In the center was a small ornamental fire in a table surrounded by a couch. She walked down the one step into the well so she could sit on the couch. "Oh my God, this is so beautiful," she said in a hoarse whisper. "I've never seen anything like it."

"And you may never again." Brett sat down beside her. "Bullard designed this and had a hefty hand in the actual creating of it."

Caught up in the fantasy of the moment she curled into the couch and sipped her coffee. "The children would just love this."

"They would," he admitted. "But of course it's not childproofed. With all the pools and fountains they'd need constant watching."

She laughed. "They do anyway."

"True." He smiled. "I imagine the two of them are quite a handful."

"Oh, they are," she said warmly, feeling the love of

motherhood inside. "But even with everything that's happened I never regretted having them."

"I think that's one of the best recommendations anybody can give."

She felt as his glance landed on her face and then darted off again. She wondered what he was thinking. "You never married?"

He shifted so he could rest back against the couch, his head tilting up to watch the sky above them. "No, I never found anybody I wanted to."

"I'm sorry."

He gave a bark of laughter. "Why?" He shrugged. "I've been busy. I'm not unhappy."

"But that's not the same as saying you're feeling fulfilled and had a glorious few years."

He rolled his head toward her and pinned her in place. "Can you say that?"

Instantly she retreated. She didn't know what to say. Because of course the answer was no, she couldn't. She took a sip of coffee and appeared to study the rings as they swirled around in her cup. She would do a lot for a change of topic right now.

Thankfully, Dave arrived just then with a laden down trolley. He quickly transferred the cutlery and plates to the table. With a full dining service being set she marveled at the luxury. She smiled at Dave, murmuring, "Thank you."

He nodded once and said softly, "Dinner will be ready soon." And he quickly wheeled the cart away.

"Such service."

"Dave was a SEAL, too."

Startled, she turned to look at Brett. "Really?"

He nodded. "Got his left leg blown off. Bullard left soon

after. Dave's been with him ever since."

She winced. "It's not obvious."

Brett shrugged. "No need for it to be."

"Well there you two are. How absolutely romantic."

Brett's face lit up like a firecracker. He hopped to his feet only to be immediately engulfed by men.

Not just men but huge, muscle-bound, dangerous looking ones.

She shrunk back into the corner not too sure what she was supposed to be doing. And wishing she could go back to the children. In the mix of that chaos Dave returned with more cutlery.

Obviously, everybody knew each other as there was much shoulder slapping. When the group realized they'd arrived at dinnertime there were more exclamations of joy. Finally the noise calmed down.

Brett turned to face Ceci and said, "These are my friends." And he introduced them one at a time.

She knew she'd never remember all the names but some were very unforgettable like the monster of a man who looked like he was ready to eat the silverware off the table. His name was Swede. And there was the silent shadow behind him who was appropriately named Shadow.

As she walked through the group she found it relatively easy to memorize certain characteristics to match their names, making it much simpler for her to tell who was who. Realizing they were all active SEALs was not only intimidating and a little overwhelming, but it also made her realize how different a world they lived in.

She'd been married to Jimmy just under three years, but he hadn't had the same presence. He'd been very fit, but he didn't have that dangerous cutting edge. These men were a cut above.

BRETT KNEW AS a group they were overwhelming. Individually they were all larger than life, but when they got together the boisterous energy of the men, although respectful and polite, was still a lot to handle. He'd seen Ceci shrink back into the corner and had maintained his position at her side the whole time. He could see the knowing looks from several of the guys, but it wasn't until the last man joined him that he realized how it looked. Chase was his best friend and had recently found somebody special. Chase's gaze immediately landed on Ceci and then back over at Brett, one eyebrow raised. He stepped forward and held out his hand to Ceci and said, "Hi, Ceci, Nice to see you again."

Ceci smiled up at him and shook his hand. "Thanks, it's been a long time."

At that time Dave returned with a larger cart and what appeared to be enough food for dozens of people. That shifted the energy as everyone took a seat.

Dave disappeared and then returned with two high chairs.

She jumped to her feet. "Are they awake?"

Dave pointed. She turned to see Bullard with one child in each arm. Around her she could hear the questioning atmosphere as if people were trying to place whose children they were and what her role was in this place.

The children reached for her, cries of delight in their voices. Unlike her they weren't intimidated by the sudden number of men. She hugged them close, kissed each of their cheeks, all the while whispering little nothings to each of them, then tucked them into the high chairs. It was dark out but she knew their sleep patterns would be completely off because of the drugs. Bullard managed to squeeze into a place at the far end of the couch and sit down.

He laughed. "Dave's in his glory. He's always telling me to bring people over so he'll have somebody to feed. Now you guys are here and he'll be cooking for days."

"And we'll be happy to eat Dave's cooking." Swede laughed. "It's good to see you, Bullard."

"And you. Why the hell haven't you come around before now?"

"I didn't need a job," Swede said with a big grin. "Neither did I require your medical services."

"Maybe you haven't but I heard that several might. What's this about Dane and Cooper?"

"Both of them are actually doing fine. Even Levi, Merk, and Rhodes are well on the mend."

"I heard about them." Bullard's voice deepened. "That's never a good thing."

Dave spoke from the sidewalk, large platters of food in his arms. He placed them on the table. "What about Stone?"

There was a heavier silence. Mason spoke up, "Stone is on the mend. There's obviously an adjustment. As you well know."

Dave nodded. "Maybe I'll give him a call."

Chase spoke up. "Do that. He'd appreciate it."

After that the topic turned to lighter issues. Everyone dug into the platters of ribs, chicken, potatoes, and vegetables. Brett kept a close eye on Ceci as she fed the children. Leaning closer to her, he whispered, "Are you getting any food?"

She flashed him a bright smile. "I'm getting lots to eat."

Brett returned to his own meal until Mason pushed his

empty plate back and said, "Brett, what the hell's going on at the embassy?"

In a quiet voice Brett explained everything that had happened since his arrival. As he concluded he added, "Ceci did say right from the beginning she felt unnerved, that instinct told her to run. She hadn't seen anything that would explain it, but if we'd run earlier we'd have avoided all of the rest of that mess."

"In which case, Amanda would have likely died."

Brett turned to face Ceci. "True enough."

With the men tossing ideas back and forth the conversation went from the military to the US and back to the embassy as everyone discussed the outcome. Mason piped up and said, "The US is not admitting to an attack at the embassy, but they have assigned a team to take back control."

"The place was empty when we left. So there likely isn't anything to take control back from." Ceci looked at him. "Besides, what team is that?"

He grinned. "Us."

CHAPTER 10

S HE WASN'T SURE how she felt about that. She understood the team was here on-site so that made it logistically the best answer. And as they hadn't seen anybody at the consulate maybe they wouldn't be in danger. But it bothered her to think of these men going back into that nightmare. Yet, as she stared at them she realized they were looking forward to it. She shook her head. Who knew?

Jimmy wanted out of his high chair. Having slept long he was full of energy. She tried to keep him entertained for a few minutes, but as soon as Jennifer was done eating she unbuckled both and carried them over so they could look at the lights. Jimmy squirmed to get down. She let him stand but held on to his hand firmly. She quietly explained what the problem was with the water, but Jimmy was already a good swimmer and he just wanted to go in.

Dave appeared magically at her side. Towels in hand. "If the children want to go swimming let's take them over to the shallow end of the pool where they'll be safe."

She looked at him in surprise. "The shallow end? A pool?"

He nodded and led the way. She'd seen the lights in the distance but hadn't realized it was a large pool decorated with colored lights. Jimmy started screaming hysterically with joy. Within seconds he was stripped down to his underpants and jumping in.

Comfortable in the water, he paddled and laughed in the shallow end. Jennifer cried out to go in too but that was a different story. She couldn't go in unless Ceci went in. And Ceci had no bathing suit.

Hell, she barely had any clothing. If she got wet now, she was stuck.

She slipped off her shoes then rolled her pants up above her knees. That was as high as they'd go. At the stairs, and after stripping Jennifer down to the buff, she let her play at the edge of the water.

With the lights, it looked magical. She longed to go in but at the same time it was nice just to sit here on the top step with her daughter. At the sound of a heavy splash she looked up to see Dave diving into the far end. He swam all the way across the pool to pop up beside Jimmy, causing him to break out in a full set of giggles. That's when she realized he'd come in to help with the children. She smiled her thanks.

Dave didn't seem to notice. He was just too busy having fun with Jimmy.

For the first time in over a week she could feel some of the tension slipping from her shoulders. After everything they'd been through this was a much needed idyllic break.

Brett sat down beside her on the edge of the pool, his jeans pulled up over his knees and his feet bare. "Bullard has a selection of bathing suits for everyone if you would like to go for a swim."

She brightened. Then sagged in place. "No, I should probably stay with the kids."

"Why?" He reached over and picked up her hand. "I'll stay here with Jennifer. You can go into the bathhouse right there." He nodded toward a small cabin looking structure on the side. "See if you can find something to wear. We are here so you might as well enjoy it. I doubt you did your time on the yacht at all."

She laughed. "No, I really didn't. It was hard with the kids."

"Here you have almost a dozen built-in babysitters. We're all very capable of looking after these two. Go," he urged. "Remember you have to live a little and enjoy life too."

She hesitated then with a big smile she hopped to her feet, handed Jennifer to Brett and ran to the small bath-house. Inside was an amazing array of bathing suits for both sexes of all ages. A closet door stood open with a sign at the top that said *ladies*. Another one said *men* and another one *children*. Jennifer's was big, but it was good enough. Then she found a bathing suit that might fit her.

When she put it on she realized it was a whole lot small-er than she'd expected. Then again since motherhood she was a whole lot more endowed. She yanked on a beach cover up then spied the towels. She grabbed three and took them out to add to the pile Dave had brought.

Self-conscious but grateful the men weren't staring, she dropped the towels beside Brett, eased off the cover and jumped into the pool water. As soon as the water closed over her head she knew she'd done the right thing.

Her body rejoiced as she floated carefree. So damn re-freshing and freeing.

GOOD, HE WAS glad she decided to go in. His mom had filled him in on her last few years of life with and without

Jimmy. Brett had deliberately stayed away, not wanting to deal with any more hurt and anger. It hadn't been easy for her. But she'd devoted her life to raising the children.

He could well imagine that going on a yacht for a week would be a gift. And he certainly didn't blame her for that. Everyone needed a break. It hadn't turned out the way she had expected, but here she was actually managing to find some enjoyment in the current situation. He admired that.

Knowing she was self-conscious, he'd kept his gaze away from her as she dropped the robe. The water couldn't camouflage the mermaid in front of him though. She was beautiful inside and he already knew she was outside as well, but motherhood had given a ripeness to her figure that was hard to mistake. It looked good on her.

Jennifer wanted to go back in the water so he walked over to the stairs and stepped down so she could paddle around on the wide stairs, his hand holding her safe. This cherub was truly adorable. He hadn't been around babies very much, but because of his mom's extended family he had a lot of experience with children.

Ceci swam close and held up her arms to Jennifer who squealed and threw herself into the water. With a laugh Ceci swam out a little further away just letting the baby float. Brett sat back watching mom and baby.

There was a Madonna look to the two of them. As a man, there was a certain reverence to the scene. Something he couldn't access for himself. And had never been interested in having before. Now he wondered if he had a child of his own, would they have a similar bond?

Footsteps approached. He recognized the sound before his friend opened his mouth.

"Is this serious?" Chase asked. "And are you nuts? She hurt you once already."

Brett raised an eyebrow. That wasn't quite the question he'd expected. "There's been no time to answer that," Brett said with a smile. "I've been trying to keep her safe." He glanced up and said, "She's also different now."

Chase frowned, his gaze on the mother and child in the water.

"Is she? I just don't want to see you get hurt again."

"I'm not planning on it," Brett muttered.

Chase wandered back to the other men, leaving Brett to his thoughts. And none of them were good. Ceci was all he'd ever wanted, but she'd broken it off with him. He'd been devastated at the time. He wasn't as young now and the world had narrowed. He wasn't sure he could go back to that time, and could he trust her again. She had torn his life apart and left him broken. There was no way he wanted to go through another session like that.

Besides, she'd shown no interest in him. Or in anyone that he could see. She'd lost someone dear to her, and she might not be ready to move on. And there was a much bigger issue – two children.

The phone rang behind him. He heard Bullard answer and then a shuffle of chairs as he made his way past the group still collected around the table. A few moments later he hung up the phone and called out, "Our injured guest from the embassy is awake."

Several of the men got up and walked inside the house to where she lay. Brett watched them leave. He was torn. He wanted to go question her himself, but he didn't want to leave Ceci alone here with the two kids. He caught Dave's eye who motioned toward the house.

Brett nodded and stood up, pulling down his damp cuffs and followed the group inside.

CHAPTER 11

"THANK YOU AND good night." Ceci closed the door behind Dave. She still carried Jennifer bundled up in a towel and Jimmy walked beside her dripping water everywhere. "Let's get you a quick, hot bath." She walked through the gorgeous guest room to the large bathroom. Marveling at the modern contemporary look, she quickly filled the bathtub with warm water a few inches deep for the kids and set about rinsing off the chlorine. With both of them shampooed, and rinsed and now showing signs of being very tired again, she got them dressed in PJs and tucked into bed. She picked up the only book they had and read a bedtime story. It wasn't long before both kids dozed off.

That was her cue. She was still wrapped in a towel herself. She stepped into the bathroom, quickly tidied it up then pulled the plug and turned on the shower. Finally she stood under the hot water letting the heat wash over her body. It was warm outside, almost humid, but the water had been cool. She wished she'd gotten an update on the poor woman. She rinsed her hair and then shut off the water. After wringing out her shoulder length locks, she opened the door and grabbed a towel to wrap around herself. Stepping out she grabbed a second one and dried off her hair. Wandering back into the bedroom, she froze.

Brett sat on the large armchair.

"I'm sorry, I didn't mean to startle you. I did call but you didn't answer." He shrugged. "After what we've been through I needed the peace of mind of knowing you were safe, so I came in."

She raised her eyebrows but didn't say anything. Under the circumstances maybe that was understandable. "And now you know that we are fine."

She walked to the closet and opened the double doors. She gasped in delight. She'd wondered after seeing the fully stocked bathhouse if there would be more clothes in the room, but she hadn't contemplated such a variety. A robe hung on the back of the door. She quickly pulled it on then dropped the towel.

Feeling better she carried the towel to the bathroom where she hung it up to dry. Back out in the main room she sat down on the only other chair. "How's Amanda?"

"Unconscious again. She woke briefly, but was groggy and barely coherent. She said something about change of staff recently, and having no warning until they were rounded up at gunpoint."

Ceci sank back against the chair. "That would've been so terrible," she exclaimed.

Brett nodded. "Exactly. It also means they had an inside man. Someone had to know the bulk of the people were going to be leaving the embassy that day. Making it perfect timing."

"Normally everybody would know about staff changes weeks in advance," she said thoughtfully. "So they had to have some kind of a reason why a switch like this was made so fast."

"Apparently there was a major shuffle in the department.

She's now thinking maybe they had an idea of the mole."

It was so damn unbelievable that it actually made sense. Ceci was sorry for all those poor people who had died through this attack, but she was glad it was not on a more global scale. "So now what?"

"A couple of things. The US is almost finished processing your passports so we should be able to get you home soon – possibly tomorrow. Are you okay to stay here with Bullard until they come through? And did you have enough interactions with any of the people from the embassy that they might be concerned about you identifying them?"

At his first comment her smile lit up until he continued and finally finished talking. Her heart went back to pounding under major stress again.

Cautiously she said, "That's good news about the passports. I'll be happy to stay here." She frowned. "Yes, I could identify some of the people. I was there for several days."

He nodded. "That's what I was afraid of. We're getting photos of the staff who were killed. And trying to get video feeds from the embassy during the takeover. Let's see if you can identify any of the attackers as having been part of the staff you interacted with."

"In other words you want to know if I can identify any of the bad guys in particular."

He nodded.

Her breath pushed out in a big gust. "That's scary."

"Yes, but you're safe here."

Her gaze flew to the sleeping children, wondering what it was going to take to get home safe and sound. "Even if I can identify them that does not mean they are going to come after me, right?"

"We can't say that. It depends on how high a position

the mole has obtained and whether it's important his or her identity be kept secret. The US is already working to take back the embassy. That means whoever is left in office is going to be in danger."

"Of course." She shook her head. "How did my life come to this? All I wanted was to raise my children in peace." She glared out the window. "Was this punishment for actually thinking I could have a vacation on the yacht?"

"Just because you ventured out of the safety and sanctity of your home doesn't mean all this bad stuff happening is your fault. I don't know how you ended up in the middle of it, all I know is that when it's over you can expect to go back to your safe life, and it'll be fine."

"I wonder about that." The good news was they were safe here. And she had no doubts it would take quite an army to breach this place. It was also an idyllic spot to stay so she was happy to be here. "Go on, go save the world. Again. I'll be fine."

He laughed. "That's not exactly what I was planning on doing."

"Oh, why was that?"

"'Cause somebody needs to stay and keep an eye on you."

"And I suppose you volunteered for that job?" she said in a dry tone. Inside she was happy to know she wasn't going to be deserted by everyone. As much as she loved the surroundings she really didn't know Dave or Bullard. And she had no idea how many other men were here.

His voice turned cool as he said, "It was a group decision, but it wasn't a hard one to make considering the children are most comfortable with me."

Immediately she felt like an ass. He was right. The children had come to accept him. There were a lot of men downstairs and the kids had been fine at dinnertime, but that didn't mean they were going to be very happy to be passed from one to the other. Her gaze slipped over to where the baby slept. In a soft voice, she murmured, "You're right. I'm sorry."

"You don't need to be." He stood up and looked around the room. "I'm in the room next door if you need me. You can pound on that wall." He pointed. "If I don't respond feel free to come into the room. I won't lock the door."

She shook her head. "We'll be fine."

He nodded and walked back to the front door. "Good, then I'll say good night."

He went out and closed the door abruptly. She trailed behind and stood feeling like a fool. An ungrateful one. She opened the door and peered outside to find him staring down the hallway.

"I'm sorry," she said. "I really do appreciate everything you've done for me. For us."

And hit a nerve.

He spun, his eyes dark. "The last thing I want is your gratitude." He walked inside his room and slammed his door closed.

And that just made her feel much worse.

BRETT WALKED A few feet into his room and bowed his head. What an ass. What was it about the situation that was setting off his inner stupidity? Sure they had history, but they didn't have anything now – this was a job. He had to remember that. It was also damn near impossible to forget the smell of her in his arms, the sight of her body in that damn bikini or that absolutely unbelievable sensation when he watched her cuddle Jennifer.

Her kids were great, and he knew at one point in time he would head down that same road with a family of his own.

But he'd never considered taking on a ready-made family until now.

He was being an idiot because there was no way in hell she was interested in him. Neither did he want to go down that road with her again.

There was a knock at the door. He bowed his head, knowing who it was. He briefly considered not opening and then realized that was just being foolish too.

He pulled it open and said, "Now what?"

Shit. He was being an ass.

She bit her bottom lip in a move that was causing a distraction. He reached out, cupped her chin and said, "Stop that."

She glared at him. "And what if I don't?"

A half laugh escaped. "If you don't then I'd have to do this."

He tugged her chin toward him then bent down and covered her lips with his own. When he pulled away, the absolute look of disbelief on her face made him smile.

"What's the matter?" he teased. "Have you forgotten how to do that?"

She shot him an odd look, then added, "I haven't forgotten *anything*."

As the heat flashed between them she turned and walked back to her room, and it was her turn to slam the door.

He stood in the doorway in a state of shock of his own. What had she meant by that?

CHAPTER 12

"THAT'S A DANGEROUS game you're playing," Ceci whispered to herself as she sat down in the chair. Tremors rippled through her body. What had happened to that nice complacent life she'd lived? After Jimmy died she'd been determined to stay single and just focus on raising her children. She had a clear purpose then. But since this mess? It was like she didn't know who she was anymore.

And inside she was afraid all she'd been doing before was hiding.

Now it was like everything had been blown wide open.

What she was... She shouldn't have this confusion over Brett, there shouldn't be this heat... Not anymore. She'd walked away.

Passion had never been the issue between them. So what had been the problem? Still dressed in the bathrobe, her feet up on the coffee table, she mulled on the past. Just because he'd kissed her didn't mean he wanted a relationship, and she couldn't do anything less. Not with the children.

Besides, she wasn't ready for that either. She might never be again. She had changed. Older, a widow, a mother. She viewed relationships differently.

As much as she'd enjoyed a lot of things about being married, what she hadn't was her relationship with Jimmy. He'd said he wanted to be a father but he hadn't. When he found out she was pregnant with Jennifer things became *very* difficult. She often wondered if he'd asked to be sent overseas. Anything to leave. That was just one of those little horrible fears inside that wouldn't go away.

She closed her eyes and murmured, "Jimmy, what the hell happened to us?"

What she did know was if Jimmy hadn't died they would probably be separated by now. A sad acknowledgment of her relationship. And part of the reason she feared she'd been hiding out instead of living. Was she happy to use any excuse to avoid getting involved again? Avoid making the wrong decision again. Avoid getting hurt again. Yet, was it really feasible to consider being alone for the rest of her life?

She's a young, healthy female and didn't the children need a father? She'd seen lots of single-parent families out in the world and some of them did really well. Others not so much. She didn't want hers to fall in the "not so much" category.

She got up and wandered over to the closet looking to see if that magical selection of clothing would offer anything for her to sleep in for the night. There was a pair of pajama pants she paired with a T-shirt. When she was finally ready for bed she turned out the lights and snuggled in close to her children. Unbidden, tears came to her eyes. She'd do anything to keep them safe. She wrapped her arms around both, kissed each on the cheek and let herself slowly relax into sleep.

Just as she was about to drop off she thought she heard a ruckus outside. She bolted up from her bed, checked on the kids, saw they slept and raced to the window. It took her a moment to realize it was the dogs barking in the back corner.

She opened the patio doors and stepped out. The evening was balmy and warm, but as she watched men slide through the back fantasy garden, guns in hand, she realized the fantasy part was a mirage. That same hellish world existed beyond those secure gates.

And someone was trying to breach them.

So just how secure were they?

"It's okay, Ceci. Go back to bed."

She didn't turn to face Brett, knowing he was on the identical patio just a few feet away. "Is it? Something's bothering the dogs."

"The men will handle it."

Right. She didn't want to know what that meant. With her arms tight around her chest, she turned to glance at him. Then gasped and spun back to stare out into the cool evening as heat flashed up and down her spine, awakening nerve endings from their dormant state. She'd forgotten what kind of physical shape he was in. Even before he'd become one of the elite, he'd been heavy into sports. He had bulkier muscles now, his body lean and so damn sexy. Dear God, where was her willpower? And why was this hitting her now? Stupid. She was more than a set of idiotic hormones.

She shook her head. "How the hell was it that you came to rescue me on the yacht?"

"Is there any reason it wouldn't be me?"

She raised her gaze to the moonlight shining high above. "In all the years since we broke up it never crossed my mind I'd be in a situation needing your help."

"My help was always there, but it wasn't something you would accept."

She pondered that. "Maybe. But it always seemed like your version of help was giving the solutions when I needed to find my own way."

"Good enough. Did you find it?"

That was another one of those very important questions. Had she? No. She'd found part of it. But as she hadn't shared so much back then it seemed pointless now to bring it up. Yet, her secret felt like a stumbling block to moving forward.

She shook her head. "I'm not sure," she admitted. Deciding it was time to leave before the conversation got even more dangerous, she turned and headed toward the glass doors, calling out, "Have a good night."

"I'd have a better night if I was with you," he muttered softly in the evening air.

She froze in the middle of the doorway and turned to look at him. "Do you mean that?"

He glanced back at her. "What?" he asked brusquely. "You've always known how I feel about you. It should be no surprise now."

He turned to gaze at the corner of the yard where the soldiers had converged.

"No," she said forcibly. "I knew how you *felt*. I have no clue how you feel now. Why would you still care? I walked away years ago."

He nodded. "Yes *you* did."

The thought that he might still care for her was just a little too heartwarming to leave open like this. Scary too. But she'd made a lot of mistakes in her life. He was one. She didn't want to repeat it. In a soft voice, she said, "Are you saying you still care?"

Silence.

Maybe that was a little too far. She waited, studying his impassive face – the cool night air brushing against her sensitized skin.

Finally, he shot her a shuttered look and said, "I just said that, didn't I?"

Of course, the real question was how *much* did he care? But she wasn't comfortable asking that. And apparently he wasn't willing to add more either.

With something potentially starting between them, both unsure, each a little hesitant, she gave him a quick smile and said, "That might be nice."

She went inside, closing the door firmly behind her.

"NICE?"

He shook his head at her as she disappeared from sight. What the hell did "nice" mean? He turned his attention back to the group in the far corner of the property. What was going on? Deciding that action was better than inaction, he turned to his room, quickly dressed, and raced down to find out. If this had anything to do with Ceci he needed to know.

"Brett?"

Hearing Swede call from the left he quickly changed course. Swede was in the shadows keeping an eye on the situation.

"What's happening?"

"Two armed men. Dogs brought them down." Swede grinned darkly. "Bullard trained his dogs to sit and wait and when the enemy climbs over the fence they get them."

"Isn't the fence electrified?"

Swede's grin widened. "Bullard shut it off so the men could enter."

"Smart." It also let him know if they were serious threats and not just scoping the place out. "It helps that Bullard also keeps fully armed men here."

Swede studied his face. "You do know Bullard runs special assignments from this location, don't you?"

"I knew he did something along those lines, but I wasn't sure exactly what."

Swede snorted. "*Nobody* knows exactly what."

"Still, it's nice to know there are options for later." He didn't specify what. Swede knew. It wasn't something the men talked about, but with Levi and his unit forced to consider their future options it was on everyone's mind. Ten years went by quick and that was about the max for SEALs. It was nice to know there were other things he could do to help the world out. There was always going to be a war somewhere.

"As long as one of those options isn't going into the regular Navy then I'm good." Swede slapped him on the shoulder and slipped around behind the trees. "Might be fun to go private. Less rules and regulations that way."

Brett followed Swede through the path down to where the guard had two men pinned on the ground. Bullard's crew pulled a balaclava off one of the men. Lights were shone in his face.

"Jesus," Brett whispered.

Swede turned to look at him. "You know him?"

Brett shook his head. "Not *know* him. He and a woman passed me on the way up the stairs. They'd just shot three of the embassy people and the two men they'd left behind were trying to rape Amanda, who's now in Bullard's clinic." The group glanced at each other and then back down at the man on the ground.

One of the men reached out and pulled the balaclava off the second. On cue everybody turned to look at Brett.

He nodded. "He was one of the two assholes attacking

the woman." With a change in his voice he added, "I guess I didn't hit him hard enough."

"Guys like this, just shoot them dead."

Bullard's team split into two groups with four men picking up the intruders and carrying them up to the house. The others set up positions around the yard watching.

Always watching.

Of course, Bullard had exceptionally trained people on his staff. When one had been the best, only the best would do again.

Swede nudged him. "Let's go see what these guys are after."

Brett fell into line beside him. "I don't need to ask. I already know what they're after." With a sharp look he added, "They want Ceci and the kids."

And they weren't going to get them. Not while he was alive.

CHAPTER 13

SHE COULDN'T SLEEP. Who could knowing something was happening outside? Frustrated and getting pissed off the longer she lay there waiting for sleep to come, she wondered what the chances were of being able to find out anything. Then again, she glanced over at the children, knowing she couldn't leave them. There was nobody here to babysit, and she was not going to leave them alone in a strange place. If they woke up to find her gone they'd be devastated.

Not happening. She lay back down on the bed once again.

Heavy footsteps came down the hallway. She bolted for the door, opening it before she allowed herself to think. Sure enough it was Brett. Fully dressed once again. "What happened?"

"Why aren't you asleep?"

She shot him a look. "Who can sleep with all that's going on?" She tapped the floor impatiently. "And you aren't answering me?"

"Two men from the embassy. One who passed me on the stairs and one I knocked out but not hard enough. Both are here."

She gasped. "Oh my God. Are they after me?" she asked incredulously. "Why? Besides, how would they know where we are?"

At that he winced. "There might've been a GPS tracker on the truck."

"What?" He was serious. "We led them right here to us?" This was too impossible.

He shrugged. "Can't say searching for a tracker to disable was at the top of my mind. I was trying to get the three of you out of there safely."

"Good Lord." Of course, it wasn't his fault. And he had rescued them from a horrible situation. But apparently that brought the assholes right here, and put everyone in danger. "I must apologize to Bullard."

Brett laughed. "He's probably opening a bottle of champagne. If things get too dull he gets bored."

She grinned in relief. "Nice to know this is the right place for this kind of stuff because almost every other person I know would be completely freaked out."

"He would never do that."

"Your mom would," she teased. The humor lightened the guilt slightly.

"Let's not bring her into this. She gives me enough trouble these days."

"She's adorable," Ceci said. "But I can imagine she's a little demanding in her wishes."

"You think?" But he smiled at her. "There had been just the two of us for so long that she figures it's her right to meddle as I won't have anybody else around to do it." His grin widened. "She's terrified I'm never going to get married."

"Marriage isn't all it's made out to be," she muttered.

"I imagine marriage is more about what you put into it. But I've never been there so who knows." He shrugged as he walked past her to his bedroom. "Are the children still sleeping?"

"Yes." She retreated into her room, hating this awkward dance of a new relationship. The uncertainty, the questions. It was one of the reasons she'd been happy to marry Jimmy. She'd wanted to find the "one" and settle down before she was too old and life passed her by.

That realization was a bitter pill to swallow.

"What's wrong?" He stepped toward her and reached out to grasp her by the shoulders.

She shook him off. "Nothing, just a difficult realization."

"Tell me."

He didn't ask, he demanded. But then maybe he had the right given the circumstances. That didn't mean she wanted to share. "It's really nothing. Just something I understand better about my actions now than back then."

He waited, indomitable. "If it has something to do with me then I would really like to hear, please?"

She winced. She'd pretty well destroyed his life back then. Without giving him an explanation. "After you, I went through several short-term relationships looking for what would be a permanent one, and when I found Jimmy he seemed ready to settle down," she said. "I jumped at it, not so much because I loved him but I was in love with the package. I wanted to be married, to start a family. But what I *just* realized is back then I figured, if I didn't do something fast, I was going to miss that stage of life."

She dropped her gaze to the floor. What the hell did she just do? That was such a stupid thing to tell him.

When he didn't say anything for a few minutes she looked up and felt the impact of the shock even now.

"Why didn't you tell me?" he asked. "We never talked

about marriage back then. I thought you weren't ready." He turned to face his door as if ready to leave. "You married Jimmy within six months of us breaking up because life was passing you by? How long did you even go out with him before you knew you were magically in love with this man?"

He knew when they got married? Of course his mother would've told him. Ceci wasn't very impressed with herself, but he was going to be even less so if he knew everything.

She took a deep breath. "I hadn't realized how uprooted and insecure I felt. Something happened that made me want to run and hide for a while, then when I came out of my cocoon, I returned to living with a vengeance. Feeling like I was out of time, panicked that if I didn't get married soon I'd miss that too. I'd just had a hard lesson on the fragility of life, the preciousness of good relationships and I really needed to take that step. Only I couldn't explain why – not then at least."

She walked into the hallway and started pacing. "The men I dated were all losers. When I met Jimmy, he seemed like the answer. He wanted to get married too. But toward the end…" her tone trailed off.

"You weren't happy?"

She shook her head. "Not once Jimmy Junior came along. Jimmy was happy to be married, but he wasn't about fatherhood. We started having major trouble when he found out I was pregnant with Jennifer. That really finished him. I'm pretty sure he asked to be sent overseas. As if death was better than his life."

"I'm sorry. I hear what you're saying but that was five or six years ago. I'm sure as you look back you can see there was no need to feel that note of desperation."

She paced a little further and spun to see him. "I understand that now," she admitted. "That was a realization I couldn't figure out then, but I do know something else I haven't told you."

Dare she tell him? If she started a relationship with him again she wanted it based on honesty. She hadn't been with him years ago, and she should have. It would have changed everything.

She took a deep breath and said, "If we're being honest with each other, and I need to be if we're looking at starting something," she said. "Then I need to tell you the truth about back then. You aren't going to want anything to do with me afterwards."

"I sincerely doubt that." He shook his head. "But if there is an explanation about why you broke up with me, I'd like to hear it."

She dropped her gaze to the floor then slowly raised it to stare him in the face. "It's going to be hard for you to understand. Hell, I didn't for years."

"I can't understand anything if you don't tell me," he said in exasperation, but he never broke contact, the look in his eyes intent. Watchful.

"I broke it off with you because… I learned I was pregnant only to lose it within weeks of finding out." She took a deep breath, watching his eyes darken in shock. "I walked away after losing your child."

"WHAT?" HE SLOWLY straightened and took a step toward her. She retreated. He stopped and stared at her. "You were pregnant?"

"I was." She looked at him nervously. "But not for long."

"And you didn't tell me?" He couldn't even begin to process this information. "Why?"

"Because I wanted you to want to marry me because you loved *me*, not because I was carrying your baby." She opened her arms. "I needed you to marry me because you cared not because it was the right thing to do." He held his hand out as if to grasp hers and then let it fall weakly to his side. He was stunned. He'd had no idea.

He turned and stared at his doorway blankly. What was he supposed to say? To think? To feel? A part of him felt betrayed at the most deepest level. He could have had a little boy like Jimmy or a girl like Jennifer all his own. Only it had ended before really starting. Confused, he didn't know what to think. Yet at the same time he wanted to grieve the loss of something that, although it was long ago, felt like today.

Confused, his emotions in turmoil he asked, "If you hadn't lost the baby, would you have stayed?" He leaned closer, needing to see the truth in her eyes. "Or would you have taken my child and left?"

"Oh my God." She ran toward him and threw her arms around his chest. "I'd have stayed. I would never have done that to you."

He slowly wrapped his arms around her and held her close. He whispered against her temple, his heart aching with the loss he hadn't known. "Why didn't you trust me enough to let me know? If you had we would have been a family, had kids of our own by now."

He pulled back so he could look down at her face. "You pulled away from me so suddenly, and I had no idea what I'd done. Or what I could do to fix it." He gave her a little shake. "You gave me no chance to."

"I just knew I was hurting. As I hadn't told you about

the pregnancy I didn't feel like I could tell you about the miscarriage. It was like I'd closed the door and didn't know how to open it. I turned and walked away and I didn't even know why."

Her eyes brimmed with tears. "Even afterwards there was desperation with every other relationship. As if I had to find a man who would give me a baby to replace the one I lost." In fact, she'd walked away realizing she'd made a mistake but couldn't reverse it. Instead, she tried to get it all back again but with someone else. Silly. Stupid.

She pulled back and wiped tears out of her eyes. "I know it makes no sense. I don't even understand, but that convoluted thinking made sense at the time. I can tell you it wasn't any one thing you did."

He snorted.

"I know that doesn't help much."

"What it comes down to is trust. You didn't trust me."

She reached out and cupped his cheek.

"No," she whispered. "It was me. I didn't trust myself."

With tears passing down her cheeks, she turned and walked back inside her room.

CHAPTER 14

THE NEXT MORNING she stared at the mirror in dismay. Her face was puffy, her eyes red and swollen. There was nothing she could do to hide the ravages of a night of crying. She'd done her best to keep silent so as not to disturb the children, but even after a hot shower she looked the way she felt – like shit. Why was it only now she understood her actions from so long ago?

She'd hurt him badly then, but she'd just slashed open that wound and hurt him twice as much now. She should've kept her mouth shut. What good had it done? And just like that the tears started again. The loss was fresh and as hot and painful as if it just happened. She'd gone on to have two beautiful children, but she'd never found the same beautiful love.

Staring out on the balcony in the early morning sun, her arms wrapped around her chest, she whispered out loud, "Dear God, what have I done?"

"Are you okay?" Chase's voice reached across the other patio from behind her.

She sniffled and wiped her eyes. "No, but I will be."

"Funny, I think I heard that exact same response from Brett this morning too."

"He'll get over it." She may never, but that was her cross to bear.

"Well, instead of being a martyr, get dressed and bring the children down for breakfast. If nothing else Brett needs to know you're okay. He's worked himself up over you." Chase's voice had a hard edge to it.

She nodded. "You never did like me."

"I liked you just fine, but I hated you when you hurt Brett." And on that note he turned and walked back inside.

That was one thing about Brett and his friends. They always had each other's backs. Something she never had. She'd grown up in the foster care system with no siblings or parents. Lots of extended family but none willing to take on raising a young girl. She'd been close to no one and had instead chosen to isolate herself to heal the hurt inside. Their presence in the background had kept the relationship with her foster family on good terms. She'd been well cared for. Only it left her relationships with a touch of neediness to them.

As evidenced in the ones she'd had after Brett.

History repeating itself.

Stupid really.

And it needed to stop.

She was no longer the same young woman. She was now a mother with two small children of her own to raise. She turned back to see Jimmy sitting up, rubbing his eyes. She opened her arms and swooped him up into a hug. God, she loved her children.

"Can we go back in the water, Mommy?" he asked sleepily.

She laughed. "Maybe later."

He got dressed with little help from her. As he tugged his shirt down over his head Jennifer started to wake up. Her early morning smile made Ceci's heart ache.

The next hour was filled with fun and laughter as she got both kids up and ready for the day. She quickly dressed herself. Carrying Jennifer and holding Jimmy's hand she walked back down to the main part of the house.

The place was big and she had no idea where she was going. Dinner had been outside on the lovely patio, but she didn't think that would be the same place for breakfast. As she walked down the last few stairs Dave magically appeared.

She smiled at him. "I have two very hungry little children," she said.

In a move that totally surprised her, Dave held out his arms to Jennifer and she threw herself into them. He gave her a tiny hug and said, "Follow me."

He led them outside to a different area where there was a large table that would hold at least fifteen people. At one end were two chairs for the children. Dave buckled Jennifer into the high chair as Ceci assisted Jimmy up onto his chair. Jimmy kept up a continuous chatter of questions.

And Dave, with the patience of a saint, answered every one of them as best he could. "No I don't understand how they make these chairs. Some kind of woven plastic from my understanding."

Jimmy ran his fingers over the chairs and smiled. "I can make chairs with Legos."

"Legos are good for making all kinds of things," Dave said. "I'll return soon with breakfast."

In a giggling high-pitched voice, Jimmy said, "Food, food, food."

And he started smacking the table. Jennifer immediately followed his lead. It took several minutes to calm them down. When they were finally happy to just sit and look around at the garden Ceci settled back into her chair hating the fatigue inside. She'd slept but hadn't rested.

She also wasn't looking forward to seeing the men. All of them were Brett's friends and by now all knew the two had a history. Only none of the men showed up. Instead Dave returned with bowls of cereal and toast for the kids. "What would you like for breakfast, Ceci?"

"Coffee. Other than that, I'm good."

Dave frowned but he didn't say anything. He disappeared to return a few minutes later with coffee and a tray of food to obviously tantalize her into eating.

There was yogurt, granola, and a fresh fruit bowl as well as several kinds of muffins and a cheese platter. She stared down at the wonderful selection. "Okay, now I'm hungry."

He disappeared as silently as before. Once the children saw her platter they immediately wanted some, so it was a case of share and share alike. That was her world with children.

She loved it. By time they finished there was still no sign of anyone else. She frowned as it was an idyllic scene here, but it didn't stop the fact that last night they'd had two intruders connected with the embassy. She wanted to know more but wasn't even sure where to find answers.

She was finishing breakfast as Dave returned with a trolley and a warm washcloth. He proceeded to clean up both children's hands and faces. She marveled at him. "Looks like you have a little bit of experience with this."

He stilled and in a low voice said, "At one time I did."

He helped Jennifer down from the high chair and handed her to Ceci. Realizing she'd opened a wound, Ceci stayed quiet until he was done with Jimmy. She stood up and looked around, not sure what to do with herself and the children now. That was the trouble of being a guest, you could never be quite comfortable and do what you would do if you were at home.

"The playroom might be a good place for the children now."

She turned to look at him. "Playroom?"

Jimmy started jumping up and down. "Playroom, playroom, playroom."

Ceci, the kids in tow, followed Dave as he led them back into the house. "Why would you need a playroom here?"

Dave explained. "Sometimes patients arrive with families that often have to wait for hours. So Bullard had this room put in."

They came to a large double door with glass panels. He opened the door and turned on the lights.

She stopped in amazement. There was a big slide in the middle of the room plus little activity centers at each corner. Off the center was a slick little kitchen area and a big sandbox full of trucks.

This was a slice of heaven for little kids.

Jimmy pulled his hand free and raced toward the trucks. He sat down in the middle of the sandbox and proceeded to make loud engine noises, moving the vehicles around.

Ceci turned back to Dave only to see he was gone. "The man is a bloody ghost." Putting Jennifer down she let her toddle around trying to see everything. When she managed to pick up a ball with flashing lights she giggled. Ceci let the children play and explore, happy there was a space that was safe for them. What a marvelous idea. There was a beanbag chair to one side. She plunked herself down close to the children and relaxed. When a voice called from the doorway she didn't recognize it. But when Brett called her a second time she bolted to her feet.

"Sorry, I didn't mean to disturb you," he said. "I couldn't see you but I could see the children."

She motioned to the chair tucked out of the way. "I was just resting."

"Bad night?"

She shrugged. "I've had better."

As the awkward silence's lengthened between them, she stepped in and asked, "What about the men last night?"

Instantly the atmosphere changed. Brett stepped closer, bending down to say hi to both Jimmy and Jennifer. When he straightened again he said, "Neither man is talking. Bullard is handing them over to the US military for questioning. Hopefully they'll be able to get more information out of them."

She nodded. "Yesterday you said I might be able to go home today. Are we still on track for that?"

Again he nodded. "We don't have the passports yet. As soon as I know more I'll let you know."

She turned to look at the amazing playroom. "This is a great place to stay in the meantime."

"That's Bullard for you. He's always thinking about everybody else."

"Is there anything I can do to help the investigation along?"

"Actually there is. It's one of the reasons why I'm here. I was hoping to get you to look through the images we have collected."

"I don't have a problem with that as long as I can bring the children."

"If you're okay with it, Dave will babysit."

She raised her eyebrows. "I'm sure Dave has more important things to do."

Brett's voice softened. "No, I don't think Dave has anything more important to do than visit with the kids."

Remembering Dave's reaction earlier, she nodded. She didn't know the story but he obviously loved children. "As soon as he's available then I can come."

Once again in that slick way of his, Dave appeared behind Brett and said, "I'm here."

Ceci let Brett lead the way back down toward the clinic, but detoured him into a large room first. As they entered she whispered, "What's with Dave and children?"

Brett looked at her then lowered his voice and said, "He lost his wife and two children about ten years ago."

She cast him a shocked look. "Dead?"

"His wife took the children and moved back home without telling him when he was away on a mission. He finally tracked her down only to find they'd been killed in a car accident two days earlier."

"That's terrible," she exclaimed in horror. "He lost them twice over."

"Exactly."

And that just pointed out something she knew but had ignored until now.

Everyone had a story. Everyone had strife, trouble. Some were small, others were big. Some were a long time ago and some right now. In ten years this would be a minor blip in *her* world. She needed to make the most of this time and then go home knowing she'd never see anything like this again.

Inside the boardroom there were several laptops open on the table. She presumed other people would be coming to join them. Walking to a set of empty chairs, she sat down and accepted the stack of images.

She glanced through the first dozen or so without recognizing anybody, but at the last set she stopped.

She tapped the man's face and frowned. "I think he was at the embassy." She placed the photo down on the table and flipped through the others. "I don't recognize anyone else in these."

She handed the stack back to him. "Are there more?"

He motioned at the laptops. "We have a couple video feeds from the embassy set up for you to watch."

Almost as soon as he started the feed she stopped him. "Him. He's the one who checked me in. I completed the paperwork with his help, and then he showed me to my room."

He switched her over to another feed. When she came to the woman walking beside another man, she said, "I've seen her around, but I don't know in what capacity."

Brett made several notes, then glanced up and smiled at her. "Thank you for taking a look."

She got to her feet a little awkwardly "Anything else I can do to help?"

He shook his head, "No, that's it."

She could feel the door shutting in her face and she hated it. With that distance between them it seemed an impossible line to cross, but she had to try. "This probably isn't the right time, but there may not be another that's better than this one..." She reached out a hand. "Look, all I can say is I'm not the same person I was six years ago. I was young, confused, and grieving. I wasn't thinking straight and I didn't mean to hurt you. I was too hurt myself to see anyone else's pain. That's not an excuse, but it's what happened."

On that note she spun on her heels and found the doorway full of men. Damn. They'd probably all heard. Avoiding eye contact she brushed past them and quickly ran back to her children.

At least there she felt safe. So what if there were no other relationships in her future. She knew what her role in life was. She was Jennifer and Jimmy's mother. That would be enough.

"TROUBLE IN PARADISE?" Markus asked as he walked in. He slapped Brett lightly on the shoulder. "I just got in. Sorry I missed last night. Sounds like it was a lot of fun."

Brett's grin was instinctive. He understood Markus's intent gaze, checking out if he was okay.

"Sounds like you and Ceci have some history?" Markus raised an eyebrow. "Anything to do with the children?"

And that was Markus, direct and to the point. Brett knew the others were listening in as well. He also knew they would understand that anything he said to them was private and personal. But maybe it would help them to know the dynamics going on.

He took a deep breath. "Ceci and I were in a relationship six years back. Only she got pregnant and miscarried and left me right after. I didn't know until last night. I spent months wandering around in confusion then picked myself up and carried on. She married a military man six months later, who died in Iraq two years ago."

Several of the men winced.

"That would have been tough on her." Markus pulled up a chair and sat down. "What's she got to do with this mess?"

Not sure if the others had heard all the details Brett sat

down and brought Markus and the others up to date. He tapped the face she'd identified. "She says this is the man who set her up with a room and started the paperwork to get her passports."

"And no sign of him yet?"

"Right, and neither have we found the staff that went for the meeting and never returned to the embassy."

"Shadow has a line on that. We'll be heading out soon to check into it."

"What kind of a line?"

Mason picked up the story. "An embassy vehicle was seen parked at an abandoned warehouse several miles away. They can't confirm the license plate, but there's no reason for it to be in that location. We're going on the expectation the staff have been taken hostage."

Brett shook his head. "Go on the expectation they've been murdered." He motioned at the videos on the laptops. "The woman I found was the only one left alive in the building."

"And we'd like to talk to her."

Dave spoke from the doorway. "She's awake again. You can have a few minutes now."

As the whole group stood up Dave studied them and said, "She's pretty nervous, so keep it to just two men."

Mason motioned at Brett. "You're the one who rescued her so you and Markus go."

With Markus walking at his side Brett hurried behind Dave. "How's her condition this morning?"

"Better. The swelling has gone down."

"That's good to hear." As they walked into the clinic he could see Dave's words were true. The woman was sitting up and looking around. Although her gaze was still full of pain, there was a cognitive awareness in her blue eyes.

Bullard was standing at her side. As Brett and Markus approached, Brett overheard Bullard as he quietly explained to her who they were.

She held out her hand and said in a warm voice, "Thank you for rescuing me."

Brett shook her hand, liking there was a strong grip behind the frail looking body. "I'm glad I was there in time."

She smiled. "Me too."

Markus stepped up closer. "What can you tell us?"

She launched into a recital of her day's events. "We had no warning," she said. "We were taken at gunpoint down to the garage. The men were interrogated and when they had nothing to offer they were shot one by one." She splayed out her hands. "They beat me. One of the blows to my head was hard enough I just blacked out. So unfortunately I don't know what else I can tell you."

"Did you recognize any of them?" Markus asked.

"I didn't. But I think one of my coworkers did. Chester was shot first." She shrugged. "There was also an odd smile on the man's face when he shot him, as if he knew a bullet wasn't what Chester was expecting."

"Do you think Chester was involved? That he was betrayed?" Brett asked. "Ceci, who was staying at the consulate, was rescued as well. And she identified one of the men in the security tapes, saying he started the paperwork for her and gave her the room she and the children were staying in."

"That would be Chester." She stared up at them. "I don't know what was going through his mind. I'd never have thought he'd do something like this."

"We never really understand what's going on in people's heads," Markus said. "I'm sure the investigation will find that there was some kind of mitigating factor. It could be as simple as money."

Her gaze flew up to his. "Chester was a reformed gambler. But lately it seemed like he was getting more nervous about something." She reached up to rub her temple.

"Any idea how the men got in? I presumed they didn't just stroll in the front door." Markus walked to the end of the bed.

"No," she said. "I have no idea. Chester may have had something to do with that." Pallor washed over her face as if she was just now understanding the enormity of the betrayal by her coworker and friend. "It was terrible," she whispered. "The gunman just up and shot them. He didn't care."

"We often find that's the case." Brett reached down and patted her hand gently. "You're safe here. Focus on getting back on your feet."

She turned her attention to Bullard and asked, "Am I safe here? I heard a commotion sometime in the night. I wasn't even sure where I was."

"Do you recognize these people?" Markus held up several photographs.

"The woman. She's been to the consulate a couple of times."

Markus nodded and held up two other photos. "What about these?"

She studied them and her face turned red with anger. "The one on the left is the man who shot Chester. I don't recognize the other man but I couldn't see everybody. There was somebody talking in the back of the garage. I don't have a face to identify him."

"Good enough. These two men were caught outside the gardens here last night."

She shrank back into the bed. "They're here?" she cried

out. "How did they find us?"

"I stole a truck from the embassy car parking lot," Brett admitted. "I didn't realize it had a GPS tracking unit. Or that these men would have access to it."

She stared at him as her comprehension was a little slow, and then her face flushed again with anger. "That would be Chester. He insisted our vehicles get trackers. Said it was for our own safety," she snapped. "Sounds like it was more for his own ass."

"Well he won't be worried about anything anymore as Chester is dead."

She turned her head away and stared at the blank wall. "Anything else or do you mind if I just kind of fall back asleep? I'm really tired."

Brett was ready to let her rest, but Markus had several more questions. By the time she answered she was definitely looking on the weak side.

Bullard stepped in and said, "That's enough for now. You can ask more later. Right now it's time for her to sleep." He shooed Markus and Brett back out the door. Brett wasn't sure what to believe. But they'd known there was a mole in the embassy. Now they had a name.

"I'll start running what I can find on Chester."

"No, you go back to Ceci and the children. We'll handle this."

Brett turned on him. "Why?"

"Because you're too involved."

"Is being involved a bad thing?" he protested.

"Let me rephrase that. You're too distracted. Go settle up your differences with Ceci. We can use all hands on deck, but we need your head on straight."

Shit.

A T JIMMY'S INSISTENCE Ceci walked the kids out of the playroom into the main foyer hoping to see Dave. They really wanted to go for another swim, but she didn't know if she needed permission. It would also be better if the children had bathing suits this time.

"Mommy, they're over there." Jimmy pointed down the hallway where the voices were coming from.

"No, Jimmy, *some* people are over there. Does that mean Dave is?"

He tried to take her hand and pull her in the direction he wanted to go. "Dave there," he said.

She could hear the voices, but she wasn't hearing the tenor of Dave's. She shook her head. "No, Dave is not one of those men."

"That's because Dave's behind you." She spun to see Dave standing there with a big grin on his face.

"I'll never get used to how silent you all move."

Jimmy ran the few steps and reached up his arms. Dave picked him up, slinging him high onto his shoulders. "I hear he'd like to go for a swim."

"Swim." Jennifer waved her pudgy hands at Dave.

He reached out and gave her little fingers a shake. "It's this way. Let's go."

"You sure you don't have something more important to

do?" she asked. "I hate to take you away from your job."

"My job is to make the guests happy." He bounced Jimmy on his shoulder. "So right now that is what I'm doing."

He led the way to the pool and bathhouse again. This time she struggled to get the kids changed as they were very eager to jump into the water. Finally, she had them both into bathing suits and back outside to the water. Dave stood in swim shorts waiting.

Jimmy jumped in on his own, and Jennifer did the same right after. Dave reached out and swung her up into his arms then dropped her back under again to her great delight.

He motioned to Ceci. "Now you go get a suit on."

She did not need to be told twice. She raced back to the bathhouse and quickly changed into the same swimsuit from yesterday, only freshly washed.

She snagged up a bunch more towels and walked back outside. After dropping the towels at the edge of the pool, she said, "Thank you."

"Don't thank me. I should be thanking you." Handing Jennifer over to her, he went to the pool room where he pulled out several inflatable toys. There was a big blowup swan that he placed Jennifer in the middle of so she could paddle around safely and a pirate ship Jimmy quickly claimed. With Dave there to help watch over the kids Ceci took the opportunity to swim laps.

It seemed like a long time since she'd been able to do anything physical. She was out of shape and this was just too good an opportunity to pass up. When she finally slowed and lifted her head to float back toward the children she heard a different male voice. Brett.

She was going to have to face the music sometime. Bolstering up a happy wave she said, "Hi."

"Hi yourself." Dave swung Jimmy off the pirate ship and tossed him over to Brett and that's when she realized Brett was in the water too.

Jimmy squealed with joy as the two men tossed him back and forth, letting him drop into the water just enough to set off his laughter. It amazed her how these men were with the children. It was not something her husband had taken the time to do. He hadn't really understood what having a child meant, and had therefore missed out on a lot.

Dave excused himself after a few minutes and said, "I'll be back in a little bit. How about a cup of coffee and maybe a treat for the kids?"

She smiled up at him. "Thank you. That would be lovely." She watched as he walked away, for the first time seeing his prosthetic. She hadn't even noticed it before. "It never occurred to me the prosthetics could go in the water."

"Bullard and his team are working on several prototypes. What you see today could very well be a very different model for tomorrow."

She liked the sound of that. "Good, maybe eventually they can grow him a new leg," she half joked.

"Who knows? Maybe down the road." Brett sat Jimmy back into the pirate ship and gave him a push out across to his sister who was busy playing with the movable wings on the swan. An awkward silence descended.

"Any update?" It seemed to be the only thing she asked him these days.

"Just a little bit from Amanda."

She listened while he explained what they'd learned, realizing although there were small bits and pieces of the puzzle filling in, none of it affected her situation. She was still in stasis waiting for the passports.

"I'm sure you guys will figure it out. You always get your man…or woman," she added at the end with a big smile. "Don't you?"

He gave her a flat stare. A reaction she hadn't expected. "Or not."

He dove under the surface. She studied him as he moved through the water as sleekly as a dolphin. Obviously they still had a lot of things to work out but she was hopeful. She wanted him as a friend if nothing else. He'd been instrumental in saving her and the children, and for that she was grateful.

Lifting Jennifer out she wrapped her up in a towel and sat on the side of the pool watching Jimmy paddle around in his boat. The sense of wrongness had disappeared. She felt safe. Even though there had been two intruders there was a sense of confidence in Bullard and his people. Maybe she was wrong to relax, but her body had a mind of its own.

Dried off, Jennifer toddled over to the grass where she sat down and tried to pick up several blades in her fingers. They were too short but she kept grabbing at them. She giggled at the handfuls as they fell from her fingers.

Sitting where she could see the two children Ceci kept her eagle eye watching both.

It wasn't long before Dave returned with a tray. He set it down on the table and called to Jimmy. "I brought fruit and some cheese. Do you want a snack?"

Jimmy immediately jumped over the side of the boat and swam his way to the stairs. He was up checking out the contents of the tray in seconds. Ceci picked up Jennifer and gave her several pieces of fruit to eat.

Dave set a cup of coffee on the table and said, "Here you

go."

There was only one cup. She looked up at him. "You didn't bring a cup for Brett?" Dave nodded toward the pool. She turned to see Brett walking away to the bathhouse to get changed.

"Damn," she whispered softly under her breath.

"Some hurts take longer to get over." On that cryptic note Dave took the tray back with him leaving her and the children by themselves. And this time she'd never felt lonelier.

BRETT WANTED TO walk away but he couldn't. Not only was he responsible for keeping her safe right now, but he knew he couldn't leave with the distance between them. He came out of the bathhouse with a towel draped over his shoulders and forced himself to sit down at the table.

The children appeared to be happy and content and that said much about their mother. He could even understand the shock she'd gone through with the miscarriage.

He didn't understand her silence with him. He'd always been there for her. This wouldn't have been any different.

Trust was a hard thing. Once broken it took a long time to heal.

"I've said I'm sorry," she said in a low, sad tone. "There's nothing else I can say to make it better."

He slouched back in the chair and closed his eyes. He wasn't sure he had an answer for that. He sensed movement from the side. Opening his eyes he watched Dave place a large mug in front of him. With a pat on his shoulder Dave turned and walked away again.

"How is it that he knows and sees everything?" she exclaimed softly.

"One of Dave's specialties is reading people."

"I didn't know that was something that could be taught."

He turned to look at her and said, "Would it make a difference if it could?"

"Back then, probably not. The shock was horrific. I wasn't happy when I found out I was pregnant, just numb. By the time I realized I *was* actually delighted – it was too late and I lost the baby." She shook her head. "And the numbness spread."

"And here I thought we were working toward something back then. Something serious. But your actions…"

She turned to glance at him. "That's why I told you." She shook her head. "I don't want any more secrets. I am who I am. But I'm not who I once was."

If there was one thing he could understand it was that. He took a sip of his coffee and considered where to go from here. "You've had time to get over that shock. For me it's like it's real right now."

"Every day I wish things had been different. But it's also over and I can't do anything about that." She played with her hands. "But I wish I could."

He gave a bark of laughter. "Thanks for that."

This time when he smiled it came from deep inside. And she burst into tears.

<h1 style="text-align:center">CHAPTER 16</h1>

"MOMMY, WHAT'S WRONG?" Jimmy cuddled up against her shoulder, his hand awkwardly petting her hair and cheek. He placed his cheek against hers and wrapped his arms around her neck tight. "It's okay, Mommy."

Jennifer started to cry beside her.

And that only made her cry harder. Wrapping her arms around her son, she held him close. They'd been the mainstay of her life, the force that had kept her going all these years. She loved them both so damn much.

The world tilted at an awkward angle as she was lifted, both kids still in her arms, and tucked up on Brett's lap and held tight in his embrace. When he brushed a gentle kiss against her temple more of her walls came crumbling down. Ones she hadn't even been aware she'd put up. God she'd loved this man. He'd been her everything. And then she'd lost the baby and somehow he'd become something to run from. He was right, she should've told him. But she'd been too shocked, too much in pain. All she'd wanted to do was run away. And she had.

Where did that leave them now? She came as part of a ready-made family. It was a lot for him to take on.

With his breath against her ear he whispered, "Easy, Ceci, take it easy. You'll make yourself sick."

She tried to bring her emotions back under control. It was hard. Once that dam burst it wasn't easy to stop. But this wasn't the time. Her children were upset and going to be more so if she didn't get herself back in control.

And in true miracle fashion Dave appeared at their side, held out his hands to both of the kids and said, "You know, I think it's time for ice cream."

Jimmy's face lit up like a rocket. "Ice cream?"

Then he glanced back at his mom and said in a teary voice, "Mommy is hurt." That set Jennifer's tears off again.

Dave scooped up both kids and said, "You know, I think Brett can handle Mommy right now. She's not hurt, she just needs to cry a little bit. And I think your tears will heal much better if you have some ice cream." He turned and walked the two children back up to the house, leaving Brett alone with Ceci for the first time.

"Dave's a smart man," Brett said in admiration.

"He's a conniving man. And I really appreciate him taking the kids right now."

"You haven't given yourself much of a chance to grieve, have you?"

She shook her head. "Not for any of it. At first I didn't know how, then there was no time." Her shoulders lifted in a helpless shrug. "How does one do that with children? The necessities of getting through the day take over. It's in the darkness of the night that the pain hits."

He shifted her gently in his arms to a more comfortable position. "Maybe everything had to happen this way. Look at us now. You're single again and back in my arms. I find it hard to be upset about that."

"Even after what I told you?"

He nodded. "Even after. I'll need a little time to adjust.

There's no doubt it was a shock. It hurts," he admitted. "I'd like to have children of my own someday."

Curled up in the warmth of his embrace Ceci wondered how she'd actually managed to come out on top. She figured he'd want nothing to do with her. Brett was such an honorable man. He was good inside – not just good at what he did. Spending a few moments like this with him in private was a gift. One she was determined to enjoy. The children would be back soon enough with ice cream, but in the meantime they had an opportunity to mend some bridges. "I really *am* sorry."

"So am I," he whispered. He opened his mouth to say something else, but she never heard it for the sound of rapid machine gun fire splintering the air. She jumped to her feet, but Brett was already sprinting toward the house.

She raced behind him, screaming, "Oh my God, the children. Where are my children?"

The gunfire ceased for a moment only to erupt in another part of the house.

Glass shattered and she heard swearing. And then there was the sound of a vehicle ripping away.

Dear God, please let them not have taken her children. She bolted inside trying to avoid the glass as she headed to the kitchen. As she didn't know the layout of the house, she didn't have a clue where the kitchen was.

"Over here," Brett yelled running down a long hallway. She followed in a panic.

Several of the other men joined them. In the kitchen she burst through the double doors to see Dave sporting a lot of blood dripping down his head, two guns in his hands, standing in front of both children. They might have been crying at one time, but at the moment they were more concerned about the ice cream in their hands.

The relief damn near killed her. She swung them both up into her arms ice cream and all.

Jimmy cried out, "Dave has guns. He has big guns."

"Yes he does. Nice for him." Her arms were shaking so badly she didn't know if she could carry them very far. There was a very large circular set of chairs in front of a window off to one side. She walked over and collapsed.

She didn't think she could take another step. Neither was she ever leaving these children alone again. She glanced at the men who were huddled together talking. Then they split up and disappeared.

Dave arrived at her side, the guns nowhere in sight, a wet cloth pressed to his head. He sat down and asked, "How are they? Are they okay?"

Tears flooded her eyes as she nodded. "Thanks to you."

"I don't think they were after the children. But I do think they were after you." He studied her intently. "There has to be a good reason why."

She shook her head. "I don't have a clue. I didn't do anything. I wasn't there long enough to get involved in anything. I pointed out the one man I'd seen but that was it."

She stopped and looked at him. "Well and the woman…"

His gaze sharpened and he leaned forward. "What did you see?"

"I just remembered when I saw her. It was the first evening we were there. I went to the dining room and sat by the doorway. There was a group of men at the corner who didn't notice me. They were talking about plans." She shook her head. "I didn't really understand any of it. I was so happy to be there but still nervous. I just wanted to go back up to my room with the kids. The woman from the video came from the kitchen. She spoke to them briefly and then laughed. Before she left her gaze swept the room and she looked at me." Ceci sat back and stared at Dave. "Would that matter?"

"It might. That woman is part of the military splinter group. They are trying to take over the government." He nodded thoughtfully. "She must consider you a loose end."

"Wasn't there just a coup here recently?"

Dave grinned. "Absolutely. Just a couple of months ago, but new government takes time to solidify. So another coup right now makes sense."

"And she's leading that group?"

Dave nodded. "She is. But she can't be associated with the attack on the embassy. That would be a traitorous move and she can't show her hand yet. Timing is everything, particularly in a coup. There's been rumors about her for years."

"There has to be a lot of people who saw her at the embassy though," Ceci protested. "I'm nobody."

"You're exactly what she can't allow to have happen." He leaned back. "Think about it. The only ones who survived the attack are right here at the house."

She sank back deeper into the chair, her mind consumed with the mess. "How quickly can I leave? Get away from all this?"

"We could possibly have you home tomorrow night." He paused. "But did you consider that going home may not be any safer than here?"

She shook her head. "No, surely not."

"They have your personal information."

She turned and looked at him and bit her lip. "I just

want to go home." She turned to study the group of men walking forward. "Anybody hurt?"

"Two guards. The attack was to break out the intruders from last night and take down Amanda." He gave a thin smile. "The men were handed over to the authorities this morning, and Amanda was moved an hour ago."

"So we have nothing?"

All the men stared at her. It was Mason who piped up and said, "That's not true. We have you."

BRETT WAS TAKING the first watch with Ceci and the children. But he knew there was going to be two of his unit nearby at all times. He wouldn't want it any other way.

The second attack had come too close to the first. Too fast. Bullard was having a fit. Not only was he doing surgery on his injured men, but his place had been attacked. And he wanted answers as to how and why. If there was one thing Bullard hated it was to be shown to be inferior in any way. He would get to the bottom of it and fast.

In the meantime Ceci and the kids, although they'd never really been alone, would now be under constant guard.

He hoped they could get her home as soon as possible. That wasn't going to guarantee her safety though. It *might* be easier to keep her safe at home. On the other hand, once back into her normal routine, she'd become complacent because she was removed from the situation.

And that he didn't want to happen. She must never lose her sense of awareness. Her guard must always be up until this was dealt with.

And dealing with it wasn't going to be that easy.

CHAPTER 17

WHEN SHE FINALLY slipped the hidden spare key into the lock of her own house and walked inside there was such a sense of overwhelming relief it brought tears to her eyes – yet again. Hadn't she cried enough this last week? After the last attack, all attempts had been made to get her back as fast as possible. The decision being that as long as she was over there everyone else was going to be a target. And that it would be easier to protect her on home soil.

She didn't care about their reasoning.

She was home. She wanted to dance and sing for joy. Instead, she had two cranky children to settle first. Brett, who had been at her side steadily for the last two days, was busy unloading the luggage. Bullard had sent them home with several outfits the kids had worn at his place and Dave had loaded them up on toys and treats. The last day had been tense. She hadn't relaxed until she got onto the flight, and at that point in time the children had lost patience and were miserable.

She dropped her purse on her table, kicked off her shoes and quickly stripped off Jennifer's coat and shoes. Her poor little girl was exhausted. It was very late. The flight had been uneventful. They'd even managed to get their luggage and clear customs in record time. But still the traveling was hard. They were all tired and ready for bed.

In Jennifer's bedroom she quickly changed her clothes and tucked the little girl up in bed. She barely made a whimper before she succumbed to sleep.

Jimmy wasn't quite so easy. He was too wired and at the same time stressed. But she got him into pajamas then carried him out to the kitchen for a warm glass of milk and a snack.

It was Brett who finally picked him up and carried him into his bed. She followed, dropping a kiss on his forehand and tucking him in.

As she stood in the doorway, dirty clothes in her hands, she smiled down at her son. Thank God they were home, but that did not mean she got to rest. Not with her kids. She went to the washing machine and loaded the clothes they'd brought home. In the kitchen she found Brett rummaging through the fridge.

"We've been gone for weeks. There's no food," she reminded him.

He nodded. "Any problem with me ordering pizza?"

"Go for it." What she really needed was a shower. Food could wait. She headed to her bedroom and turned on the light. Her room was exactly as she'd left it. There was a certain amount of comfort in that.

She stripped down to her skin and stepped under the hot water. And almost cried out in joy.

After scrubbing her hair twice she got out of the shower, wrapped herself up in a towel and padded, still damp, into the bedroom where she opened up her double closet doors and smiled at the contents. Finally, she had clothes of her own again. She quickly pulled on her pajamas, added her dirty clothes to the laundry and started the machine before walking back out to the kitchen still brushing her wet hair.

Brett was in the process of opening a box of pizza. She hadn't even heard the doorbell ring.

"Wow, how did you get that so fast?"

He just smiled at her and said, "Do you want a piece?"

Hell yeah, she wanted a piece. She cheerfully munched through two. When she was done she stood up and asked, "Are you planning on staying here tonight or are you going home?"

He froze, shot her a glance and asked in a humorous tone, "Is that an invitation?"

She shook her head, "No, it's not. But I wasn't sure at what point in time the security detail was over."

"Are you nervous?"

She shook her head and laughed. "No. It feels marvelous to be home."

"Good. Get a good night's sleep. I'll crash on the couch."

"That's not going to be very comfortable." She frowned. That was hardly the way to treat someone who'd done so much for her.

"Don't worry about me." He reached across and picked up another piece of pizza and took a bite.

She watched him eat with such obvious enjoyment. That was another thing about Brett she had always loved. He could enjoy the little things in life. Where she got hung up on worrying about every little detail, he had the ability to let most brush off his back and just enjoy.

"I'll find blankets and pillows for you." She walked back to the bedroom closet for the bedding. A moment later, she returned, her arms full and stared at the small couch. That was not going to work.

She would love it if he'd sleep beside her in her bed, but

she didn't want him to think she was ready for more. Because she wasn't. Not yet. Maybe not ever. How long had it been since she'd made love and how awkward she already felt at the idea. A warm hand landed on her shoulder. "I'll be fine here. Don't worry about it."

"It's awfully small," she warned.

"Unless you're offering a half a bed to sleep in, the couch is what's available. Besides, we're both tired. I won't have any trouble sleeping here."

Making a sudden decision she turned, looked him square in the eye and said, "You're welcome to half the bed to *sleep* in, if you want. It would be much more comfortable than this."

He raised his eyebrows and grinned. "I wasn't planning on more, you know. Not if you weren't."

She winced. She had emphasized the sleep aspect a little too much.

She brushed that off. "We both know we're heading toward a relationship," she said. "I just need you to know I'm not ready for that part." Her tone was flat, cool. But when she felt his hands grasp hers and lift her clenched fists, she realized she still really wasn't dealing with this well.

"We'll have to talk about this one day. And yes, thank you. I will accept half a bed. I could use a good night's sleep," he confessed. "And if I get a chance to just hold you in my arms then that would be a blessing too."

He tucked her into his arms and just held her, dropping a kiss on her temple and resting his cheek against the top of her head.

Hot tears burned her eyes. It felt so good to be held by someone who made it obvious he cared. She was a fool. And an exhausted one. She smiled up at him and stepped back.

"I'm going to bed now," she said. "I'll leave a light on for you. Feel free to come in when you're ready."

At the doorway she called out, "Good night."

She brushed her teeth and climbed into bed. She wanted to fall asleep, she needed to, but she was too keyed up knowing he'd be joining her soon. It was foolish. She'd slept with him for over two years. He was a hugger. At night he'd often hold her and she'd loved it. The comfort of knowing she was part of a special twosome.

There was no feeling like it.

WHY DID IT feel strange to sleep with a woman he'd had a long-term relationship with? He knew it was different now. He knew she was too, as was their relationship. Obviously those were givens, but there was an awkwardness he hadn't expected. He didn't like it. She'd always been natural about sex. She was more uptight about her physical appearance now. And there was a lot going on in her head. He suspected a lot of it wasn't terribly healthy. She hadn't said she regretted marrying Jimmy, but neither had she said she'd been happy with him.

Then he was a realist. Marriage like everything else took work. There were good days, bad days, highs and lows. The thing was right now she was single again. And she had two beautiful children. He'd already slid past the point of questioning whether they were children he could live with because they *were* children he *wanted* to live with. It was too early to know more than that. But he wanted to take that journey and see what more there was to feel. It was all new again. It was as simple as that. He quickly cleaned up the kitchen and walked into the bedroom. Sure enough, she'd left the light on. She lay facing the window leaving more than half of the bed closest to the door. Just like old times. He stripped down to his boxers and crawled under the covers grateful for a good night's sleep himself.

She lay stiff on the far side of the bed.

He lay back and let out a heavy sigh. He wanted to drop off to sleep but there was something about her rigid spine that spoke volumes. He couldn't leave her like this. He reached an arm around her waist and tucked up against her spoon style. She gasped softly, but after a few seconds her hand crept down to cover his. And slowly she relaxed into sleep. He smiled. Perfect.

He didn't know if she understood or not, but he was never one to slide back and lose the gains he made. As far as he was concerned, now that he was sleeping in her bed, that was where he was going to stay.

CHAPTER 18

S HE WOKE TO the birds singing and a sense of comfort and peace in her heart and soul. A feeling of time having reasserted itself – of life finally being back on the right track and moving in the proper direction. As if a mistake made a long time ago had been corrected.

Brett's arms were wrapped around her and hers were around him as she lay with her head against his chest.

In a weird knowing, she understood another truth. She'd finally come home.

His hand gently stroked up and down her back. "Good morning to you. Did you get some sleep?"

She smiled and propped herself up on one elbow to stare down at his beloved face. "I did. Did you?" She reached up and stroked the dark shadow across his chin.

He winced. "Sorry. I'll have to unpack my shaving kit."

"Not an issue."

She tried to sit up but he pulled her down and said jokingly, "What, no morning kiss?"

She knew it was dangerous. Knew she'd be playing with fire. They were in a bed after all, but she also had children likely to be waking up. Although it was still very early. She reached down and dropped a kiss lightly on his lips. "There you go."

"Not quite." He slipped a hand up her neck and through

her hair to urge her head back down. Just before his lips touched hers he murmured, "*This* is a good morning kiss."

And he proceeded to kiss her thoroughly, heat fired up to envelope them both in a warm cocoon.

When he finally released her head, she looked at him in bemusement and sighed with contentment. "If you scramble my brains in the morning, how am I supposed to get through the day?" She rolled off the bed and went to the closet to pull out clothes.

"You could come back to bed." He pushed himself up to lean against the headboard, the bedcovers resting down to his waist.

She didn't dare look. As a male specimen he was unbelievably gorgeous. And she was *not* immune. Hell, her body hummed with pleasure just from his kiss. "The children will be up soon."

"Sure, but they aren't up yet."

With her back to him she quickly dressed. Her movements efficient and practical. She could sense him watching her. As he'd watched her millions of times before. But when his husky voice cut across the bedroom she froze.

"You're really beautiful, you know that?" he said. "Before there was an air of innocence around you. But now after giving birth, there's maturity and a ripeness that's even more attractive. I didn't think it was possible for you to be even sexier – but you are."

With her bra and shirt clutched to her chest she turned slowly to stare at him in shock. And saw only sincerity on his face. And heat. Lots of it. Something she never thought to see in a man's eyes again. Certainly not in Brett's. Her body flooded with warmth, but her stomach cramped with uncertainty. She wanted to shake her head at him for being so blind. To point out the stretch marks that had ruined her belly and gave her breasts a rippled look. They were fuller, heavier. The truth in his face said he didn't see any of those things. That he didn't care about any of them.

And he never would. Because it was who he was. She'd been a fool to not have realized that before.

She walked closer to the bed, her heart in turmoil. Her mind confused. Unsure of her next step. He threw back the covers and stepped out of bed to stand before her. He wore boxers but there was no hiding the erection straining the material. She swallowed hard. Dear God, she wanted this…him.

"I can see the insecurity in your face. The fear that you've changed, that you're not as beautiful now as you were before. That things are different now that you are a mother…" He tilted her head toward him. "It *is* different, *you* are different. I'm here to tell you that honestly…you're even better."

And he lowered his head and kissed her.

She closed her eyes and sank into the sensation. Jimmy had been gone for over two years. Two years since she'd been held by a man in any kind of loving embrace. Two years since anyone kissed her as if he cared. The six months before Jimmy's death had been rough. Ever since he found out about Jennifer's impending arrival he'd been pretty distant.

She almost laughed. Distant wasn't quite the word. He'd slept on the couch since she told him.

Brett deepened the kiss, pulling her mind back to him. Unable to help herself she reached up and wrapped her arms around his neck and held him close. She wanted this – him – so much…but she couldn't relax. She didn't want to feel awkward but she did, she didn't want to feel ugly but she did. He lifted his head, his hands coming up to cup her face, and as he gazed into her eyes she knew he could see into her soul. His next words confirmed it.

"Stop thinking," he whispered. "Relax. We're good together. We always have been."

He kissed her eyelids. Tiny little feathery brushes across her cheekbones and then her temples. His fingers gently massaged her skull, threading through her hair, the loving caress making her moan.

Brett knew her well. What she liked. What she needed. Maybe even more than she did. She melted a little more against him only to realize he was walking her backwards to the bed, his erection insistent against her pelvis.

Her bra and shirt had become trapped between them. But as he dropped her to the bed he whisked the offending material away. And sucked in his breath, his gaze hot.

Instinctively she covered her breasts.

"Don't." He reached down, his finger slowly peeling her hands away. "Don't hide. Don't you understand how beautiful you are right now?"

She shook her head. Her gaze downcast. "I don't feel sexy. I feel like a mom. There is something very wrong about a mom feeling sexy."

He chuckled. Not a mocking laugh but one full of warm compassion and understanding.

"You're so wrong there. You're the epitome of womanhood. You embrace all that is right about being a mother. You've created two beautiful children and the changes in your body are nothing in comparison." His fingers stroked across the stretch marks on the side of her breast. "They are badges, medals of honor for a job well done."

She stared up at him in wonder. "You really mean that?"

"Absolutely." He narrowed his gaze at her expression and then sighed. "Jimmy didn't feel the same way, did he?"

She shook her head. "He hated how long it took for me to get rid of the baby fat," she muttered. "Nor did he like the permanent changes from giving birth." She shrugged. "I tried hard but it didn't seem to matter. I was no longer the young woman he married."

"And you feel like you're a dumpy old lady that can't enjoy her body. Who shouldn't be making love anymore?"

She dropped her gaze yet again. "When you say it like that it sounds stupid."

His fingers stroked up over her ribs to cup her breasts, squeezing them gently, his thumbs rubbing over the taut nipples. His voice dropped to a husky whisper. "It doesn't matter if it's stupid or not. It's how you feel so you have to deal with that. In my opinion you're just listening to his garbage."

He smiled, a corner of his mouth quirking. "You used to love sex. You used to walk around naked, totally relaxed. To see you now so lacking self-confidence, it hurts," he admitted.

As she listened to him she could see how Jimmy's influence had impacted her. It was her fault in that she hadn't been able to let Jimmy's comments roll off her back. But over time even a stone wore smooth. And just because she'd acknowledged the problem didn't mean she was going to be able to get over it and move on just like that.

But it did mean she no longer had to keep the same beliefs. Brett was right about one thing. She had always been quite comfortable with her body when around him. Now she realized it was more about her lack of self-confidence rather than his acceptance.

And that was a balm to her aching soul. She smiled, her fingers reaching up to clasp his hands. "Maybe instead of trying to tell me how it used to be," she whispered, "you should show me how it is now."

With his breath mingling with hers, his smooth skin feeling like a heated blanket over her already sensitized skin, he whispered, "With pleasure."

It didn't take long for her to realize she'd forgotten nothing. He'd always made her feel she was the only woman in the world, the most perfect female in the universe. He'd always kept his focus on her. On her pleasure. Her needs. Her body. It was intoxicating. She felt connected and...loved.

She missed that the most.

He rolled onto his back, pulling her onto his chest.

"You're still wearing too many clothes." He slipped a finger along her waistband reminding her she'd pulled jeans on before coming to bed with him. She laughed self-consciously but more at herself now.

Standing up, she shucked off her jeans, kicked them to one side and then with a simple flick of her fingers dropped her panties to the floor. As she stood there she studied his long muscled form.

"God you're beautiful," she whispered reverently.

He jackknifed into a sitting position and said, "No. You're the beautiful one."

He stood up and kicked off his boxers releasing his erection. She stretched out a hand, unable to resist. Her fingers wrapped around the lean length, loving it when he sucked in his breath. In a surprise move he lifted her off the ground, wrapping her legs around his hips. A shriek of laughter escaped. "I know you're strong, but this strong?"

As if challenged he walked several steps to rest her back against the wall, a glint in his eye. "I guess we'll find out."

With his erection teasing the heart of her, she found it hard to keep still. She wanted to lower herself. But he was holding her too tight to move.

She wiggled against his hips, trying to loosen up his grasp. He laughed and dropped his head to run kisses down her throat and across her shoulders then back up under her chin.

She moaned. "God that feels good."

"Good. How about this?" He swept a finger between her legs, pinned as she was he had full access and she had none. When he dipped his finger in the moisture and spread it over her sensitive skin she gasped and wiggled harder. Taking his cue from her he slipped his finger in again only to withdraw to circle the nub this time. Then he slipped inside only to retreat. He did it again and again and again. Each time she cried out, her body twisting against the wall, trying to force herself down onto him.

But he wasn't having any of that.

"Damn it, stop teasing me."

He laughed hoarsely as he changed her angle and then slowly released his hold. With her back against the wall – she slid down onto him – but only as far as he'd let her. He pinned her again against the wall, not letting her slide any further.

She leaned forward and bit him on the shoulder.

He gave a shout of laughter, releasing his grip a little more and she slid lower to his shaft.

But not quite home. She shuddered. Need clawing at her.

Well, she could fix that. She leaned forward and pulled

his head down for a hot passionate kiss. As she kissed him she released all of the years of pain and guilt. Instantly the void was filled with the drive to be one with him.

Her hips rocked from side to side, slowly up and down. Her fingers stroking his back before sliding down to cup his heavily muscled cheeks.

Without warning she dug her nails deep into his skin and tightened her inner muscles – hard.

"Jesus," he swore, throwing his head back, his hips slamming her into the wall.

Driving himself deep inside her.

Now she was where she wanted to be. With a lusty laugh she used her nails to scrape gently up his back, caressing every inch she could reach as she dropped tiny kisses across his chest.

He kissed her again and again, his arms shaking with the need. She leaned forward and gently bit his nipple. And he lost it. His hips slammed into her again and again.

She reveled in it, matching him thrust for thrust. Tension twisted her insides ever higher.

He reached down his hands gripping her cheeks, holding her immobile as he pounded into her.

Harder.

Faster.

Higher.

At the next thrust she exploded, her cries of joy resounding in the bedroom. He immediately clamped his mouth down on top of hers to stifle the noise.

At which point she remembered the children sleeping in their beds.

He shuddered, his body plunging one last time as his climax ripped through him.

She wanted to laugh. She wanted to cry. She wanted to hold him close – forever.

Slowly recovering, he lifted her higher and carried her to the bed where he laid her down and collapsed down beside her – still joined.

God, she'd loved this man.

And maybe still did. Was that possible? Did one stop loving because a relationship stopped? Or was it more a case of when love stopped the relationship did? If so, what the hell had she done and why?

She'd always loved him. Maybe that was never going to change.

THAT WAS NOT what he'd expected to happen. But he was pretty damn glad it had. He tucked her close to his side and relaxed.

"I should get up." But she didn't move.

He kissed her temple gently. "I don't hear them yet."

She yawned. "They'll be awake soon enough." Pushing herself up, she sat on the edge of the bed and glanced down at him. "I'm going to sneak in a quick shower."

He watched as she made her way to the bathroom, hearing the hot water turn on soon after. She hadn't sent him an invitation, but it was a great idea.

He got up, put his boxers back on and wandered out into the small kitchen. He peeked into the kids' bedrooms, checked they were still asleep then with a smile still on his face, he put on coffee.

What a difference a day made. This was what his life was going to be like if he got back with Ceci. Trying to find time to be alone because the kids were going to come first. He grinned. It was fun. And as such, what the hell was he doing here? He gave another quick check on the kids, but there was no sign they'd be waking up anytime soon. Good. Back in the bedroom he kicked off the boxers again and stepped under the hot water.

Ceci let out a startled shriek, followed by laughter as he reached for the bar of soap.

"I checked on the kids. They're still sleeping. I put on some coffee. But I figured we might just have five minutes."

Her delightful laughter rang through the bathroom. "So now you need only five minutes," she teased. "I thought for sure the idea was to last longer, not shorter."

He chuckled. "Let's just say I'm adaptable." With his hand slippery from the soap and her body slick from the water he proceeded to show her how adaptable he was.

When they finally stepped out of the shower both felt much more at peace with each other and the world.

He grabbed a towel, quickly got dressed and walked back to the kitchen. He poured two cups of coffee and realized he still wasn't hearing the children's voices. Not knowing what their routine was he went to Jennifer's room and found her bed empty.

His heart cramped with fear as he raced to Jimmy's room.

And found both children asleep on the one bed.

Only they weren't alone.

CHAPTER 19

CECI COULDN'T HEAR the kids. They'd been through so much she didn't begrudge them a normal sleep. But surely they'd return to a routine soon.

She wandered into Jimmy's bedroom, Brett sat on the bed, one hand resting on each child. Jimmy just now rubbing his eyes as he woke up.

He stood up, his face hard, his gaze cold.

"Take him out to the kitchen, please." But his tone was icy and demanding, yet quiet at the same time.

She stared at him in shock. "What? Why?"

He cast her a warning look and handed her a sleepy Jimmy. Jennifer slept curled up against Jimmy's pillows. "Jimmy is looking for food," he said gently. "I'll explain in a few minutes."

And she had to be satisfied with that. As she held Jimmy she realized something else. His blanket, the one he loved to carry around and sleep with, was covering something very large on the floor. She opened her mouth but Brett said quietly, "Don't."

Her mouth snapped shut as she hurried into the kitchen, but inside tremors were starting. Dear God, what was under that blanket? She hadn't been away from the kids very long. And Brett had checked on them earlier and said they'd both been sleeping, so what had happened? And when.

Jimmy yawned. "That lady is really tired. Brett put a blanket on her, so she could sleep."

Ceci stiffened in shock, but her voice was calm and quiet when she said, "We all need to sleep sometimes."

"We've been sleeping lots," he announced. "And I'm still tired." He slid down to the floor and walked to the couch. After curling up in the corner, he picked up the remote and put on his cartoons. With a happy sigh he settled back.

"I thought you were hungry?"

"I am." But his attention was riveted to the cartoons. Saturday was always his morning for watching cartoons on the couch. She rarely put a limit to the time because it was only once a week.

Sure that he was okay she casually went back to his bedroom and found Brett carrying Jennifer. Jennifer gave her a toothy smile and started blowing bubbles. Ceci reached out and accepted the cherub then walked back into the kitchen to put her in the high chair.

She went through the motions. All she had to do was focus on the routine. To make everything look normal even though it was a hell of a long way from it.

She could do this.

She *had* to do this.

Ceci put on toast for the two kids and stared out the window.

Inside she knew what was under the blanket. And it made her sick. She'd known the possibility existed that someone could follow them here. It just never occurred to her anybody would care enough to do so.

She was nobody. Why come after her?

When she had a moment she'd ask Brett for an update on the scenario at the embassy. But right now...there was a problem about a woman in her son's bedroom. Christ. Was she dead? Who the hell was she? And what had she been doing there?

She quickly buttered and cut Jimmy's bread into squares and took it out to the couch for him. Normally eating in the living room was not allowed but today…well maybe this would help him.

With Jennifer happy for the moment gnawing on her toast, she quickly escaped back to Jimmy's room. She stood in the doorway, her gaze taking in the empty room. Where was Brett? She forced herself to look at the floor. But there was nothing there. And the blanket was missing.

She knew Jimmy didn't understand what he'd seen. And she was sure hoping she hadn't either.

Back in the kitchen she sat down beside Jennifer and waited for Brett to show up. Two vehicles arrived instead. One a big Jeep and another a big truck. Maybe some of his unit had come to help out. Instead of making her feel better, panic ensued. Dear God, had that really been a woman in Jimmy's bedroom? And if so, how the hell was she going to keep these kids safe? No one had even heard the woman enter. She could have killed her kids while they slept. She felt ill. If she wasn't safe in her own home, was she safe any-where?

BRETT MET HIS team. He took them to the garage where he'd placed the woman's body. Swede asked, "Is she dead?"

Brett nodded. "I didn't mean to kill her. But I gave her a hard chop shot to the throat before she could move. She wasn't expecting it and dropped like a log." He shrugged. "Her Glock is beside her."

He handed Mason the contents of the woman's pockets. "This is all I found on her."

Shadow asked, "Any vehicle?"

Brett shook his head. "I have no idea. I didn't want to leave Ceci and the kids long enough to look."

Shadow nodded and disappeared into the neighborhood.

Brett watched him. If there was anything, Shadow would find it. Hawk, not saying a word, headed outside in the opposite direction of Shadow. Those two were the best hunters in the group. Brett could only hope they found out if she worked alone. Before someone decided to come back looking for their colleague.

Mason bent down and pulled the cover back off the woman's face. He studied her features for a long moment then glanced up at Brett. "Do you know her?"

Brett nodded. "I don't *know* her, but she passed me on the stairs during the embassy attack."

"So she is involved." Mason nodded in satisfaction. He straightened. "Go over it again for us."

Just then they both heard a noise at the side door. Brett turned to see Ceci standing there, her hand over her mouth. He opened his arms and she ran into them. She peered down at the woman and shuddered. "It's true? She really followed us here?"

Brett nodded.

"If we're not safe here, where will we be?" she cried.

Brett rubbed her shoulders gently. "Go back to the kids, I'll come in a few minutes and explain."

She nodded and ran back inside.

Brett took a deep breath. "I went to Jennifer's room but she wasn't in her bed. I ran to Jimmy's where both kids were laying on his bed. Jennifer still slept. Jimmy was just about to wake up. The woman couldn't have been in there longer than five minutes." He took a deep breath. "I didn't want him to see her."

His fists clenched. "She warned me what would happen if Ceci said anything about what went on at the embassy. I know it was just talk, but she pointed the gun at Jimmy's head…" he shrugged. "So I attacked."

"Looks like you broke her neck," Swede said.

"She was after the kids. For that she deserves every bit of hell she gets." Brett walked to the edge of the garage. "Do you think it's over?"

"No." Mason shook his head. "We need to find her accomplices first – if she has any here."

"They would've taken off when she didn't return." Brett turned to look at Mason.

"Maybe," Mason said. "If they have a visual on the house they would know the operation failed."

"Good." Swede smiled, but it wasn't a nice one. "Better than us going after ghosts, knowing there could be an attack anytime."

Brett stared down at the blanket wrapped body. "I'm not sure what to do about Ceci and the kids. They can't stay here."

"That's a given."

Chase came in the side door from checking the backyard. "There's no sign of anything back there."

"I didn't expect there to be, honestly," Brett said. "It wouldn't have been hard for her to get into the house. There was no security to speak of."

"She'd be better off at your house," Chase suggested. "We can keep an eye on her and the kids there. Like we did with Amrit and Peter."

Brett smiled. That was exactly what he'd been thinking. His house was ideal. "What we have to do is find the woman's cohorts and take them down."

"You let me handle that," Mason said. "I'll talk to the commander. Once he realizes what we're up against you know we're all going to be pulled into this."

"First thing first. We need to find out everything we can about her."

Swede nodded. "That will lead us to the others."

"She acted and spoke like she had the authority to pull off that embassy attack." Brett admitted. "Partly why it never occurred to me she'd come after Ceci herself."

"Which means she's following someone else's orders. There's no other reason for a high ranking official to be pulling off a job like this."

"Unless it's so secret she can't afford to have anyone telling tales. As in this is *her* operation." Mason pulled out his phone and stepped outside of the house.

Swede turned to look back at the woman on the ground. "She wouldn't have been working alone."

"I agree." Brett glanced toward the kitchen door and added, "She probably walked right into the house, saw the kids and realized with the coffee brewing we'd be out anytime. If I hadn't been here…"

"Don't even think about it, man." Chase gave him a light slap on the shoulder. "You *are* here. And that makes all the difference."

"And what if one time," Brett murmured, "I'm not?"

CHAPTER 20

B ACK INSIDE HER small house, Ceci tried to focus on the kids. But it was as if her entire world had flipped. There was no normal anymore. She'd been sure that going home would solve everything. That life would return to the way things had been.

Although having Brett with her changed everything too.

Shaky, she sat down at the kitchen table, a coffee at her side, and helped Jimmy slather peanut butter on his second piece of toast. She swore he had more on his chubby fingers and cheeks than he did on the toast. But it wasn't in her to admonish him for trying to do something on his own. He was going to need that independent spirit when he grew up.

Because it gave her something to do, she stood, found a washcloth and did her best to clean up some of the mess. There was no point in giving Jimmy a complete wash down because he was still eating. Jennifer sat in her high chair chewing away on the crust of her toast. She still looked tired. Hell, they all were.

"How are the kids?" Brett asked as he walked inside.

Jennifer came to life and started banging her tray calling out, "Brett. Brett. Brett."

His eyebrows shot to his forehead as he sat down beside her. "Well hello, little lady. I didn't realize you could say my name."

The toast was jammed into her mouth and she gnawed away on it for a few seconds as she stared at him, silent once again. Brett turned his attention to Jimmy and the peanut butter mess. He winced. "Hey, Jimmy, what are you doing with all that peanut butter?"

Jimmy was a very generous soul at the best of times. He immediately reached out his piece of toast stuck to his fingers, offering Brett a bite.

With a big grin Brett said, "Thanks, buddy, but I'm not hungry yet. You go ahead and eat up."

Jimmy shrugged and shoved the last piece in his mouth.

"Jimmy, that bite was too big," Ceci said.

He just looked at her, grinned, hopped off the chair and ran to the bathroom where he stood on his little footstool so he could reach the taps. She went in to help but it was too late. The taps were already covered in peanut butter. She grabbed a cloth and proceeded to scrub him down. He giggled then headed toward the living room. She went back into the kitchen and collapsed.

"It's never going to stop, is it?"

"This might actually put an end to it," Brett said. "But first we need to find out who traveled to California with her."

She studied him. "And what good will that do? Do you expect them to confess to being involved?"

"You're such a cynic," he said with a smile. But she sensed the seriousness behind that twinkle.

"I was wondering something," she said. "Why a woman?"

"Not sure, but maybe she thought the children would be less afraid of a woman."

"That's smart of her," Ceci admitted.

"Not smart enough. She's dead now."

At that reminder Ceci stared down at the cup in front of her. "Then why do I want to go out and kill her all over again?" she cried out in pain. She muffled her voice as much as she could. She didn't want her son to hear her talking about killing someone.

"That's a natural reaction. Someone tried to hurt those you love."

She gave a hiccup of a laugh. "That is very true."

Restless, she got up to wash the few dishes and stared out the window. Something else bothered her. She half turned back to look at him. "How did she get in?"

"She broke in through the garage door." He got up and wrapped an arm around her shoulder, dropping a kiss on her temple. "I hate to say it but you need a decent security system."

"It's not my house." And she doubted her uncle would pay for one.

She busied herself playing with the soap suds. Not a whole lot she could add to that. She didn't have much money as she was living on what she got from the government after Jimmy died. Choosing to stay home and look after Jennifer rather than putting her in a daycare wasn't an option most people would choose, but as a single mom she wanted to be there for her children as much as she could. Particularly after losing Jimmy. Of course that left her financially strapped a lot of the time. She did babysitting part-time, which helped, but she didn't have money for luxury items. Which was why the vacation on the yacht had been such a godsend. But a security system? How was she supposed to come up with the money for that?

On the other hand how could she *not*? There was nothing more important than keeping her children safe.

"Maybe I should go away for a few days," she said abruptly.

"Where would you go?"

Her shoulders sagged. "I don't know. I could pack up the car and just drive. Find a hotel somewhere I can afford to stay for a week or two." After everything they'd gone through already, all she had been able to think about was getting home. Letting go of that dream was really hard for her right now. But when compared to her children's safety – it was an easy decision.

"Alternatively I suggest I move in and we put in the security system." He smiled at her. "Even when you come back you'll need to feel safe. That means a security system."

"Will I feel safe then?"

He reached across the table and grasped her hand, his thumb slowly stroking up and down hers. "You will." He looked out the window. "We just have to finish this and with any luck that will be today." He stroked her hand again gently. "However, the best idea is for you to move into my place. I have lots of room. We might need to anyway as it will take a few days to put in a security system."

His phone rang and he dropped her hand to pull it out and check the number. "It's Mason."

"SHE FLEW IN with two men and booked a flight home on the last flight out today. They were staying at a hotel close to the airport," Mason said.

"So what? A quick flight in, take care of business then fly home?" Brett thought about the number of times he and his unit had to do something similar. It was all too possible.

"One of the two men was giving a talk at a business conference in the hotel. He appears to be related to her. The other one is at large."

"That's the one we need to speak with then. I presume the man at the conference has an alibi?"

"Tight as a drum."

"Of course he does… What's his relationship to the deceased?"

"Waiting on confirmation now but it looks to be her brother." Mason spoke to someone briefly in the background. "We're assuming he had a legitimate reason for coming, and she took the opportunity to join him."

"Right. Can you send me photo IDs of the two men? That way both Ceci and I will be able to identify them if they come around."

"The brother is still at the conference. We have one man keeping an eye on him to make sure he doesn't leave. The second is the deceased's lover."

"And he could be coming here for all kinds of reasons."

"Exactly. Watch your back. As soon as we track down the second man, I'll let you know." Mason hung up. Brett turned to study Ceci's face. Quickly he told her what they knew, and then he added what they didn't.

"So we have no idea if he's coming after us. Considering they were lovers he may very well want to come for revenge. If she was the leader, the one pushing for an attack on the embassy, the military government is going to bend over backwards to say they will handle this issue. And of course they must apologize to the US government." She leaned back and snorted. "Are we really going to believe she was masterminding this little coup on her own?"

"One thing to remember is that when there's an unstable

government," Brett explained, "people in the ranks below like to take the opportunity to rise up themselves. So I have no trouble believing that's exactly what she was trying to do. With the attack on the embassy the government would have been blamed, further weakening their position. A perfect time for her to take advantage."

SHE MULLED OVER the information. If he was right, with the woman dead the problem over in Somalia was going to be brushed under the table. The embassy would once again re-staff and carry on. "What about the missing staff members in the van?"

"They've been found. Alive, but in rough shape. They were held in an empty building close to where the vehicle was found."

"At least you found them in time," she cried. "It would have been terrible if they'd all been killed."

He nodded. "Another day or two and they'd likely have died. No one would have known."

That was a horrible thought. "It feels very much like a large chessboard and the next move is somebody else's. I can do nothing but wait to see what their strategy is going to be."

"That's a good way to look at it."

She held out her hands for Jennifer who Brett had cleaned up and removed from the high chair. It was amazing to have somebody around who did something, to not have it all fall on her shoulders. Still, she didn't want to become complacent and expect it. "Thank you very much for looking after her."

He lifted Jennifer higher and dropped a kiss on her pudgy cheek. "No thanks required. She's a joy, not a job."

She smiled up at him realizing she could get used to this. When she thought about having another relationship it never occurred to her she would find somebody who would love her children as much as she did. Having been such a bad judge of relationships up until now she didn't figure her luck was going to change anytime soon. But maybe she was wrong.

She put Jennifer down on the floor, opened the fridge, and checked her cupboards. "We've been gone for a while. I do need to go shopping." She reached out an arm toward the living room. "We could order in, but it would be good for the kids to get out and visit some of our usual places."

"What does that mean?"

"A little shopping, a walk in the park. Potentially meet a friend for a play date this week."

At that Brett shook his head. "No play dates. We can't put anybody else in harm's way."

Her shoulders sagged at that. "You're right. That's not what we want to do. So no play dates. Instead we could rent a movie or some games and maybe just spend lots of time at home doing stuff we like to do. Jimmy loves crafts and math."

At that Brett's eyebrow shot up. "Math? How far along is he?"

She gave a proud smile. "He's already got his numbers one through one hundred, and his addition with small numbers down pat. Now he's working on subtraction." She grinned. "He loves to use Lego blocks for doing math."

"Sounds like he's going to be an engineer one day,"

She laughed. "He can be whatever he wants to."

Brett's phone rang again. He glanced at the number and groaned. "It's Mom."

"Go ahead and answer it."

He rolled his eyes, clicked on the talk button and said, "Hello, Mom."

He listened for a moment and then said, "Ceci is fine. Yes, the children are too." With a wicked grin he said, "Here, you talk to her. She's right beside me."

He handed the phone to her and Ceci immediately tried to pull her hands back, but he wasn't having anything to do with that. "Go on, talk, Mom, Ceci can hear you."

And he got up and went to the children.

She shot him a glare. "Hello, Mikka, how are you?" It really wasn't a hardship to speak with Mikka because in actuality no one got a word in edgewise. She bubbled away about how concerned she was for the children and how sorry she was about the vacation turned nightmare, plus she'd heard from Jason and he was really upset, and why didn't she phone him and let him know she was okay. The man was really interested in her, and it would be good for her and the children. Making the appropriate nods and murmurs Ceci got through the bulk of the conversation. Then there was an odd silence. Followed by a gasp. "My Brett is there?"

Ceci knew she was in trouble as Mikka finally stopped talking long enough to connect the dots. "Yes. Sorry, I have to go. Bye."

And she hung up quickly. Then giggled.

Brett popped his head back into the room and gazed at her suspiciously. "What was that for?"

With a twinkle she handed him his phone back. "She just realized you're here with me." She turned and walked away, turning back to say, "Have fun with that."

On cue his phone rang again. She heard his muttered oath and laughed out loud as he tried to decide what to do.

He shot her a look and said, "You have a mean streak." Then he answered the phone and walked back into the living room. "Hello again."

As much as she wanted to hear the conversation she also really didn't. He was going to get grilled like a red-hot barbecue right now.

She also knew his mom understood how badly hurt he'd been before, so it wasn't going to be an easy phone call. Maybe it was mean of her, but she didn't have any more answers than anyone else as she had no clue what was going on between them. Just that they'd taken a step this morning she'd never thought would be available for her again.

BRETT DIDN'T EVEN bother lowering his voice. "No, I'm not sure what I'm doing, Mom, I just know I have to do this." He listened as his mom ran on about how badly hurt he'd been. "And none of that matters. Because this is where I find myself right now. I never stopped loving her. It's she who walked away from me."

"And that's what I don't want to have happen again," his mom said in a pained voice.

"You're the one who told me how unhappy she was with Jimmy. How difficult her life was after his death."

"That didn't mean I wanted you to step in and save her," his mom protested.

"There's no need for that. She's doing just fine on her own. Now I'm at work so I'll talk to you later."

As he hung up he realized his conversation had been overheard. He spun around to see Ceci leaning in the doorway, tears in her eyes.

"You still love me?" she whispered.

Self-conscious but never one to back down or surrender – unless it was the kind that was great for both of them – he said, "Why does that surprise you? I loved you years ago. You were everything to me. That hasn't changed."

Her lip trembled. "But I hurt you." Her eyes welled with tears again.

"Yes, you did." He shrugged. "Apparently I don't let go easily." He stared across the distance wondering what it was going to require to cross the divide. "The good thing is I stay true to my heart."

A small gasp escaped. "And I don't?"

Feeling like he was heading into a minefield with horrific consequences if he took a misstep, he shook his head. "I think you got hurt and didn't know how to handle it, and you did what you are quite used to doing."

"Running away?" she said bitterly, her body stiffening as anxiety washed over her.

"No. Hiding." He walked closer, his steps calm and sure. "What was it about Jimmy that attracted you?" He didn't touch her. He just stood in front of her not really giving her a chance to back up or move forward. "Think about it," he urged.

She shrugged. "I thought I loved him."

"But what you actually said was that you loved the package. That you were looking to settle down and have a family."

She nodded. "Yes, I said that."

"But there was something else about Jimmy you really liked," he said quietly. "That you needed at that point in your life."

"And what was that?" She frowned up at him. Not upset, but curious. Good.

"He was safe. He didn't have a dangerous job. He was a records clerk. He didn't do any heavy sports. He looked like a family man. He left the house, went to work every day, came home and watched TV most nights." He tilted her chin up. "Right?"

It took her a moment then she gave a short jerky nod.

"So think about this." He gently rubbed his thumb against her bottom lip. "When you lost the baby you were hurt, and you ran. You went through a series of relationships looking for a place to call home. In Jimmy you found that. He could give you the babies you wanted. In your mind you had a safe place to hide out and not have to deal with the rest of the world anymore. A world that had hurt you, where you now felt insecure and unstable. Jimmy gave you a safe, stable home."

"That makes me sound foolish," she protested.

"But you weren't thinking rationally, likely you weren't thinking at all. You were reacting. To the pain. The loss. All the hurt you'd stuffed inside."

She raised her gaze to his. "Don't you resent the children?"

"Of course not," he exclaimed. "Why would I do that?" Just the thought of feeling that way was so alien to him he could hardly believe she'd asked.

She frowned and dropped her gaze to the floor. "Jimmy did."

If Jimmy were standing in front of him right now he'd probably knock him down then wait till he stood up and knock him down again. How could he have made this beautiful woman feel so insecure and believe her children were so unlovable? Then as he thought about it he wondered if he'd been the same because when she'd been hurt she'd run. Instead of coming to him for comfort or reassurance she'd taken off in the opposite direction.

He took a deep breath reminding himself that had been then and this was now. They'd both changed, matured.

"That was Jimmy's problem. Remember, we don't carry his problems forward. They need to stay buried with him."

"I'm not the same person I was when I went to Jimmy," she replied quietly. "I did a lot of soul-searching after he died. That's not the same dream I want now."

He tilted her head and studied her. "And what dream do you want now?"

She opened her mouth to answer.

He leaned in to hear but gunfire rippled across the front of the house, bullets spraying the living room, sending them screaming to the floor. As the smoke and dust settled, Brett heard a vehicle racing away. He grabbed his phone and contacted Mason.

"The children," Ceci cried, crawling toward the two on the floor crying.

Brett rushed to the kids and found no blood. They were scared, but unhurt. He snagged them up. "Take the children to the bedroom and stay there. I'll be right back."

And he bolted outside.

CHAPTER 22

HUDDLED TOGETHER ON the unmade bed from her romp with Brett, Ceci hugged the children tight. Both buried their heads against her chest, their bodies trembling in fear.

This had to stop. The kids were going to be traumatized for life. She expected to hear chaos outside, sounds of people running around trying to figure out what happened. Not this time apparently.

She looked around her small home. There was no way she wanted to stay here. Now the living room was covered in glass and wasn't habitable considering she had little children. Then there was the fact that someone was trying to kill her, and they knew where she lived.

It was one thing to pack up when she was in the embassy but now… She shook her head. This was a full on move. Not something she could do quickly. She had family to call on for help but was loathe to do so. The extended family to call if need be, but that wasn't her style – at least it hadn't been.

She'd been happy with her foster family, but she'd let that connection fall away too. She glanced down at her children, realizing how little she'd actually contacted them over the years. Something else she needed to change.

She looked back on her history, her patterns and fears,

realizing that as much as she didn't want to admit it she had been hiding. Since forever. Her foster parents had brought up a discussion about adopting her. She'd been seventeen at the time. It was almost too late to be adopted by then. More than that it had seemed like a betrayal of her own mother. She'd gone into hurt mode.

She'd moved out soon after. She'd contacted her foster family in the beginning but had already started to distance herself before she'd left. Why? They'd made her an incredibly generous and loving offer but instead of accepting she'd pulled away. When she'd lost the baby she should've known Brett would be there for her. He'd never let her down before. But she'd been hurting and she pulled away. And again, why?

Because like any injured animal she'd gone into hiding to heal. She hadn't *run* as much as hidden.

When Jimmy died, she hadn't been able to hide the same way because she had the children to look after. They'd been her rock. She'd had to be strong for them. She was all they had. They were all she had. And as she studied their sweet faces, she realized that if something happened to her, she'd want someone to adopt her children.

The last thing she wanted was for them to feel alone and unloved – like she had. As she thought about it longer, she realized it was as if she felt she hadn't deserved their love. That she'd been to blame in a stupid way for her mother leaving her. More than that was the fear she was going to lose anyone else she loved, so better not to love. It was the only way not to get hurt. But such truths were harsh.

And didn't change the fact she had a pattern, and it wasn't one she particularly liked to look at. Time to change it. She gently stroked Jimmy's hair back off his face. "Time to get your hair cut again, buddy."

He sniffled and laid his head against her chest. "Don't wanna."

She smiled at his return to baby talk. "Still needs to be done," she said cheerfully. "But maybe not today or tomorrow. How about next week."

Holding the children safe in her arms she snuggled deeper into the bed and whispered, "I think it's time for all of us to have a nap."

"You too, Mommy?"

She closed her eyes and snuggled down close to Jimmy. She wouldn't sleep – but for the chance to hold her babies after such a close call – oh hell yes, she'd take it. "Yes, me too."

BRETT SLIPPED BACK into the house. He hadn't been able to shake the feeling the drive-by might've been a way to get everyone out of the house. The last thing he wanted to do was allow another intruder inside. He'd felt pretty stupid this morning.

So far it didn't appear Ceci was blaming him, but he blamed himself. He didn't know what he'd do if anything happened to his family.

He damn near froze. *His* family? With that thought moving around in his head for a couple of twists and turns, he smiled. Yes, they *were* his family. This wasn't about her children from a previous marriage. This was about Ceci and her children being his. And he'd be damned if he'd let anybody hurt them.

She lived in a nice little residential area. The cops were already on their way so that was going to be yet another mess, but it was necessary.

Still, the children didn't need to be here for this. It'd be better he got them to his house. The place he'd bought after his breakup with her – as if sensing he'd lost more than he knew with Ceci and had bought a family home and lived in it alone, waiting for her…

He could congratulate himself now because it was a perfect place to bring a family. He was also jumping the gun because he had no idea if she was interested in moving in or not. It was one thing to have a relationship, but it was another thing entirely for her to accept him as a father for her children.

First they had to put this behind them.

He could hear noises in the master bedroom. At the doorway he stared, a smile curving his lips. They were asleep. All three of them. And interestingly enough she'd curled into the spot where he'd slept. As if she already knew she'd be safe in his arms.

CHAPTER 23

S HE OPENED HER eyes to the afternoon sun. Who knew she'd fall asleep? With both children still tucked up against her she smiled and kissed each on the top of the head. She slipped out from under the covers and walked into the living room, stopping at the devastation in front of her. Through the big open space where the window used to be she saw people in the front yard. She froze when she saw the cops, then relaxed.

Of course there were going to be cops. There'd been a drive-by shooting. As far as they were concerned this was their case.

But she really did not want to answer any more questions.

From where she stood she could see Brett at the corner of the garage. Beside him stood Swede and Mason. There was a heated discussion going on that she didn't want to get involved in. But it was her house, her family, and she could no more walk away from this than she could from anything else. At her own wording she wanted to laugh, because of course, she had walked away – from almost everything. But she wasn't that person anymore… She'd do anything to keep her family safe.

She stepped out of the side door and walked toward Brett. He frowned but immediately held out a hand. She slipped her fingers in and locked them with his as she faced the police.

"When can we leave?" she asked the policeman.

He glanced at her and said, "Were you inside when the shooting happened?"

"I was with Brett and my children were playing in the living room."

"Anyone hurt?"

She shook her head. "Not physically."

He nodded in understanding. "We'll need to get a statement from you, and then it would be best if you did leave the house so we can go through and do what needs to be done."

"I'll pack now."

She dropped Brett's hand or at least tried to but he wouldn't let her go.

He tucked her closer and wrapped an arm around her shoulder. "If one of you wants to come into the kitchen we can give our statements there, and then leave with the children."

The young officer who'd been asking questions nodded. "I'll come in."

"I'll come too," said a second cop as he came around from the back of the house.

All in all, she'd been outside five, ten minutes, maybe fifteen at the most.

But when she walked back inside she knew something had shifted. There was a malevolence to the air.

Ice filled her veins. Dear God, no. She bolted from the doorway to the master bedroom and froze. Both children were missing.

She spun around and raced through the house screaming, "Jimmy, where are you?"

She raced back to Mason. "They're gone." Tears of terror filled her eyes. "I just woke up from the bed, snuck outside and spoke with you guys so they can't have gone far."

Already she could see the front yard was empty as everybody raced to find the children.

She ran out to the backyard and studied the small fence. It wasn't intended to keep anything in and it sure as hell wasn't going to keep any intruder out. It was only now she realized how unsafe the house really was.

None of it mattered.

Her children were gone. She started to shake. She couldn't figure out if it was anger or fear, but underneath it all was a hatred she'd never felt before.

Brett snapped, "Stay here with the police." And he vaulted over the back fence into the neighbor's yard.

She could hear vehicles on the street. No way to know who the drivers were. The children couldn't be gone. There'd been no time.

She could hardly move.

She was so frozen inside.

The cops she'd been with had stayed inside, searching her house.

Alone she paced the open garage. In her head she could hear them crying, calling out for her. Her heart wrenched with every cry.

She stopped because damn it, she swore she could hear them. She spun around and stared at her small house. She bolted back inside and stood in the living room, spinning in a circle as she tried to sort out the sound in her head. She knew her heart and mind were screaming at her to do something, but was she hearing the children or was that a mother's imagination?

One of the officers asked, "What's the matter?"

"I can hear them." At the look of pity on his face, she cried out, "I can. I can hear them."

And she bolted for the master bedroom again. Just as she reached the doorway she heard an odd sound. One she recognized. Her feet refused to move, dread clutching at her heart. Her mind screamed at her to run, instead she turned. And watched as the younger of the two cops slowly fell to his knees and collapsed face down on the ground.

She raised her shocked gaze to the second cop who held a gun pointed straight at her.

A fury she hadn't known existed inside came to life. Aware for the first time she could kill a man and never think twice. She stared at the man responsible for her missing children. "What did you do to my children?"

He laughed. "You can still hear them crying," he mocked. "It doesn't matter if you hear them crying anymore or not. They might get a chance to live. You, however, will not." He raised his gun and pulled the trigger.

BRETT JUMP BACK over of the low fence wishing he could see the children in front of him. So far no luck anywhere. They'd managed to stop two cars on the road they had suspected of being involved, but it was just kids with new vehicles showing off. They knew nothing about the kidnapping.

He bolted back to the side of the house but she wasn't there. That's when he heard a sound that made his blood run cold.

Gunfire.

He crept around to the open kitchen door and slipped inside. He had his handgun in his hand. Since he'd arrived back on US soil he'd never been without it. Not that Ceci knew. It would've been just a reminder of everything she'd been through. From where he stood he could see Ceci on her knees. Her hand on her chest, blood blossoming over her shoulder.

The gunman laughed.

"Stupid bitch. It wasn't even worth making the trip over here for you. And instead of you dying, my beautiful Lena is dead. It's your fucking fault."

He raised his gun.

Brett raced forward. When Ceci saw him she sent him the sweetest smile.

Shit. He lined up a shot and fired.

The gunman dropped, rolled, shot wild and came up behind Ceci. The gun to her head.

"Drop it," he snarled.

"No," Ceci snarled. "Shoot the little bastard." The gunman wrenched her head back, making her cry out in pain.

The killer needed to lower his hand just enough that Brett's bullet would take him out and not have his trigger finger fire off a shot that would kill Ceci.

That he couldn't afford to have happen.

"Let her go," he ordered.

"No fucking way."

Brett knew this bastard was going down. The guy knew it too, and was going to make sure he took Ceci with him.

What happened next took place so fast, his eyes didn't believe it.

Ceci lurched up, a long piece of glass in her hand, and she stabbed the gunman in the throat.

Brett raced in and kicked the gun out of the man's hand as he gurgled his last breath. In his eyes, there was only hate.

For Ceci. For Brett. For the whole damn world.

Then he couldn't see anything as death took him under.

"Good riddance," Brett murmured. He turned to Ceci as Swede and the others poured into the room. He ignored them.

Ceci stood, wavering on her feet. Blood in her eyes, more dripping from her palm where the glass had cut in deep – and then there was her injured shoulder.

"Sweetheart, he's gone. You did it. You killed him."

She lifted her head to his, her gaze huge as she struggled with the shock of her actions. "I should feel bad," she whispered. "I killed a man. In cold blood. But I don't," she said, her voice dazed. "I don't. All I can feel is…relief."

He holstered his gun and reached out gently, grabbing her wrist and slowly, carefully, opening her fingers. "Let this go. Just drop it."

Her gaze fell on the weapon she still held in her hand. With a shudder, she opened her fingers, letting the weapon drop to the wooden floor.

She turned to the men crowding in behind them. In an unnaturally calm voice, she said, "There's an injured cop in the master bedroom, help him please."

Several men raced back.

With a heavy sigh, she looked up at Swede and said, "I can hear the children. They are in here somewhere. Please tear this place apart and find them."

With her hand reaching out weakly for Brett, she whispered, "Look after them for me. I really do love you."

Her eyes rolled into the back of her head and she collapsed into his arms.

CHAPTER 24

EVERYTHING HURT. WHY? She rolled over and felt her stomach start to heave.

"Take it easy. You're just waking up from surgery. Your stomach might be a little upset. If you're in a lot of pain, we can give you something to help you go under again."

Surgery? What the hell happened to her? As she lay back at the nurse's insistence she tried to make sense of what was going on, but her mind was full of the greasy waves of nausea making her want to puke. She shuddered, then a warm blanket was wrapped up around her shoulders and neck. She moaned as the warmth seeped into her bones. Her eyelids drifted closed.

"Just rest. Your body needs to heal. Sleep."

Instead, she opened her eyes to stare up at the blurry features in front of her, trying to make sense of her world. Memories flooded through her psyche and she shuddered as remembered panic hit. In a voice that was more cracked and broken than audible, she asked, "What about my children?" She coughed. "Are they okay?"

The nurse smiled. "Your husband said that was going to be the first question you asked and I'm to tell you the children are fine."

Ceci sank back into the pillows, relief taking over. It didn't matter how badly hurt she was as long as the children were safe. She'd heal. But to lose those babies… That would be too much pain to bear.

"Now that you know, just sleep. Everything is going to be fine."

She smiled, and then remembered the word the woman had used. "Husband?"

"Well husband-to-be. If that little bit of difference matters." Brett spoke from the other side of the nurse. His footsteps were strong as he approached. "But in order to discuss that concept you have to go back to sleep so you can heal."

"Already getting bossy, pushing me around," she grumbled. But there was a smile on her face. Husband. Now that had a nice ring to it. She closed her eyes and slept.

When she woke up the second time it was to find Mikka sitting in the chair beside her. She lay quietly for a moment studying Brett's mother. The woman had a remarkable capacity for patience and love, but could be irritating as hell. And she loved Brett.

"I know you're awake. I'm glad to see it. I would not want to be dealing with my son if something bad happened to you."

Ceci smiled. "Brett's a very special man." Her body ached and she didn't want to move. But this conversation was a little unnerving. The relationship with Brett was too new to analyze, to even understand.

"Not only is he a special man, but he is completely devoted to you. And I'm here to tell you that if you hurt my boy again…" She let her voice trail off.

Ceci stretched out a hand, happy when Mikka reached forward and grasped it in her own.

She couldn't open her eyes but she could reassure the

woman. "I've always loved Brett. I went a little haywire after my miscarriage. I don't really understand what happened to me, but all I can say is life is finally back on the right track. I love him. I always have."

Her fingers were squeezed, her hand dropped. She sank back down into the pain filled haze until a warm set of lips landed on her cheek.

Brett's voice whispered in her ear, "I always believed that you still loved me."

She opened her eyes.

He smiled down at her. "Even when you were with Jimmy I always knew you cared. It tormented me for years until I realized you had to sort yourself out. Now you're home, back where you belong."

She reached up a hand and stroked the side of his beloved face. "Only I don't come alone anymore." She needed him to understand. "Jimmy and Jennifer need a father who will love them too. Who will keep them close and treat them as his own."

He sat down on the bed beside her and smiled. "Personally, I think all of our hearts have been through the wringer and maybe now we can settle down and become a family."

She studied him. "Do you mean that?"

"Of course. We can't keep this up," he whispered. "We love each other and always have. Waiting for you to find your way home was hard, but now you're here. Of course I want Jimmy and Jennifer. I already love them. And if possible, I'd like to have more."

She smiled and a gentle glowing warmth from inside spread throughout her body and soul. "I'd like that," she whispered. "I always wanted a big family."

"Good. Then we're going to have to make it official. I

don't want to lose you again."

She chuckled. "I promise. I'll be at your side forever. As long as you want to keep me there."

A snicker from the hall surprised her. She swiveled her head to see the doorway full with a half dozen dangerous looking men lounging in the small space.

"What's so funny?"

Mason smiled. "We have a tradition. Once one of us finds a woman he wants, he needs to decide if he is keeping her or not."

She frowned, not sure where this was going, or if she'd like it.

Brett groaned and said, "Don't listen to them."

She reached out a hand to him. "Shush."

He turned to glare at the grinning men. Swede took a half step forward. "The thing is, we all have the right woman in our lives. We were hoping Brett would find someone too."

Ceci studied his face. "Go back to Mason's comment earlier. What happens if the man doesn't want to keep the woman?"

They grinned.

"No idea," Swede admitted. "Because SEALs aren't known to be stupid and so far, each and every man has kept the woman of his heart and not given the others a chance to woo her away."

"And it's no different this time," Brett snapped, glaring at them. "Go away, will you?"

"Nope, not until we hear it."

She chuckled at the discomfort on Brett's face. "You know something... I think I want to hear it too."

He snorted. "Like that's going to happen. Not with an audience."

At the doorway there was a commotion as Shadow stepped into the room, both Jimmy and Jennifer in his arms.

"Mommy!" Jimmy cried, trying to dive for her.

Jennifer bubbled up with joy.

Her eyes misty, she reached out to hug them with one arm. When she could speak, Jimmy beat her to it. "Mommy, can we keep Brett?"

Speechless, aware of the sudden silence in the room, she asked her son, "What do you mean?"

"He's been with us a lot. I like him. Can we keep him? Can we?" he added craftily, puffing out his chest. "Jennifer needs a father."

Brett grinned and gave him a tiny shove on the shoulder. "And you champ? Do you need a father?"

Jimmy looked him in the eye and said, "I want a father…"

Brett opened his arms. "In that case, maybe I will do."

Jimmy fell into his arms. Then turned to look at Ceci on the bed. "Mommy?"

And she knew what he was asking. "Yes, we can keep him."

"Forever?" Jimmy asked cautiously with the wisdom of someone who already knew some things didn't always last.

"Yes," she said, tears running down her cheeks and to the cheers of everyone else in the room, she added, "We'll keep him forever."

DEVLIN

SEALs of Honor, Book 12

Dale Mayer

CHAPTER 1

THERE WERE TRAINING missions, and then there were training missions. Devlin Hayman was in Afghanistan as one of two SEAL teams training Afghan military groups in new open-warfare tactics.

Between the dust, dirt, and language issues, he was just about fed up. But he was here to help the Afghan military's elite, and that made it worth doing. Although this afternoon was a whole different story because he would be learning something, training with the new drones.

And not just for the Afghans, but for the SEALs as well. Currently teams ran the drones in very specialized operations throughout the world. But definitely something for the SEALs to know and understand. Devlin had worked on some of the basic models. But this one was high-tech. And he wanted in on it. The manufacturer had sent a representative from its design team. He should be here now. At thirteen hundred hours, training would commence.

What a great way to spend his last day. He shipped out tomorrow, heading stateside. He couldn't wait. He'd been here for three weeks—eaten a pound of dirt, he was sure. Reconsidering all the time he'd been here, he'd probably eaten three or four pounds.

But it wasn't so much that. The training had gone well. Just his patience was running short. It seemed like every trainee looked forward; yet they all forgot to look behind. And it was damn important to always watch your back.

Still this type of training was essential. These men were allies. Besides, the process had gotten a whole lot easier once Easton took over—another member of Devlin's team, who had the patience of a saint. He was right up there with Swede from Mason's unit.

Ryder and Corey rounded out Devlin's crew.

Four of Mason's unit were here too, including Mason himself, plus Shadow, Markus and, of course, Swede. A lot of personnel switches in and out of various specialties had been worked through to get the appropriate men to this drone training. Swede, even with his size, was patient with the tech stuff. And always just off to the side was Shadow. That man was lethal, quiet, and silent. You never heard him arrive or leave. Like the stealth drones themselves.

Devlin walked over to Ryder and Corey. The training session would be called in another twenty minutes.

At the sound of a mechanical whine, Devlin glanced in the sky to see a drone far to his left. Making sure everything was good in front—and back—of them, he nudged Ryder and pointed for Corey. They twisted to look.

This one was more bat-shaped—looked almost like a stealth fighter plane, only smaller.

"That's one of the new ones," Devlin said.

Corey grinned, practically bouncing on his feet. "Can't wait to play with those."

"I heard the engineer arrived already," Ryder said.

"Good. I'm looking forward to learning about those things." Devlin watched as Corey followed the drone in the air.

"Not sure I am," Ryder said. "I'd much rather have a

gun in my hand than a remote."

Devlin laughed. "You can have both, you know?"

"You're the one who's good with those things," Ryder said. "Me, I'm a big ole grunt."

"Like hell. You're the best IED man we've got."

Ryder shrugged. "Sure, I can handle anything that goes boom in the night. But that thing, in the night? I'm not so sure about."

"Well, this afternoon you'll have a chance to find out."

"I can get the whole war over and done, take out the enemy before he sees anything. But to think a drone can pinpoint and deliver a shot with the accuracy *these* machines can, and have nobody even see them ..." Ryder shook his head. "That's like, *freaky*, man."

"You guys ready to call it?" Markus walked over behind them.

"Absolutely," Devlin said. "I can't wait to get to those." He motioned at the drones above.

Markus nodded. "I've heard a lot about them. The private sectors have moved forward with them at a rapid rate too."

"That's just wrong," Devlin said in protest. "We need the latest technology. They can go to hell with that one."

"Tell Levi that," Markus said with a grin. "You heard how bad his unit was blown to shreds. Well, they made a comeback and have taken revenge on the rest of the world by getting the biggest and baddest of everything."

"Shit." Devlin tossed one last glance up at the drone and turned to face the rest of the men.

They had a short talk, and then they dispersed for lunch. But he couldn't forget Markus's words. Levi and his unit had been blown to shit—the whole lot of them. But they'd survived and gone on to build Legendary Security, a fast-growing, incredibly well-respected private security company. They'd only been in business for a few months, and they were already snagging top jobs.

But, of course, why wouldn't they be, considering they'd already recruited some of the top men from the military. Hell, so far, they only had former SEALs working for them, as far as Devlin knew. Even Flynn, who'd been drummed out.

And Flynn was a hell of a good guy too. Then Devlin remembered the nicknames for Levi's company. "Levi might have some of the best tech toys, but some very romantic nicknames sure followed him."

Markus laughed. "The latest I heard was Heroes of the Heart."

Ryder snorted beside them. "Last I heard was Heroes for Hire."

"Yeah, *heroes* being the common denominator," Markus added. "Seems every time another woman moves into the compound, she comes up with a new name for the company. Levi's beside himself thinking that one of them might stick."

Devlin glanced at Markus and said, tongue-in-cheek, "You should know. You're part of the *Keepers'* unit."

"That's hardly our call sign, as you know." Markus grinned. "But, since I understand where that name comes from, I can hardly argue with it. Besides, I could discourage it until I'm blue in the face. Mason already tried that a million times, and we can't get anybody to ignore it."

"Probably because you argued it so often and heavily," Ryder said with a big grin. "Besides, how the hell did every one of you end up with some kind of perfect romance?"

Markus slapped Ryder on the shoulder. "Dude, if you

tried it, you wouldn't knock it. We'd never thought to find partners like we have. Yet look at us. And the total count is something stupid, like ten for ten now."

"We included Levi because that relationship is fantastic too," Ryder added. "I'm really happy for Ice. She's one hell of a pilot. Dozens of men had their sights on her, but she's never had eyes for anyone but Levi."

"I tell you," Markus said, "if they ever have a wedding, they'll invite half the military to the ceremony. Although, from what I hear, the compound's almost big enough for it."

"Compound?" Devlin asked. "Is that really what they have?"

"Yes. Fully gated, fully secured. Bullard's even in on the act. He helped set up the security on the place. And Ice, well, she's got two helos there. Talk about a perfect setup. I tell you, they are in for some serious business."

It boggled the mind. But given the people involved, it made a lot of sense. Devlin had never met Bullard but had heard lots. He was an icon in his own world, even though he'd set up his business in Africa. *Less rules and questions,* he'd said once, when asked about his choice. Just as much a legend as Levi was. The name Legendary Security was perfect for anybody in the business. And Levi had a hell of a lot of connections. He and Ice. Those two would be unstoppable. Devlin was happy for them and maybe jealous. He hadn't given any thought to his future after his life as a SEAL. Just no time for that.

His military life was everything to him at present. So he didn't understand the whole relationship thing Markus had talked about. Devlin had no time for that shit. He was one of the few who were more into a short-term relationship because it came with no strings. He didn't worry about it when he headed off into the field. And he was doing mission after mission too. If not being deployed, he was learning or teaching. And it was all good but, at the same time, just provided no room for a relationship.

So kudos to Markus and the other men who made it work. No way in hell was Devlin after the same thing.

Not that he was superstitious or anything, but when Ryder had talked about not wanting to hook up with the Keepers—in case it was contagious—Devlin had privately agreed. The last thing he wanted to do was end up as part of their group. Ryder felt the same. Now several Keepers were already married. Yet more of Devlin's SEAL buddies were going through their own current struggles with relationships, and then a whole mess of them were single—and not by choice, like Ryder for instance. Divorce rates were high. Military wives didn't have it easy. The Keepers' group somehow knocked down the number of singles, one by one.

Still Devlin needn't worry; a relationship wasn't in the cards for him.

Now he could fully get into some of that specialized drone training. And all the men here were the best of the best. But there were, of course, specialties. From IEDs to snipers to drone operators. Sure, several would be trained on the basic ones, but these babies were special. And Devlin wanted to play too. The drones were to become standard equipment moving forward. And that would be one hell of an arsenal.

If he found the engineer, it'd be a great opportunity to speak with him about what he was currently working on.

Devlin glanced around and stepped back. The guys had just wrapped up the morning teaching session. He walked toward where the drones were. Several men talked with

Mason. When he caught sight of Devlin, Mason motioned him over.

Perfect. He introduced himself. He got the first man's name, Brent, but he didn't appear to be the engineer. Three women were nearby. One was tweaking a remote in her hand. As for the other two, they were operating drones. He figured something must be wrong with one of them as the woman really struggled to move hers.

He wanted to grab the remote from her hand and take over. But he probably knew less about it than she did, considering she was already handling one.

At that moment her drone did a very erratic movement.

"Whoa," he said. The men turned and watched it.

One of them called, "Bristol, bring it back."

"We can't," she responded, watching as another woman tweaked the remote. "Something's wrong with the controller."

The other woman shook her head and offered the handset to Bristol.

"Thanks, Morgan," Bristol said, who then slipped off the cover. Whatever she did stabilized the drone. With the same skillful movement, Bristol, now holding the handset, brought the drone in for a perfect landing on the ground in front of them.

This close, Devlin could see it was six to seven feet in length. Bigger than he had thought. And yet, in the sky, it looked no bigger than a falcon or hawk.

At first glance anybody would expect it to be a bird.

The men returned to their conversation. Devlin listened with half an ear as he watched the women setting up tables for this afternoon's training. First would be a demonstration, then a simulation on laptops, and finally they would form small groups to work with the actual drones, providing three were in full operation. As he understood, the women were the instructors.

Devlin could get behind that. Generally he got along well with females.

And they really liked him. Then again, he was very amiable.

Ryder, on the other hand, who tended to be curt most days, wasn't looking forward to the training. He was also dealing with the end of a long-term relationship. And that was hurting him. He wasn't looking at women in the best light currently.

Poor guy.

Another reason why Ryder wanted nothing to do with the Keepers.

Devlin cast a glance around, but not seeing any reason to stay, he walked away from the group of men still discussing this afternoon's schedule and headed toward the women. As soon as he took the next step though, two MPs stepped in front of him.

"Can't allow you to pass this point, sir."

He nodded. But kept his eye on the three female trainers. He hoped he got the one with blonde hair. He was always partial to blondes.

CHAPTER 2

BRISTOL STARED AT the small panel in front of her. It wasn't taking kindly to the sand and the heat of the region. She'd had the cover off too many times. What she really needed was her small handheld vacuum to clean this out. In normal operations, the units would never be opened. But here she dealt with prototypes far from ready. She understood the rush, the need to get these things into active missions, and to get that done as fast as possible. But why the hell did it always have to be before the drones were ready?

The bosses pushed, and everyone caved in. That was why she was in Afghanistan, dealing with three units that had been on her lab worktable at home, getting them ready for the training session this afternoon. One was doing just fine. But, of course, that wasn't enough. She needed the others.

Colleen muttered, "Can you fix it?"

Bristol looked up at her assistant. "Do I have a choice?"

Colleen sighed. "Sorry, but I just couldn't control it—like it's possessed. Never seen anything this screwy."

"It might be the controls or a broken wire. Hell, it could be the software. Let me take it back to the tent, and I'll see what I can do."

She got the handset, and recalling the drone, she and Colleen walked to the work tent the women had been given.

At least some attempt had been made to keep out the sand and dust here. Bristol replaced the computer chip pack, a normal step. She'd brought dozens with her, just in case. But they too were being modified so each one she used had to be upgraded first. She was doing that as well.

To open the pack and change out the computer was simple. It was smaller than a cell phone after all. She brought up the handset and entered the new code. Using her laptop, she found the match for the new computer chip set.

She handed it over to Colleen and said, "You mind taking it out and seeing how we're doing? I'll be there in a minute."

Colleen walked out ahead of her. Bristol covered up her gear and followed. Within minutes Colleen had the drone up in the air, and this time it appeared to be working fine.

Patting Colleen on the shoulder, Bristol said, "I'll go inside and see if I can fix the other one."

Back at her table she grabbed the damaged unit, quickly typed the serial number into her laptop and noted what had gone wrong.

The soldiers needed a lot of training, but today was a crash course only. The drones needed more testing time. Hopefully they'd be ready when the real training began.

When the tent flap flipped again, she thought it was Colleen. "Now what?"

"Nothing. I just came to see how these awesome drones are doing."

She looked up and did a double take. Tall and blond with that air of command. Shivers whispered down her spine. He was … She swallowed hard and reined in her emotions. She didn't have time for this. She couldn't afford any distractions.

She studied him for a long moment and then said, "You don't belong here."

He grinned at her. "I'm sorry, ma'am. Just a big fan of the drones. I was wondering if I could see some of the detailed work you do."

She shook her head. "Not today. Not any day." She stood and pointed at the tent flap.

The smile fell from his face, and his gaze narrowed. He gave a clipped nod, turned and walked out.

She breathed a sigh of relief. She'd been in the industry way too long to allow somebody to sneak under her guard like that. Nobody ever saw the work she did. She wasn't just repairing; she was the designer of these drones. The modifications made on a standard-issue drone were her baby. And no way in hell did she want anybody to see her work.

She operated alone, always, and always would. Hence, starting her own company.

On the other hand, it was a hell of a lonely life. But she had no time to fill it with friends, and, as for family, … that was just painful. All she did was work. Turning her attention back to the pieces on the table, she checked her watch and realized she was almost out of time. Just that two-minute conversation had made her lose focus. And she didn't have time for that shit.

Colleen walked back in just then. "This drone tested out fine. Did you fix the other?"

Bristol shot her a fulminating look. "If the men would stop coming in here, it would be a whole lot easier to work."

Colleen grinned at her. "I saw the man walk in. Got to love that long, loose-limbed walk of his. And how the guys know to single out the ladies and grab us when we don't have anybody else around."

"Like I need that shit today." Bristol returned to her work on the table. "How much time do I have?"

"Twenty-two minutes and counting."

"Right, of course. So I miss out on lunch again."

"Sorry, we were late getting in. Without having everything ready for us, it's been a bit nuts."

"A bit?" She hadn't wanted to come in the first place. She should be back at her lab, working on changing out these developments so they weren't so finicky. But again, it went back to that whole issue of no time for testing. Everything was now, now, now. And, of course, her contract had a deadline with many conditions if she couldn't meet it. If she defaulted, she'd lose everything. Still it was a major contract and a huge step forward. She owed Brent for this opportunity. He had received other bids, but she appreciated him giving her this chance. She didn't understand why, but wasn't about to argue.

Everybody wanted results and money. Brent didn't care how the hell they got it. And if she couldn't do the job, she'd get the hell out of the way because he'd find someone who could. And in fact, already had a backup in place according to him. She'd been listening to that for a long time.

She'd known better. She should never have signed this contract.

When she looked up from her work twenty minutes later, she found Colleen standing there with a cup of coffee and a muffin in her hand. She held both out to Bristol. "It's the best I could do."

Bristol nodded gratefully. "It's a hell of a lot more than I had, so I'll take it. These are ready to go. If they break down this afternoon …" She shook her head. "Well, not a whole lot I can do about it."

Bristol motioned toward the broken pieces on the table. "I can't even take it back like this. I wish I didn't train today and could leave that to the others. I have so much to do. But I have no choice. Morgan can handle one, you and I the other two groups."

"What about having David take one?"

Bristol snorted at that. "He's good with a pencil, but he sucks on the drones, as you well know."

"I know, but there's a need …"

"No, I'll do it. Which means no dinner. By the time I get all this shit packed up, it'll take me right through until tomorrow morning. You know that too."

"I'll help."

"I was counting on it."

Bristol smiled at Colleen. The two had worked together for the last four years. Colleen was great on hardware, but she didn't do software or design. However, she was a great operator, and that made her perfect for training. Bristol took one last look around and said, "Let's go. It's time."

Muffin in one hand, coffee in the other, Bristol walked out with Colleen to where the training would be—and realized they would have a larger audience than normal.

"Great," she said under her breath.

Colleen smiled at her. "You can do this. You always do."

DEVLIN WATCHED AS the women walked to the center. He wasn't sure what it was about the blonde that caught his attention so. She was prickly, like a porcupine, but when you stroke them right, those soft quills lay down smooth. He just knew something good was inside.

He often found that the bristlier a woman was on the

outside, the softer she was on the inside. Usually somebody had given her a reason to not trust anymore. But he wasn't here for women. He was here for the drones.

But one thing he did recognize was, when she spoke, she commanded attention. He listened to her rehearse her speech for the afternoon and realized not only would she be doing the demonstration but she was the engineer he'd been looking for. This latest technology allowed these drones to target a dime on a sidewalk at an incredibly unnerving distance.

He wanted to know more about the accuracy, having heard rumors of a built-in retargeting system as well. He hoped so because that would just make their life so much easier.

It also explained why she'd been so prickly when he had walked into the tent unannounced. She had a lot of her parts and pieces there. Probably thought he was after intel. Although they should be safe in a camp like this, he understood security measures. Men should've been standing guard at the edge of the tent, but no MPs had been there. That's why Devlin had walked in. He realized he may have shot himself in the foot.

Just then her gaze landed on him. Her lips downturned.

Shit.

Then she turned, grabbed her remote and sent one of the drones soaring into the air. And she carried on.

"Good afternoon everyone. We set up several targets on the ground up ahead," she said. "I'll demonstrate the three drones we're working on. If you all will keep quiet for the next twenty minutes or so, we'll show you just how accurate these drones can be."

And what followed was an intense, awe-inspiring session.

The drones danced in midair, flipped and turned, rolled easily, and then went into what she called flight-and-mimic mode—the soaring motion of any bird in the wind. "Watch the target," she called out, pointing to a setup on the far side, a good 250 yards away.

A hard *ping* sounded, and the target took a shot right through the dead center of the bull's-eye.

He grinned. "Oh, *hell*, yes."

Not only had the first drone fired, but the second had too, leaving a matching hole in the target right beside the first. The third did sweeping maneuvers around the other two. But at no point did the drones allow that to stop them. When the blonde brought all three to a smooth landing, the crowd erupted into applause, and nobody clapped louder or harder than Devlin. Damn, she was something.

For the first time, she smiled. "Gentlemen, you've all been assigned to a group, and we will work for the next four hours with these three drones plus six more. The other six do not have the same capability. These are the elites. When you've mastered the basics on the six, then we will carry on to training with the three. However, if you think all the training is done with the drones in the air, you're wrong. I have a lot of computers set up. This is an extensive group so we'll work in subgroups. I needed several days to teach this, but apparently you're getting a crash course today. We're here this afternoon only so let's make the most of it."

She turned and walked off. The other woman, who had been with her damaged drone, stood and said, "I'm Morgan, one of the instructors. Get into three groups as assigned, and please go to your allocated station." She grabbed her handset. "I control one of the big drones." It flew over her head and stayed above her as she headed to her training station.

Devlin watched in amazement as she led group number three to the right. "Amazing."

He hurried over to his group, which was group one. He could see another drone hovering over another woman as she headed to a different location. He had no idea what instructor he had. He hoped he would have the engineer he'd met, but he had no way to know.

Then he caught sight of the third drone. As it came on this side of the area, he knew where it was headed. He quickly followed as the crowd swelled around him. He had hoped the trainee groups would be smaller, but he quickly understood that half the crowd here were just spectators. Twelve men stepped forward, of which he was one. Then he realized he'd lucked out. He had the engineer, Bristol. Perfect.

She gave instructions clearly. They would work with computer simulations, not the real drones yet. He was positioned with Easton at a laptop. Six laptops, six remote controls. She ran them through simple navigational training. Remote control was something they all had worked with at one time or another. But not at this level of fine-tuned control.

He watched as Easton's fingers managed the basics but lost out on the commands. He itched to grab it in his own hands.

Only, when his turn came, Bristol had walked behind him, and he had completely flopped at everything— slamming the drone on the computer screen into the wall and then crashing it on the ground. And yet she never said anything mocking. He expected it, especially after their earlier meet. He shook his head.

Easton just said, "It's way harder than it looks."

"And you're trying too hard," Bristol added. "Pull back the tension on your thumb. Consider it like a video game controller and pretend you're just playing against a buddy."

At her words Devlin relaxed. Because this was exactly that—a training session, just a simulation. Like the remote in his hand was quite similar to a controller. But he only had one toggle to control and two thumbs that refused to listen to his commands. His thumbs kept getting in the way of each other. "Could you make this controller more hand-friendly?" he asked.

"It's in progress. But this session was moved forward so I couldn't finish them."

That also accounted for some of her disgruntlement. She'd probably been pushed to bring the equipment here when she needed more time on it.

He nodded. "Sorry," he said in commiseration. "A typical story. Everybody wants everything now."

She glanced at him, and he caught the glimmer of another smile when she murmured, "Isn't that the truth." Then she walked over to another pair in the group.

But it was enough. He glanced back down at the laptop and made another run at the simulation. This time he reached the end without killing it.

As progress went, this wasn't much. But he'd take it. He handed the controller back to Easton and said, "Your turn."

Easton grabbed it and said, "What? Are you going to hunt your ladylove?"

Devlin snorted. "Did you ever see anybody less likely to sign up for the position of my ladylove?"

The derision in his tone had Easton laughing. But they both settled back down and got through the simulation. Once again with a good lineup and they reached the end with a relatively smooth performance. The instructor returned and set them up for the second simulation.

Devlin turned and smiled at her. "You introduced yourself at the very beginning, but it was hard to hear. I'm Devlin Hayman," he said and held out his hand.

Her smile widened. "I'm Bristol McEwan. Now get back to work."

Devlin smirked at her retreating back, losing his sense of humor quickly. The drones were finicky and complicated. Way more than he'd expected. To do a decent job was one thing, but to excel at these was much harder.

After they had a break, she separated the groups further, taking several out of each and moving them off to the side. Thankfully, Devlin was one of them. Each person now had a drone and instructor of their own. And yet, once again, although it looked easy enough to do, it wasn't.

The coordination and control of the drone was very difficult to fine-tune. Devlin tried hard. He could get it up; he could move it around and over trees, but he clipped a tree, and his landing left a lot to be desired. Not to mention repairs were needed.

And the other guys didn't appear to be doing any better. Behind them, Ryder and Easton were still working on the simulations. But Devlin knew their hearts weren't in it. So that was all good. He was where he wanted to be. But he sure as hell wasn't putting his best foot forward. And that sucked. By the end of the day he was frustrated and fed up. He joined Ryder and Easton and walked over to where the rest of Mason's unit worked with the Afghani soldiers.

Mason and Swede talked with several other men. Devlin and his buddies approached, not wanting to disturb them, yet at same time ready for a change of pace. One of the guys motioned toward them and grinned. "Heard you crashed a drone today. Nice job."

"I didn't crash it. It just had a little rough landing."

The others laughed. Swede said, "Not very easy to handle, is it?"

"It's definitely more difficult than I thought." He shrugged. "I'm not doing that bad though." As he spoke, he saw a look of shock spread over Swede's face.

"Fire!"

Devlin spun to see one of the tents—close to where he'd been practicing with the drones—going up in flames.

Cries ripped out across the small compound as everyone rushed into action. He was only halfway there when he realized the tent was the same one he'd walked into earlier. The tent where Bristol had been working on her drones.

He raced toward the disaster as the flames easily ripped through the canvas tent, quickly spreading to those on both sides. But these were all military men and well trained. Very quickly they had a fire brigade moving in, putting out the flames.

Once the fire was completely doused, everyone stood and stared in shock at the remains. The fire had started in Bristol's tent. The table was gone; a mess of melted plastic left instead. The temporary wooden flooring had burned up, adding fuel to the fire. His heart jumped as he worried Bristol was inside. He pushed his way through the crowd until he stood at the edge and could see for himself. The murmurs rose.

Then they cut off in silence as quickly as they had started. But Devlin had to know for sure about Bristol. His gaze flowed over the water-soaked area and landed on the floor in the middle of the small space.

And spied the charred body among the black ash. Not as badly burned as the rest of the place. Enough for a positive ID as one of the women working on the drones. His gaze scanned the crowd, and there, off to the side, he saw Bristol, standing, her hands over her mouth, tears in her eyes as she stared at the remains. Several men stepped away from her. The hell with that.

He approached quietly and asked, "You okay?"

She turned and stared up at him wordlessly. Her eyes were huge and tear-stained.

He stepped between her and the body.

She closed her eyes briefly, then opened them again. "Is it Colleen?"

"I'm not sure," he said calmly. "But from the hair and bits of clothing, it's likely."

Her lower lip trembled, and she looked for a moment like she couldn't remain standing. Then she straightened her shoulders and gave a clipped nod. "I need to ID the body." She dashed around him and stepped into the blackened nightmare.

He stayed with her, knowing military police in the compound would take over. But he wouldn't leave her alone. From the looks of it, everybody else stayed well away from her. Which said much about her cool personality. But nothing was cool about it at present. Shoulders shaking, she bent down beside the woman on the ground. He heard one hiccupping sob.

Then she straightened and faced him. She gave a nod and said, "It's Colleen."

He led her out of the way, knowing the men rushing toward them weren't happy they were in there. He held up his hand and was instantly surrounded. "She just identified the body. Her associate Colleen …" He turned toward Bristol for more information.

Bristol said, "Colleen Palmer. She works for me. We're here today for the drone training."

Two MPs led her several tents over, where they sat her down and asked questions. He hadn't planned on following. He had his own work to do and people to be with. But when she glanced at him, he saw that look of hope in her eyes, and couldn't leave her alone. He immediately caught up with them and stayed with her. At the entrance to the tent, one of the MPs turned and shot him a hard gaze. "Who are you, and what are you doing here?"

He quickly identified himself and added, "I'm with her."

The MP turned to Bristol to confirm. She gave him a shaky nod. With that, Devlin stepped up behind her to give silent support. She gave him a grateful look and then murmured, "Thanks."

He reached down and gripped her shoulder, squeezing gently once, then dropped his hand and waited for the questions to start.

And start they did. The men were kind, yet firm. "Where were you before the fire broke out?"

"In the mess tent, getting a coffee."

"Were you with anyone?"

"No. But I was seen by many."

"Where was Colleen when the fire broke out?"

"Obviously in the tent," Bristol said. "I don't have any idea why."

"When did you last see her?"

"Before I went to get coffee. We were talking outside the tent."

"What was she doing in there?"

"Recalibrating one of the drones that had a rough landing."

Devlin stiffened at that. She turned and looked up at him with a smile. "Don't worry. We're used to it."

Still he hadn't wanted to be the one involved in this.

"Did you see anyone set the fire?"

She looked startled. "Are you saying it was arson?" Her hand went back up to cover her mouth as she stared wordlessly at the men. After a long moment she said, "I thought for sure it was an accident."

"No determination has been made at this time."

Devlin studied the man's face, but Devlin knew the MPs obviously had seen something already. Devlin hadn't had time to look. He'd been too busy dealing with Bristol. He also wondered how Colleen had died. She could've been overcome by smoke inhalation. But what was she doing that she didn't recognize the fire in a tent that size?

Inside his gut an ugly suspicion grew. He wanted to ask her several questions himself, but the MPs were still firing them at her.

"Did you have any problem with Colleen?"

She shook her head. "No."

"Did Colleen have any problems with you?"

This time she shook her head even more. "Why are you asking me these questions?"

"Just answer them, please. This work you do with the drones, how important is it?"

At that she dropped her hand to glare at him. "It's very important."

"We want you to go back into the tent with us and see if there's anything missing."

She looked at them in bewilderment. "Missing?" Then

she sat back, the color draining from her face. "As in stolen?"

The man stared at her. She bounced to her feet. "Let's go. I have to see. I was working on some very definite prototypes. If my work was stolen …"

She shook her head and then cried out, "Oh, my God! Listen to me! I'm so worried about my data and Colleen … Dear God, poor Colleen." She started to cry, quietly wiping her hands. "I'm so sorry. I'm trying not to break down, but just the thought of that beautiful woman dead …" She turned to look at the men. "If you tell me that she was murdered, I just don't know what I'll do."

"Why would you assume she was murdered?"

She stared at them. "I'm not assuming she was, but you just asked about arson, and she's dead inside the tent. Was it to cover for her death? Or was she overcome by smoke? Or was this just all one horrible accident?"

"Was she tired?" one of the MPs asked. "Would she take a nap in the tent?"

"No, it's a work tent." Bristol frowned. "It's not very comfortable. She may have dropped her head in her hands for a moment, but I doubt she'd have slept through the fire. Surely she'd have woken up with that." Impatiently she asked, "Can we go back to the tent and check my equipment, please?"

The two MPs at the entrance to the tent stepped out of her way. She passed Morgan on the way in for her own questioning session. But Morgan was military, on attachment to this training post. The two instructors grabbed for each other's hands and gave a quick squeeze as they both walked on in opposite directions.

Devlin watched as she stormed ahead to her work tent. The two guard MPs looked at him. "Do you have anything to say?"

He shook his head and walked out casually behind her. But she had brought up some interesting points. Had Colleen been murdered? Had the fire been set? And if either of those answers was yes, was Bristol's research and equipment the reason for it?

He glanced around the compound. Several people still studied the mess. But a lot of the crowd had dispersed. He reached the tent just behind her. As she was about to stumble, he reached out and grabbed her. "Take it easy. Let's do this methodically."

She turned, recognized him, and her shoulders sagged. "It's the thought that she may have been murdered. It's driving me crazy. I can't think of anything else."

He nodded. "Obviously that's a huge issue. But we can't assume that, and we don't want to start rumors." Devlin motioned to the men working. "Everything you do and say here will be recorded, so take it easy."

She took several deep, controlling breaths, and then, as if a little more centered, she stepped into what remained of the tent and walked to the table. The laptop was burned beyond recognition; the cases that held the drones were as well. She froze. Under her breath she said, "Oh, shit."

Devlin was close enough to hear her, as were several other men. In a low voice, he asked, "*Oh, shit*, what?"

She turned and stared at him. "Bertha is gone."

<h1 style="text-align:center">CHAPTER 3</h1>

"**B**ERTHA IS GONE," she cried out again in shock. "She was in a big case sitting right here." She pointed to an empty but charred spot on the floor. "I must have that case and its contents."

"Why?" Devlin asked.

The space filled as the other MPs joined them at the burn site. "It's the project I'm currently working on," she said, her tone much quieter. "And yes, it's definitely something somebody might kill for."

Eyebrows shot up on everyone's faces.

"No one mentioned that to us," one of the MPs stated.

She gave him a flat look and added, "Good, no one should have known." She turned her attention back to the other boxes and cases. Not much was left. "What a bloody disaster."

"Are all the other drones here?" the same MP asked.

She turned to look at him. "A couple are still in the field. I intended to bring them back and work on them after I got my coffee. I've had some issues with one of them. I wanted to know why. So they are still out there." She gave a very tired sigh, hating what this would do to her progress. Sure, she had more parts and pieces back at her lab, and she could certainly put together several more drones. But she'd need Bertha to finish her contract. She had lots of equipment to rebuild Bertha, but didn't have the time.

Because of the extended contract deadline looming, she had brought work with her to get caught up, hoping that, on the flight and while here, she could fine-tune these components. But they were all damaged. Destroyed. Burned to God-only-knew-what now. She glanced around, caught her breath, her throat closing as tears burned in her eyes. She spun and bolted outside. Holding the tears back she paced back and forth. Only to find herself standing outside the tent with their personal belongings. She and Colleen had been assigned two tents, along with Sandra, Brent's assistant. Morgan's was on the other side of the camp.

Devlin as always, stood at her side. Why? Not that she didn't appreciate it. "You don't have to stay with me, you know."

"I know that," he answered. "But you're still pretty stressed out and in shock. This is not easy for anybody. And we need to find Sandra."

At that her steps slowed. She pulled out her phone, brought up her Contacts and hit Dial. *Please let her answer.* When Sandra answered the call, Bristol cried out, "Oh, my God, Sandra, are you okay?"

"Yes, of course I am. What's wrong?" Sandra's voice was curious but not unduly alarmed.

With her sleeping tent in front of her, Bristol ran inside and sat down on the bed. She was almost shaking. "Did you hear about the fire?"

"Sure. I was sitting down to coffee and dinner. I decided to stay here, as it looked like everyone else went out to take a look," Sandra said in a wry tone. "Enough people are around there, so I didn't want to get lost in the crowd too."

"It was our tent."

Silence.

"What do you mean, our tent?"

"Our work tent. All the equipment is ruined. Even worse." She caught her breath before she went on. But the tears were clogging her throat. "Colleen is dead."

"What?" A shocked silence was followed by "Oh, my God! Oh, my God! Oh, my God! Are you serious? How? What happened?" A wail on the other end broke into a sob. Finally Sandra asked, "Where are you?"

"I'm in our quarters," Bristol said quietly. "I was questioned by the MPs. I went through the burned-out tent to see what I could salvage, but everything has been destroyed."

"You sure it's Colleen?" Sandra cried quietly.

"I'm sure. I'm the one who identified her."

"Stay there. I'm coming."

Bristol ended the call and just sat here. She wasn't sure what to do. With a heavy weight in her heart, she looked up, startled, realizing Devlin was still here. As he'd been since the fire. A comforting presence. So far he'd asked nothing of her but was here for support. And she needed that right now. "Thank you for staying," she said sincerely. "Sandra is on her way. I'll be fine then."

He nodded. "Is Bertha really that important?"

She nodded. "Bertha is my prototype for the next level of drones. I can't really give you all the details, just that I take what is out there and make it that much better. Espionage is always an issue when it comes to this level of technology. It never occurred to me that Bertha would be in any danger while we're here in the middle of a military compound." She shook her head. "I told them I didn't want to come. We're so far behind, I didn't have time to waste, even a few hours being here, not working, so I brought

Bertha with me."

"When you say, *them*, I presume you mean the company buying your drones. Did they know about Bertha?"

She nodded. "Yes, and Brent and his boss are both here." She looked out the open tent door and said, "I should contact them."

"Later," Devlin said. "They will have heard the news. I'd expect them to track you down themselves."

"Not likely," she said bitterly. "Brent will only worry about the drones. They won't spare the time to worry about us workers."

"But you're actually the design engineer, aren't you?"

"Yes, and it's my software. No matter what they want to do with it, it's mine. I'm under contract with the company though."

"Why were you having trouble with the drones?" Devlin asked.

"Because they aren't ready to be demonstrated," she said simply. "I'm trying to get to the bottom of a weird software glitch." She shook her head. "We shouldn't even be here."

"I'm sorry for the loss of your friend. But we don't know anything yet, so don't go jumping to conclusions."

"Yes, we do know a lot," she said bitterly. "Bertha is gone. No sign of her. And she's not some small worthless creation of mine. The woman standing guard over Bertha is dead. Those are two inescapable facts. Put them together, and that's bad news."

She closed her eyes, crossed her hands over her forehead and shut him out.

HE DIDN'T NEED to be here any longer, but neither did he

want to leave her alone. Not right now. Just then he heard some racing feet, and a woman—one of the women he'd seen earlier—burst into the tent, tears streaming down her face. "Bristol?"

Bristol immediately sat up and opened her arms. Sandra threw herself into them. Closer now to the two women, he could see Sandra was younger, maybe mid-to-late twenties. Whereas Bristol looked to be in her early thirties. Colleen had been a little older; he'd estimate her age to be around thirty-five.

He watched the two for a long moment, but they didn't even recognize his presence. He stepped outside and headed back to the crime scene. Because that was what it was. With the theft of a prototype, he had no doubt Colleen had either stumbled onto something or had been in the wrong place at the wrong time. She could possibly have been involved and cut out, but that wasn't as likely as the other two scenarios.

As he walked, he heard someone call his name. He spun around to see various members of the two SEAL units, standing in a group talking. He detoured to join them.

"What the hell's going on here?" Mason asked. He studied Devlin. "What's this about a dead woman?"

He quickly filled in the men and added at the end, "I just escorted Bristol back to her tent. She's pretty whacked out. Another woman just arrived, so it was safe to leave her alone." He motioned in the direction he was headed. "I wanted to take another look at the crime scene."

"*Crime scene?*" Swede asked.

Devlin realized he hadn't told them about Bertha. He quickly explained and asked, "The question really is, was Colleen part of the theft? Was she at the wrong place at the wrong time? Or was the whole thing just an ugly accident?"

"If Bertha is missing," Mason said, "I'd rule out an accident. That tent went up pretty fast."

"The MPs should be able to tell very quickly if she was dead before the place caught fire or not," Swede said. "Not that they would tell us."

"Honestly," Devlin said, "from what I saw, it's possible an accelerant was poured over her. I'm just hoping she was dead first." He stared off in the distance, remembering the heavy physical damage to the body. "In fact, her body was substantially burned for the short amount of time that fire was alive."

"It might've started with her." Swede crossed his arms. "We've all seen way too many scenarios where somebody used fire to get rid of evidence."

Devlin nodded. "Trouble is, we can't do anything over here. The MPs are all over this."

"And it has nothing to do with us either." Mason studied him carefully.

Devlin looked back and said, "I agree. I just happened to be there and found Bristol. She's pretty upset obviously." He glanced around at the others. "This doesn't affect my return stateside tomorrow, does it?"

"No, you're good to go," Mason said. "I'm still here for another couple days."

Devlin wasn't sure Bristol would be allowed to leave tomorrow, but he hoped so for her sake. Not to mention they had to transport home the body of her friend. "The company contracted for her drones has two representatives here. They are schmoozing with the brass."

"If Bertha was so important, why is it even here?" Mason asked.

"I asked her that actually," Devlin said, "and she said

something about the company bosses didn't want to give her any time off, and she was behind schedule, so she was forced to bring it all here to keep working through the day and evening."

"That's rough," Swede commented.

"It's also very convenient if set up ahead of time," Mason said. "A great way to get Bertha out of the lab."

"That may not be her only prototype," Devlin said.

The men stared at him.

He shrugged. "If it was me, you know I'd have backups."

Mason nodded thoughtfully. "That's a good point. You should ask her."

"I plan on it. I was giving her a little bit of time alone. The two women are grieving the loss of their friend. Makes it a little hard to intrude."

"But the question needs to be asked. And they need to be asked now." Mason turned in the direction of her tent. "I just met her briefly this morning, so I don't know her that well, but I'd still like to get answers to these questions because the MPs won't be sharing their information."

As Mason strode in the direction of Bristol's tent, Devlin jogged to join him. "I'll go with you."

Mason smiled. "You don't have to."

"It's no problem."

At his side, Mason chuckled.

Devlin shot him a look. "It's not like that."

"Of course it's not. By the way, it wasn't like that for any of us either."

"I doubt the Keepers' effect is so strong that spending a few weeks with you will turn us into one," Devlin joked. "But just in case, you can expect Ryder and Easton to run to the far side of the compound and stay the hell away from you."

"Like hell," Mason said good-naturedly. "You'll be damn lucky if you find what we have." He stopped at the tent and saw Bristol and Sandra. "As a matter fact, if you make this happen, Devlin, you'd be a better man than I'd ever have expected. From what I've heard, Bristol is good people."

Mason stepped inside, leaving Devlin standing behind, wondering what the hell Mason meant.

CHAPTER 4

B RISTOL ROSE, LEAVING Sandra seated on the bed, wiping away tears, to face Devlin and another man beside him. "You're Mason, aren't you?"

He tilted his head and studied her, then gave a short nod. "I am. You're Bristol, I believe. I've heard a lot about you."

A grin swept her face. "From Tesla. She's one of my best friends."

At that he relaxed. "Then you're truly blessed."

She laughed and nodded. "I see you are too. She's a wonderful woman."

"She is, indeed." A note of heavy satisfaction hung in his tone that made Bristol warm inside. She looked at Devlin. "What can I do for you two?"

Mason said, "The military police won't give us too much information, but we'd like to have a few questions answered, if you have a moment."

She frowned at him. "Are you part of the investigation?"

He shook his head. "You understand how we're on a compound full of some of the most elite fighting machines out here. And we deal with this kind of stuff on a daily basis. Maybe not exactly like this but—"

Devlin interrupted, "But like this."

She nodded. "I do remember Tesla telling me all about

who she married." She looked over to Devlin and asked, "Are you one of Mason's unit?"

"Same team, different unit. I'm here with three from mine, and Mason with four from his. We were all part of the drone training though."

She'd heard from Tesla that Mason was a SEAL. She hadn't known if the SEALs were actually here or not, but it made sense. Nobody ever mentioned that name. All very secret and hush-hush. Devlin had the same look about him—one of those men who could handle anything. He had been a big help this afternoon. She didn't break down often, but, seeing her friend burned to a crisp … Well, that was enough to shake anybody's composure.

She motioned at one of the other beds and said, "Have a seat."

Mason sat down with Devlin beside him, while Bristol reseated herself next to Sandra.

"What was it you wanted to know?" Bristol asked.

"I'm confused as to why Bertha would actually be here," Mason said. "And is it the only prototype you have?"

Her eyebrows rose at that. "She's one I was working on. I had made some tweaks, which is why losing her costs me time and effort. Can I recreate them on my other prototype back home? Yes. So you're concerned about the espionage aspect?"

"It could very well be the reason behind your friend's death."

"I think it is actually."

She glanced at Sandra, who stood and gave her a hug. "I'll return later."

Bristol looked back at the men. "Colleen and I both received *propositions*, shall we say. Offers of a good sum of money to look the other way on a project we were involved in over a year ago."

She held up her hand to stop the questions already forming on the men's mouths. "Neither of us took it seriously. However, it was a reminder that the work we do is always coveted by others. I don't say this from an egotistical perspective, but I'm at the top of my field. When a designer speaks, other people sit up and listen. That's one of the reasons why I refused to let the company have a blanket arrangement where they get all my inventions. I'm always working on new products."

"Okay, but that still doesn't answer the question."

She shook her head. "No, of course it doesn't. Because the answer is that, although Bertha was unique, she wasn't 100 percent so, but the modifications I made since I left the lab are, indeed, special for this model."

"How many people knew you were bringing Bertha?"

She shook her head. "I didn't even know I was bringing her until just before I left. So only those who saw Bertha here knew."

"Why did you?" Mason asked.

She stared at him, the corner of her lips turned down. "I have a contract that is really ugly. The problem with people who expect genius without understanding what goes into creating it is that they have a deadline, and it's a hard one for them. One thirty-day extension, but no others without severe penalties. It doesn't allow for problems, troubleshooting, thinking time, or figuring out answers. And when I run into some problem, it takes time to fix it." She shook her head. "This setback will be the financial end of my company."

As the three talked, an interruption came at the tent

opening. Two MPs stepped inside. They nodded to Mason and Devlin, then turned to Bristol. "Ma'am, if you would come with us, please."

She stood up slowly, frowning even more. "Of course. Can you tell me what this is about?"

"It's part of the investigation, ma'am."

She turned to look at Mason, an eye on Devlin also. "Why is it that I don't like the sound of this?"

Mason smiled reassuringly at her. "Go. We'll keep digging ourselves."

She tried to look reassured, but she glanced again at Devlin, wondering if he'd come with her this time. Then she straightened her shoulders and realized she needed to just face this, whatever *this* was. She hadn't done anything wrong, and there shouldn't be any reason to feel like she had.

She reached for her purse and walked confidently toward the two men. Devlin caught her arm as she went past. He bent down and whispered in her ear, "Do you have a lawyer?"

She gave him a horrified look. "Are you telling me that I need one?"

He glanced at the MPs. "Does she need legal representation at this time?"

The two MPs looked at each other, at her, then at Devlin. "Not at this time."

"Not sure I like the hesitation in that answer." He glanced at Mason. "I'm going with her."

Mason nodded. "You do that. I'll phone Tesla, see what kind of resources we can dredge up to help."

"I didn't do anything," Bristol protested. "It's my research material that's been stolen, and my friend who's been murdered."

One of the MPs said, "*The company* is suggesting other-wise."

She froze. "ENFAQ? Really?" She fell silent, figuring it out. She shook her head. "No way. I have no idea what the hell you're talking about, but I would never do anything to hurt Colleen or to jeopardize my work."

The second MP opened the tent flap. "Ma'am."

She nodded, glanced at Devlin and whispered, "Would you mind?"

He reached down and grasped her hand. "I won't let you go alone into this unknown." He shot the two MPs a cool look and followed her from the tent.

TOO BAD HE didn't know any lawyers. He had a modicum of legal knowledge, enough to get anybody in trouble. That was not where his focus had been. Law held a fascination for him, but he'd always be cheering for the underdog. And although he really liked Bristol and truly believed she was innocent in all this mess, he'd been fooled before by liars and cheats. Some people were so damned good it was impossible to tell, until they were caught in a lie. He just couldn't accept Bristol might be one of *those* people.

Something odd was going on here, and Mason and his connections would get to the bottom of it damn fast. The trouble was, Devlin had no right to do so. But that didn't mean he couldn't stand by her and see what information came out of this meeting. As he entered the room behind her, he heard the murmur of conversation. His presence was unexpected. Too damn bad. She was entitled to have support.

Bristol stood tall and straight in the center of the tent.

She was not offered a chair. Not a good indication.

"I believe you gentlemen have some further questions for me?"

Several MPs sat at the table on the far left side with Bristol in the middle of the room. Others stood to the right, watching the proceedings, almost like a trial. Devlin had no problem taking two steps to stand at her side. The man in the middle seat looked up at her, his gaze hard and cold.

"There's been some discrepancy between your statement and that of someone else."

"And whose is that?"

"We're not at liberty to say."

"And yet I'm being judged and not allowed to face my accuser?" She kept her voice cool. "Gentlemen, I have not lied in any way, shape, or form."

"And yet you led us to believe all was well at your company."

Her eyebrows shot up. "At my company it is. If you're asking about at ENFAQ Ltd., that's a different story. You never asked me about the atmosphere or the relationship between me and that company. So I'm not sure where you assume that answer is from my lips."

The middle MP lifted a sheet of paper. "It says here you were, indeed, asked that question, and you said you were perfectly happy at the company, and, as far as you knew, there were no problems in terms of working relationships there."

She held out her hand. "I'd like to see that please."

He handed her the statement.

She looked at it, then snorted. "Are you telling me that you can't see this is a different handwriting from up above? My signature on the bottom, when I wrote that, did not have that paragraph included. And besides, I would've been happy to tell you what the working atmosphere was like between me and the company. And it's … tense." She stepped back and crossed her arms.

The MP looked over the sheet of paper and said, "That's a serious charge, to say somebody altered your statement."

"I don't care how serious a charge you think it is. That statement was added after my signature." She glared at him. "Therefore, anything you say or do at this point will be suspicious, and as such, you have a problem on your side of the bench."

The men seated at the table put their heads together.

"I'd like to face my accuser myself." She turned her gaze, zooming deliberately to a man standing on the right side. "Brent, could you please answer that?"

The man Devlin had met earlier straightened and glared at her. "Answer what? You're the one being interrogated."

Her eyebrows matched her lips in a sneer. "And how is it that I'm being interrogated? *My* friend was murdered. *My* research was stolen. Did they look at you for that?"

He cast a look around in shock. "How could you possibly blame me?"

"And yet you apparently have no trouble blaming me."

"I didn't. I just said they should look at you a little closer."

"Which is blaming me." She turned back to the three men watching the conversation avidly. "What you need to understand is that the research was mine. I'm under contract to the company, but I own that particular project until it's completed and handed over. He essentially owns it upon completion. It is not completed."

"But it should've been," Brent said in frustration.

"You're behind schedule."

She snapped, "Yes, but I still have ten days left on the extension. *Ten days.* That's it. And why is it that I'm behind? Because you didn't supply the help you promised and indeed, are contracted to, nor the materials you were also contracted to." She stood in the middle of the room and tapped her foot on the floor. "To tell them to examine *my* motives for losing *my* own research is just too unbelievable."

"Well, as it's insured, and if you've lost it, there would be a huge payout, it makes sense."

"If my software doesn't work, my name and reputation go down the drain." Her glare deepened. "And, of course, if I don't make my deadlines—"

"Which you're not."

"With a thirty-day override still counting down, of which I have ten days left," she added in a hard tone. "Then I owe you a percentage of the contract for every day I'm late. But it's not to that point yet, as I still have ten days to complete it." She snorted and waved her hand. "However, my research is missing, my assistant has been murdered, and I am in real trouble of meeting my deadline. That means I'll pay a hefty penalty, even though I did all the work." She took a deep breath. "So in what way in hell would murdering Colleen, my friend and assistant, and losing my research help me?" She lowered her voice to a lethal softness and added, "If anyone here benefits from this nightmare, it's you."

Nothing but silence ensued.

Devlin watched the two of them with a great deal of interest. He dragged his gaze away and studied all the other men in the room. She'd made a very valid point. What she'd lost would cost her both financially, not to mention the loss of her reputation, and she'd incurred an emotional loss too, with the death of her friend.

As he gazed around the room, he caught a sudden understanding on one's expression, an agreement in the face of another, and disapproval in one, likely somebody who didn't think a woman should hold that type of research hostage. But then again, if she'd been a man, he probably wouldn't have any trouble with that scenario.

The session didn't last long after that. The MPs had a couple more questions, which she answered easily. The man Devlin kept his eye on said absolutely nothing. Devlin didn't know Brent, but would damn sure find out who he was.

By the time the MPs said she could leave, Devlin had the man's face memorized. He pulled out his cell, casually turned to face her and snapped a picture of the three men standing on the right. He wrapped an arm around her shoulder and escorted her from the room.

He didn't want any of the others to see her legs were shaking. She'd withstood the questioning quite well. And had answered with just enough bravado to hide her anger. And the hurt. Her fiery fury was draining; all she could do was to keep going. He led her straight back to her quarters.

Sandra wasn't back yet. At her bed, Bristol collapsed and buried her hands in her face. "Oh, my God! What will I do?"

He realized the question was rhetorical, and he had absolutely no answer. She was about to lose everything.

CHAPTER 5

THE TREMORS RACKED through her system. It was all she could do to not bawl. In a way she was glad Devlin was here. His presence enabled her to have a modicum of control. She couldn't remember another time in her life when she'd been at the edge quite like this. And she wanted to crawl away and hide. But there was no hiding from this.

And still there was Colleen. Beautiful, friendly, outgoing Colleen. Not only was Colleen a friend, she was also her assistant. And she'd been instrumental in getting Bristol's timeline together. What would she do now?

She had Sandra on loan for the training session, as she'd worked with her several times before, but that wasn't the same thing as having Colleen. Not that Sandra wasn't good, but she didn't have the same drive or meticulous attention to detail that Colleen had. And, of course, Sandra worked for Brent. Sandra was young. She hadn't yet matured into understanding how important every aspect of the job was. She was still about having a good time, not necessarily a long one.

Bristol shook her head; she was lost. "I need to get home as soon as possible."

"When is your flight booked?"

"Tomorrow at noon," she said. She shifted so she could lie down on the bed and allow her trembling limbs to relax.

She knew it would be a good thirty to sixty minutes before the tension vibrating up and down her back would ease. "But I can't wait. Not after today. I've lost too much—my prototype, special parts, more time, ... Colleen." She turned her distraught gaze to him. "Yet, if I leave early, they'll say I look guilty, won't they?"

He frowned. "I wouldn't worry about what they say. You have a job, contract, and a deadline. And a huge mess on your hands. You have to handle all that, and you need to pull it together." He reached out and grasped her hand in his. "You want me to see if I can get your flight changed?"

"I don't think they'll let you," she said. "It was a military flight arranged by the company."

"Did you ever consider that, because you didn't want to come, maybe the company actually had something to do with the theft?"

Her eyes flew open wide, and she studied Devlin in confusion. "But how would that help them? If I don't supply the drones actively working, then I'm in breach of my contract, and they don't get their product."

"I wondered about that too." He settled back, pulled up one leg and ran his hands around it as he thought. "Any chance he had somebody else on the hook for these drones? Maybe someone ENFAQ has invested in? If they can get rid of you—and even better, completely trash your reputation at the same time—then the new company could jump in, grab the contract, and this person—yes, maybe that's Brent—gets a big chunk of money."

She sat up slowly and stared at him in horror. "I don't like the way your mind works," she whispered. "That would be just too..."

"Realistic?" He shot her a sideways glance. "In my line of

work I see some of the worst things people can do to each other almost every day of the year. Nothing surprises me. But power, love, money, and sex are the rulers of almost everyone's actions." Devlin waved at the open tent flap. "No love is lost between you and Brent. As you hold all the power, he's helpless and will hate that. If he can make money another way, and at the same time destroy you, well, you have almost a perfect set of motives right there."

She flopped back down on the bed and groaned, closing her eyes. "You can add sex to that too." She felt him give her a startled glance but didn't open her eyes. "No, we weren't lovers, but he damn well tried hard. I kept refusing him."

"Why?"

She snorted and looked at Devlin. "Because I wasn't attracted to him. Because he was pushy as hell. And he's one of those guys who thinks sex is the way to control a woman. And when I go to bed with a man, I do it because that's who I want to be with at that moment. Not for any other reason."

He grinned at her. "Good. Glad to hear it," he said cheerfully. "We agree on that point."

She frowned at him. "Why do I think that is like a tick box in your head?"

"Because it is. Now we can move on to the next." He patted her knee and stood. "And that wasn't meant as a patronizing pat, by the way. I was checking to see if the tremors in your legs had calmed down."

"It was pretty bad, wasn't it?" she confessed. "I'm not used to justifying my actions or defending myself like that."

"Yes, it was pretty bad, but even though you were nervous, you handled yourself really well while being questioned. You stuck to your guns and logically defended yourself."

She nodded. "But still, there's that sense of *what if they come back?* What if somebody else ..." She hopped to her feet. "I have to pack. I need to get going. I must get the hell out of here." She looked around, then threw up her hands. "There's nothing salvageable from the work tent. I barely have anything left to pack."

Devlin grabbed her shoulders and gently made her sit back down again. "Stop. Did all the drone elements go into the work tent, or did you have anything stored somewhere else?"

She stared up at him, her gaze huge. "It was all in there, except my personal bag and the training materials. Everything else is back in my home lab."

"Where?"

"California."

"Then you need to get back there before that goes too. You should go home, sort this out."

"*Before that goes too,*" she whispered, now fully aware of what Devlin was telling her. She had to remain calm. She took a deep breath and straightened again. "You're right. I'll see if I can get an earlier flight home."

He shook his head, pulling out his phone. "Let me talk to Mason. If anybody can pull some strings to get you home faster, it'd be him."

She waited—patiently she hoped—as he quickly brought up Mason's line. She was still afraid of looking guilty, like she was running away. And, if the MPs got wind of it, they wouldn't let her go. She felt like she was trapped here—on a military base in the middle of nowhere. Not exactly someplace where she could turn around and catch a commercial flight home. She could travel to the closest city, which she thought was Mosul, like that was a safe place to go. Hell, anywhere off base would be a nightmare. She'd come over on a military flight, and she'd expected to go home on one.

She heard Devlin talking to Mason. She zinged her gaze to him and listened in. He was being incredibly helpful. She needed that. Hell, she needed him too. A feeling she had trouble reconciling with the rest of her life. She had never leaned on anyone. Was it so wrong right now?

"Mason, she needs to be home and sort this out. All the materials she had in the tent are totally unsalvageable. I don't know if you heard what happened at the meeting today." Devlin nodded. "Yeah, word travels fast, doesn't it? Then you understand she has to get back home and get to work, otherwise she loses everything. And that's probably what the motive behind this is. Somebody sabotaged her entire life in one swoop. But she needs to do what she can to pull forward." Devlin listened to something else Mason said, then nodded. "Yes. Is there any chance she can pull out of here tonight? Like within the next couple hours would be great. She needs to get stateside and regroup."

He ended the call and turned to face her. "Mason is minutes away. Give him a chance to see what he can do, and he'll get back to us."

She nodded, her smile bright. "Thank God."

DEVLIN WATCHED AS she lifted a shaky hand to brush the hair off her forehead. It was short and blonde. Efficient. Businesslike, just as she was. But he could see she was still trembling. She'd been put through an ordeal. He didn't think she should go home alone, much less remain that way. "Do you have family you can stay with? I'm not sure you should be alone."

"I'll be in my lab full-time for the next ten days," she

said. "Even then, I have no hope in hell of meeting the requirements of my contract."

"What if you had help?"

"Only somebody who knew how to handle hardware could help me. I don't have time to train anybody. And I'll be completely whacked out just doing the software changes, dependent upon whether I can get all the supplies. But I did order an extra load, just in case. We had problems with some of the plastics cracking before."

"If I could line up a couple people, would you see if they'd work for you?"

She raised her gaze and stared at him wide-eyed. "You know any IT people?"

"We all know some." He smiled. "It's a matter of finding the right ones."

"The other thing would be the security issue."

"What if they were former SEALs?"

She frowned at him. "Who do you have in mind?"

He grinned. "Harrison and Rhodes are both damn good with hardware. Harrison's a whiz, and Rhodes isn't far behind. They're also damn good with software."

She shook her head. "Those names mean nothing to me."

"No, but they might in the future. They were SEALs and currently work for another SEAL friend of ours at Legendary Security. They deal with a lot of hardware."

"I'm not in any position to say no," she said slowly. "Certainly if they're in a security company, they'd be bondable. It depends what skills they have, if they're available, and if I can afford them," she confessed.

He nodded. "I know most of the guys who work there," Devlin said. "We might make something happen here." He stopped and looked at her. "How many men would you actually need?"

"As many capable hands as I could possibly get."

He pursed his lips and thought about that. "Well then, I'll see what we can do."

He strode over to the tent to take a look outside. He didn't want anybody else listening in on this conversation. He didn't trust her boss, at the very least. The last thing he wanted anybody in the company to understand was that there was any hope in hell of her pulling off her contract. And, on that note, he realized her tent could've been bugged. "Shit."

"Shit? What do you mean by that?" she asked in alarm.

He shook his head. "I just realized I assumed this was a safe place to talk, and that's not a good thing to do."

He pulled out his phone and sent a text to Ryder.

Do you have a bug detector to check Bristol's quarters?

Ryder replied,

I'll grab one and be there in a few minutes.

Devlin put away his phone and said, "My buddy's coming. We'll check it out to make sure."

She just sat here with her mouth open, then said, "Oh, my God."

He nodded and held his finger up to his lips. "We may have already blown this. But let's check it out. We'll be as safe as we can from here on out."

Ryder walked in only minutes later. He took one look at Bristol sitting cross-legged on the bed and smiled. "Ma'am." He tipped his fingers to his head on the imaginary hat he always wore when he was off duty.

She smiled up at him. But it was tremulous and shaky.

Ryder handed the tester to Devlin. "Do you want to do the honors, or shall I?"

"Just push the Down button."

Ryder turned it on. But the button was green, and it didn't flash. Ryder slowly searched the room. "It's clear."

Devlin nodded. "Good. I wish we could get into the work tent to see if one had been there. But it's likely to have been burned to a crisp too. If it had been functioning, it certainly isn't now."

"And the problem with that is, we don't know if someone gleaned any information before the fire took place." Ryder turned to look at Bristol. "Ma'am, any idea if you were discussing anything important prior to the fire?"

She stared at him with a glazed look. "Honestly? I don't remember very much from before the fire at all. It's like there's now my life before and after." She shook her head. "We were talking about the drones. We've had an odd problem with them, but I didn't have time to dig into it to. I was forced to come here."

Bristol waved her hand around the base. "Earlier Colleen said something about it being possessed. That was her word."

She slowly got to her feet. "That's it. One or two of the drones might still be in the training areas. I have to go see. Sandra was supposed to clean up and take everything back to the tent, but maybe she didn't get that far." Bristol rushed out of the tent.

Devlin pointed to the tester in Ryder's hands. "Keep that handy." And Devlin bolted after her.

CHAPTER 6

S HE RACED OUTSIDE, back to the drone training area. With any luck a lot of parts and pieces were still out here that she could use. What she really needed were the drones. The laptops were incidental, but if she didn't have to replace them, that would be great. Devlin ran behind her. She said, "Check over on the far side, where you were training earlier."

Sandra appeared to have cleaned up the training area. If that was the case, where were those laptops? And the drones? Had she taken them back to the tent, and they burned too? Sandra was notoriously bad about putting equipment away. She would just dump everything on her bed and leave it until later. Only there'd been no sign of them in their quarters. Bristol pulled out her phone and called her. "Sandra, did you put away all the equipment used this afternoon?"

"It's all in the truck. I figured we probably wouldn't be packing them up until tomorrow morning."

"Truck?" she asked. She spun around. "What truck?"

"Brent parked one close by so we wouldn't have to haul the stuff back and forth."

Devlin raced to her, shaking his head. "No sign of any-thing."

She hung up on Sandra and shared the information

about the truck.

"Was that to help or hinder?" Devlin frowned at her shrug. "Sounds like this guy has been working against you for a long time."

She glanced around. "I need the drones and anything else available. It's all my property."

He nodded. "Then let's go find it." He pulled out his phone and called Mason. His message was short and sweet. "I need everyone we can trust."

She watched him, wondering if he knew just what was at stake. He'd been here for her since this started. And always seemed to have a way forward. So, yes, maybe he did.

Within ten minutes they had a dozen men standing around them. And when they realized what was going on, completely disappeared—all in different directions. They worked from some sort of foundational organization, but she didn't understand it. She felt certain though that everybody was out looking for the truck holding the balance of her equipment.

If anything was left to find.

She had to get home to her lab. If this was sabotage here, then there was a bigger chance somebody was heading to destroy her base lab too. And that was deadly to her and those she employed. If her lab had been hit, in no way could she fulfill her end of the contract, and she would lose everything. She'd been beside herself over signing this contract in the first place. But it was just too damn big a deal not to try. However, from the back end, facing opponents like this, what was she supposed to do about it? She didn't have the manpower or the know-how to stop the sabotage from happening again. She might still complete the contract at this point, ... maybe, ... but this was all bad news.

She turned to Devlin. "What are we to do while they search?"

"First we'll talk to Mason." He nodded behind her.

She spun around to see Mason walking toward them.

Mason had a smile on his face. "Flights have been changed. You leave in two hours."

She threw her arms around him and gave him a big hug. "Oh, thank God. If we could only find the damn equipment, it can go home with me."

"We'll find it. Don't worry. Did you make sure nothing was usable in the work tent?"

She shook her head. "Honestly I haven't. Is that an option?"

"It should be. Let's go see."

Flanked between the two big men, Bristol walked back to the burned tent. She hated to see the charred remnant of her friend's body again, even in her mind, as she knew Colleen's body had been removed. Inside, tension curled tightly around her back and shoulders again as she stepped into the work tent. She needed to be realistic about the whole scenario. If something could be salvaged, she needed to find it. She'd lost so much already.

She swept away the tears threatening to take over and strode forward. Even a screwdriver was one less thing to replace.

Looking around, she realized there wasn't even that much. This was probably her only opportunity to actually take a closer look, so she moved forward, resolutely walking past where she'd seen Colleen lying on the floor. Her computer chip components had been on the side. She'd had plastic parts and pieces as she tried to build more of the small motherboard for the drone control panels. The plastic melted around the blackened skeletal metal pieces were still connected to the cables. It was all garbage. She continued to search, but nothing was really here.

Finally, when she couldn't find anything, she had to accept the truth. She turned back to the others. "There's nothing I can salvage from here."

Devlin looked down at his watch. "It's been half an hour. Let's get you packed and ready for the flight. You need anything to eat before you leave?"

She shook her head. "My stomach feels queasy."

"Which is usually when you should make sure you eat," Mason said quietly. "At times of major stress and loss, your body still needs fuel."

"I think I have a few granola bars in my bag. That will sustain me until I get home." With one final glance around, she turned and left the tent. "When can I have Colleen's body released?"

"Not for a while. The next of kin has to be called, and it will be their choice."

She nodded. "I'll talk to her mom when I get home."

"Good idea." Devlin led the way back to her quarters. "What about Sandra?"

"She was here earlier. She's found a group she's been hanging out with. She's very social. I'm sure it wouldn't be hard to track her down. She flew with Brent and the rest of the company personnel." She spun back to Mason and said, "Still no news on the truck?"

He held up his phone. "They'll contact me when there is."

Inside her quarters, she sagged down on her bed once again, unable to think clearly. She glanced around the small space, then reached under the bed, pulling out her single bag. This was to be a short trip, so she hadn't brought much. She grabbed her sweater she had left at the foot of the bed—needed at nighttime or on planes—put it on, threw her backpack over her shoulder, and then brought out her laptop bag from underneath the bed. She rose and turned to face the men. "I'm ready."

Devlin's eyebrows went up. "That's it? You travel light?"

"It all went up in flames." She hefted her laptop bag and said, "This is the other half of my life."

"Let me check that it's all secure."

She frowned. "It rarely leaves my side, though it has been here through this whole mess." She sat down again, unzipped her bag, pulled out her laptop, and quickly opened and booted it up. Once it turned on, she took a few minutes to check if anybody had accessed it. But her login had come up as normal. When she ran a history of the last twenty-four hours, it didn't show any signs of anyone having hacked into it. With a sense of ease, she closed it down, put it back into her bag and said, "It looks to be fine."

"Good."

Just then Mason's phone went off. He took a few steps away and answered it. When he spun around, he was still talking. "That's great news. We'll be there in a few minutes."

A grin flashed on his face. "They found the truck. It's parked only a few tents over, beside your company's tent."

"You mean, Brent's company, not mine. Which way?" she asked, already turning to the left.

Mason called to her, "This way. Follow me."

He took her around several tents until he came to a truck, guarded by four men. As she approached, Brent came dashing out, yelling, "You can't touch any of that."

She shot him a look. "All this is mine."

"I still own you for another ten days as per the contract. This is mine. Our lawyers will be talking to you," he roared.

"Send them. I'll be waiting." She turned to the men guarding the truck. "I need all of it loaded on the plane that is leaving with me in the next hour."

As Brent fumed, totally without any rights in the issue, the men quickly packed up the drones, laptops, and remote controls.

She looked at the few boxes and shook her head. "This is pittance compared to what I brought. It's completely worthless in value as to all I lost today." As she walked away, she turned back to see Brent. "If I find out you had anything to do with the sabotage …"

"Then you'll do what?" he snapped. "You're just a fraud. You don't know what the hell you're even doing," he said. "I saw that drone drop from the sky. Without Colleen, you won't be able to control it. You don't have anything to hand over. Nothing but shit."

She smiled at him. "But it's my shit, not yours." And she turned and walked off.

DEVLIN TOOK NOTE of the confrontation. He wasn't exactly sure what was going on because he didn't expect this type of behavior from somebody with a contract for really high-tech drones designed by Bristol that Brent could easily sell to the Department of Defense for a bundle. Something was going on here, and Devlin didn't like it one bit. Brent had to have something at stake for things to be going down this way.

As far as Devlin understood, Brent was not at the top of the company. ENFAQ Ltd. was huge, so this made little sense to Devlin. He caught up with Bristol as she stormed down the road. "Brent doesn't own the company, correct?"

She shook her head. "No, but he's the one responsible for swaying the others to give me the contract. I was an employee first, before I set up my own company. When the opportunity came, I put in a bid. They already knew my work."

"Oh, his ass is on the line." At her nod he added, "It does make his behavior a little more understandable."

"Understandable, yes. Justifiable, no." She stormed ahead and was about to go in the wrong direction again.

"Ease up. We could have just stayed with the truck and been driven over to the airport, you know."

She came to an abrupt halt and closed her eyes, swaying in place. "I'm sorry. I'm just so angry."

"We can't do anything about that right now. Let's just get you home safe and sound." At the sound of a Jeep, he turned to see Mason behind the steering wheel. "Here's our ride. Mason's got all the boxes. Let's get you and your laptop out of here."

Within twenty minutes, they drove up to the plane. The gear was locked and loaded in the back. She made it through all the paperwork to get on. Almost before she had a chance to realize it, Devlin made sure she was seated and locked in.

He walked back outside and spoke with Mason. "I hate to see her traveling alone."

Mason nodded, and pointed to a duffel bag in the back of the Jeep. "That's why we packed your gear. You have four days' leave coming. This just became it."

Devlin smiled. "I was wondering about asking for that."

"You don't need to ask. If you find any evidence, or something else goes screwy, call me. We'll make it as official as we can. Then you won't lose your days."

"Thank you. I would rather not lose them," Devlin said. "But what's going on here is a travesty. She's about to get a major shaft."

"I agree," Mason said. "I'll get a handle on this end while I'm here as long as you stay in touch. I put a call into both Levi and Tesla to see if anybody can help Bristol." He held out his hand and shook Devlin's, staring at him intently.

As he was about to board, a second Jeep flew toward them. He stopped and took a look. Ryder, Easton, and Corey hopped from the vehicle. "Hey, guys, I'm taking four days' leave. This kind of changes things a little."

The men nodded. Each grabbed a big bag, shouldering them, and Ryder said, "The commander just changed the entire shift. With the murder and all, everybody's backtracking. We were due to leave tomorrow anyway, so they cut it short. We're on the way home too."

They stared at Devlin, the same way Mason had.

Inside Devlin hope bloomed, and he felt that complete sense of brotherhood he never had anywhere else. He gave them each a curt nod and said, "Good timing."

"Always. We got your back." Ryder glared at Devlin as he stepped past, going into the small plane. "How the hell did you think you could leave without us?"

Easton didn't bother saying anything. He just shot Devlin a look and walked past.

Corey grinned. "I didn't know what the hell was going on. I turn around, and your butt is hanging in the wind."

Devlin stared at Mason. "Is this your doing?"

"I might've made a suggestion that they could go home on your flight. What they do when they leave the base is up to them. Besides, everyone here wants to know what the hell is going on. Sabotage at a military base is serious business.

We can't afford to let her work fall into the enemy's hands."

"And yet it's still not official?"

Mason waved a hand. "Some things take time. Give me something to take to them, then we can make it official, otherwise this has to be unpaid leave."

Devlin boarded and closed the door behind him. Mason was right. Devlin was already sticking his neck out.

And he had to, for Bristol's sake. He walked in and took a seat beside her.

She looked at him with pleasant surprise. "You going home?"

He nodded. "My whole unit is."

She smiled, seeming at a loss for words.

"I'm supposed to be on four days' leave. I'm going stateside to give you a hand. These guys are my unit so they're being sent back and will be in Coronado."

"Nah, I've got four days too," Ryder said. "And I don't have anything better to do with my time."

Easton said, "Me three."

"Hey, Bristol, any chance of getting a beer at your place?" Corey asked with a big grin. "We also eat a lot."

In shock, her gaze went from one man to the next to the next. "Why?"

"We'll figure it out. Chances are good Colleen wasn't the target, but you and your work were. Colleen's death was likely an accident, and they meant to sabotage the project," Devlin said. "And we're here to ensure the killer doesn't get a second chance."

"I NEVER CONSIDERED that ..." She shook her head. "Oh, my God! How does anybody get into something like this? It's not how I envisioned my life. When I said I didn't want to come on this trip, I meant it. And I'll work through my nights because I know how damn short on time I am. But I could've made it, had things gone smoothly, with Colleen to help."

Ryder nodded. "You'll need to figure it out on the flight home."

"I presume the company won't provide any kind of security for you?" Easton said.

"I never asked for any," she said quietly. "Not that the company will do anything for me now. Security was never an issue before. But then this is my first big contract, so I'm new to this. And apparently bit off more than I could chew."

"Not at all. Someone is making sure you choke," Devlin said.

"Not to worry," Corey said with his hard-to-keep-down grin. "We won't let anybody get a second chance." Corey looked over at Devlin and smirked. "I see you've been hanging around Mason just a little too much."

Devlin shot him a hard frown.

She didn't quite understand what the reference was. But she wouldn't allow any slight to Mason. "Mason's a really nice guy. Tesla is a friend of mine. I don't want to hear you saying anything against him," she scolded Corey.

He chuckled. "I'd never do that. Mason's a great guy. And Tesla"—he shook his head—"she's dynamite."

"She is that."

Devlin looked at Easton. "Buddy, how's your hardware skills?"

"Guns and bombs?" Easton asked quietly. "Can't say too shabby with either."

"I didn't quite mean it that way. You're an expert with both of those. I meant computer hardware."

"Pretty damn decent. Why?"

"Devlin, do you really think so?" she asked doubtfully. "My work isn't really firepower stuff."

"Of course it is. You got that technology down so far, it's incredibly accurate."

"Those drones are actually all working well. The firing boxes didn't get shipped yet, so with any luck, they will be fine. But as for the rest of the drones, we'll put them together."

Corey gave her a winning smile. "Right. I'm not as good on computers as Easton and Ryder are, but I'm really handy with mechanics."

"Anybody who can handle a screwdriver and follow a few simple directions would be a big help," Bristol said quietly.

Devlin quickly explained to his guys what the problem was.

Easton shook his head. "Now that is some shit." He stared out the window as he contemplated the implications. "This is definitely sabotage. And that's a screwy deal. I presume we're talking big money here?"

She nodded. "The biggest. I'll be bankrupt if I can't make the deadline." Her lips quirked. "Like I said, I bit off more than I can chew."

"Could you have made it without any of these problems?" Ryder asked. "I'm always happy to help the underdog but prefer it to be a reasonable fight from the beginning. Or were you seriously in dreamland?"

"I honestly thought I could do it." She leaned back and closed her eyes. "But there have been a series of setbacks. And then this."

In a sharp tone, Devlin's voice snapped, "Setbacks?"

She turned her head toward him and opened her eyes. "Yes, software bugs, viruses, possibly hacking." She shrugged. "I haven't been able to do a whole lot with it as something else would pop up. I'd solve one problem, and then another would appear. I was so damn close to having this put together, ready and done." She shook her head. "I would've made the original deadline, if not for all those problems."

"All were normal research-and-development issues?" Corey asked. "Because everybody figures in a certain amount of time into every project for stuff like that."

She shook her head. "No, at least I wouldn't say so. All just little stuff. Like I couldn't get the shipment of plastics because the warehouse was broken into, and they had to redo most of the molds as everything had been stolen. That shouldn't have anything to do with me. It was their problem. But at the same time, it delayed me by weeks. The final software is the issue. My servers crashed. I lost time immediately when that happened. I have an extremely expensive server bank for all this, but I'm pretty damn sure somebody was hacking it. I lost forty-eight hours rebuilding a security system they couldn't get into. And since then I've been free and clear from any hacking attempts or viruses."

"Sounds like a long-term sabotage to me," Ryder said, his voice hard, implacable. "And something you should have looked at a while ago."

"I brought it up with Brent. I asked for assistance, and he said it was my problem." She stared at Ryder, frowning. "I had two fantastic programmers, and they both took jobs elsewhere—on the same day." She knew exactly how that sounded, what it meant. "I finally understand that people don't want me to finish this contract. This business is brutal." She leaned her head back and closed her eyes. "As Tesla well knows."

She could feel when all the men just kind of relaxed at the name Tesla, because sure enough, that woman had been to hell and back with her own programs. "We're targets no matter what we do," Bristol said. "I just put a bull's-eye on my forehead when I got the contract."

"Was there a lot of competition for the job?" Devlin asked. "I don't mean this in a negative way, but why did you get it?"

"I was up against some big guys," she said. "But my prototype has exactly what they wanted. They were frothing at the mouth to get it. They didn't want to wait." She smiled. "And that was for renditions earlier than Bertha."

"Bertha?" Corey exclaimed. "I know what it is, but why call it that?"

She heard the snickers from the other men. "You guys don't like her name?"

"What kind of clunky name is that? Makes me think of Big Bertha," Corey said.

She smiled a secret smile. "Exactly." She'd meant it to look that way, because then nobody would know what she really looked like.

Instantly the men sat forward. Nothing guys liked better than stealth toys. At least, she didn't think so. And Bertha's flying model was anything but clunky. But Bristol didn't want to say any more because, although they were on this plane, and it felt secure, other men were here—though seated farther down at the back of the plane, not crowded around in the group they were in, but it wasn't exactly safe.

She motioned at the other men, and Easton nodded. So far nothing had been said that would get her in trouble, but she didn't want to start now.

Neither did she want to say anything to get these men in trouble. They'd been wonderful to her. Especially Devlin. She closed her eyes again and asked, "You guys mind if I just nod off for a few minutes?"

She relaxed back and let herself drift into that half-asleep, half-awake state where she did most of her designing work. A troubleshooting, problem-solving state where she could just let go of her current world and drift into one where none of this mess existed. If ever she needed to be there, this was the moment.

In her head she went through the logistics of building the number of drones she'd promised and fixing the software so it ran as it needed. It was possible, if she had the parts. But she needed capable hands, and people to build the drones, install the software and chips, and test the drones. And then there were her software issues.

She still had a few tweaks left to make, not many granted, but she knew how difficult those few could end up being. Just because she assumed it would go fast didn't mean it would. Problems always arose. And she was pretty damn sure she understood what had gone wrong with the training drones. She just had to figure out how and why, and if any signs of that same problem were in the others. And if there were, she had to figure out how to get rid of it.

She'd spent her whole life building and creating. She found it very hard to deal with the other aspects—kicking out people who had their nose in your business when they shouldn't. Espionage in her field was unbelievably bad. And she'd spent a lot of time building security systems to lock down her projects. She had no way to know who it might be at this point. She thought somebody might have remotely taken over control of the drone, just to make her look bad.

The problem was they'd succeeded in a big way.

DEVLIN WATCHED HER rest. He could see her eyes moving under her lids, so he knew she wasn't in a real sleep, just half-and-half, preserving energy. On a computer, you called it Sleep Mode. But on humans,…well, not so much. What she really needed was several good hours of recovery time in a deep sleep to get past the emotional trauma of what just happened. She'd been under a lot of stress for a long time. Obviously small problems had built to bigger ones until this biggest of all messes. That alone had to be killing her, but she had an air of almost calmness to her that he didn't recognize.

Yet he knew she was taking the death of her friend pretty hard. He couldn't help but wonder if maybe Colleen had been a target or if she had actually been the one sabotaging Bristol's work—either alone or in cahoots with someone else. If that was the case, and she was meeting up with that person at the base during the training session, maybe her partners decided to take her out. A splitting of ways, so to speak.

Still he liked his original theory: Colleen having been in the wrong place at the wrong time. Or they could have assumed she was Bristol and taken her out. It would've been a shock when they realized Bristol was still alive, in which case, her life remained in danger. And if somebody made one attempt, chances were very good they were about to make a second.

And he wouldn't allow that. In his world, he fought— long and hard. Right to the end. And he knew every one of his men would agree. That was how they were made. SEALs don't stop; they do what they do best: they go to battle. So, whoever Bristol was up against, they'd better watch out because they'd taken on the wrong woman. They had assumed she had nobody around to help her. They were wrong; she had friends in very good places. And not one of them would let her be taken down without an all-out war.

CHAPTER 8

"BRISTOL?"

That voice drifted into her subconscious. One she'd been dreaming about only minutes before. She opened her eyes and blinked owlishly up at Devlin, realizing something had shifted. She straightened in her seat and looked around. "Are we here?"

"Yes, we'll be landing in a few minutes."

She wiped the sleep from her eyes and made a trip to the bathroom. When she returned, she sat down and buckled up again. "I'm really glad I managed to sleep. I hadn't realized how tired I was," she confessed.

"Nothing's better than sleep to heal a lot of what's wrong with us."

They were another two hours landing, clearing, loading her gear and everyone's personal baggage into vehicles, driving to hers, and then to her place. She lived half an hour out of Los Angeles. Although what she called the outskirts was the boondocks to him. Devlin chose to ride in her car, with the rest of his unit in the others, escorting her drone hardware.

"Is your lab at your home?" he asked.

She nodded, tossing him a grin. "Yes. It's one of the reasons why I live where I do. I have space." She glanced behind them to see the rest of the men following. "They don't really have to come, you know." She tilted her head at Devlin. "I feel bad about taking their leave."

He laughed a hard bark that made her wince. "It's better they have something to do on their days off anyway. Ryder's coming out of a bad relationship. Corey would likely just party or get into trouble, and Easton … Well, he's one of those guys who would much rather fill his time wisely than spend it alone."

It took her a few minutes to digest all that. She realized they might as well come and help. She could sure use the hands. "Then thank you, all of you, for coming and helping."

"I need your address so I can send it to Levi."

"Levi?"

"Yes, he's sending Harrison and Rhodes your way. Both of them are aces with computers. Harrison's elite when it comes to software and hardware."

She frowned. More people. She needed them, but were they all safe to let into her lab?

He shot her a glance which she caught from the corner of her eye. She took a turn off the highway, checking to be sure the guys were still behind them. Her small car versus their two vehicles—one large Jeep and a truck. She just didn't get it. What was it about men and Jeeps?

But that was a thought for another day.

"It's tough to trust strangers," Devlin said, "but you have to trust someone, so it might as well be me. Levi is a good man, and he has good men. Levi's nothing if not ambitious. Between him and Ice, they already have a corner on some of the most black-ops private-security missions going."

"Ice," she repeated. "That's right. I've heard that name before. Isn't she some kind of top-notch helicopter pilot or something?"

"The best." Devlin nodded. "I've never had a chance to ride with her myself. Kind of wish I had. She is supposed to be something."

"She walked away from the military too?"

"Let's just say she stuck with Levi."

"Ha." And that was something Bristol understood too, even though she'd never had a relationship where she'd been willing to do the same. But if she ever did, if it was worth it, she'd walk away too. She couldn't help herself from sneaking a glance at the man beside her. Yeah, she was a fool.

"Address?" he prompted.

She rattled it off. "They need clearance to get inside."

"That's to be expected. How big a place is it?"

"Big. I've got a full-size hangar and a large testing pad outside. I needed the acreage in order to test drones," she said. "I have various places I take them out for some finite tuning, but I have enough space for the drones that I can actually run them at home."

As they drove farther and farther away from the outskirts of the big city, into more open country, he said, "I think another friend of mine actually lives out here too."

She glanced at him. "Sounds like you know everybody."

"No, but Hawk and his sister own property in this area. She runs an animal rescue. When she first hooked up with Swede, another SEAL, she and her brother were living out of state. But she and Swede couldn't stand being apart as often as they were. It was too far for him to travel back and forth, and she couldn't leave her animals, so the siblings sold that first property and bought another down here." He studied the neighborhood. "I'm sure it's nearby."

"There is a rescue not too far from my place. I can't remember the name of it, but they handle animals of all kinds."

He laughed. "That's likely it. You might've seen Swede in Afghanistan. He was the monster-size guy."

"I remember him," she exclaimed. "You're saying that's his place?"

"I believe it's part his. He and Mia hooked up. Both the brother and sister needed to buy the property, so I think they all own it or something like that." He shrugged. "No idea how it works. The three of them do really well together. And, of course, Hawk is currently engaged to his sister's best friend."

"Oh, that's perfect then."

"Do you think so?" He laughed. "That was the dig that Corey made earlier about Mason." He quickly explained a little bit about Mason's Keepers.

She laughed. "Good for Mason. There should be a little bit more light and sunshine in this world with all this nastiness." She flipped on the turn signal and headed right. "We're almost there."

She took several more turns, then ended up outside a very large steel gate with security cameras mounted on both sides. "Welcome to my home."

DEVLIN'S EYES WIDENED as he took in the stone walls all around the property and the large double security gate. She drove up to a center post, punched in numbers and waited for it to open. He glanced at her. "I hadn't expected this level of security."

"My father installed it years ago," she said. "Otherwise it wouldn't be here."

"Your father?"

"Yes, he's an inventor, a mechanical engineer with an interest in all things computer."

That explained some of her history.

She pulled the vehicle through the gates just enough to drive to the far side and park. "I have to let the other vehicles through."

She hopped out, walked back and hit a button that kept the gates open. The two vehicles with the rest of his unit drove through. She quickly hit a series of buttons on the computer panel, waited for the gate to close and returned to the car.

When she was back in her seat, she said, "We're good to go."

He wondered just how safe she thought she was once inside the gate with all the cameras and security codes. His mind was already cataloguing the easiest way to get in and access her place. It wouldn't take much. The fence was not high enough, nor electrified. Cameras were around, but he didn't find too many. It would be easy to take out the entire system first, depending on the time frame.

She pulled up beside a ranch with Spanish tiles on the roof.

He smiled. "At least a roof like that you don't have to replace too often."

"Again, my father. Everything he did, he did for long term."

"Does your dad work here still?"

She shot him a hooded glance and said, "Somewhat."

She opened the car door and got out. He followed suit. They walked over to the truck where the rest of her gear was packed and helped the men unload. They stood with the stack on the ground, and he turned to her. "Where do you want these?"

She smiled. "Follow me."

She walked to the front door and inside the house. Devlin, with one large box in his arms, followed close behind. The house was an open floor plan, tiled and spacious. He fell in love with it immediately. "This is perfect," he said. "I love the windows."

The entire back wall was nothing but windows. And from here he could see a huge pool. The ranch wrapped all around the pool on three sides.

"This way," she said as she took a left.

He saw a very large elevator door and frowned. "Not too many people have a service elevator inside their house."

"You have no idea what's downstairs." She laughed. "I grew up in this house. To me it's normal, but for the few times I have people over, to them it's anything but."

The elevator was big enough for all of them. As he looked around, he realized five people were in the elevator, all with their arms fully packed, so it could easily hold ten to twelve men comfortably. He checked out the panel, noting two levels. And yet a pool was outside, and her home was on flat ground. He shook his head. "Nobody would realize there's another level to this place."

She gave him a hooded look again. "Exactly."

And he realized what she had meant about security. How could anybody infiltrating her company know about this?

The elevator doors opened on the first subfloor. She walked out into a massive lab. He could hear the gasp and whistles from the guys behind them. They all appreciated a good work center, and this was state-of-the-art. To the left was a massive bank of computers and several workstations. To the right were more computers, but these were set up with hardware. Huge long tables—twenty to forty feet each—were put together. Almost like a production assembly line but on a much smaller scale.

"Was Colleen working with you here?"

"Yes."

"What about Sandra?"

She shook her head. "No, she's Brent's assistant at ENFAQ. Whereas Colleen worked full-time for me."

"Was she on the payroll at ENFAQ as well?"

Bristol looked over at him and frowned. "I actually don't know, but I don't think so."

Devlin exchanged a glance with Easton. "Espionage is always easiest when somebody is within the company." If it was just her and Colleen, then that didn't look so good for Colleen.

"Anybody else work for you?" Ryder asked.

"Bookkeepers, accountants, and lawyers." She laughed. "Some come here, some don't. Very few have been downstairs."

"Can you tell us who *has* been down here?"

She turned to study Devlin, her gaze assessing, figuring out what his angle was.

"I'm looking to see who might have had access to place bugs, to see the actual setup and type of software you're using, and also who could have assessed the security you have in place." He shrugged. "The more information we have, the easier our job."

"Just what is your job?" she asked.

He grinned. "Saving your ass."

That startled a surprised laugh out of her. "I can't argue

with that. As far as answering your original question, the insurance agent came through. He didn't believe me when I said I had the electronics and setup I have in here. I had to insure everything, all the intellectual property and equipment."

"That's something we need to know. Exactly how much is this insured for?"

She glanced at him and in a low voice said, "Seven million."

Silence came first. "Wow."

She nodded. "I believe the property assessment came in at three. The rest of it is the business."

"What has to happen in order to get a payout?" Ryder asked.

Devlin winced at Ryder's tone, but these questions needed to be asked.

She stiffened. "Basically full loss of property and business. I think a major fire or bomb." She shrugged her shoulders. "Anything on a large scale like that."

"I bet your insurance guy didn't like the pool above here," Corey said in a light tone. "Just imagine the water damage."

She chuckled. "No, he did not like that one bit."

Devlin turned around. "I see you have a filter system. You work with gases and chemicals here?"

"The system is here, but it's not connected. I was looking at doing other work. I just haven't gotten there yet."

"Other work?"

She groaned. "My father was a weapons designer. The HEPA filter system was my suggestion for some of the work he did."

All four men stiffened at the words *weapons designer*.

"That's how you got into these drones?" Devlin asked.

"Yes. But my father is not the man he used to be. It's one of the reasons for the security." Then she clammed up and wouldn't say anymore.

After an uncomfortable few minutes, Corey stepped forward and said, "I'm not just a pretty face. I'm quite capable too."

She grinned. "I sure hope you mean that because we have one heck of a lot of work to do."

CHAPTER 9

I T WAS HARD not to like the men. Corey's lighthearted attitude seemed to permeate the entire group. She quickly had them unpack the bits and pieces she'd brought home. She set it all up on her main workstation. Then she led them to one of the large cupboards she used for storage. She opened the doors, relieved to see all the parts she needed for her work. Maybe they could pull this off.

"The initial order was for fifty drones. After that, if they were pleased, we're to manufacture two hundred more. But that was just in discussion, not in the contract. It's the fifty drones that we have to deliver in less than ten days. I have the bulk of the plastic here. We had a problem with a couple coming through with cracks. Quality is very important when we do our testing."

She led them inside the storeroom where everything was neatly organized and labeled—shelves stocked to the left and right. At the back of the room she showed them the racks of sheets of plastic and the machinery to do the cutting.

"This is just the plastic." She looked over at them. "You understand that, right? I use the term loosely."

The men nodded.

"We read up on your work," Easton said. "These are state-of-the-art materials, superlight, no reflective shiny surfaces for the sun to illuminate. Almost textured nylon."

"And bulletproof," she said quietly.

The men's gazes zoomed in on the material.

She nodded. "It's one of the reasons why these are state-of-the-art. It'll require a rocket launcher to take them out. Sure, a bullet might send it off course, but that's why I'm working on the software. Because once targeted, they should be locked on, and any deviation of their position should be automatically corrected."

The men looked at each other, smiling in anticipation. "We need these babies," Easton said.

She nodded. "I'm doing my best to get them for you. But when I say that screwing up on any of these is big money, you know what I mean."

The men turned with a whole lot more respect and studied the stacks and full shelving.

"Well, okay then. Let's get to work. Anybody here good with software?"

Ryder nodded. "I'm not bad. Easton's good too."

"And when I say, *good*, I need to know, can you program web languages? Would you consider yourself an expert, intermediate? If not, you get to work on hardware."

She tried to keep ego out of the question because she understood that often programmers became extremely competitive. Hackers lived in a subculture, and often the challenge for them was beating their own or somebody else's work. She was hoping a couple were in this group. But they would have to own up to how good they were, because she couldn't let anything less than an intermediate programmer or a solid hacker touch her babies.

"I'm good," Easton said. "I can hack but I've never tried to do anything too extreme."

Ryder took a minute before he answered. "I'm slightly

below that."

"Good to know. Hardware."

Both nodded.

She turned to Devlin and Corey. "And you two?"

"We're okay with computers," Devlin said, "but in terms of operating—not fixing or hacking."

She reached behind her and pulled out two screwdrivers. "Your tools."

The group cracked up.

"You two will start with the bulk and frames. These have to be 100 percent aerodynamically sealed units. Let me show you."

She went through the process of building the starter drone. It took her ninety minutes, start to finish, but then she'd been working on these a long time.

When she was done, she looked up at them and asked, "Any questions?"

Devlin shook his head. "We have it on video. If we have any, we'll ask. And yes, we promise we will destroy the video before we leave."

She nodded. "It may not matter, if we don't get these done on time." She turned to the other two. "If you follow me, I'll put you to work on the boxes."

"Boxes?" Ryder asked.

She took them one table over, a completely different space.

There was an odd Plexiglass wall with a series of doors and walls. She undid the security, opened it and let them in. "This is a dust-free zone. I do the best I can to minimize any interference. You're to build the computer boxes. I had all fifty. However, the chip sets were faulty, and every one needs to be switched."

Easton said, "You do the first. We can handle the rest."

She looked at him, and with the reality and truth of his statement, she felt something inside her settle. "Did I say 'thank you' yet?"

Ryder smiled, nodded at Easton. "You can say it when we're done. Let's just get at it. We don't have any time to waste."

Two hours later she let herself out of the room. She walked over to check on how Devlin and Corey were doing and realized they'd set up an assembly-line system where they each did one part. She watched for a moment and smiled. "You guys are used to working in teams, obviously."

"Teams have saved our ass more times than we can remember," Corey said. "One can only go alone in life for so long."

She nodded. "Although I work through the night, I can't expect the same of you guys. So I figure we'll call it in two hours. Then I'll take you upstairs for some dinner and show you to your rooms."

Corey brightened. "Food! She'll feed us too!" He reached out and smacked Devlin on the shoulder. "Damn, man, we are lucky."

Devlin grinned. "You do realize the guys are kind of big eaters?"

"You do realize I am too?" She smiled right back at him.

She'd already warned her upstairs housekeeper, Carmelita, that four men would be here for dinner and to bring on the beef. Bristol needed to check on her father, but that would wait a little longer. She'd said two hours, and she meant it. She didn't dare waste time.

She walked over to what she had left from the testing and quickly ran through it, checking for damages. They all appeared to be working. That was something—not a whole lot though. She set her security to do a full sweep on every laptop and locked away the drones. They would need a whole lot more work. But she didn't have time for that now. After dinner she'd come down and tear that drone apart. She had an idea what had gone wrong, but had to prove it. And that could be a lot more difficult.

Ten minutes before she was ready to call the time, her phone rang. It was Carmelita. "You've got more company. I let them in the compound."

Mystified that she'd do that, Bristol glanced at Devlin. "Are you expecting anyone?"

Devlin pulled out his phone as it rang too. Answering it, he turned and looked at her, nodding. "Looks like you have more help."

She stared at him in disbelief. "Really? Capable help?"

He gave a crooked smile that made her heart tilt. "Oh, yeah."

She rapped on the window for the guys in the computer room and called time. They laid down their tools and walked out. With everyone in together, they went upstairs to the main floor. She headed to the front door, unlocked and opened it. And burst into tears.

"Bristol," Tesla cried, then threw her arms around her. After she hugged her, she asked, "May we come in?"

Immediately everyone inside moved back to allow entrance for the new arrivals.

Bristol shook her head, now understanding Carmelita's actions as her housekeeper knew Tesla well. Bristol wiped her eyes but clung to Tesla's hand. "I can't believe you came."

"Of course I did. I can't believe you took that damn contract. I told you not to." But no hate was found in her voice. She'd been in that situation and understood.

Bristol smiled up at her, then studied the new arrivals.

The first man stepped forward. "I'm Harrison."

The next man did the same. "Rhodes."

She glanced at Devlin.

"We owe you guys." The two men shook hands with Devlin.

"You talk to Levi about that. As far as we're concerned, when one of us goes down, we'll always be there to help."

Bristol understood the sentiment; she just didn't know what she'd done to deserve it. "Come in, please. Welcome to my home."

Tesla looked around the place. "It's still the same."

Bristol smiled. "Of course it is. It's home." She led the way toward the dining room. "You've arrived at dinnertime."

Harrison said, "We didn't mean to disturb your meal."

She sent him a sharp glance. "Does that mean you can't eat?"

He grinned. "Ma'am, I can consume food at any time of the day."

She glanced at Rhodes, already rubbing his tummy. She shook her head. "Let's go." As she led the way into the massive dining room, she motioned to them and said, "Grab a seat. I just need to check in with my housekeeper."

She walked away, disappearing into the kitchen, and found Carmelita bustling around. In a low voice, she said, "Three more arrived. I'm sorry."

Carmelita laughed. "No worries. I have lots."

Relieved, Bristol turned and headed back to the dining room. Her father's place at the end of the table was empty, as was the spot beside his chair—waiting for the presence of her and her father.

She nodded to the men and said, "Excuse me while I get my father to join us."

She turned and walked away again. She felt the surprise of the group behind her and knew it would only compound while she was gone. But she lived with this reality. She went into the library to see her father dozing.

She gently patted his arm. He woke with a startled look at her and frowned. "Its okay, Father. It's dinnertime."

She helped him to his feet and led him into the dining room. Devlin stood and walked around the table, pulling the chair back for him.

Her father looked at her, Devlin, then back at her and asked, "Do I know you?"

She smiled sadly at him. "Yes, Father, you do. Come and sit down. Your meal is coming."

He sat down. With a look of thanks at Devlin, she took her own seat.

Before any need for conversation, Carmelita pushed in the food cart. Devlin hopped back up and helped her. He lifted platters laden with roast beef onto the table. More were full of vegetables, a huge salad, and Carmelita's favorite addition to any meal, rice.

She pushed away the empty cart and came back with a single plate, which she placed in front of Bristol's father.

Bristol reached over and stroked her father's hand. "Father, your food is in front of you. Please eat."

He looked at her and frowned. She placed the fork in his hand, and in a very shaky motion, he spooned up some of the soft food on his plate. But he ate. And for that she was grateful. With a close eye on him, she motioned at the others with a smile and said, "Please serve yourselves."

The men dove in. She put a little bit on her plate, with

her eye forever on her father. It was so damn upsetting how he didn't recognize her. He didn't miss her when she was gone and didn't know her when she returned. She'd been living with this for the last few years. And it was getting worse. She would do something more permanent soon. But she hoped to keep him home as long as she could.

If she didn't fulfill the contract, she'd lose the house and also the ability to care for her father. With tears rising, she forced herself to finish eating. Her father dropped the fork and it clattered to his plate. She studied the amount he had eaten and nodded. It was about as good as it would get.

Carmelita appeared almost instantly. "I'll take him back to his room."

Bristol nodded and stood. With her father on his feet again, she reached over, kissed his cheek. "Have a good evening, Father."

But he didn't acknowledge her in any way. He hadn't for a long time.

As soon as they were gone, she took a deep breath, swallowed hard and sat back down at her plate. She took several bites to regain control and then glanced at the men. They'd been watching—of course they had—but they were all eating now.

Devlin asked in a quiet, understanding voice, "How long?"

"Two years. It's been that long since he last knew who I was." She settled back to eat. "Just one more reason why this contract is so important."

"And a very long two years," Tesla said with sympathy. "He was such a vibrant man." She glanced around the table at the others. "Bristol and I did a stint at MIT. I came here a couple times on holidays. Her father was fascinating. He had his fingers into a million different designs. He was doing everything from computer programs to chemical warfare."

"The trouble is, I didn't realize over the last five years how he was already sliding," Bristol said. "So when he started into the chemical warfare—and a few other adventurous things—it got a little scary."

"I'd say." Corey shook his head. "Chemical warfare is a science all on its own."

Bristol smiled. "And yet my father has several PhDs."

Stunned silence filled the room. Then Ryder groaned. "This is where I get to say I'm probably the most uneducated person seated at this table."

"You might be," Devlin said, "but you're the best at reading people, and you can't be taught that from a book." He glanced at Bristol. "Ryder's gotten our asses out of trouble just based on that alone."

"Interesting," Bristol said. "That's a fascinating concept." She shrugged. "I really suck at that. But I can tell when people are hungry, and your plates are empty. There's lots of food here, so please help yourselves to more."

Several of the men did. But ten minutes later Ryder stood and said, "Thank you, ma'am. That was excellent, and I'd like to get back to work now."

All the other men rose and followed suit. Bristol glanced at Tesla, who was grinning like a fool. She leaned forward and said, "Yes, they mean it."

Bristol stood then and said, "Well, I'm not one to stop the work train. Let's go." She turned and led the way back downstairs. Only this time, Tesla was at her side. And damn, it was good to see her old friend.

DOWNSTAIRS THE TWO previous groups of men returned to their assignments. Rhodes looked at Bristol and said, "I'm here to help you build the drones, but both Harris and I are pros at finding hackers and security breaches."

Her eyebrows shot up. Devlin grinned. He had been listening but didn't know if she believed it or not. "Bristol, that's what I said originally about these two."

She nodded. "I'm torn between having you tear apart my system to figure out what is going on or having you help with the software I need to build."

"Both," Harrison said. "Let's do what we can on the first, see if there is a leak, and if so, we'll plug it. That way nothing else goes wrong. We can't have anybody knowing you have all this help, with the potential of making your contract good. Because they are likely to up their agenda. Let them think you're a limping duck today, heading for the slaughter."

Devlin winced at the analogy but saw she got it.

She nodded. "What do you need from me?"

"Permission to access your system."

This time Bristol winced.

Tesla reached a hand over and squeezed her friend's shoulder. "I know exactly how you feel. But you need to do this."

She nodded. "I'm not sure exactly what you need access to. The laptops on the table were all over Afghanistan at the training session, and my main server is through that door."

Harrison turned toward the server.

Devlin stopped what he was doing, walked to Bristol and said, "You'll need to let them into the server."

Her breath rushed out with a *whoosh* and said, "Fine." She opened the double doors.

Devlin trailed behind. He halted when he saw the banks of servers. "Really?"

But Harrison was in the middle of the room, rubbing his hands together gleefully. "Oh, I do love it when people put money where it belongs."

Rhodes whistled. "This is nice."

"I'm glad you approve," Bristol said. "It took a lot of money to do this. The trouble is, for all I know, someone is coming in the back door to hurt me hard."

Harrison looked down at his watch and said, "You've got a lot more going on here than I expected, so I need a few hours. I also need you to logon, and let me and Rhodes work."

Devlin held his breath. It was a huge moment of trust for Bristol. But given the situation she was in, she didn't have much of a choice. If she didn't trust these men—the ones who could potentially help her—then there was no way to save her. But if she could, then she just might make this happen.

She stepped forward, dropped the keypad onto its lower level and quickly typed in her password. Instantly a four-wall bank of monitors turned on.

She glanced at Harrison and asked, "You do know what you're doing, right?"

"I'll be fine. Let me just go take a peek."

She shook her head, and with a shudder, she turned and walked back out. At the doorway, Devlin wrapped an arm around her and tugged her in for a hug and kissed her temple. "Trust. Remember that."

She looked up at him, her eyes wide, confused. "A little hard right now."

He nodded. "But you'll lose everything if you don't let

us help."

She nodded, and he dropped his arms and returned to Corey, who'd been watching them with interest. Devlin turned to look back at Tesla, taking Devlin's place, wrapping her arms around Bristol. It was obvious the women were close.

It looked to him like her life revolved around her work and father. Colleen would've been a mainstay. And with Colleen murdered, well, it appeared one more support post was gone in Bristol's life.

Her father. Her contract. And the thought of somebody sabotaging her—that would've finished it for most people. But Bristol was strong. Her back was straight, and she was already back to business. Tesla was at her side as the two examined the drone. He wished he were over there, learning, listening. The bits and pieces he did hear made no sense to him. They were talking at a level way above his knowledge. He was damn glad Tesla had joined them. Bristol needed her. Hell, she needed all of them.

CHAPTER 10

"I 'M SO GLAD you came," Bristol said.

"I would have earlier if I'd known you had this kind of problem." Tesla's voice was low and filled with compassion.

"I was handling it until this mess," Bristol said louder than she realized. She forced herself to refocus. "Right. I think this is the problem we need to work on first."

The two had been poring over the laptop, testing the software in the drone. It went along with what Harrison and Rhodes were looking for. Troubleshooting software, debugging code—almost a full-time business.

"Colleen told me how she had trouble with it. Called it *possessed*. At the time, I thought something was wrong with the hardware, like a shorted wire. You know what can go wrong with poor connections."

Tesla nodded. "But you're thinking the software was tampered with, like somebody doing a remote control takeover?"

"I was wondering about that," Bristol said. "But if so, it was poorly done as it couldn't fly properly either. Just doing these crazy dips and turns. The goal could have been to take control, but they only made it that far."

"If they changed your software just a little, that would be enough to mess things up. But it was only one of the computers?"

"Yes, this laptop." She tapped the machine. "Using this controller." She pointed to the remote. "It's connected to the system."

"Let me take a look."

Bristol sat back and let Tesla study the code while Bristol glanced around the room. She'd never had this many people working for her or helping her out. And yet, even though six extra men were here, it didn't feel crowded. Her lab afforded a ton of space to work without bumping into another person.

"I've got it."

Bristol lowered her gaze to see Tesla pointing at a series of commands. "They are typed incorrectly, but it's to screw up your main commands." Tesla kept going down, searching and highlighting text.

Bristol realized somebody either didn't have the skill or the time because only that one line was off.

"Down here they got it right."

"Somebody had access long enough while I was in Afghanistan."

Tesla looked at her and asked, "How many people were there?"

"Hundreds, if not thousands, at the base. As to how many people actually had access to my tent? Not very many. The company, Colleen, Sandra, Morgan, David, and myself. And the odd person who came in and went out. A few of the MPs."

Tesla nodded. "It's also possible someone could access this remotely."

They both looked over at the double doors to the server room. "Let's clean up the code."

"I need to take it out for a test run, confirm what we've done has corrected the problem, and see what Harrison and Rhodes came up with."

Tesla stood. "And I fully expect to help you build the rest of these. I've taken the week off. From the sounds of it, we are very short on time. And you need fifty units to fulfill the contract?"

"Yes." Bristol glanced at her friend gratefully. "If we could do that …"

Tesla reached around and hugged her again. "We can do anything it takes to ensure you don't lose this house."

"It's my fault. That damn contract. You were right all along."

"Hindsight is twenty-twenty. We can only focus on what's in front of us," Tesla said firmly. "Let's just get our heads onto this problem, lean our shoulders in and fix it." As her arm fell away, she added, "You're not alone any longer, remember?"

"Thank you," Bristol said with a smile. She bent her head, intently working on the issues.

When she next looked up, rubbing her temples, scanning the room again, she realized not one of the men had called it quits. If they were tired, they weren't saying so. They were determined to keep forging ahead. But she also knew, pushing too hard for too long caused accidents and mistakes. Neither of which she could afford.

She glanced at her watch and gasped in horror. "Oh, my God! It's after two in the morning." She bolted to her feet. "You guys have to be exhausted."

Tesla yawned on cue. "I am, now that you mention it," she admitted, glancing around at the others. "You'll have to call a halt to this. The men won't stop until you do."

"Right."

Bristol rubbed her eyes, walked over to the server room and saw the men standing with keyboards open, working like crazy. She cleared her throat. They didn't notice. "Harrison? Rhodes? How about knocking off for the night and getting started bright and early in the morning?"

The two men spun and looked at her with two pairs of laser eyes. She instinctively straightened.

Harrison looked at the computer in front of him, glanced at Rhodes, and then said in a very polite voice, "I'd rather not. We just had a breakthrough. I don't want to come back in the morning and find out somebody saw what we were doing and created a wormhole, going in a whole different direction."

She held up her hands. "Your decision. I just don't want you to work 'til you drop."

The men snorted. "Hardly done anything yet."

She shook her head, stepped from the room and walked to where the rest were working. She reached up to touch Devlin on the shoulder, feeling the heat emanating off his body. He glanced down, wrapped an arm around her and tucked her up close. She really shouldn't let him do that. They hardly knew each other. But the comfort was just so damn nice that she leaned into it and accepted what he was offering.

"I was thinking it was bedtime," she said to the men. "You guys are really working your asses off."

Corey snickered.

At first, she didn't understand his meaning, but when she did, she could feel the heat flash up her neck. She glared at him. "We're no longer in high school."

At that he laughed uproariously. "But we had some really good times back then."

"Maybe for you," she muttered. "Not so much for me."

Devlin glanced down at her, a smile at the corner of his lips. "Too many brains?"

"Too many brains, not enough social skills, and a very strange father." She shrugged. "You name it, I just didn't fit in with anybody."

"Doesn't matter, sweetie. I left school behind a long time ago."

Devlin smiled, making her sigh, almost wishing she were back in school for the teenage feelings washing through her. Who was this man who stirred her so? Who'd come to her rescue over and over again?

"Exactly."

At Corey's snicker, she rolled her eyes, pulling her emotional tide back in tight again. So not the time or the place. "I was trying to say, it's time to knock off for the night, so you can get a fresh start in the morning."

Devlin glanced around the room to see that nobody had stopped working.

She followed his gaze and realized even Tesla had gone back to work. "I didn't intend for you to work through the night, you know."

"Harrison and Rhodes? Are they ready to quit?"

"I don't think you can say anything to make them quit," she emphasized the last word. "And apparently they are at some kind of breach, and don't want to walk away just yet."

"Good enough. We'll keep pushing until they got it. If we all leave together, we can start again fresh in the morning at the same time." Devlin's arm squeezed her shoulders gently, and then he dropped his arm, returning to his work.

She shrugged and walked over to the last two. "I doubt it

makes any difference," she announced, "but I was telling people to knock off for the night."

Easton and Ryder looked up at her, and she knew they had caught a glimpse of everyone and heard what she'd said.

"I gather nobody listened?" Ryder asked with a smile. "We're not real big on quitting."

"I see that," she said in exasperation. "But even SEALs need to be fed and watered on a regular basis."

Easton chuckled. "Look at that. She's funny."

She glared at him. "Does it matter that I might be ready to quit?"

Instantly the men stopped and stared at her.

She chuckled. "Okay, I'm kidding. But soon. Maybe another hour."

"One hour it is."

She turned back to Devlin, her gaze connecting with his and repeated, "One hour."

He nodded, but didn't say anything.

As she walked past the server room, she called out, "One more hour."

Tesla grinned at her when she reappeared beside her.

"Are they always like this?" Bristol asked in an awed whisper.

"They so are."

WHEN THE HOUR was up, not one person stopped working. Devlin knew she was right—they needed rest. But he also knew nobody would quit until Harrison and Rhodes had done what they needed to. Devlin was curious about how it was going. But for the muttered expletives coming out of that room every so often, he figured things were less than ideal.

Suddenly a cheer rose up. Rhodes stepped out and said, "We've got it."

"Got what?" Bristol asked.

"We set a trap. We couldn't find out who was coming into your system until they reentered again, about forty minutes ago. Your system caught and quarantined a key logger, but there have been other attempts. I closed a couple holes," he said with a big grin. "Harrison's working on backtracking where it came from. In the meantime, we're putting in new security systems and a couple extra layers of protection."

Devlin watched Bristol's jaw drop. "So I *was* being hacked?"

"Oh, yeah," Harrison said with a grin, joining Rhodes. "I can tell you it came from inside ENFAQ Ltd., but no lead as to who is responsible.

"Any idea how long?" she asked faintly.

"Fairly recent, but we don't have any idea how far the previous attempts might've made it in. We'll find out though soon."

She nodded. "I'm very glad to hear he's been booted out."

"Booted out, locked down, and the system reinforced. No way to know who and what yet, but I'll be working on that tomorrow." Harrison stepped toward the server room again, stopped, turned. "But I can tell you it'll take a hell of a lot more to get back in again."

Devlin grinned. "I told you they were good."

With a dazed look in her eyes, Bristol studied him. She nodded, turned to face them all. "Thank you all so much."

"That hacker mess is related to the drone problem," Tesla called out. "We figured somebody was accessing the computer, centered on the remote controls, and screwed with the commands, with the ultimate idea of taking over the drones potentially."

"Like in Afghanistan, when the drones weren't responding to Colleen's commands?" Devlin asked.

Bristol nodded. "That's what we figure. We have to make sure these guys didn't cause any other damage while they were in there. And that's a lot of code to check. Plus, we need somebody who can handle the drones for testing. And you can't just be a beginner." She glanced at Devlin. "I'm sorry. I know you really wanted to do this, but it needs to be someone with a much higher skill level."

"Tomorrow's problems," Devlin said quietly. "We'll all think better in the morning."

"True enough. Let's pack it in for the night." She turned back to Harrison. "Is the server set for the evening?"

He nodded. "Tomorrow I'll show you what we've done."

"Good. Let's go." She led the way to the elevator.

As the rest stepped into the elevator car, Bristol set a special security code inside the room, then joined them. Behind her, Devlin watched as infrared security beams crisscrossed the room.

"Nice," he said.

She nodded. "As state-of-the-art as I can produce it. Those are relatively easy to set up, but the computer stuff…The hackers are constantly evolving, and are sometimes the most difficult things to lock down."

"A lot of businesses make their way in the world from hacking, especially military weaponry."

On the main floor the doors opened. She led the way

through a hallway Devlin had yet to see. There she opened the first room and pointed to the others and said, "Each room has its own bath and two king-size beds. Hopefully you'll be comfortable here." She kept walking and opening doors. "I don't care who goes where or how many. For now you can have your own room, but if I bring in more people, we might need at least two per room."

Harrison and Rhodes took the first room. "We'll be fine. It's way more comfortable than what we have a lot of times."

As Devlin glanced inside, he agreed. Huge windows, balconies, French doors, and private bathrooms. He glanced over to the guys and said, "Nice way to spend a few days off."

Both men grinned, and Harrison said, "You can call us back here anytime."

Tesla was at the far end of the hall, talking with Bristol. The two women hugged, then Tesla went in and closed her bedroom door.

Bristol turned to the door across from Tesla's, pointed at it, and told Devlin, "That's your room."

Devlin frowned, staring at her. "And where's yours?"

She frowned back.

He could see the confusion in her gaze, deep circles under her eyes.

She pointed to the left hallway and said, "The master is down this way. My father's bedroom is as well."

"And if there's trouble, how will any of us get to you?"

She chewed her bottom lip and reached up to run her fingers through her hair. "One spare bedroom is down there, if you want to be closer, and sleep better."

He nodded. "I'll take it. Somebody needs to be close enough to hear if you call out."

As she brushed past him, she said, "I never thought of that."

She showed him the room, pointed out her father's room and then hers. He walked into hers, took a good look around, assessed the security. There was very little. He walked to the windows and doors. The ground dropped a short way down on the back side, and he could see the huge pool from earlier, surrounded by the large courtyard.

He turned and looked back at her. "You lock all these doors and windows at night?"

"I haven't been," she admitted. "But I guess I'll start."

"Tonight and every night that this is going on." He studied her to make sure she understood. When she nodded, he gave her a quick hug. "Now off to bed." He walked to the door, where he turned back. "Don't lock this door in case I need to get in."

He pulled the door closed and tested the security of the latch. It closed with a quiet whisper. He did it a couple times, memorizing the sound, and then turned to his room. He stood in the doorway and smiled. It really wouldn't be a hardship staying here for a few days.

His balcony faced the other part of the property. He could see a large cement area, maybe a landing pad. Several outbuildings and what seemed to be two separate triple-car garages were at the far end. He'd love to spend some time just exploring, seeing what was here. As he studied the landing pad again, a thought occurred.

He quickly sent off a text and hopped in the shower. When he came back out, he collapsed on the bed. Tomorrow was a whole new day. They hadn't set a morning wake-up time. But he knew the guys would be up within six hours. They were just that way. Always ready for action.

He could do no less.

CHAPTER 11

BRISTOL WOKE THE next morning, groggy and disoriented. She heard a weird whirling sound, but didn't understand. She bolted out of bed and looked outside, though she couldn't see anything. She quickly dressed and raced down to the main living area. She stepped outside and watched in stunned amazement as a helicopter landed right in front of her. She shook her head, waited for the blades to slow and walked closer.

Someone reached out a hand and grabbed her. "Wait."

She turned to see Devlin, standing beside Rhodes and Harrison. "You guys expecting someone?"

Just then a tall blonde woman, eyes pale blue—like ice that had been frozen too long—walked toward them. She was dressed in black jeans and a black T-shirt. She was long, lean, and looked like she meant business.

The helicopter lifted up behind her and took off.

The woman's gaze swept the four of them. She nodded at the men; then her focus locked on Bristol. She stopped in front of her and held out her hand. "Hi, I'm Ice."

Bristol gasped, her hand immediately reaching out to shake the hand offered. "Oh, my goodness. I've heard of you. But I had no idea you would be coming here."

Harrison grinned. "You will soon be amazed. She's a hell of a drone operator. You needed somebody to test."

Bristol turned to look at Harrison and caught the devilish grin on Devlin's face. "You did this, didn't you?"

"Last night you and Tesla discussed how you would soon need somebody to run the drones, and it couldn't be a beginner. She might not be up to where you are, since you're the inventor of these things, but I've heard how good she is." He turned to Harrison and Rhodes. "And she's half of Legendary Security, who these guys work for."

Bristol didn't know what to say. She'd never considered so many people would step up to help. She was a little confused, wondering if a price was attached. One she wouldn't be able to pay if this all blew up in her face. But they all knew the stakes here and came to help regardless. Amazing.

"Thank you so much for coming." She glanced at the helicopter, disappearing in the distance. "Is that yours or a friend's?"

"A friend. I flew into San Diego, and he gave me a lift. It's a long way for me to come from Texas in my own." Ice smiled. "Besides my babies are at home getting upgrades."

Harrison and Rhodes peppered her with questions. "What upgrades? What are you adding, Ice?"

She grinned. "A drone storage bay and some extra handheld remotes, with a few perks," she said.

"Perks?" Bristol asked. "What kinds?"

"Just a little extra added artillery," she said smugly.

The guys brightened.

Devlin laughed. "We all want to hear, but we're also desperately in need of breakfast and coffee."

At his reminder Bristol smiled. "Please follow me." She led them back inside, the others talking behind her.

Devlin walked at her side. He said in a low voice, "I

hope you're okay with this."

She shot him a sharp look. "Though it's much appreciated, I'm not sure how she'll be able to go all day without any sleep if she's been traveling all night."

Rhodes overheard the two of them. "Show her the room where she'll be staying. That woman power naps like nobody I've ever seen. If she needs it, she'll take it."

"Really? She'd go all day and night?"

"Often has and still will," he confirmed. In a much lower voice he continued, "She's Levi's partner."

Bristol had to admit, she only knew a little about Levi and what Devlin had said about Legendary Security. And with Ice at his side …

She led the way to the dining room, making a quick stop in the kitchen. Her housekeeper was busy putting together breakfast. She stopped and said, "There is one more."

Carmelita smiled. "I heard the helicopter. So I prepared more food."

Bristol smiled. "Good thing. I only knew when it arrived."

"They are doing a good thing for you. You need the help." Carmelita returned to the pancake she was busy flipping.

Bristol could handle codes, machinery, and any number of finite little pieces and parts. But when it came to making things in the kitchen taste good, she was a complete failure. And those pancakes looked divine. Already she could feel her stomach growling. "Those look great."

"You do love my pancakes."

Bristol left the kitchen and returned to her guests, happy to see they were already in the dining room, with the sideboard set up with brewing coffee. As she walked to the pot, hoping there was still enough for a cup, Devlin stepped in front of her, holding out one. She smiled. "I was afraid it was all gone."

"It is," he said cheerfully. "A second pot is dripping."

She nodded at Devlin, delighted to have house guests who not only knew boundaries but also when to cross them, like putting on another pot of coffee. They were so damn self-sufficient that she was amazed at just how much they could accomplish. For the first time in a long while, hope lived in her heart. Maybe with their help, she could make this happen.

"After breakfast, Ice, I'll show you to your room," she said, taking Rhodes's advice. "Then, if you need to crash anytime today, please feel free."

Ice nodded that regal head of hers and said, "Thank you. That would be lovely." She glanced around at the place. "Maybe, with any luck, we can all go for a swim later today too."

"That would be a great idea," Bristol said. "We'll all need a break from work."

Harrison laughed. "Not to mention the fact that Ice wants Levi to put in a pool at the compound."

"Really?" Rhodes turned to Ice. "That would be awesome."

She laughed. "Wouldn't it? But Levi's not quite convinced yet."

"Ha! All SEALs love water. He'll come around. I'm sure it's more about budgeting than anything."

"It is, but with good reason," she said. "We bought the parcel of land beside us."

After a moment of silence, Rhodes and Harrison pumped their fists in the air with a collective "Yes."

"That's unbelievable. Awesome job, Ice."

She tilted her head and smiled. "It's hardly just me. A lot of finagling went on over that piece."

"Still we could use the expansion."

"And who could possibly think we would need that?" Ice asked. "We already have a massive amount of property."

"Yeah, but I bet the helicopter pad will get thrown over on the new piece."

She grinned. "And we're planning for a third chopper."

The men just stared at her, big grins on their faces. "So maybe there will be room for a pool?"

Devlin said, "I don't believe it, but I think I'm actually jealous."

Ice turned to study him. "We have the room and space for you anytime you want to make the move."

Bristol had been watching the exchange. The dynamics between these three people who obviously worked together showed a depth of affection and trust she rarely saw.

She realized Devlin, Easton, Ryder, and Corey were all still in the military. The other three were no longer in, but worked for Levi's company. "It must be a great relief to know, when you're done with military service, there is a place like Legendary Security to go."

Easton nodded. "I was just about to ask Ice if they needed more people."

Ice's gaze zeroed in on him, and she smiled. "When I said there was room for Devlin, I didn't mean just him. It included you and the others. I can't imagine ever turning down a SEAL, though there may be one or two who might not work out so well," she admitted. She turned to explain to Bristol. "We're a tight-knit group. It takes a special person to fit in. The thing about SEALs is they're driven badasses. A lot of alphas among them. But they're used to following orders. And that makes up for a lot."

Rhodes was already seated at the dining table and slouched in his chair. "We are badasses," he admitted. "But with several of us picking up partners recently, we've calmed down."

"Partners?" Devlin asked. "The last I heard it was just Levi and Ice."

"Then you are out of the loop in a big way," Harrison said with a snicker. "Along with Heroes for Hire, there's Heroes for the Heart, and Heroes for Heaven. The damn compound is becoming a matchmaking service."

"What? I thought Mason's Keepers' group with Tesla here was bad."

Tesla walked in, rubbing the sleep from her eyes. She stopped to survey the group with a smile on her face, "What was that about Mason?"

Ice chuckled. At the confusion on Bristol's face, she explained, "Tesla and Mason started the trend. Mason's unit— and quickly those by extension who went out on missions with him—found new relationships." She continued. "And all are still lasting relationships and doing very well, thank you."

Devlin added, "Ever since then, Mason's group has been nicknamed the Keepers. Any man who goes out with Mason's team inevitably finds love right then and there. One at a time, another falls."

"Get it?" Tesla grinned. "Because all the men are *keepers*. So the name sticks." She turned to Ice. "Heroes for Hire though, that's perfect."

Ice nodded. "I'm afraid I started that. Levi was not impressed. But with a few more women on board, each offered their own version. The company is called Legendary Security, but I'm afraid the Heroes for Hire, Heart, or Heaven has stuck."

"I love it," Bristol said. She glanced at Easton, Ryder, and Corey, then around to Devlin. "So which one of you will fall next? I saw you all there, working with Mason in Afghanistan."

That started the others laughing. "It will be one and then another for sure," Ice said. "The chain hasn't been broken yet."

Easton glared. "Well, if it looks in my direction, I damn sure will break it." He shook his head and sat at the dining table, his nose in the air. "Smells like breakfast."

Bristol called out, "It's probably ready. We can move to the table, but that won't change the subject, Easton."

"Then it'll be Devlin," he said, with a knowing look at Bristol.

Instantly she could feel the heat crawl up her neck. She liked Devlin just fine, but that alone was a long way off from having a relationship. "Even if it is Devlin, you're still on the hot seat."

"Like hell," he said cheerfully. "Somebody's got to catch me first."

Just then Carmelita arrived, pushing a large trolley. Everyone still standing then walked to the table and took a seat. Devlin helped Carmelita unload the platters of food. From golden buttery scrambled eggs to sausages, to hot buttered toast, and great big mounds of pancakes, the platters held a ton of food for everybody. Bristol was delighted. She shook her head, wondering how she'd gotten so lucky with Carmelita.

"Dig in everyone. There's lots."

DEVLIN IMMEDIATELY STABBED three pancakes, putting them on his plate. A lot of food was before them. He didn't feel the need to hold back at all. This could be a long day with a lot of work, and he needed his energy. He was also running short on sleep. It hadn't been the easiest thing to go to bed, knowing Bristol was in her room on that massive king-size one all alone.

She was so small she would be practically dwarfed in that bed. But his room had been incredibly comfortable. Not luxurious, but not far off. Elegant and tasteful. And finding out that Ice had flown through the night to arrive and help, well, it was pretty damn hard to be anything but delighted.

If ever Bristol had needed renewed faith in humanity, this should do it for her.

That the guys had already found and stopped the hacker was huge. If they could plug the leak of information, and the rest could rebuild the drones, then she need not worry. They had hope of pulling this off.

That damn stupid contract. He wanted her to see a lawyer about that. The trouble was, she'd signed it. Contracts like that killed you.

She might not have gotten it if she had tried to rewrite it. And he could certainly understand her taking a chance. It would put her on the map. "Will I be starting back in the same place as last night?" he asked. He sat beside her yet again. He looked down at the little bit of food on her plate and frowned. He reached over, grabbed another stack of pancakes and dumped them on her plate. "You need to eat."

She turned and glared at him. "I've been feeding myself for quite a long time, thank you."

"And you're pale and tired."

He turned back to his plate, reached for the maple syrup, realizing this was the real stuff, and poured it liberally on top of his pancakes. Then he dug in yet again.

He could feel her seething beside him. He glanced over at her. "Get used to it."

In a low voice she responded, "Get used to what?"

"Somebody looking after you for a change." He glanced around the table. "Where is your father? Did he have a decent night?"

"He should still be sleeping. I hate to disturb him in the mornings."

He nodded. It made sense. Also with Ice's arrival, Bristol's normal morning routine had been thrown off. "Maybe by the time breakfast is finished, you could slip out and spend a few minutes with him."

In a low voice she said, "That's what I was thinking. I'll bring his breakfast to him and see how he is."

"I can take everyone down, if you need me to."

She glanced over at him and smiled. "You're really a nice man, Devlin."

He winced. "There's nothing nice about me."

He caught Rhodes's grin, glared at him and watched as it spread around the room. But nobody said anything, and with them all being silent, he returned to his meal. He quickly finished what was on his plate and pushed it back.

"Your housekeeper is wonderful. That was terrific. Thank you." He reached for his cup of coffee, walked to the sideboard to fill it up and returned to his place. Noticing her cup was empty, he did the same for her.

As he sat back down again, she said to everyone in the room, "I need to spend a few moments with my father to start the day. Devlin'll take you all back downstairs. I'll be there in about ten minutes." She glanced over at Tesla. "Maybe you could explain to Ice what we've been doing."

Tesla smiled. "Be happy to," she said cheerfully. "I'm sure she will love the new drones."

Ice said, "To be honest, I haven't heard very much about these."

"Stealth, bulletproof, and even when shot off target, it's still capable of realigning."

Ice immediately dropped her knife and fork, and stood. "Let's go."

"Ha!" Tesla pushed her plate back, grabbed another cup of coffee and said, "Is everybody ready?"

The group stood, refilled their coffees, and then, with Devlin leading the way and Bristol watching, they left.

<h1 style="text-align:center">CHAPTER 12</h1>

B RISTOL WATCHED THE elevator doors close in front of her. She opened a panel beside the elevator and turned off the security to the lower floor.

Carmelita came to stand beside her. "These are good people."

She turned, putting her arms around her housekeeper. "They are the best."

Carmelita patted her shoulder. "Your father's breakfast is ready."

Bristol walked into the kitchen, grabbed the tray already laid out and went to see her father. She knocked on the door and heard a confused murmur from inside. Pushing the door open, she walked in. He sat on bed, a book in hand, looking at the world from the foggy filter he lived in now.

"Good morning, Father. I brought breakfast."

He glanced at her. "Good. I'm quite hungry today."

Relieved he was coherent, she placed a small breakfast tray over his lap, sitting down on the bed with him.

He brushed her away. "I don't need anything else. You can leave."

With a heavy sigh she stood, realizing that today was just a normal day. He didn't recognize her for who she was. Still she persisted. "I'm your daughter, Father. I came to visit with you."

He looked at her and shook his head. "I don't have a daughter."

Right. One of those days again. The good days when he remembered his life were nonexistent. Every once in a while, there were glimmers of awareness, not recognitions of her, but at least of himself. They were little golden lights to help make the rest of it so much easier on her.

She stood, turned to him and gave him a gentle kiss.

But he was irritable and brushed her away again. With a hand he pointed to the door and said, "Go."

Sadly she turned and walked out. As she closed the door, she held her breath and willed back the tears. It was so damn hard to see him like this.

But today of all days she had to focus and get on track. She straightened her back, brushed away the tears in the corners of her eyes and headed downstairs. Everyone here had come to help out. The least she could do was show up and be the person in charge.

As the elevator doors opened, she walked into her lab to see everybody back at their stations, with Tesla and Ice bending over the laptop programming the remote controls she'd had in front of her last night.

She never considered anybody here might actually spread any secrets. And she'd never asked or had anybody sign an NDA. She probably should have. She certainly wasn't a lawyer or anywhere near as worried about things as her team of attorneys would like her to be. But there hadn't been any time. When able-bodied people had been willing and ready to help, well, she wouldn't have insulted them by asking them to sign something like that.

Besides, she imagined, in their business, they did this all the time. Secrecy bred secrecy. And these men and women lived with it. Bristol was damn glad they were here.

Not only was Ice supposed to be an exceptionally good drone operator, but she was intuitive and understood the inner workings easily. She was a huge asset right now. Of course, under Bristol's test conditions, she wouldn't get to see Ice really letting loose and being creative with them, as there just wasn't the time for fun, only for work—yet not enough hours to really do this job justice either. Very quickly they took the drones Bristol had brought back from Afghanistan off the rack, put one of the new chip sets in each, and the three women each carried one of the drones outside. Bristol shot it into the air. It handled just fine.

She gave it to Ice and said, "Run it through its maneuvers. You won't have a clue as to all it can do, so this is a really good test from a new user's point of view. I want to watch and see what's happening. I've got some tools here that will give me a better idea of the controls as I go through the field with her."

She held up one of the special testing devices she'd developed and watched as Ice began working with the drone. Not only was she careful, but she was good. The drone was up and flying overhead in a beautiful straight line.

Bristol set up the tracker that would measure the drone's flight and matched it to the commands. They had to be exact for accuracy.

She spent the rest of the afternoon fussing, tweaking, and getting more and more frustrated. Finally, by late afternoon, she had the adjustments pretty damn close. Ice had gone to lie down.

Bristol had the drone flying in the sky, pulled out the remote, recalibrated it and ran the drone through a series of maneuvers. No way could she do this enough. Every damn time the calibrations had to come back perfectly. The only way to do it was to run the drone, have her tester measure absolutely every movement it took, and then compare that against the code and results. Then she'd tweak it again and send the drone back up once more. Finally, she was satisfied she'd gotten as far as she could with her current time constraints. Her notebook open, she made several notations, locked down the code, grabbed up her remote and walked to the back of the property.

She hadn't even considered asking anybody to come out and help. Everyone else was busy inside. Tesla was also lying down, having not gotten much sleep last night. Besides, this was a whole different stage of testing. And these results needed to be exact, so it was best she did them herself.

She had several targets set up. For her, practice was very important. The drones were ultimately weapons. In order to be so, they had to have accuracy second to none. Having finally locked down the code at this stage, if the lucky charms were working for her, she could sort out the bugs in this part of the program. She buried herself in them, running the drone through the tests. She did single-shot, rapid-fire, evasive maneuvers, and then, with the drone flying high, she reached into the box she'd brought and pulled out a hand-gun. She aimed and fired. The drone took the hit, bounced to the side and immediately fired on—and hit—its target. She set it up and fired again, watching its movements.

She stepped around to see the tracker downloading all the data. Every one of the targets was hit in the bull's-eye center. So far, so good. What she needed was something so much bigger and heavier. She had an assault rifle. She didn't have a rocket launcher, so she'd wait for military testing to confirm those results.

She went through the weapons she did have available. She had emptied all three, and the drone was still in flight—looking a little worse for wear but holding its own. She opened her strongbox rifle case, locked the weapons away, then turned back and grabbed her laptop and tester. She had to download the information. This was the critical part.

As far as she was concerned, the performance had been about 90 percent, so there was room for improvement. But she'd come a long way, and because of that, she felt a heck of a lot better. As she turned to head toward the lab, she realized she wasn't alone. She stopped and saw everyone, minus Carmelita and her father, staring at her. She raised an eyebrow.

"You didn't think we'd ignore gunfire, did you?" Corey asked with a smile.

"That was quite a performance," Devlin said. "I didn't know you could shoot."

"A basic skill in my line of work," she said calmly. She walked toward them and realized they all walked backward. She turned to look behind her and then said, "What's the problem?"

Ice pointed above her.

She glanced up to see the drone, always hovering right above her head. She studied Ice's face and said, "Yeah, it's one of the tricks these guys have. It's locked on my position and will follow me." She handed her the remote. "Try to take control."

Ice accepted it, but with a frown, she asked, "Is it still weaponized?"

Bristol laughed. "It's out of ammunition, if that's what you're asking."

Ice played with the controls. "I can't get it to do anything. Why's that?"

"I added an antitheft device. The drone is locked on me. Even though it's in sad shape at present and needs repair, it's above my head until I tell it not to be."

"And how can you tell it that?" Devlin asked. He motioned to the hovering drone. "I saw this in Afghanistan. It was a pretty cool display."

Bristol pulled out her cell phone. A series of musical beeps played, and the drone came down and landed right beside her. "At the moment, I have access on my cell. I can actually coordinate to almost any computerized device. As long as I can access the codes, I can have the drone lock and follow." She pressed a different set, and the drone shot into the air. She backed up; the drone followed. She said to Devlin, "Catch."

He held out his hands, and she tossed him her phone. Immediately the drone flew over and hovered above Devlin.

"Whoa, nice control."

She grinned. "You think so?" She lifted her tablet, hit one button, and the drone returned to her. "And in case you lose your cell, you can use another device, code it, and control the drone's home placement. I call it *fostering*. No matter where it goes or with whom, the Home button will bring it back."

"It's fascinating," Ice said. "I've always loved drones. Of course it's flying, so to me it's just part and parcel of what I really love." She grinned. "But these are big and bulky."

"They are indeed," Bristol said. "In the first delivery, it's for the size. The prototype after this is already one-tenth the size. The plan is to make the prototype after that one-tenth the size yet again. The problem is making it small enough that it's good for stealth but large enough to carry the weapons."

"Do you have a prototype built to the smaller size?" Devlin asked. "And is there only one kind of weapon for this?"

Bristol shook her head. "That's another reason for the initial delivery of the larger ones. The military wants to do testing for different kinds of weapons. Size will be determined once we know the weight it will carry. Weight drains power. More power means more noise, and that means easier detection." She smiled. "I'm not reinventing the wheel. Drones are big business. What I'm producing are very small individualized ones. This is another aspect to one of the upcoming models. There will be foldable drones, almost to the size that one can keep in a carry-on."

That shot many eyebrows up. "Applications for something like what?" Tesla asked.

Bristol gave her a wry look. "War. Although what I would much prefer is to use this for scanning. I can put in heat sensors, metal detectors, and ..." Bristol motioned at Tesla. "What about ground-surveying software? I mean, the applications are endless. I'm not interested in building the large UAVs. The Hellfires out there are doing a bang-up job of dropping bombs upward of one hundred pounds of payload. Smaller, elegant, and hidden are much more my style."

She pulled out her tablet and shifted the programs. Then she held up an arm, and the drone above her head rose up slightly higher. Then using her arms, she told the drone to land. It came down slowly to the ground. She watched as it lowered itself, and seeing the wobble, realizing some of its damages.

Completely ignoring the others, she checked the drone's

fabric. "Still weak on that joint. I need to fix that."

"Really? You tried to shoot it down a half-dozen times. What did you expect?" Easton stated in disbelief.

She shot him a look. "I didn't expect to weaken a joint. They're already weak, so I reinforce them so they don't become worse. In this case it wasn't enough." She pulled out her tablet and typed notes while everybody watched.

Tesla spoke up. "This is truly amazing, Bristol. I had no idea you were working on this."

Bristol sighed. "I'm working on so much, so many cool things these guys could do. But I'm stuck with a stupid contract."

"Why do they want so many? I don't understand that," Devlin said. "Usually a contract is to develop one. And when they like it, they turn around and order more."

"True enough. But these are specs. I've already delivered a basic prototype and showed them an upgraded version I had with me at the time. It's those they ordered fifty of. But what they wanted was the more general drone, size-wise. They don't even know about these other prototypes. My goal was to give them the fifty they requested as part of the contract. While I was there, I'd hoped to show them some of the new developments and get a better contract for the next one."

In a quiet voice, Ice said, "What you should do is get one advanced prototype and see if you can interest the military directly."

"So your contract isn't with the military?" Easton asked.

"No, it's with ENFAQ, under Brent's recommendation. So it doesn't make any sense that he'd be sabotaging my work."

"Unless he's being paid to have your contract fall

through somehow," Tesla said. "I wouldn't put that past him."

Ice looked over at Tesla. "That makes a lot of sense. Do you know Brent?"

Tesla shook her head. "No, but I've dealt with military contracts." She shook her head. "Most of them are not much fun. And if Brent is an asshole, well …"

She turned back to Bristol. "You were really excited about the contract in the beginning and then quickly soured on it. But didn't you tell me something about personal differences between you and Brent?"

"He wanted more from me personally than I was interested in giving," she said. "Originally our verbal agreement was for just five of these units. Then he handed over the contract and had upped the delivery to fifty. He told me that he could make it easier on me if I'd do the same on him." She shrugged. "I didn't ask details, just said no thanks. But the contract was written. So either I could sign it or not. My choice. It was for more money, and I had hoped it would lead to bigger and better things."

"I'll talk to one or two people about this," Ice said. "I'm afraid this contract is something you're stuck with, and we'll do our best to help you meet it. But if the military saw what you're doing here …" She shook her head.

"Too bad Brent was intent on screwing you over."

"Almost literally," Bristol said with a laugh. "He didn't take my rejection well."

"Tough shit," Tesla said strongly. "Why should a woman have to sleep with a guy in order to get a contract?"

"I agree," Ice said. "But you can't change the way of the world overnight." She smiled at the other two women. "We just have to be better." With a laughing glance at the males, she turned and walked inside.

Harrison groaned. "I think that was a *dis* on us guys."

"Like hell," Rhodes said. "We're not second to anyone. But I agree with Ice. Women shouldn't be either." He motioned at the drone. "Can I carry this inside for you?"

Bristol grinned. "Yes, please. Thanks for the help. They can get heavy by the end of the day. I really don't want to fly it anymore until I can fix that wing."

"That's also a very special material. The military will be interested in that."

"As you can see, it's bulletproof." Bristol grinned. "It's also superlight. Although, if I can make it lighter yet again, that would be better."

"Not today," Devlin said beside her. "You need to show the military your new drones. Then they can negotiate with you directly. In the meantime, we must ensure nobody else knows what the hell you're up to because this will attract a lot of attention, especially the wrong kind."

With a final glance around, Bristol nodded and went inside her home. At the back doorway, she turned and asked, "Would you guys mind bringing in those weapons? I locked them in the case down by the target practice. But I really don't want them to go missing." She reached into her pocket and held out the key. "I have a weapons room in the lab."

Ryder snagged the key from Bristol's hand. "I'll get them. Nothing I like better than a little weapon time."

She chuckled as he walked away. "These guys are terrific."

"They sure are." Devlin looped an arm around her shoulders as they entered the kitchen. "This is a hell of a place you built yourself here."

She laughed. "Thank my father for that."

Just as she walked by the dining room, an alarm broke out across the house. She froze, dropped all her gear and raced for the stairs. She heard Devlin's voice behind her.

He yelled, "What is that?"

"The chemical lab," she cried out. "My father."

She bolted through double doors and raced downstairs. She could hear footsteps coming behind her. She hit the bottom door at full speed and barreled out into the short hallway. She stopped and stared. Her father's lab was under double-lockdown as normal. Cautiously she approached. None of the sensors outside revealed any leak. But the alarm noted somebody had entered.

She stared through the window in the door but couldn't see anything. No one was inside. Frowning, she turned. Most of the others milled around her. "The alarm went off, so somebody entered this floor." She pointed at the chemical room. "That room is the concern, but it's still secure. I don't see anybody in there."

"Could they have left already?"

She shrugged. "I don't know." Her phone rang. "Carmelita?"

"Your father is missing."

She groaned. "Okay, I'll look for him." She glanced around at the others. "My father's gone missing. This is his lab. Can you guys spread out and see if you can find him?"

They all went into this crazy stealth mode and disappeared. She'd never seen this many men move so quietly in her life.

She keyed in her passcode and stepped into her father's lab. "Father, are you here?"

Silence. If he hadn't recognized her this morning, then he likely wouldn't now. But she could always hope. She headed straight for his office, pushed open the door, and with Devlin behind her, she stepped inside.

Someone blasted past her, pushing her out of the way. She barely caught sight of the man in black as he slammed up against the brick wall named Devlin.

Instantly the man was on the ground, and Devlin was on top of him.

She leaned against the wall, hand to her chest. Thank God it wasn't her father.

She looked around, then down at the man struggling to breathe under Devlin's knee. "Find out if that guy did anything with my father."

Devlin shot her a look and nodded. "Look inside the office. Maybe he's in there."

She checked but found no sign of him. "No, he's not here." She called Carmelita back. "Any sign of him?"

Her housekeeper answered in a tearful cry, "No." Then she started apologizing. "I was cleaning all the rooms. I never thought to check on him. So many people are here, it never occurred to me that he could leave without someone seeing him."

"When did you last see him?" Bristol rubbed her temple. Her father had disappeared before but not for a long time. Normally he never got as far as the front door. If he did, he couldn't get out of the grounds. That was one of the things she counted on.

As the men collected around the intruder, she said, "He's still missing. Could you please go out and search the grounds?"

Again they all disappeared.

"Let's take him out of here." He quickly hooked hand-cuffs on the man's wrists behind him, pulled him up on his feet. "Recognize him?"

She glanced at the man's face, then shook her head. He looked more of a bruiser than an intruder. She walked up to him. "Why are you here?"

He gave her a sideways glance but didn't answer.

She was such a fool. These guys never talked. She said to Devlin, "Maybe you could just run his prints, and we'll figure out who he is. Then we can call the military and see if they want to talk to him."

"Military?" the man asked. "Why would you hand me over to them?"

"Because I'm ultimately working on military defense weapons here," she said quietly, "and you breaking into my place means you're either after my material or to sabotage my work. In that case the military might be very interested in you."

"Oh, no, you don't," he snapped. "No way am I getting into that. I was just sent here to determine how far along you are, then to get the hell out. I saw the drone demonstration outside. While you were all there, I came in. But no way in hell are you handing me over to the military."

She studied him carefully. "If you saw the demonstration, who the hell do you think I'm working for?"

He glanced nervously from Devlin to her. "I heard you stole the information. And you have a contract you won't be able to make. They want to know how much you've done."

"So you work for Brent?"

"I have no idea who that is."

She believed him. Brent wouldn't have hired this guy himself. He would've gotten somebody else to do the dirty work.

"Do you work for another company that's building

drones?" Devlin asked. When the guy pinched his lips together, Devlin nodded. "These are military-grade weapons. You'll pay the price no matter who it is you work for."

The man shook his head rapidly. "I told you. I've got nothing to do with the military."

"I don't care what you say," she snapped. "I don't have time for this. Devlin, call the DOD. They can do whatever the hell they want with him, including throw away the goddamn key. For all I know, they still line up guys like you and shoot them with a firing squad."

She turned and headed back toward the elevator, intent on going upstairs. The priority at the moment was her father. She trusted Devlin to keep this asshole in check. She didn't believe all the intruder had said, but half of her realized he'd been told only part of her story. She had no idea how he'd gotten onto the property, though getting inside had been easy. She'd left the rear entrance open while working in the backyard. That guy had no idea how lucky he was, considering the chemical lab was down here. She didn't even know what to do with most of them. Her father had walked out one day, and she'd never caught him in a lucid state since. For all she knew, working with those chemicals had brought on her father's mental condition.

And it sucked. Big time. But that level was locked off for that reason. She needed to get a chemical engineer to go through the place and ensure it was safe. Her father had had several accidents. When they'd actually found him, wandering around with full-blown dementia, she'd been out of town for several weeks. She'd seen the onset coming but only in a minor way. She hadn't realized how bad it was until she came back and saw him, still in his lab coat, obviously distressed after an accident of some kind.

Immediately afterward she'd gone downstairs, locked up all the rooms, set up security passcodes on the dangerous lab, and that had been the end of it. She'd forgotten about it. She'd do away with it at some point because it was a ticking time bomb. But at least one safely locked up for now.

She ran to her father's bedroom, found it empty, then checked his bath and on to her room. By the time she went through all the guestrooms and back to the living room, she found no sign of him. She headed out to the garage.

Once before her father had tried to drive away in his car. Somehow he had gotten into the vehicle, turned it on and hit the garage door but hadn't even closed the driver's door. He had still been prepared to drive out nonetheless. He'd also been in his pyjamas and bare feet.

No sign of him in the garage. She raced outside and checked the front. On the driveway she caught sight of his robe belt. The one that always hung askew from his bath-robe. But as she raced to the gate and saw the security system was off and the gate hung slightly ajar, she realized the truth.

He was gone.

And not likely by choice.

DEVLIN PULLED OUT his phone and called Mason. His friend answered and he quickly explained the situation.

"An intruder? Jesus, she's got her hands full of trouble already."

"Yeah. I don't know anything about the intruder yet. He's here beside me. I'll send you a picture." He quickly took a snapshot of the man's face and sent it to Mason. "Her father's still missing too. Everybody's searching the grounds, so I can't say at this moment just what the problem is, but it could be bad news."

"Right. Let me hear as soon as you know something. I got the photo. I'll run it through facial recognition." His voice slowed as he said, "I don't think I recognize this guy. I'll call you back if I find anything."

Pocketing his phone, Devlin took the prisoner to the garage—a safer space for a little more interrogation—taking him closer to the workbench, where Devlin grabbed several bungee cords and a chair, and sat the guy down away from the workbench off to the side. Then he quickly wrapped one of the cords around the man's ankles. He wasn't going anywhere. Then he looped one around his handcuffed wrists and the chair. "Now you stay here," Devlin said with a chuckle.

The man struggled and said, "You can't keep me here."

"You're the one who trespassed on Bristol's home and property, intent on corporate espionage, finding military secrets."

"I told you how it's all a mistake. The company's just worried she can't fulfil her contract."

"You mean, the company is worried she *can*, and they want to know how far along she is because they want to replace her." At the guy's startled jerk and his darting glance to the side, Devlin realized he'd hit the nail on the head. "So as soon as we can pinpoint who your company is, we'll know exactly who is behind the sabotage going on in her world."

"Hey, I haven't done any kind of sabotage," he said. "I'm just here looking for information."

Just then the garage door burst open, and Bristol raced toward the intruder. She reached back and with a heavy hand, smacked the guy across the face. Distraught, her voice breaking, she said, "No, you're not. You're the diversion.

Somebody took my father." Tears were in her eyes. "He barely knows his own name. How could you do something like that to him?"

The man shook his head. "No. No, I'm not part of that."

"*That?*" Devlin asked in a hard voice. "So you knew about the kidnapping?"

The guy shook his head wildly, as if understanding finally just how dangerous a position he was in.

She glared at him. "If he won't talk to us, take him out back and shoot him. Better yet, let him run. I'll test my drones out for real."

"Whoa, whoa! You can't do that. That's not legal to do something like that," he protested. "That's inhumane."

She shoved her face into his, grabbed his ear and twisted it hard in a circle. When he yelled, she said, "So was taking my father, asshole." She belted him again.

Devlin caught her in his arms and held her close. "We'll find your father. Take it easy. This guy, he's nothing."

"He's garbage." She glared at him. "Just kill him." She turned and walked into the house.

"Hey, man, I didn't have anything to do with her father's kidnapping," the intruder protested in a panic.

"Yeah, but we don't believe you, so I guess I'll do what the lady asked." Devlin kept his voice calm, quiet, unconcerned. Enough that it sounded like this guy was just one more irritant Devlin didn't need.

"I'm serious, man. Okay, so the company asked me to come and check to see how far along she was because they were concerned she might actually make the contract. I don't know anything about sabotage or kidnapping. I was asked to come here, take videos, and figure out how well she was doing. That's it."

"Then what the hell were you doing downstairs in the chemical room?"

He shook his head. "It's not where I wanted to end up, I tell you. I thought her lab was on the bottom floor. When I made it that far and saw the warning signs, Jesus, I thought for sure I'd walked into something out of a horror movie," he cried. "Then I couldn't figure out how to get the hell out without setting off more alarms."

"But you were outside watching her demonstration?"

He nodded. "Yeah. The company just wanted to make sure she couldn't make her contract." He shook his head. "I shouldn't even say that much."

"Well, you'd better keep talking," Devlin said. "I have a lot more questions."

CHAPTER 13

B RISTOL HAD HER father's bathrobe belt wrapped around her hands in the middle of the driveway, staring at the damaged gate. Her mind couldn't quite compute the evidence in front of her. She wanted to believe her father had left on his own. But no way could he damage the gate. Not unless he had taken a vehicle. She spun and stared at the garage, her mind mentally cataloguing the vehicles there. He had a classic he liked to drive in good weather. But he was also protective of that baby. It was hard to imagine he could have damaged the gate with the classic car. But she had to check and make sure. She raced to the second garage on the far side.

Actually it was a three-car garage but with only one vehicle inside. She punched in her security code and went in the side door. The '69 Mustang was still here.

"Oh, dear God." She stepped back out, locked it up and pulled out her phone. No way could he have left on his own. Not unless the intruder had raced out, damaging the gate, and her father had seen the opening and walked out. That was just too much of a coincidence. Talk about a comedy of errors.

"Who are you calling?" Tesla asked, racing toward her.

"The police. I don't know who else to call." She raised her ravaged gaze to her friend. "Dad's gone. There's no sign of him, and the gate's been damaged. We have an intruder in the other garage. Devlin's holding him. I want to torture him to tell me where my father is. He says he doesn't know. But I don't believe him." She cried, "I just want whatever information he has."

"Let's check the security cams first."

Bristol stared at her in shock. "Oh, my God! What's wrong with me? I'm not even thinking straight." She had trouble putting her phone in her pocket with her shaking hands. "I have to get a hold of myself so I can help him."

"We'll find him. Come on. Let's get to the security camera feed."

With Tesla at her side, they raced to the security room. The one she hadn't even shown the others. Of course Tesla knew about it. Bristol quickly unlocked the room, which was barely big enough for all the computer equipment, and stepped inside. The others—except for Devlin, still with the intruder in the garage—had followed and gathered around her.

Once Harrison saw this, he whistled and said, "If you know what you're doing, great. If you don't, let me."

She turned to look at him in confusion.

His voice gentle, he said, "Bristol, let me handle this."

Tesla gently propelled Bristol out of the small room so Harrison could enter. He sat down at the security camera feed, and within seconds, had the front gate brought up. "You recognize this vehicle?"

Bristol neared to stare at the TV monitor and shook her head. "Black sedan, smoked windows. But no."

Rhodes, standing out in the hallway, said, "I'm already running the license plate."

She nodded. "You guys know what to do with this. I

haven't a clue. Please help me get my father back. I presume the same people who did this were sabotaging my work. Just one more distraction to stop me from getting ahead."

The others froze for a second, contemplating it.

Corey said, "It makes the most sense. We just can't stop looking at other options."

"Shouldn't we call the police?" Bristol asked.

Ice shook her head. "Not yet. We will once we know something."

"How do we track the vehicle? How do we find out who the hell is doing this and where they've taken my father?"

"They had the security code for the gate," Harrison said.

"What?" She watched as he replayed the video, showing where the black car drove up, punched in a number and the gate opened.

"No way should they know that. I just reset it when I got home."

"It's easy enough. They took out your system, and they changed the code themselves."

"But I have a special override."

She watched in shock as her father was led through the front door and into the back of the car, losing his bathrobe belt in the process.

As the black car sped toward the gate, it started to close. The driver sped up, made it through, but the gate crunched the back end of his car.

Harrison looked at her. "Is that your override protection?"

"Yes," she said. "It's a rebound call. If after a certain time, I don't punch another number the gate automatically closes and locks."

"Nice." He nodded in approval.

She shook her head. "But useless. They still got out. They weren't supposed to."

"And that means they knew exactly where your father was, got him out and took off before the override. That doesn't mean they knew about it, they just happened to get lucky. They weren't here"—he checked the monitors—"even five minutes."

She sighed. "And the override is set for five."

"I presume then," Tesla said, "the asshole Devlin's holding in the garage knew where your father was. Maybe even helped move him toward the front door so he could be picked up faster."

"That is the most likely scenario." Harrison quickly ripped through a series of other cameras and said, "They came in the front door, and look here."

He pointed to two people walking down the front hall they'd all entered the day before. There she saw her father coming around the corner and yes, a gloved hand on his shoulder. Her father was grabbed roughly, confusion on his face, fear in his eyes, as they moved him when he protested. One of the men bent, picked him up and ran out the front door.

"A snatch and grab. Inside intel. And they were gone."

"And the plates are coming up stolen."

"Of course. They knew they'd be inside the compound, and the license plate would be easily seen. They'll ditch the car as fast as possible because it's got obvious damage from the gate."

Bristol leaned back against the doorjamb and sagged. "Oh, my God! My poor father."

Tesla squeezed her shoulder. "We'll get him back. Stay strong."

She nodded, reaching up to rub her temple. "Satellite would track that, wouldn't it? Could it have seen them as they drove away?"

Harrison turned to stare at her. "You have satellite?" he asked incredulously.

She shook her head. "No, I don't." She straightened in shock. "But I might have something better. I have to go to the lab. Now."

She bolted from the room, ran back down the hallway to the elevator and dashed to her lab. She forgot the security code, having to enter it twice she was so frantic.

"Easy, Bristol. Just calm down. This isn't helping anything," Tesla told her.

Bristol reached up, smashed the doorframe, the frustration eating at her. She took a deep breath and then tried again. This time the light switched from red to green, and the door unlocked. She walked inside, headed for a cupboard on the far side and pulled out her baby. "You've never seen this before. I would really appreciate it if you don't tell anybody about it."

They gathered around her, like kids in a candy store. She opened the box and pulled out what appeared to be a common everyday swallow. But it was a mechanical one.

"Oh, my," Ice said in awe. "Is that what I think it is?"

"It's actually more than you think it is."

She brought up her laptop, quickly accessed the server and typed in the code she needed. She plugged the swallow into her USB cable and downloaded the coordinates she needed it to follow. She started the GPS tracker, double-checked it was at full power and said, "I don't know for how long this can run. It'll depend on the wind conditions. But I need somebody on the ground right now to follow it."

"How can anyone follow the swallow?" Ryder asked. "It's damn near impossible to see."

She looked up at him, her eyes hard, her gaze almost dark and said, "Exactly." She pivoted the laptop so they could see the beeping that showed the location it was at. "I set the coordinates for my father's implant. And just like the drones that follow me overhead," she said, "this is geared to find him. And it will give us the GPS directions as it travels."

A moment of silence passed as everybody inhaled that information, then a fervent whisper came from Ice. "Oh, my God. That's so damn perfect."

"Shit. Did you actually build that?" Harrison asked, right before his phone rang.

She nodded, snatched up the swallow and laptop, and ran up the stairs. "I have three of them."

She raced out the front door and did something that made the others wince. She took the swallow and threw it high into the sky as far as she could. The swallow hovered above for the first second. A series of low clicks and taps followed, then it shot off into the sky. "Go, go, go."

She searched the crowd. "Devlin?"

He was at her side instantly. "What did I miss?"

"I'll explain as we go." She tossed him her car keys, not bothering to ask what else he had gotten from the intruder. She trusted he was secure regardless. "We need to go, and now." He raced to her car. She hopped into the passenger side, calling out to the others. "We'll need backup."

"We've got it."

She saw Easton and Ryder run to the jeep. She had no idea about the others. Devlin was already maneuvering her car around the busted gate.

As they shot off down the street, he asked, "Where to?"

"Head toward San Diego. Take the highway. I'll tell you when to get off."

"I'm at least ten minutes getting to the highway."

"Hopefully you won't be," she said. "We may not have that long." She appreciated his foot-to-the-floorboard technique as the car zoomed ahead. "If you don't know where you're going, just tell me."

"I'm familiar with the area." He shaved off three minutes while she tracked the signal heading straight toward the city. "You want to explain what the hell we're doing?"

She gave him the short version. Tapping the monitor screen, she said, "This is the swallow. It's tracking and gaining proximity to my father."

"What's the distance?"

"Half a mile. It has a burst in the first thirty seconds as it reaches out for the signal. After that the distance is short-ened. If I could figure out a way to keep up the power during all this, I could probably extend the distance." She felt his stare. But ignored it. She just kept talking. "I think there's a lot of usability for something like this."

"You think?" He shook his head. "This is huge."

"Well, not really. The swallow has to be able to track something. In this case, both my father and I have embedded chips." She pointed to her forearm at a spot just before her elbow. "We had them implanted a long time ago. That was my father's security precaution when I was just a toddler. But they are old. He built a tracker, but never bothered to update it, and thirty years of change in technology is a lot. But he never thought his daughter would be creating something to keep him safe." Her voice turned bitter at the end. "I should've kept him safe."

"You're doing what you can. It's a hell of a lot more than

most people have. A method to track their loved ones."

She settled back into her seat. "I should be able to track more than just that. Wait 'til you see what I can find out about his vitals."

DEVLIN WAS GRATEFUL that Harrison and Rhodes had arrived when they did to look after the intruder and also to give him a quick update on Bristol's whereabouts. Devlin told them the little bit the guy had shared but left them free to get more. As he ran from the garage, he heard the intruder cry out, "No! I don't know anything."

"Well, these two will figure out if you do or not," Devlin called back.

Once he joined Bristol, the two of them were in her vehicle within seconds, driving after her father.

He was still wrapping his mind around the idea she'd built a drone to track her father. One she could change the code in to track something completely different when needed. The applications were endless. And hers resembled a swallow, but it could be any shape. She presently tracked her father's vitals to see if he was alive and how he was doing.

Kudos to her and her father. Devlin and his team had come up against ID chips on kids of wealthy families but those were specific microchips for tracking and modern tech devices. Her father had been way ahead of the game decades earlier. Talk about being beyond Devlin's capabilities. He shook his head. "What you've done is fantastic."

"It would be if it worked," she snapped. "But so far every damn thing I'm doing has failed."

He knew the reality, however. He couldn't give her enough assurances to convince her what a hell of a job she was doing. But those on the outside knew. He wondered if these people ever reached a state of perfection, those with minds that could conjure up ideas and create them. Were they ever satisfied with their products?

He'd once asked Tesla why she wouldn't stop tweaking the code on her programs. "Why not just build a new one?"

She had laughed and said, "I am. But so many things could be done to improve it that, as I learn something new, I feel compelled to backtrack. At some point the old system becomes faulty. Just too many upgrades and changes in patches. The new software hopefully will be ready to slide in over the top." She shook her head. "But at this point I can be tweaking and planning for the next upgrade."

He imagined that was very similar to what Bristol went through on a regular basis. As he thought about the drones she was building, he knew they were actually light years ahead of the others, and that the military would really want them. But he had to stop Brent and this company. Devlin understood the middlemen were making money off people like Bristol. But it was damn time for her to step up and the world to recognize that she did this. And she didn't need Brent.

Devlin's contacts didn't include anybody that high up in the military. But certainly a lot of people were around who did know such valuable people. Tesla's father had a lot of connections. So did Mason. For that matter, so did Levi. Hell, a lot of former military personnel were in their worlds. Surely somebody knew somebody. If they could get Bristol to connect directly with the military, she could dump the middlemen.

With the work he had seen of hers already, he knew she'd make a killing.

"He's still alive," she said in a hard, thin voice. "But his heart rate is erratic and slowing."

"*Slowing?* I thought it would be faster from the stress and fear."

"I'm afraid they've given him a sedative." She lifted her head and gazed at him.

He glanced at her, but from the almost blank look in her eyes, he figured she saw something she wasn't telling him about.

"He becomes quite irrational when he's upset. He'll lash out, hit, walk away, cry, and yell. He won't understand, he'll be upset and won't be afraid to let anybody know."

He understood. "It must've been a very difficult few years for you."

"Much harder for him. He just didn't understand. And no way could I make it any clearer to him." She started clicking on the keyboard. "I'm getting the coordinates now. It appears they've turned off the highway."

He looked for the exits. "Left or right?"

"Stay in the right lane," she said. "I need to see what turnoff they took."

He waited.

Finally she said, "Take the East exit."

"The sign for it just whipped past. It's right here," he said. "They can't be too far ahead of us then."

"In a way just barely enough for me to track the swallow," she admitted. "If they were already at their location, we could map a route. But instead I'm waiting for the location to show up and figure where that is exactly as I don't have the GPS on Google Maps. I'm taking the coordinates, typing them in and finding locations."

"Something you can integrate later?"

"Yes, definitely. I've never actually had a chance to run this program, so I had no idea what was required."

He could almost hear the wheels of her brain turning, figuring out a better method. He saw the aerial view on the laptop. And, of course, that didn't lock on street signs.

He slowed, took the turn, ran the car around the corner and checked behind to see that the other two vehicles were following. Then he merged into the new street, drove down it for another couple miles, and pulled up to a stop light. "Anything new?"

"They're taking a turn, just blocks up," she said. Her voice was distracted. Her fingers busy.

He pulled out his phone and called Ryder, quickly relaying the updates. He said, "I'm leaving the phone open on the seat between us. As she gives us instructions, you'll hear them too."

Ryder said, "Sounds good."

"Take a left," Bristol said.

He pulled up to the fourth block and put on his left turn signal. When there was an opening, he took it onto the side street. They were in a half-business, half-residential district. Lots of suburban businesses on the bottom and apartments on the top. As he drove down the side street, the apartments gave way to small houses and condo complexes.

"The signal stopped."

He glanced at her, startled. "Have you lost it?"

"No, as in the vehicle has stopped, and so has the swallow. And my father is up ahead."

Ryder's voice came through the phone on the seat between them. "How far ahead?"

"Four, three, two," she counted the blocks. Devlin slowed the car at the next intersection. "The block ahead of us?"

"Yes."

He studied the street. No sign of the car. Large properties were here, separated by fences high with cedar hedges. Not much visibility. He wouldn't see the car until he drove in. "Can you see how far down?"

She said, "Turn the corner here, park on the side. I can find the swallow."

Doing as instructed, Devlin pulled forward, took the left corner and parked around the far side.

She hopped out, remote in her hand, and set up a signal. She turned in a circle and tracked it. "Second house from the corner."

Ryder said, "We'll take a walk, one in front, the other in back. We'll check out the house from here."

Devlin grabbed the phone. "Right. I'm here with her. You guys stay out of sight."

She said, "I want to go into the house."

He shook his head. "You did what you needed to get us here. Your job's done. Let us take over."

She opened her mouth, snapped it shut, stared for a long moment, and then nodded. "Let's hope you do a better job at recovering my father than I did at keeping him safe."

Devlin shook his head. "We're so having a talk about that. But later. Right now this is all about finding your father."

CHAPTER 14

S HE STAYED BEHIND the tree, leaning casually as she played with the remote in her hand. She knew she wasn't visible from the house, unless somebody actually came out past the cedar hedge to look. She reached inside, grabbed her laptop, and then sat behind the car, sitting cross-legged with the laptop balancing on her legs. She had the address now. She could get all kinds of information.

She could hear Devlin talking to Ice on the phone, bringing her up to date, giving her the location. Bristol could only hope things went smoothly from here. Somebody had gone to a lot of trouble to take her father. They wouldn't let him go so easily.

When he was done with his phone call, she said, "The house is registered to the Sunset Corp."

"It's probably a holding company," he said. "Do you recognize any of the names on the Board of Directors?"

"Looking now." She sighed. "They own ENFAQ. It's one of their companies."

"So that's the company Brent works for?"

She nodded. "Yes."

"Well, that answers that. Chances are it's the same people then."

She nodded. Inside she was just plain sad. "I had such high hopes for this. Why the hell are these people such assholes?" She stood, put the laptop back inside the car and locked it. She turned to him. "Now what?"

He gave her a hard glance. "We wait. We trust Easton and Ryder." Just then the phone rang. "What's up, Easton?"

"Looks like somebody's on the second floor. We found the vehicle, in the back garage. Ryder's inside. He confirmed the damage on the back right-hand side of the car. He's getting the VIN number for us."

"Any other vehicles?" Devlin held the phone so she could hear.

"No. But her father didn't come alone so expect at least two more people."

"Right. Chances are there are twice that many."

Easton's voice changed. "I just saw somebody on the main floor. I can see an open window downstairs. I need to get in and do a floor-by-floor search."

"Not alone."

"No, Ryder's joining me from the garage. We'll check back in five." He clicked off.

Devlin stared at the house. He hated to have two men go in. Especially when he was so far away. He turned to study the houses on either side. The one at the corner was for sale. No way to tell if it was currently occupied or not. But if he and Bristol could get into that yard, it would provide better access to the house they ultimately needed to get into.

In a low voice, he said, "We'll walk over and take a look at the house for sale. Act like a married couple, looking to buy the house. My men are in the house doing a floor-by-floor search.

She gasped. "Isn't that dangerous?"

He just stared at her.

She said, "Yeah, I get it. You do danger."

"We do big danger," he said with a whisper. "Don't you forget it." But he winked at her and wrapped an arm around her shoulders, tucking her up gently as he led her across the street. They walked toward the house for sale, stood on the driveway and stared.

"It's actually not all that bad," she said in a half-strangled voice, her body stiff. She was so close to the house. Were they being watched?

He chuckled. "But not all that great either."

At his nudge, they walked up to the front door, then around to the back as if looking for the Realtor to see inside. On the other side, out of sight from anybody else, he walked to the fenced side between him and the house where her father was being held. The wooden fence was solid and in good shape—also a good six feet high with an alleyway access.

He stepped out with her hand in his, keeping her shielded by his body. He peered around at the house.

THERE WAS NO sign of them. But he could see the open window. As an invitation? A trap? He'd seen it all. It was hard to plan for every contingency. But failure was not an option.

The biggest problem was he didn't want to go in to help search and leave Bristol alone outside. Given what she'd said, there was no guarantee her father would calm down at the sight of her, so they really didn't need Bristol for that, but it was the best option they had. Her father could potentially be very unruly.

His phone buzzed. That was the signal. The downstairs was clear. In a low voice, he told her that. Immediately she stuffed her fist in her mouth and buried her head against his chest. He wrapped his arms around her and said, "Take it easy. That's good news."

She shook her head. "How can you do this? My nerves are stretched so thin it feels like butter spread onto bread."

He gently rubbed her back up and down. "It's what we do. The nerves and the adrenaline get to us sometimes. However, we're doing exactly what we need to do."

A second buzz came through. He pulled his phone out and checked. The text simply read:

One down.

He showed her and watched as her gaze widened. She wanted to peer around the hedge again, but he pulled her back. "It's a really tough time."

She gazed up at him, not understanding.

"When people are under attack, their instincts go on alert. They search, looking around for what's wrong. We don't want them to look outside and see you standing here."

She let out her breath and nodded. He had to admit she was good at following orders. He kept her up tight, the phone in his hand, willing her to relax. He could feel the adrenaline rushing through him right now. He wanted to race in there and start pounding people into the ground.

The more unfriendlies who could be taken out, the better. This was also not an official mission. And the police wouldn't take kindly to them taking this into their own hands. So the least amount of damage, the better.

Afterward was a whole different story. Still he was hoping to not be the one to handle the police. He didn't have a whole lot of patience for that process.

But he'd do what he had to do. They all would. A third

buzz came through. He held it up for her to read.

In a low voice, she whispered, "Two down." She turned and stared at him. "We counted two in the house. Do you think there's more?"

He shrugged. "We'll know in a few minutes."

She reached up a trembling hand and gently stroked his face. "Thank you."

He raised an eyebrow at her. "For what?"

"For everything. For helping me in Afghanistan, for coming back with me. For bringing all these people in. For following my father, trying to help him." She gave a broken laugh. "There's no way I'll be able to repay you."

He closed her mouth with a gentle nudge of her chin. "No repayment necessary. There are some good guys in the world."

She searched his gaze as if looking for the truth and then gave a beautiful slow smile that made his heart race. "There might be good guys," she said, "but I haven't been very lucky meeting them."

He smiled. "And maybe your luck just changed."

He reached down against his better judgment—knowing it was so not the time but unable to resist the wet lips in front of him—and gave her the gentlest kiss.

His phone buzzed. "Let's go," he said. "House is clear."

"Did they find my father? Did they find anybody else?"

"Two more men down." He turned and shot her a hard look. "And, yes, to your father. But he's not in very good shape." He watched the color drain from her face. He grabbed her hand and said, "Don't faint on me. Your father needs you."

She shook her head. "I've never fainted in my goddamn life. Right now, I'm wishing to hell they hadn't knocked all four men down. I'd punch one or two myself." And she raced into the house ahead of him.

The rear door was open and showed a kitchen. At the landing to the stairs, he stepped in front and led the way. He went up to the second floor to the bedroom on the left to find both Easton and Ryder there. And on the bed, curled up in a fetal position, was her father.

"Oh, my God! Daddy."

CHAPTER 15

AND ON AT that note, things went to hell. She spun and said, "He needs medical attention and now." She pulled her phone out and dialed 911.

When she finished with the call, she turned and looked at Devlin. "What do we tell the police?"

The three men exchanged glances and asked, "The truth?"

"And our excuse for not calling them right away?"

"Think fast," Devlin said. "The ambulance is almost here."

She stared at him in surprise. "It must've been around the corner then." She ran downstairs to let them in.

The ambulance parked out front of the house. Two men jumped out, the first racing toward her.

"He's upstairs to the left."

The paramedic ran up the stairs. The second man unloaded a stretcher from the back of the ambulance.

She ran upstairs to see the paramedic checking her father over. The stretcher arrived. All four of them were quietly told to leave the room.

Her father was loaded up, covered with a blanket and strapped down.

Within minutes they had him moved downstairs and in the back of the ambulance.

Bristol hopped up in the back and said to Devlin, "I'll call you when I get to the hospital."

He nodded. "We'll wait for the police."

She shot him a grateful look, jumped back out, threw her arms around him and gave him a kiss before climbing back into the ambulance. The doors shut, and they were gone, sirens blaring, lights flashing.

Sending a last wave through the window, she turned her attention to her father and the man leaning over him.

But he was sitting beside her now, a needle in his hand. "Nice of you to join us, Bristol McEwan." And he slid the needle into her arm.

DEVLIN STARED AT the ambulance as it disappeared from sight. He shook his head and turned to find Ryder and Easton, staring at him, huge grins on their faces.

"What?"

Ryder said, "Yep, Mason's luck struck again."

He stared at them in surprise, then frowned. "Like hell," he said good-naturedly. "This has got nothing to do with that."

"No course not." Easton smirked. "Wait until the others hear about it."

"There's nothing to tell," he snapped. "Where the hell are the cops? The 911 call went out. Doesn't that mean everybody, fire truck, ambulance, and police? Why was there only one ambulance?"

Just then he heard the cops in the distance. He rolled his eyes. "Finally our city's finest doing their job."

"Go easy on them. You don't know where the hell they're coming from."

Devlin nodded. "True enough." He tried to calm down. "We need to track down who the hell was behind this kidnapping. Did you guys happen to get any ideas from the men upstairs?"

"Pictures and a couple IDs," Ryder said easily. "I sent everything to Mason and Ice. They're looking into who they are."

He nodded. "Good. Once the police are involved, we'll get hit for information."

"True enough."

Two cruisers pulled up and parked out front. The cops opened the doors, walked over and said, "You called 911?"

"Bristol did," Devlin said. "The ambulance got here ahead of you. She left with the injured man. We got four men down in the house."

"Four men down?" the officer asked, his voice turning ugly. "And who dropped them. Are they dead?"

"We dropped them. No, they're not dead. They're the ones who kidnapped the old man who just left in the ambulance."

Another siren split through the air, and an ambulance screamed around the corner and parked on the opposite side of the road. *Another ambulance?* Devlin shook his head. "You guys are late. The other ambulance already got here."

The medic looked at him and said, "What? We're the only ambulance available. Everybody's off on a call on the bad multicar pileup on the I5."

Devlin stared at him. He could feel the color bleaching from his face. He pulled out his phone, his gaze going hard right to Ryder and Easton. "I sure as hell hope you're wrong," he snapped. "Otherwise the goddamn kidnappers had an ambulance ready to take the father away, and now they've kidnapped both of them."

"You better start at the beginning. Who the hell is it that's been kidnapped?"

Devlin stared at the officer as he was dialing Bristol's phone. "Bristol McEwan, and her father, Jerome. They're both military weapon designers."

The policemen's eyebrows rocketed upward. "And you think this is connected to their work?"

Devlin nodded. "I know it is." He held the phone to his ear. In a low voice he whispered, "Come on, Bristol. Answer your goddamn phone."

But no answer came.

In shock, he turned to face his men. "She's not answering."

"Try it again. There could be lots of reasons why she's not."

"Right." None of them were good. But that didn't mean her father hadn't taken a turn for the worse, and she wasn't hovering over him. A buzzing phone was hardly a priority at that moment. He quickly redialed and held the phone to his ear. His heart pounded against his chest, and his fists clenched as he waited. Suddenly the call was answered.

"Bristol? Are you okay?"

"Bristol is fine," said a man, his voice unfamiliar to Devlin. "For the moment. And as long as you don't follow us."

And then he hung up.

Devlin groaned, his heart clenching with fear. "They've got her. We actually handed over the father and daughter. They have kidnapped both of them."

CHAPTER 16

B RISTOL AWOKE, FEELING groggy and disoriented. She
lay still for a moment, her mind grappling with the new
reality—one of pain and confusion. She wanted to move, but
this voice screamed through her head that said, *Lie still.* She
didn't know whose voice it was or if it was her own subconscious—but it was strong enough to keep her still.

She lifted her lids ever-so-slightly. She was in danger and
had no reason why. Her mind struggled to put the jumbled
memories back in the right order. Her father had been taken.
Devlin and she followed him with the swallow. They'd
found the house and her father. Relief washed through her at
that. Surely whatever happened after that couldn't be all that
bad.

And that's when she remembered the rest. The needle,
the look on the man's face as he shoved the needle deep into
her arm, and the panic and fear as she slowly slid sideways,
unable to help herself. She remembered the last cry in her
mind as she called out for Devlin. Not only had her father
not been saved, they'd both been taken.

When she thought about the sequence of events, she
realized no police had shown up. Just an ambulance. Then
how else would one cart an unconscious man around?
Particularly if they'd been forced to drug him.

Or if he needed medical assistance. But she highly

341

doubted these ambulance attendants had any medical training. They were just the same as the other men. Men who would do anything for a price. Men who didn't give a shit about the chaos they created or the pain and destruction they left in their wake.

Her body rolled with an odd movement. She opened her eyes wider to see she was laying on a bed, her father beside her. No, not a bed—more like a bench. She had no idea where she was. Outside of her father, nobody else appeared to be in the room. She rolled over to her back and frowned. She was inside a boat. Maybe the main cabin. She could see sunshine outside and graying skies. And yet she could hear traffic. Then she understood. She and her father had been stashed inside a boat towed on a trailer.

Considering she was on a boat, were they heading for the harbor? That was not good. Once they hit the shore, headed out to international waters, it would be even harder to escape.

She tried to move her arms and realized her hands were tied. No, they were taped. She studied the tape around her wrists and realized the abductors hadn't expected to run into her. They'd taken her father, who didn't need anything to keep him immobilized, but they'd had to improvise with her, using medical tape, and it was damn tight. She glanced around, looking for something to cut it with. Her thoughts forewarned her, if she was inside the boat, were the bad guys watching her? She searched for a camera. Thankfully she didn't find one.

As she sat up, she realized her feet were tied with the same type of tape. She pulled her knees up to her chest and with her nails tried to scratch and rip the tape around her ankles, but it was too tough. She needed something sharp. A kitchen was down here. She doubted she'd be able to find anything, not if her captors were smart. But she had to look. Likely they thought she'd sleep the whole journey, but her body reacted differently to most medications.

She slid her feet down to the floor and although woozy and unsteady with the jolting movement as they traveled, she hopped her way to the galley. And sure enough, although she found no knives, there were various other instruments. One looked like a meat fork. She grabbed it, sat down on the floor, and stabbed at the tape. Anything that would break the integrity of the material would allow it to be ripped apart easily. In less than a minute, the bindings on her ankles gave way. The trouble was her bound hands would be a little bit harder to get to.

How did one stab something holding the hands together tightly? She reversed the tool, and with her feet together holding the fork, she plunged her hands up and down against the prongs. Several times she stabbed herself, but she persisted.

Panic started to set in. How long had she been gone? Had Devlin figured it out yet?

As soon as her hands were free, she found the chip below her elbow and, with a great deal of pain, pressed down on it hard. An alert button should send a signal back to her central control. With any luck, Tesla or Ice might see it.

She didn't have the swallow with her; it was back in the car with Devlin. Did he have enough knowledge to switch over the programming? Tesla should know. Bristol had left the instructions with them. She shook her head. But she hadn't taught anyone. It never occurred to her that she'd also be kidnapped.

Now free, she grabbed a napkin and pressed against the

blood flowing from her skin. She didn't bother cleaning up the blood droplets on the floor. If anything happened to her, that trace of evidence might help fill in the trail of her abduction.

Back on her feet, she made her way to her father. He appeared to be unconscious, but from the state of his skin and the lax way his body laid, she figured he'd been drugged. She reached out a hand and gently brushed the wispy white hair off his forehead.

She considered how to contact somebody. Anybody. She peered out the window to see traffic going by. Lots of traffic. How the hell would she get somebody's attention? Quickly she searched the cabin, looking for anything that would help. There wasn't much.

She went back to the tape that had been her bindings and ripping apart the multiple rounds they had used, and with a black pen, she taped the word *Help!* on the window. She'd already checked her pockets. Her cell phone was gone, and her father didn't have anything on him either. Although the cabin appeared to be wired with radios, she didn't see any electronics she could put together to contact anybody. Neither could she see what vehicle was pulling the boat.

She went to the cabin door and tried to open it, but it appeared to be chained shut from the outside. Of course, it was probably just locked. She ran back to the galley, grabbed the meat fork, went back to the door and worked on getting it open. The fork broke off in her efforts, both pieces falling to the floor. If this didn't work, she would start smashing windows. On the third try, something gave way. She propped open the door and slowly climbed to the deck. She waved frantically, screaming for help. As the traffic roared past, several people stared at her in surprise from inside their vehicles.

She screamed, "Help! Help me please."

She saw several people grabbing their phones, but she had no idea how long it would take before anybody came to her rescue. She dashed back inside, checked on her father, grabbed the sheet that covered him, and quickly took it outside, flinging it up and down in the air. If there was ever a universal sign of distress, it was the white flag.

Just then the truck pulling the boat slowed, and she realized she may have caught their attention too. Turn signals blinked on the truck, and it turned right. She screamed louder and harder, and hoped somebody had called in the license plate number, if there was one. She had to do something fast. If she found a place to jump off, then she would take it.

Only … how could she leave her father behind?

DEVLIN SET THE swallow on top of the car, the laptop beside it. "Tesla, I don't understand what I'm doing here." He'd been following instructions to send the swallow back up again; thankfully all the programs had been left open. "She also said she had the same tracker."

Tesla, in a calm voice, said, "As long as she has it on, we can track her right now." She gave him careful details on how to start the program.

When the swallow lifted in the air beside him, both Easton and Ryder stepped back, whispering, "Whoa."

Devlin realized he was finally getting somewhere. He took another couple steps, and the swallow shot off into the distance.

"It's gone, but where the hell is it?"

Behind him, Ryder said, "I'm driving. Easton, sit in the front."

They helped get Devlin and the laptop into the back of the Jeep.

In his ear he could hear Tesla asking, "Can you get to the GPS page she had open?"

He quickly tabbed through until he found the program he was looking for. "Yes, it's here, and some blinking thing is in the center."

"Check the beep and tell me what the number is."

He gave her the numbers that showed up.

"Okay, that's her father's tracker. Can you see any kind of location?"

He remembered Bristol tracking the GPS coordinates. He moved the coordinates into Google Maps and said, "They're heading toward the harbor." He quickly gave the street name to Ryder, and within seconds, they were headed down the highway.

Devlin tried to stay calm and kept an eye on the tracker.

"Ice is beside me," Tesla said. "She said there's chaos on one of the highways. Apparently a woman is in the back of a boat with a sheet, screaming for help."

Devlin raised his gaze and stared blindly out the windshield ahead of him. "A boat. It would certainly be a unique camouflage."

"Reports are coming in from all over the place. She taped the word *Help!* on one of the windows. We don't know if it's connected. We're trying to get an image, but she doesn't have satellite here. We're connecting through the compound. Levi's setting it up."

Devlin shared the information with the men in the front.

"So they transferred her from the ambulance to a boat?" Easton asked. "It's not bad. Boats have space below. It would hold her father, and if she was unconscious, they had a place to put her too. Obviously she's woken up, and, if they'd restrained her, she's gotten loose."

"Yeah," Ryder said. "What do you think they'll do to her when they see she's out in the back of the damn boat, shaking a white sheet?"

Silence descended in the Jeep. They all knew exactly what would happen to her.

"We won't give them that chance," Devlin said in a hard voice. "We must find them before they separate. If she gets off that boat, we have the tracker for him, but not for her."

"She has a number for herself, right?" Easton asked.

"Yes, Tesla's trying to find it."

"Jesus. People are being microchipped now but way back when? Who thought such a thing was even possible."

"It happens in wealthier families. In this case her father was involved in big military warfare experiments. And he'd had one put in her when she was a toddler."

The others shook their heads.

He gave them the new coordinates. "They're taking a turn off the main highway."

"I presume the swallow goes from point A to B. It doesn't follow the roads, correct?" Easton asked. "That makes the most sense, but not if it's coded to follow some kind of a navigational system."

"I have no idea. Never thought to ask her that. Why doesn't she just have a system where she can punch her father's code into the laptop? That should work. Why have the swallow in between?"

Ryder said, "That would be the easiest, but I think her

mind leans toward complicated details."

"Her father must've been quite something in his day."

"Besides, this was done a long time ago. ID chips are different now. Bristol and her father's were probably never upgraded. They just created a new program to find them." He shook his head. "I'm sure Tesla would understand that."

"Tesla does understand that," Tesla said in his ear. "And you're right. These chips are quite old. Bristol and her father had always talked about getting upgraded models, but because these were deep in their flesh, it wasn't something they wanted to remove. At the same time there was no need to because they were perfectly capable of finding each other." Her voice dropped as she said, "I just never considered we'd be tracking both of them down. Of course, the swallow has another purpose as well," Tesla said. "Don't forget it's weaponized."

"When you say weaponized, how close does it have to get?"

"The instructions have a spec sheet attached. The last model had to get within one hundred yards, which is a hell of a long shot. But Bristol said she did a ton of improvements on this one. She liked this one more for personal protection. But not everybody will sit around with a drone flying close by. We often argued on the applications for each of these because without a market, inventions are hard to sell."

Devlin nodded. "Right. But if we could alert the drone that the person they were guarding was under any kind of imminent threat, that would be a huge help."

"I believe she was working on something like that. Some kind of early camera awareness that some person was holding a weapon. The problem is, a person can hold lots of weapons that would put someone else in danger. How do you determine if a person is holding a weapon in a threatening manner or just showing off a weapon for others to see?"

He sat back and stared out the window. "It's hard to believe what she's doing is even possible."

"Hundreds of people around the world are currently working on this. She just happens to be one of the most gifted in the area. But she's also the most underfunded. She's doing this on her own. If the military had any idea what she was capable of, they would do a complete flip out and offer her half the world."

"Sure, and if the enemy found out, they'd do a complete flip out, and they'd offer her the *entire* world. Tesla, we need somebody in the military to look at this."

"I know. I've been thinking about that." Her voice had a distant echo ring to it.

He smiled. "Surely between all of us, we know somebody."

"Between all of us, we know a lot of somebodies. But it's a matter of knowing the right somebody." Then she gasped. "I'm getting feedback from the swallow," she exclaimed.

He frowned. "What does that mean?"

"Now that the swallow is up and targeted, we're getting the vitals on her father. Because it's close enough. I'm not sure I can switch the swallow over to her. But that would allow us access to the condition she's in."

"And her father?"

"Probably sedated from the looks of his vitals," Tesla said. "But he's alive. And we'll hang on to that."

"Right."

"It's closing the gap on the GPS location. The swallow's still flying, but its speed is slowing. Let me check." Silence was on that end of the phone for a moment. "Yes, speed is definitely slowing."

Ryder asked, "Coordinates?"

"The swallow is not far ahead," Devlin said. "According to Tesla, the vitals for the father are low, but stable. She's assuming he's sedated. We don't have an update yet on Bristol's condition. However, the police have been alerted. Apparently at this point about a woman crying for help."

Ryder said, "I still need new directions. It feels like I should be turning here somewhere soon."

"Turn on the roadway exit coming up," Devlin said. "Then go four blocks forward. And take a left." With those instructions completed, Devlin added, "We're almost on top of it. We're looking at another couple hard rights." He quickly read off the address and glanced out at the streets. "This is a much different area than before. This is a very high-class community. And it's gated."

"That'll be a bit of a problem," Easton said.

"Like hell it is," Ryder said. "We'll just go over the top."

"Why the hell aren't a ton of police vehicles around here? If she was standing on the back of the boat, screaming for help, surely a half-dozen cop cars would be on her tail very quickly."

"Unless the kidnappers got out of traffic immediately and drove in here and parked." Devlin hated to bring it up. "No guarantee they are still together."

Into his phone, he said, "Tesla, we're outside the gated community. The swallow coordinates that we have say the McEwans are in there. I don't know how to bring the swallow back."

He now stood outside the parked vehicle with the laptop on the roof of the car. The men had already gone to check out access to the community. In the daytime, chances were they didn't have any kind of electrified fence over the top of the wall. This secured compound wasn't to keep people out; it was to keep vehicles out.

"Okay, got the instructions here," Tesla said.

Devlin quickly typed in the commands, made several mistakes and had to retype it. Finally, by the time he was done, he looked up to see the swallow coming in for a landing on top of the car. He stared at it. "That's amazing."

"It is, but are you sure you wanted to call it back?"

He said, "I've got the small remote thing she had as well. If we keep this on standby, she'll be able to control it if I give her the handheld, right?"

"I'm not exactly sure how her new system works," Tesla said. "But when she puts the swallow on alert, she should be taking the remote with her. Otherwise how would it work?" She shook her head. "Don't forget I'm only helping out. These aren't my babies. Even with the instructions, I can only absorb so much, so fast."

When Devlin finished, he put the laptop back inside the vehicle, and the swallow sat atop the car, which he was hesitant to leave. But he didn't know what else to do.

His phone buzzed with a text from Ryder. "We found a house, and the boat is parked in the driveway. It appears to be deserted. But of course, there is no guarantee. Easton's gone to check the boat."

Quickly Devlin sent back confirmation he was on the way. He walked around, looking for the easiest place to scale the stone wall. He clicked on Ryder's GPS and followed the trail to where he stood. He walked up to him behind a cedar hedge. "News?"

Ryder pointed to a house two doors down, the one with

a large sailboat, schooner-type thing, on a trailer parked in the driveway. Then he saw the boat window. "Oh, my God, you can still see the word *Help!* on the side."

"Yeah, that means it's the same boat as seen on the highway. So she did get herself free, but we have no idea what happened after that."

They didn't wait long. A vehicle drove up, parking in the drive next to the boat, and two men hopped out. Ryder took as many pictures as he could from where he stood with his cell phone.

Devlin waited, knowing Easton was inside the boat and could get caught any time.

But the men marched up to the front door and went inside. Devlin and Ryder crept along the side of the house and came up on the blind side where the boat was. In the garage Devlin could see the truck used to pull it. What they needed to do was disable all the vehicles.

Devlin opened the driver's door, reached underneath and disconnected the wires behind the panel. It was a simple enough trick to put it back together again, if they knew what they were doing. But at the moment, he didn't think anybody inside had that kind of know-how. He searched the truck quickly but couldn't find anything of interest. Back outside, he checked out the area. Ryder and Easton both stood at the edge of the garage, out of sight. They motioned him over. He stuck to their side.

"The boat's empty. Found blood at the front area, and a bit of a mess in terms of cut tape and a sheet. No sign of either of them."

"Are we assuming they're in the house then? In that case I want to disable that car."

Easton snorted. "Screw disabling. Let's go take out the

tires." He pulled out his pocketknife, opened the blade casually and walked down in the shadow of the boat. He peered around the edge, then dashed to the car.

They couldn't see what he did, but Devlin trusted him to stab both tires on the far side. He came back around the front, reached under and cut the side wall on the front tires as well. He closed the knife, slipped back alongside the boat and rejoined them.

"Two vehicles are not moving. Let's go into the house."

They could gain access via three doors that they knew of. One door went inside the garage, plus the front door, and potentially at least one, if not two, rear doorways. Devlin chose to take the back. He slid around the house and did a full check. Found a large porch, downward stairs to some kind of a basement entrance as well as double French doors off the deck. A nice house. A large swimming pool. It was fenced but only four feet high. The easily scalable backyard was empty.

He slid down to the basement entrance, and his phone buzzed. He pulled it out and checked it. *Tesla.* She'd set the swallow onto Bristol's coordinates. According to the reading, Bristol was in the house as well.

Exactly what he needed to know.

CHAPTER 17

S HE COULD HEAR sirens in the distance. She was sure help was coming. But it was obvious the driver had suddenly been aware of something going on, and she was likely responsible. The vehicle made several high-speed turns and corners. At one point she was afraid the boat would go sideways, sending her crashing to the ground. The truck came to a sudden stop, and the vehicle following behind them stopped too. Two men came out of it and held a pistol at her.

Slowly she raised her hands in the air. Had she done enough that the cops would find them, or had she just been stupid, putting herself in a worse situation? One of the men jumped into the back of the boat; the others got into the vehicle.

She sat next to her father. She crossed her arms and glared at the man holding a gun on her. The boat proceeded, once again back on track. But they only drove for another few minutes. Then suddenly she was inside some residential community with big fancy houses all around.

The vehicle drove into a garage with the boat remaining outside.

"Now I'll take you inside that house. I'm totally okay just putting a bullet in you right now," the man said. "But they seem to think you're worth more alive than dead."

She had no idea why he would think that because she was still a nobody. At the moment she was just one screwed, bankrupt inventor, who thought she could do better.

The gunman was talking again. "I'll put you in a bedroom with your father. If you're good, we'll leave you together. If you're not, well, … I want you to go very quietly. You're not to attract any attention. The bullet doesn't care whether it's you or your father. As a matter of fact, it would be a hell of a lot easier to just kill him here."

"No, I'll be good. I'll be good," she said quickly. "Just don't kill him."

He shook his head at her. "From what the guys said, he's crazy anyway. What the hell do you care?" He motioned her to go ahead of him.

As she got to the deck of the boat, to the back where the ladder was, she could see two men waiting for her. And really she had no choice or chance to escape. She slid down the ladder, and the first man grabbed her arm, moving her into the garage, then through the door into the house. She barely had a chance to look around. It had a big open layout with tile floors, which looked expensive as hell. Upstairs she was shoved into a room.

"Four men will be in this house. If you want, I can tie you up. But you seem to be able to get out of bindings, so there is not much point. However, if I see you out of this room, and I don't give a shit what the reason is, even if you need the toilet, I'll put a bullet in you. Might even start with your hands. If I see you outside this room for any reason," he repeated for emphasis, "I'll take out another body part next, probably a knee. See how you like spending the rest of your life as a cripple, and if you do somehow escape, your father is dead meat."

She sat down hard on the bed and wrapped her arms around her chest. "I won't go anywhere."

Inside she was seething. As threats, they were damn effective. Her father … and the last thing she wanted was to lose her hands. She winced at the thought.

The gunman moved off to the side as another man brought her father's frail body in. She stood, and he laid him down on the bed. He didn't say a word to her, just turned and walked back out again.

As the door closed, she sat down and buried her face in her hands. What the hell would she do? No way could she give up. She'd been so close to success by getting free in the boat. In her mind she went over and over it again, wondering what she should have done differently. How was it that nobody got the cops to her in time to save her from this?

She shook her head. Was that what the world had come to? See somebody in distress … and do nothing? She wondered how many YouTube videos would show up of her screaming in the back of the boat when nobody came to her rescue.

At the same time, this type of thinking wasn't helping. She was with her father, and if nothing else, she'd face death with him too. They'd been alone together all their lives. This was nothing new.

Her mind swept toward Devlin. On the cusp of finding somebody she really wanted to spend time with, it was all being snatched away. That was so not fair.

He'd walked into her life in Afghanistan and had made himself right at home. She didn't want him to leave.

She wanted a promise that he was meant for her. She didn't really know how he felt, but at the same time, she did realize he was attracted to her. Every time she turned around, he was at her side. The gentle gestures, the smiles, the startling little kisses. She wanted that, and so much more.

As she stared down at her father, she realized how alone she'd been for so long. She'd lost him mentally and emotionally, and it hurt in more ways than she'd really understood. But now that somebody was potentially in her life, it would make detaching from her father that much easier.

She'd been in a lot of pain for a long time. She was so ready for some joy. And these assholes were trying to take it away from her. What if she didn't survive any of this? So much had been going wrong. Even if she came out of this with her life, she worried she wouldn't with her business or house. Where would she put her father if that happened?

Instead of getting depressed, it made her mad. She'd worked so damn hard for this. Sure, she'd been an idiot. She shouldn't have signed the stupid contract. Tesla had warned her about it. But she hadn't seen any other way. Yet she knew in the back of her mind that she'd had a plan. But she hadn't expected to get screwed on it. If she could just give them the fifty drones. That was what counted, what the contract stipulated. And now she had something far more advanced and fantastic.

But she had to get out of here, and she had to do it *now*.

Where the hell was Devlin?

She walked to the window and stared out. Another vehicle drove up, and two men ran into the house. She sat down on the bed beside her father, reached down to grip his hand and whispered, "If nothing else, we'll be together." She bowed her head, waiting for the men to join her upstairs.

Still there had to be something she could do. Surely there had to be a weapon, a method to escape.

★

THE BASEMENT DOOR was locked, but Devlin had it picked and open in seconds. He quickly sent a message to Easton and Ryder, saying he was in the basement; the door was unlocked, and they were to join him.

He did a quick sweep of everything around him and found it empty, except for the weightlifting area. Several aluminum weightlifting bars without the plates affixed were on the side. He picked one up, felt the heft of it and smiled. He could do a hell of a lot of damage with this.

Hearing a noise behind him, he stepped against the wall and waited. Recognizing both Easton and Ryder, he motioned to the stairs and said, "I only see one way up."

They nodded and came behind him.

With his ear to the door at the top of the stairs, he listened. No sounds heard. Hoping for the best, he turned the knob and let the door disengage from the frame. Still nothing. He pushed it open. Then they were inside a small hallway.

With the three of them on the main floor they fanned out. And again found nobody.

Only the upstairs was left. Hopefully Bristol and her father were there.

Devlin glanced at the stairs. They were always tricky. One would creak, no matter how careful they were.

Ryder had a completely different tack. He grabbed a handrail and walked up the molding on the side. He hit the first landing, repeated the process and was up the second half in three strides. Easton followed. Devlin picked up the rear.

At the top of the stairs were four doors. All closed.

That's when he realized this was completely wrong.

No matter how many people were up here, no way the doors should be shut and not a sound heard.

And that meant the kidnappers were expecting trouble.

The three men exchanged glances, each pointed to a door they would take, and moved to the side of theirs. That they would be up against armed men was a given. Only Devlin had picked up a weight bar. But then he knew Ryder and Easton had hand-to-hand combat that was like no other. Devlin was damn good too. Plus, Ryder was a tank. Even if he took three bullets, chances were he'd take out his man before he dropped.

Easton was slimmer and damn fast. But then he had kickboxing skills too. As long as he could see the weapon before they fired it, chances were good he would take it out before it hit its target.

Ryder held up three fingers. Then on cue, each of them burst into a room. Devlin's room was completely empty. He did a quick search of the closet and came back out in the hallway. Ryder did at that time too and motioned him to the other door. Easton hadn't come out of his room.

The door was ajar. Ryder nudged it wider with his foot, and they found Easton sitting on the ground, glaring up at somebody, his hands on his head. From behind Ryder's broad shoulders, Devlin could see Bristol. Behind her lay her father on the floor.

She held a long metal pipe. The pole from the closet. *Nice.* And she'd brained Easton with it. Bristol took one look at Devlin, dropped the pipe and threw herself into his arms.

He hugged her close. Against her ear he asked, "Where are the others?"

She pulled her head back and shook it. "I have no idea. I've been in this room with my father since we first arrived. I heard men come in the front door."

The three men looked at each other, and Devlin said,

"There should be two from the ambulance and the two who came in after you. Have you checked any of the other rooms?"

She shook her head and whispered, "No. I'm not sure where anybody is."

"We've already searched the downstairs and have only one more room."

"And it's empty," Ryder said from behind him.

Devlin shook his head. "How is that possible? We came in through the basement and searched the whole house. "It's only possible if they went out the French doors as we came in." Easton growled as he hopped to his feet. "And that would mean they got away."

"But why would they go out the back?" Bristol protested. "Unless they parked out there?"

The men shook their heads.

"The truck is in the garage, and the black car is in the driveway."

They turned to look at Easton. "You must have been spotted."

He nodded. "It's the only explanation. If they were going to kill Bristol and her father, why take them here? And why leave their captives behind?"

"Cutting their losses."

Everyone turned to look at Bristol.

"It's the only thing that makes sense. If they were sabotaging me, in a way this may be enough from their point of view." She glanced at Easton. "I'm so sorry for hitting you."

He shrugged. "My fault for taking the hit." He gave her a sideways grin of apology.

The men nodded, and Devlin said, "Whatever the reason, we have to get the hell out here." He glanced back at

Bristol's father. "What would you like us to do with him?"

"He needs a doctor to check him over," she said quietly. "I need to get home and finish my work." She glanced around. "Thank you very much for finding us."

"Let's not take anything for granted. We need an ambulance here for your father, and get you home again."

"I don't have time for the police," she muttered. She glanced at her father. "Maybe we can just take him home. Have a family physician come check on him?"

The men glanced at each other and back at her.

She flushed. "Does that make me sound cruel? I don't mean to be. I'm caught between a time warp and a deadline. He requires help, but he doesn't need any more run-ins with the bad guys. At my place, I'm presuming you can protect us, and we can finish the drones ..."

Ryder bent down and gently lifted the frail old man in his arms. "I'll be a whole lot gentler than anybody's been with him so far. Let's get you home."

Devlin pulled out his phone. "I'm calling the police. They can come and deal with the house and boat." He looked around at the others. "Remember, there's been a hell of a lot of news media coverage over this boat already and the crazy woman in the back with the sheet. There could be case files and a lot of man hours wasted. I'll just tell them we're taking the old man to the hospital and you home. If they want to talk, that's where they can find you."

She relented. "You do that." She marched ahead of them, down the stairs and out the front door. When she saw the boat, she froze. Then shook her head. "I was so damn close to getting out of that thing."

"You probably could've just jumped from the back on a corner when they slowed."

She turned to look at Ryder and nodded. "I could've, but I was afraid to leave my father."

"Then don't feel guilty about it," he said. "We all make decisions. Our unit has to time and time again. But we trust each other to handle what needs to be done so we can move forward with the plan."

"I didn't move forward," she said. "I just got nowhere."

"Wait until you see the news coverage." He laughed. "You'll see that your efforts weren't in vain."

"I can just imagine."

D EVLIN FILLED IN the police quickly. Then they got the other vehicle and headed back to her house. Her father was stretched out on the backseat where she could keep an eye on him.

She hoped today's punches had no ill effects on his health. With any luck he'd sleep right through the whole thing and be back in his own bed before he woke up.

As for her, well, she had a ton of work to get done. She still couldn't believe Devlin, Tesla, and Ice had gotten the swallow up and running. "I'm really impressed you operated the swallow."

He laughed. "I couldn't have done it without Tesla, Ice, and the others. And why is it that your chips aren't GPS trackable without the swallow?"

"Because they're very old," she said. "They were done years and years ago, before it was common practice. There was no GPS software back then. Today everything is smaller, easier, and faster."

He nodded. "That's what we figured. Maybe it's time to update that."

"We discussed it at one time, but the ID chips have actually grown into the muscles, so we'd have downtime of many weeks and possible nerve damage." She shook her head. "That didn't make any sense to us. We can have new chips installed, but that would likely confuse the issue with two chips so close together."

He nodded. "And you're in the unique position of having the swallow to track you and your father."

"My father had a version to track us back then too. His own program," she said. "And I got so busy I just forgot about the chips." She took a deep breath and added, "Until now."

"At least they were there and usable." He glanced at her. "Is there anything you need while we're still out?"

She shook her head. "The only thing I need is to get home, make certain my father is safe behind locked doors with a guard posted and resume my work," she said. "Even though today's folly caused no major physical damage, it did set me back again another full day. The sabotage is working in that regard."

They approached the gate.

She gasped. "The gate's been fixed."

She hopped and out, checked the gate, realizing the entire structure had been rewelded, and the solid lock was fixed. She quickly punched in her code, and it opened. After everyone was in, she quickly secured the gate and changed the lock code on it. As she approached the vehicles, Ryder exited, and with Devlin's help, they gently eased her father out.

She opened the front door and said to Ryder, "If you could lay him in his bed, that would be ideal."

Carmelita raced toward her. "Oh, my goodness, you're back safe and sound."

She was crying and blubbering at the same time. Bristol threw her arms around Carmelita, and after a moment, she said, "Let's get him into his bed, please. Then put a call in to the doctor."

"Yes, yes, yes." Carmelita raced down the hallway and stepped in front of Ryder, quickly calling for the elevator.

Now that she was home, she could feel her tension slowly easing back. But only a little. All that had happened was time lost to her, and she had very little of that left to meet her contract. She walked back to the car, pulled out her laptop and turned around. She found Devlin with the swallow in his hand. She smiled, picked up the lifesaving device and walked inside her house. If she was grateful for one thing right now, it had to be her home.

Instead of going through the kitchen to the stairs, she punched in the elevator code and quickly headed down to the lab. When the doors opened below, she stepped inside and froze. At least another six men were in here. She raised her gaze in shock. She didn't know if she should be outraged, terrified, or delighted.

And then Tesla stepped in front of her, holding up her hands. "I know I didn't ask you. I didn't have time. You were in trouble, and it wasn't like I could ask your permission."

At that, her mouth opened and closed. "Permission?"

Tesla motioned at the new group working on the hardware and another few her side of the table. "They work for me."

Bristol glanced around to see everybody was working and realized just how much of a friend Tesla truly was. She put down the laptop and swallow on the closest table, turned and threw her arms around Tesla. She could feel the relief flow in from her friend's body as she relaxed and hugged her back. She whispered, "Thank you. Dear God, thank you."

Tesla hugged her fiercely. "You're back, and we've got

lots of work to do. We have a contract to finish. And I am working to get you a better one."

Something in her tone made Bristol stand back and look at her. "What have you been up to?"

Tesla grinned. "I do know a few people," she said, and quickly shared something she had set up.

Bristol's eyebrows rose. "Do you think that would work?"

"I'll tell you what. It can't get any worse. First, we deliver. Second, we do a demonstration." She grinned. "This time for the right people."

DEVLIN KEPT AN eye on Bristol for the rest of the day. She moved at an almost frantic pace, between rushing upstairs when the doctor arrived to check on her father, then back down again working on her software.

Tesla and Ice worked on the drones. And a production line was in progress. They had fifty to put together with a certain level of aptitude. Like Bristol had said, she'd had a breakthrough. And so much more was available today. But these assholes wouldn't get anything else from her. Not Brent's company. They'd made her life difficult enough. And from what research he'd found, Brent's business practices were questionable, like cancelled contracts or nonpayment on others.

They had approximately six days left on the extension deadline. In Devlin's heart, he knew they'd make it. He just didn't know how much Bristol could make it through. Her nerves were like edged wire. There was a sense that, if anything went wrong, she would snap. He'd seen that same wire bend and twist with a tensile strength he had never expected. But at the same time, it was a joy to see.

The days went in a blur. She now had a houseful of helpers. And her housekeeper had her hands full feeding everybody. They worked long into the night, crashed for a few hours, got up the next morning and repeated it. By the time they reached the day before the contract extension was due, he knew he had to do something. She was ready to collapse. He tugged her off to the side midmorning and said, "You need to lie down and get some sleep."

She turned to look up at him, bags under her eyes, almost a feverish glint to their inner depths. She shook her head. "I can't afford the time."

He caressed her neck with his thumb and gently tilted her chin up. "And you can't afford *not* to." He shook his head gently. "Look at yourself. You're running on empty."

"I still have the reserve tank," she said defiantly. "Look at everything. It's on target. We'll make it. But if any one thing goes wrong, if any one hiccup happens, everything is lost."

Then he saw her physically lock down, regain control and stare at him.

"I'll be fine."

He watched her walk away and sit back down. He had no idea what she was working on, but it had to do with the swallow, and something was beside it, an even smaller device. He walked over to see a tiny songbird-looking thing sitting beside the swallow. "What the hell is that?"

She glanced up at him. "You'll see when I'm finished." In an almost bitter note, she added, "If I finish."

He realized whatever she was working on was so important she couldn't afford to let herself stop. He glanced at Tesla and raised his brows.

Tesla nodded. "She must finish it tonight."

He frowned at her, wondering just what that meant, then figured he'd better get back to his job. He turned and resumed what he'd been working on. He would just wait and see. It was one thing to be involved in something like this from the peripheral level. But for Bristol, he understood her commitment was so much more, her loss so much worse.

And over everything hovered the unexpected air of the kidnapping. The men took turns doing security laps, checking the video feeds. They were running on fumes as well. And the new people Tesla had brought in were so focused on the drones that they had the freedom of hours to lock down security tight. They were also on Levi's satellite feed now. Every day Stone, one of Levi's main men, made sure no intruders were on the property.

And through it all, Bristol kept working, rarely sleeping. The worried glances of the others became more frequent, concerned, and directed at him.

He knew he had to do something.

After dinner that night, she got up from the table to go back down with the others, but she was trailing them, and he could see the pallor of her skin, the heavy black bags under her eyes.

He stepped in front of her. "No."

She looked up at him, swaying in place. "What are you talking about?"

"You're not going downstairs with them."

"Of course I am."

He shook his head. "No, you're not. You're going to your room and to bed right now."

She crossed her arms over her chest, jutted out her chin and said, "And who'll make me?"

"Me."

"You and whose army?" He took a step forward, and she took one back. She shook her head. "There's no way I can let all those people down. They came here out of the goodness of their hearts, and I can't let them work without me. Don't you understand I have to be there? I can't just quit."

"In any other circumstance, I'd agree with you." He led her to the hallway where a big mirror was and said, "Look at yourself. You're exhausted. You'll collapse. You're determined by sheer willpower and stubbornness to keep moving. You're the last one to go to bed at night, and even then I don't think you sleep. I believe you continue to work in your room where nobody else can see you. You show up every morning looking worse day by day."

She glared at him in the mirror.

"You can hardly even stand straight. You're swaying on your feet."

Her knees locked, and her shoulders stiffened as he could see her temper building up inside. He had witnessed this before. But within seconds, she sagged in place again. "I can't leave them to work alone. I'm out of time. It doesn't matter if I'm exhausted or not. When this is over, I can sleep for a week. At this moment I can't afford downtime."

No point in talking to her. She wasn't hearing anything he had to say. He bent and scooped her up in his arms.

She hit at him, crying out, "Let me down. Let me down."

He heard running feet and turned to face Carmelita, coming from the kitchen with a tea towel in her hand.

"Bristol?" Carmelita asked worriedly.

Devlin knew what it must look like. But he was quick to reassure her. "I'm taking her to her room so she goes to bed. She needs to sleep. She can't do anymore. She can barely even stand."

"I'm fine," Bristol yelled. "Carmelita, go get the others. They won't let him manhandle me."

He could see the indecision on Carmelita's face. Then the resolve.

She shook her head. "No, Bristol. You need sleep. Tomorrow morning is a whole new day."

With a shriek of outrage from his captive, Devlin quickly raced down the hallway, carrying his charge. He shifted her wiggling body over his shoulder, opened the double doors, kicked them shut, bolted them behind him and dropped her on the bed. Instantly she was off, racing toward the door.

He snagged her with one arm, picked her up and dropped her on the bed again. She rose on her hands and knees, glaring at him.

And for that, he'd never seen a more beautiful sight—spitting like a cat, exhausted, and still a warrior, doing the right thing. But her body had hit a wall. He knew what that felt like. He knew she couldn't keep this up. She would rest and come back fighting after a few hours.

Quietly, holding his voice steady, he said, "You'll stay there and rest. I can stand here all night if I must, to make sure you do. Only one of us will win this fight, and it'll be me."

She opened her mouth, and a scream of frustration ripped through the room.

But she didn't get up again.

He grinned when she rolled over in defeat. Less than a minute later, her body melted into the boneless relaxation of an exhausted sleep.

Good. He sat down in the big chair beside her to stand watch.

CHAPTER 19

S HE WOKE TO a room filled with darkness. Her instant panic eased back when she recognized her room. Her body was heavy, peaceful. She didn't want to move, but her bladder was insistent. She rolled over and froze. Devlin was asleep in the chair beside her. His big feet up on the edge of the bed. His arms crossed over his chest. She figured if she made any move, he would know. And he looked tired too.

She remembered the confab before she collapsed. Just because he was right didn't make it an easy pill to swallow. Fatigue still pulled at her. She knew how much sleep she'd had. She certainly wouldn't leave the room yet. But sometimes body functions had to come first. She wiggled down to the bottom of the bed and slipped off to the bathroom. She stared at her face in the mirror and shook her head. "God, you look like a witch." Her skin was ashen, and huge bags drooped under her eyes.

She checked her watch and realized it was just midnight. She used the facilities and washed up, brushed her teeth, and then walked back into her bedroom. She went to her dresser, grabbed her nightie and returned to the bathroom. She changed and dumped her dirty clothes in the laundry basket.

Opening the door, she crept back to her bed and got in on the far side.

"How do you feel?"

"Better," she said grudgingly as she realized he hadn't been asleep at all.

"Good. Now go back to sleep."

She didn't plan on arguing, but something about being ordered around angered her. "I was planning on it," she snapped.

"Sleep. Just sleep."

She smiled at that. He really was only being protective of her. She shouldn't have been such a bitch about it. She was exhausted. "Thank you," she said as she drifted back toward sleep.

He chuckled. "You're welcome. You're adorable no matter what world you're in."

Her eyes flew open. She snuggled deeper into the blankets and grinned. She heard him walk to the bathroom himself. When he came out and turned off the light, he sat down on the bed beside her and stretched out on top.

"Now that I'm sure you won't take off on me," he said, "I hope you won't begrudge me a few hours."

Instantly she felt bad. To keep her in bed, he'd sat up on guard, and that meant he was lacking. "I'm sorry."

He reached out an arm and wrapped it around her, tucked her blankets up against him and said, "I'm not. You're a fighter, a warrior, even when pushed past your physical limits."

She snorted. "I was a bad-tempered bitch."

"That too. But I've seen worse." He gave her a quick hug. "Back to sleep with you."

"Your ex-girlfriends?" she snapped, and then froze when she realized what she'd said. But a low soft chuckle in her ear brought a flush to her neck and a smile to her face.

He whispered, "Sometimes. What is it about me that

happens to like feisty, argumentative kittens? But as long as you're okay to take on the role of girlfriend, that would make me very happy."

With a smile on her face, her thoughts drifted over the conversation. *Girlfriend?* Maybe they had crossed a line somewhere along the way. They'd gone from friendship into something more. She could get behind that. She fell asleep again soon afterward.

She woke the second time, still wrapped in his arms, but facing him.

A thick shadow covered his chin, and he slept deeply at her side. She smiled and laid her head against his chest. It had been quite a run since Afghanistan. She'd never fallen this far, this fast, and this heavily into a relationship. But no doubt, that was where they were at. He was the most giving, caring, domineering, irritating, and yet steadfast male she'd ever met.

What a blessing he was. She marveled that he would actually be attracted to her. She couldn't think of any time in the last few weeks since she'd met him that she'd been on her best behavior. It had just been one nightmare after another. Until last night. And he'd been right to do what he did. And if their situations were reversed, she hoped she'd have enough guts to do the same thing for him. But she suspected his training would kick in beforehand and show him when he needed downtime.

She had no idea what time it was. She didn't want to move. She shifted ever-so-slightly so she could look out the window.

It was still dark. She smiled in relief. Too early to get up so she could enjoy a few moments alone with him. She snuggled in close. It had been years since she'd had a relationship with anybody where she'd let him stay over-night. She never even got close to being engaged. Her father had always been a driving force in her life. It was hard to find anybody who would match up. When he'd fallen ill, she'd been preoccupied with looking after him.

But everything was different with Devlin. He was a man's man, yet protective and caring. She couldn't resist. She stretched up and kissed his chin, grinning at the bristly feel under her lips.

Not only was he still fully dressed, but he didn't have any covers on. She'd be freezing if that were her. Not to mention deadly uncomfortable. She shifted back and sat up. Maybe she could cover them both up.

As she tried to struggle free, his arm tightened, and he dragged her back against him. She let out a light laugh. "What? I'm not going anywhere."

He snuggled closer and kissed the top of her head.

"I was covering you up. You're lying here fully dressed but without any blankets."

He chuckled, his warm breath drifting down her neck, sending shivers down her spine. "I'm fine. I'm warm."

She chuckled too. "No, you're not. You're hot."

He gave her a gentle squeeze.

She wasn't sure if he was still tired, but all she could think about was that they had a solid hour. She'd get up soon though. She'd lost a lot of hours she could have been working last night, but it was hard to make herself move. What she really wanted was something they hadn't yet gotten to.

"I can hear your mind buzzing. You sure you can't sleep more?"

She shook her head. "Absolutely not. I'm awake."

He slowly let his hand drift down, coming to rest on her thigh. "If you're sure …"

But he sounded regretful.

With that said, she shifted upward, flipped and draped herself across him. "I might have had enough sleep," she whispered against his lips, "but that doesn't mean I'm ready to leave the bed yet."

His eyes popped open.

She was focused on the firm sculpted lips in front of her. She lowered her head and kissed him gently, then tasted, nipped, and nibbled her way from one side to the other and back again. He stretched, his hands moving up her back with slow, careful strokes.

A lazy, slow morning lovemaking session. God, she wanted that. The trouble was, she wasn't sure she could do slow and lazy. Everything in her life was done at top speed. And right now, she wanted a whole lot more. She kissed him full on the lips, pouring on as much passion and heat as she could, her tongue sliding inside to find his waiting for her.

When she finally lifted her head to look down at him, she had to chuckle at the playful look in his eyes. "Good morning," she whispered.

He slid his hands up to hold her head firm, and he tugged her back down and whispered, "Good morning. This is a wonderful way to wake up." He reached up to gently brush the hair off her face. "My turn." And he flipped them, lowering his head. His kiss was long, slow, and ever-so-sweet. Just as she went to pull back, he changed the tempo, unleashing a passion she'd only suspected might lurk beneath his exterior.

She wrapped her arms around him and kissed him, fiercely matching his passion with a fire of her own. God, she wanted this man, this moment, this release, and this comfort. Need clawed at her. She wrapped her legs around his hips, desperate to have him inside her.

But he wasn't having any of it. He eased back some of the passion, dragging his lips off hers to slide across her cheek, down her neck, teasing, tasting, looking, nipping, and biting. She shivered and shuddered under his onslaught as emotions swept through her. Somehow her nightie ended up on the floor. When he lowered his head and latched onto her nipple, she cried out, her body arching in the bed. He loved the sensitive tip and then moved over to the other one. She shuddered beneath him. Her body trembling, beseeching for more. And that's when she realized he was still fully dressed.

She grabbed his shirt collar and tugged. He chuckled, sat up slightly and pulled his shirt over his head. Instantly she wrapped her arms around him and kissed him, her tongue diving deep inside his mouth, tasting, exploring all. Her hands were frantic as they slipped across his skin, exploring his massive shoulders, muscled back, and chest. But she couldn't reach any more of him. In frustration, she whimpered.

He wrapped her close and held her to his chest. "Easy, sweetheart, easy."

She shuddered in his arms, her body already desperate for release. He laid her back down, stood and quickly took off the rest of his clothes.

She watched in awe of his big muscled body, a male in his prime, and hers. He was here, for her, and she wanted him like she'd never wanted anyone else. Instinctively she reached for his erection. But he grabbed her hands and pulled them away. "I can't take any of that right now."

Her gaze surged up to his, hearing the thickening of his

voice as he stared at her. In wonder, she realized he was as close to the edge as she was. She spread her legs wide and opened her arms, inviting him in.

He dropped on top of her, his arms catching his weight, and then slowly lowered himself the rest of the way. She wrapped her arms around his torso, her legs around his hips.

He surged inside. And stilled.

She gasped, her body tight, hot, the shocking sense of fullness, and yet she was desperate to adjust.

In a thick voice, he whispered against her ear, "Did I hurt you?"

She shook her head. "No. It's just been a long time."

He lifted his head to see the truth of her words in her eyes and then smiled and lowered his head to kiss her gently as his hands set about soothing her. Long caresses swept up and down her full length before coming back to cup her breasts, giving her time to adjust to his size and the sudden invasion, stoking the fires inside.

When he suckled at her breast, gently nipping the tip, she could feel her body warming, melting around him as her muscles eased to accept him. She tugged him up higher, latching her mouth onto his, sliding her hands down his hips to his cheeks.

"Enough teasing," she finally whispered.

"We have time …"

She shifted, swung both legs high up on his hips, squeezed tight and dug her nails into his back. He lifted his head and gasped, his hips plunging deep.

She chuckled. "That's more like it."

His gaze promising retribution, he lowered his head and took her lips with a fierce passion she'd never experienced before. No longer were any pleasantries being exchanged. He dove deep and then again. His tongue and hips mimicked the same action, and she was plundered from top to bottom, held helpless in his embrace.

Her temperature soared as heat burned inside, threatening to consume her, them.

And still he wouldn't relent. He drove them both harder, higher, and faster. When she came apart in his arms, he still didn't stop. He rode her through it. Just when she figured she couldn't tolerate any more, her body proved her wrong, and she exploded once again.

When he came, his body shuddering above her, she wrapped her arms around him and hung on. He collapsed to the side, wrapped himself around her and rolled over, pulling her onto his chest. She laid her head down, tears in her eyes, completely unable to speak.

When she could talk, she whispered, "What the hell was that…and how soon can I get more?"

HE LET OUT a bark of laughter, his body already showing interest at her words, and said, "I'll need five minutes, sweetheart. Can you wait?"

She lifted her head and said, "If it means not moving anything, I can do that." She leaned her head on his chest once more. She couldn't actually believe her words. She kissed the tip of his chin. "However, considering the time of day, we should probably get up."

He reached across her and pulled his cell phone off the night table. "It's ten minutes to five."

Regretfully she sat up and said, "I need a shower. So a repeat performance will have to wait." She stood and walked toward the bathroom. He hopped up behind her, a grin on his face. She looked at him suspiciously. "Do you need one too?"

"Sweetheart, I need you and the shower. Thankfully, I'm a SEAL."

She shook her head not understanding.

He winked. "We are trained to do all kinds of things in the water." He lifted her in his arms, carrying her shrieking with laughter into the bathroom. He didn't put her down until they were both standing underneath the warm water. And he proceeded to show her exactly what he meant.

By the time the demonstration was finished, both were leaning against the side walls of the tiled shower in exhaustion. "Please tell me that wasn't part of your training."

He chuckled. "No, that was not on our schedule." He picked up a bar of soap. "Go again?"

Her gaze widened in disbelief. "I'm terrified to answer that question. But we don't have time anyway," she said regretfully. "We'll pick up later."

He bent down and kissed her hard on her lips. "Tonight then."

She gave him a smile, taking the bar of soap from him. "And then it will be my turn."

He grinned in delight. "That's a date. Let's get your hair washed and the rest of you cleaned up, dressed and down there before anybody knows we were playing hooky."

She rolled her eyes at him. "I highly suspect they already do."

Considering he'd read the text that had come in last evening, he knew everybody was fully aware of where he'd been. He also knew they approved. Hopefully he could escape teasing from anybody making the connection to Mason's Keepers.

And that was something he'd like to avoid. He'd been adamant about staying away from the whole romance side of Mason's life. But no way could Devlin have seen this coming down the pipeline, nor could he have prepared or mounted a defense. This woman had gotten behind his guard like no other. And for the first time, he realized just what Mason and his merry Keepers' unit meant when they said it all had been worth it.

And he really did know. And he'd do a whole lot to stay inside as a member now of that group. And that meant keeping her at his side. And how the hell would he do that?

But he knew it was even more important to be on guard over the next twenty-four hours.

If there would be another attempt against her life, it would happen fast.

CHAPTER 20

FEELING SO MUCH better after a good night's sleep, and a whole lot more energized after her crazy lovemaking session, Bristol was on top of her game. It was a long day, but she was there at every corner, every step of the way. All fifty of the drones were done, had computer chips installed, command boxes set up, and were arranged as agreed. They were outside testing them at the moment. Thirty-two had passed. Two had problems—one was the chip set, and she had no idea why—and they were working on the other sixteen. With any luck they'd get this done.

The ones that passed inspection were being boxed up for shipment. She would take them all with her. She had a trailer, and the men were carefully loading them into the back right now. She couldn't believe she'd gotten as far this fast. And she knew who to thank for that. Devlin. Tesla. But in actuality every one of the people who came here had pulled more than their fair share of weight to get the job done. It was a huge eye-opener into understanding how many hands made light of the work.

Tesla had been instrumental in getting some of the software issues fixed. Bristol still had no idea who had tried to hack her handsets or even her server database. But since Harrison had stepped in and blocked it, there had been no new attacks. She'd hire him to help her with alarms, lights, or something that went off in case anybody else tried. She couldn't keep on top of everything by herself. And that was what this had really shown her. She needed to hire staff. And if she could make good on this contract, she'd have enough money to do so. Thank God.

The first meeting was tomorrow morning at nine. They'd pull out by seven-thirty to set up. With everything slowly working out, she threw herself into her own small project.

They still didn't have confirmation of the second meeting at one o'clock tomorrow. But she hoped everything went as planned. Tesla had chosen that time in case they needed four hours in the morning meeting, which would be about right because every one of the fifty drones would be tested and demonstrated. Bristol hoped there were no problems. But she wanted a couple spares just in case. The second meeting had her tied up in knots. She knew Devlin was never more than four feet away from her. Always protective, always watching.

Given the tight time frame, another attack could easily happen before they got out of here. But she wasn't so sure. By the end of the day she was exhausted and wired.

At dinnertime, she opened a bottle of champagne and said, "I can't believe we actually did this—with all my thanks to everyone here forever. If any of you ever need anything, you just let me know."

They had opened five bottles of champagne before they called it a night. She was still buoyed and wired. She took her laptop into her bedroom and sat down to keep working.

She just had a few tweaks to make. It was a very specialized drone, and it would have minimal applications.

With a cup of coffee beside her and her laptop in front

of her, she continued to work away, making improvements. When a knock came at the door, she knew instinctively who it was. "Come on in, Devlin."

He opened the door and slipped inside. "I guess I should be happy you didn't call me by some other man's name."

She gave him a cheeky grin. "It's what you deserve."

"Ha," he said. "I believe a promise was made that had something to do with a bar of soap this morning."

She laughed and caught the hopefulness in his face and giggled some more. She glanced down at her work and considered if she should finish it now or later. She cast a sideways look at the man waiting for her and smiled.

There really was no contest. She got up and threw herself into his arms.

"We might get to the bar of soap," she whispered against his ear. "But first I want to explore a whole lot of other things." She slid a hand down the front of his body and covered his growing erection. "And I'll start with this."

He rolled his eyes and groaned as she squeezed gently. "Damn, this could be a long night."

She stretched up on her tiptoes and nipped him on the chin. "You can count on that."

He caught her up in his arms and tossed her on the center of the bed, covering her, then snuggling beside her. As she reached for him, he lowered his head.

A long time later she raised herself from her drowsy sleep and sat up. She glanced at her watch. It was four o'clock. What had woken her? And then she knew. The answer to her coding issue.

She gazed down at the sleeping man and realized he needed the rest after the many hours they'd spent together. She reached over and dropped a kiss on the tip of his nose and slid from bed. She took a nightie out of her drawer, pulled it on over her head and sat down at her laptop. If she could just fine-tune this work and fix the last little bit of code, she might actually pull off something major.

"Good morning," his gravelly voice said an hour later. "How long have you been working?"

She got up from the laptop and went to the bedside, throwing herself into his arms. "Just for an hour. I woke up with a solution to a problem I was working on."

He rolled his eyes. "Is that what my nights could be like? I wear you down so you can sleep for the day but instead, you wear me out and get up to work some more." His voice was half teasing.

But she could hear the concern in his voice. She reached down and kissed him. "Just this one time," she promised.

He gave her a half smile that said he didn't believe her. "Sounds like you're happy with your work this morning."

"I am." She got up and danced around the room. "I might have pulled off something major."

He sat up on the side of the bed and glanced at her. "Glad to hear that. Is it ready for today?"

She nodded. He didn't question what she'd pulled off, and for that, she was grateful. She didn't want to share it yet.

If it didn't happen, it wouldn't matter anyway.

DEVLIN WAS SURPRISED to see everybody coming to the meeting for the contract. He could understand it as he also wanted to be a part of it. But he knew they would all not likely be allowed inside.

They drove up to the company headquarters at eight-thirty. Bristol used a security code and walked inside. The guard nodded at her and said, "Good morning. I was expecting you."

She smiled at him. "Where do we set up?"

"I'm to take you around to the back, yard 14B."

She nodded.

"I'll radio ahead so they'll let you in."

It took about fifteen minutes to get inside and unload the trailer. By the time everything was set up, Devlin could see Bristol's nerves were getting to her. He stroked a thumb across her pinched lips and said, "Relax."

She rolled her eyes up at him, reminding him of this exact movement last night and he grinned.

Then she stiffened and stepped back. He turned and realized not only were Brent and his boss here for the demonstration and hand delivery of the drones but there appeared to be an awful lot of brass. Devlin straightened to attention, recognizing when Easton and Ryder did the same. In fact, everybody in the group straightened up. Ice walked forward, Tesla at her side. They nodded at the men.

Sandra poked her head out of the crowd, a big grin on her face. Bristol gave her a small wave even as she whispered beside him, "Do you know any of these men?"

He shook his head. "But I think Ice and Tesla might." He cast a sideways glance at the two women. They both smiled. Immediately he felt better.

"Chin up," he said to Bristol. "Doesn't look like Brent is happy they are here either."

He watched her gaze flow over the men from the company she was contracted to and saw her grin. "No they aren't. So that's good for me."

He reached down and gave her hand a squeeze. "Go get 'em, tiger."

She shot him a grateful look, straightened her shoulders and walked forward to meet the men. Standing off to one side were three in military uniforms, along with Brent and his boss. She reached out and shook hands, treating all the men as equals.

Very quickly she set about doing the demonstration with the drones. Everything appeared to be going well as she worked, going over the contract and exactly what was expected of her and what she had produced.

The military men weren't stiff and unyielding but neither were they relaxed. No smiles were on any face. They stood in a row, arms crossed over their chests.

Devlin watched as Bristol glanced nervously at him several times. But Brent's reaction interested him more. Brent shifted his weight from one foot to the other and kept glancing around. Suspicious, Devlin searched the crowd and seeing all the photo IDs with ENFAQ emblazoned thereon affixed to most of the people here, Devlin realized many of the company employees were outside watching as well.

With instinct riding him, he walked over to Ryder and Easton and said, "I don't like this. Get ready for action."

Both men shot him hard glances.

Corey, standing with Ice and Tesla, turned to look at him and nodded. In a low whisper, he said, "This place is a nightmare for security."

Tesla protested. "That's not true. All these people are bonded. They all work for the company. They should be safe."

Devlin studied her. "And when you were betrayed, did it come from inside the company or outside?"

The color washed out of Tesla's face. She turned to look around and said, "How do we tell where the threat is?"

He took a deep breath. "I'm not sure. It's all about timing."

He separated from the others and walked through the crowd. His gaze never left the faces of the attendees as he searched, looking for whatever was wrong. But by now, the hair on the back of his neck stood up. He could feel his fingers itching as they went from fist to open palm to fist again. His chest constricted, and he stood searching, searching, and searching.

Bristol had several drones up in the air, doing a demonstration.

He watched her for a long moment, then turned his gaze back to the crowd. He heard the collective gasp. He pivoted and watched as one of the drones took a sideways slip, ready to crash. And then another. And he realized that once again, somebody was sabotaging her work to make her look like a fool. She did something to her handheld device, and instantly the drone corrected. Brent's boss asked, "Bristol, what was that?"

She said, "It's a slip maneuver." Her voice was calm, steady.

But Devlin knew her. And she was nervous. But why? Because of the nerve-wracking demonstration process she was involved in or something else? She put down the controller, picked up a different one and sent a separate drone up into the air. Her voice carried clearly over the crowd as she explained the next requirement on her contract.

The yard was open, and so there were a number of birds. He looked at a few of them suspiciously, wondering if he'd ever see one again and not wonder if it was a drone. But they all flew around the edges of the building and took roost, only to fly again. Perfectly natural.

He turned his attention back to the demonstration.

When it looked like she was almost done, a commotion erupted in the crowd. He tried to see what was going on, but it stilled almost immediately. But his suspicions lingered.

Finally Bristol turned to Brent and said, "And as per our contract, I have delivered fifty units with all the requirements we agreed upon."

She handed him the remote. Amid a lot of clapping and cheering, Devlin locked on Brent's face. Instead of being happy, he was pissed. Devlin strode to Bristol's side.

Brent's boss stepped forward and shook her hand, saying, "Thank you very much, Bristol. We weren't sure you would make the deadline for a while."

"I never doubted it," she said quietly. "There were several setbacks, as there were numerous attempts to sabotage my work, and of course, there were others on me personally. But we survived. Delivery is as promised, agreed?"

Brent's boss nodded and said, "Agreed. We'll arrange for final financing on your contract. And if we decide to go ahead with more, can you provide the additional units if we can come up with the funding?"

She nodded. "Yes, we can fulfill another order of these same units."

Brent's boss looked pleased. He smiled. "Great. Perfect. It's been a pleasure working with you."

She nodded. "Thank you, sir."

He stepped back. "You're destined for bigger and better things, I gather."

She shrugged. "One never knows. But my company is growing, yes."

Out of the crowd came another man in a three-piece suit. His arms were across his chest, and he was angry. "You stupid bitch. You stole my work."

Devlin's eyebrows raised. How did he get into this demonstration? Devlin stepped immediately in front of Bristol. But the accusation, ugly and resounding in volume, rang out across the yard.

"Well, I don't know who you are ..." Bristol studied him carefully. "But I think I've seen you before..." She cast her mind back, figuring out where and when.

Brent's boss stepped in. "No, he was one of the bids for the contract, also an ex-employee, but I chose yours over his at Brent's recommendation."

Bristol glanced at the man. "So you're Antwerp Originals." At his nod, she added, "And how is it that you believe I've stolen your work?"

"Because my drones do the same maneuvers," he roared, his face turning a bright red. "Brent suggested I come here to see the work you were doing in case you'd had access to mine."

"Of course your drones do," she said. "Because you're the one who sabotaged *my* work and sent somebody to steal it. That's why I recognize you. We caught a member of your family inside my house." She turned to Devlin. "Can you see the resemblance?"

He studied the man. "Yes." He turned to Bristol. "Not only are you right, we've actually got our intruder squirreled away safe and sound, just for an occasion like this."

She raised her eyebrows. "I never even asked what happened to him. And after being kidnapped, I completely forgot about it, then figured the cops picked him up."

He patted her shoulder. "That's why I'm here. To make sure people like him come back when they're supposed to." He turned and nodded to Ryder.

Ryder gave a whistle. Easton and Rhodes exited their truck and brought out the intruder. Everyone in the yard gasped, and their voices rose loud and hard.

Antwerp glared. "I have no idea why he might've been in your house." he said.

"Yes, you do," the intruder said warily. "I'm so damn tired of doing your dirty work." He turned to Bristol. "I've already spoken to your men and agreed to testify against my brother."

"It would have been fine if Brent hadn't been an asshole and gone back on his word. Brent promised the contract would be mine," Antwerp yelled at his brother and lunged. But Ryder pulled the brother away to a safe distance.

"Whoa, I didn't promise anything," Brent roared.

"Not to mention that doesn't address the issue of Colleen's murder," Devlin said smoothly. "Or the hacking that came from inside ENFAQ Ltd."

Silence.

Brent's boss called out, "What? Do you have proof of that?"

Devlin nodded. "Absolutely on the hacking. And whoever murdered Colleen had to be in Afghanistan when we were." His gaze wandered the stunned crowd. "And that leaves very few options. Right, Sandra?"

Bristol cried out in pain. "No, please not Sandra."

From the center of the crowd, Ice and Tesla dragged Sandra forward into the opening.

She was crying. "I didn't mean to. She caught me going over Bertha's new adaptations you'd been working on. We fought. I defended myself. She fell and hit her head." She sobbed. "I lit the fire to cover it up."

Devlin wrapped an arm around Bristol, standing stock-still, her fist shoved in her mouth as she stared at Sandra in horror.

"Brent told me to get Bertha," Sandra said, tears rolling down her cheeks. "I never meant to hurt anyone."

Brent stepped forward. "I had nothing to do with that. There's no way I told you to touch her drones."

Sandra spun on him. "Liar," she spat. "Not only to get her drones but to hack into her system after she arrived in Afghanistan, to interrupt any of her latest upgrades. I told you how I wasn't any good at that, but you said I just had to mess it up so she looked bad."

"That was Antwerp, not me," Brent snapped.

"Like hell," said the suited Antwerp brother. "I had nothing to do with either of those issues. You're not getting me involved in murder." Beside himself with fury, Antwerp pulled out a gun and turned it on Bristol. "You stupid bitch. You ruined everything. I was supposed to get the contract, not you. Brent promised it to me."

Then Antwerp turned the gun on Brent, who immediately backed up, hands in the air. "I didn't promise it to you."

"Yes, you did. I gave you money. A lot of it. And still I was forced to do the dirty work, like sabotaging her servers at her home lab to make sure that happened," he snapped in bitterness. "And when you accepted the bribe, the contract was supposed to be mine. But you gave it to her. Then you promised me that I would get this contract because she wouldn't be able to deliver. Forcing me to get involved yet again, using my stupid brother this time as a decoy to the kidnapping. Which you orchestrated with your own men on the company payroll. Now she's delivered, and I still don't have the damn contract. You took over one hundred thousand dollars from me in bribes."

He turned the gun back toward Bristol. "You! It's all your fault." Antwerp raised his weapon higher.

Just as he went to pull the trigger, a weird spit resounded in the air. Devlin raced forward but stopped as Antwerp slowly sank to his knees, the gun falling from his hand. Instantly the crowd backed up, cries arising in a loud roar around him.

Bristol held her hand up and said, "It's all right. Everyone is safe."

And then he knew. That's what she'd been working on early this morning.

To the stunned amazement of everyone, a small songbird came down and landed on her shoulder.

CHAPTER 21

B RISTOL, FEELING PRETTY damn good at the moment, stepped forward to look down at Antwerp, his shoulder bleeding heavily, and said, "You're lucky I didn't have a chance to test my new drone's aim. If I had, you'd be dead."

He shook his head. "I don't even see the drone."

She crouched down beside him. "Yes, you do."

His gaze locked on the bird on her shoulder, and he shook his head. "That's not possible."

"Not only is it, but it's made in the same light material, so if you shoot at it, it will still lock on its target and come back on-target again."

He shook his head. "No, it's not possible. It's too small."

She smiled. "Well, that was just one of the challenges I had to work on," she said modestly. She pushed the button on the tiny remote in her pocket. The songbird rose up above her and locked on to a position over her head. She walked to the three military men and said, "Gentlemen, this is one of my latest models."

They looked at the flying drone. She opened her hands to show them they were empty and said, "The older model was just delivered as agreed. But since then, I might've made a few modifications."

The three men studied the small bird flying gently above her. "Will it lock on to anyone?"

"It can if you want it to permanently, but that would require an ID chip, or depending on what kind of characteristics, we can help it to identify a target and have it lock on somebody else."

"How did it know you were being attacked?"

"In this case, I had the drone ready, willing, and waiting," she said. "I wasn't kidding when I said I've been sabotaged and kidnapped. This last week has been a living hell. I suspected there would be yet another attack here."

She pulled a tiny little makeup case from her pocket. "This completely controls the drone's actions. So I could've given the control to Devlin on the far side, or in a worst case scenario, it's compelled to act when it sees a weapon directed at me within ten feet. Those parameters can obviously be changed, but I was in a bit of a hurry to make it battle-ready for this morning."

She turned and realized everybody who had come in to save her bacon surrounded her. She smiled and said, "Sorry, guys, I never had a chance to show you this one."

Ice stepped forward and said, "Can I order one today?" Her gaze fell on the bird in fascination. "Talk about a fantastic backup system."

"Well, I still need to modify some things, plus I should set up a few more parameters. Getting a larger chip set would help too."

One of the military brass said, "Tesla has arranged a meeting at 1:00 p.m. this afternoon. I'm really looking forward to speaking with you."

They turned as one and faced Brent's boss. "I believe a conversation is in order."

With a hard glance at Brent—being restrained by two security men, another two holding Antwerp—Brent's boss nodded and said, "We better take this to my office."

Bristol watched the crowd disperse, then she turned to the others and said, "Thank you so much."

She was immediately wrapped in hugs. When the bird whistled higher in the air, several of them stepped back, and she laughed. "I promise he won't shoot anybody."

"I hope you'll always have one of those around," Devlin said. "I can't be watching you all the time."

She grinned. "Don't worry. I'll keep my birds around me at all times."

Ryder started to laugh. "Well, if you are keeping the swallow, does that mean you're *not* keeping Devlin?"

She glanced over at him and frowned. "Sorry?" she asked in confusion.

She didn't understand when the giggles started between Tesla and Ice, or when Easton cracked up, laughing so hard he almost bent over double. Corey's grin was so wide, she knew she'd become the butt of a joke.

She put her hands on her hips and glared at them. "What's so funny?"

Tesla tried to explain in between the giggles. When Bristol finally understood, remembering the earlier conversation, she spun around and stared at Devlin. "You mentioned something about that before, but I hadn't understood it was this big."

Devlin looked anywhere but at her. Especially when Ryder added, "Of course, Devlin wouldn't have anything to do with the Keepers or its romance legend because he was afraid he'd end up in the same situation."

"You know," she said to Devlin, "I should slap your face for that."

His eyebrows rose. "You should slap mine? What the

hell did I do?" he asked in outrage.

She smiled, walked closer and said, "Because, by denouncing the Keepers' group and not believing in them"—she poked his chest—"you're actually standing on the side of life that doesn't believe in love or forever." She poked his chest harder, forcing him to back up a step. "And I've got to tell you"—she poked him again—"that I love you. So I'm staying here, and I'm *keeping* you both."

The group around them cheered.

He glared at everybody else, then looked down at her, giving her a lopsided grin. A smile that took away her breath—slow-dawning, so warm, caring, and so full of love.

He caught her up and swung her around in the air before placing her back on the ground, still holding her within the circle of his arms. "I'm damn glad to hear that," he said. "I was trying to finagle my way into your life on a permanent basis."

She laughed. "There's only one way to do that—and that's to become a Keeper."

He lowered his head. Just before his lips met hers, he whispered, "As long as I get to keep you, I'll be anything you want."

And he kissed her, a passionate promise for a perfect tomorrow.

EPILOGUE

I T'S A DAMN good thing Easton Fairchild was headed home for a few days before going up north for another training mission.

He needed the time to adjust mentally and emotionally. He couldn't have contemplated how seeing Devlin and Bristol's romance would affect him. And he needed to get that under control before anyone noticed. He'd been down on relationships for a long time.

The last thing he needed was to get sucked into that emotional quagmire. He'd had one love of his life, and she'd hated that he'd been in the military, said it wasn't natural to ask her to wait for him to come home all the time. And if their positions were reversed, he wouldn't wait for her either.

She'd walked out during their engagement, a month shy of the wedding. She'd gone on to bigger and better things, including a marriage with a dot.com executive. And Easton? Well, he'd walked away from the whole long-term-relationship thing. Some rejections hurt more than others. He'd gone on to build a shell around his heart and to live his life to the fullest he could elsewhere.

Until he watched fun-loving, never-looking-for-a-permanent-relationship Devlin fall in love—without a quibble or hesitation—with Bristol. She was well worth it, and if Easton had been more on the ball in Afghanistan, maybe he'd have hooked her first. But such a thing had never crossed his mind.

Now he wondered, had he blocked all thoughts of a permanent relationship from his mind to the extent he wouldn't see the "right" woman for him if she crossed his path?

Talk about a disturbing thought. How did one become more open to the possibility and yet not attract the wrong person while doing it? He was patient and didn't mind waiting for the right woman to show up, but he wasn't sure he was the kind of guy to reach out and grab her when the opportunity arrived.

Or like Devlin, did that perfect woman walk by, and your life was changed forever—ready or not?

EASTON

SEALs of Honor, Book 13

Dale Mayer

CHAPTER 1

EASTON GALLAGHER GRABBED several of the large packs off the back of the plane and tossed them to the stack below. The supplies had finally arrived. They'd come in a few hours later than the personnel. They were doing a joint SERE training which would include survival and evasion, resistance and escape, but the real reason they were here was the water survival. The Canadian military was known for their water purification systems. While there, they'd be doing additional training on new drinking water convertors. He was looking forward to it. He loved the Canadians, and this country was just too beautiful to ever get tired of. That Devlin, Ryder, and Corey were beside him made it that much better. He loved his unit. These guys were the best.

Although Devlin could be a pain in the ass since he'd met Bristol. Now that he'd found somebody perfect in his world, he couldn't resist matching up all the others. And that was the last thing Easton wanted. He'd gone that route once, and it ended one month before the wedding date. He wasn't trying again. Her reason was valid back then, and he assumed every other woman's would be the same as nothing in his life had changed. She couldn't take his frequent absences, worrying he might not return. Not to mention sometimes he was gone for weeks or months at a time. She never knew when he would return—or if he'd come back alive from his dangerous missions.

Easton didn't know how Devlin and Bristol would manage it, but Bristol was so wrapped up in her work she might not even notice. He laughed at that.

Devlin looked at him sideways. "What the hell's so funny?"

Easton shrugged. "I wonder if Bristol even realizes you're gone."

Devlin gave him a wicked grin. "After last night, she'll never forget."

Inside Easton could feel the envy clawing at his gut. It'd been a long time since he had felt that way about anybody. Even knowing he wasn't ready himself, he was still happy for his friend. He grabbed more gear, then carried it down the ramp and added it to the rest. As he turned, Devlin tossed him a bag that shoved him back slightly. He rolled his eyes at his buddy, grabbed the next one midair and threw them both down again.

He headed toward the big metal cases they had to unload. As he rounded a corner, a woman packing more cameras than anybody should be allowed to own, plus several bags, started down the ramp to exit the plane. He walked over to give her hand, but she turned suddenly, and a camera swung out, hitting him on the side of his face. It was hard and sharp enough that he knew it had left its mark. He stepped out of the way, ignoring the cutting pain on his cheek.

"Oh, my goodness. I'm so sorry."

He shook his head. "Ma'am, do you need any help with all that?"

Her gaze widened. "Ma'am?" She shook her head. "My name is Summer. Summer Jones." She held out her hand, but it was full. Looking awkward for a moment, she shuffled the items to her other hand so she could take his.

Instead he stepped back and motioned for her to go ahead. "Let's get you off the plane."

She beamed and said, "Thank you so much. Again, I'm sorry for hitting you with my gear."

He groaned. "You're not Canadian by any chance, are you?"

She laughed. "Actually I'm one of the few who has dual citizenship. I'm half-Canadian, half-American." She stepped around him and banged him again with her bag. "I'm so sorry."

She couldn't seem to stop apologizing. Easton took a moment to really study her. She was small with jet-black hair forming a skullcap to outline her face, with her huge Miss Congeniality grin and massive blue eyes. He shouldn't even be noticing such things, but she was hard to miss.

She smiled. "So sorry again." And she disappeared.

He spun to watch as she raced down the ramp. As he did so, he caught Devlin's eye.

"Interesting. She did smack you upside the head to get your attention. Even you should be able to see that sign."

Easton glared at his buddy. "Her camera did that. Doesn't count."

Devlin's wicked grin flashed again.

Easton grabbed one of the big two-hundred-pound gun cases and carried it out on his own. He needed to vent all his frustration on something. Hauling this should do it. Of course, once he did that, the other guys raced in to prove they could as well.

As soon as all the gear was off-loaded, they filled the back of the jeeps and drove to the main part of the base. He was looking forward to the next couple weeks. The first was in-camp work; then they'd be in the backwoods for the next. And he couldn't wait. This wasn't a Navy operation. He and his unit were meeting the equivalent team on the Canadian side. Friendly training, camaraderie, and information-sharing. All good fun.

Not only did the Canadians have a new gadget for making freshwater out of saltwater that they used for their humanitarian efforts all around the world, but they had a much smaller version that could be used for backwoods travel. Which meant, anytime they were stuck out at sea or where the water was less than ideal, the gadget converted it to drinking water.

Besides, being in Canada was almost like going home. Easton had spent a lot of summers up here. He was in northern Ontario this time, but he'd traveled from one end of the country to other. He couldn't tell which part was any better than the rest. It was just so diverse.

Back at camp, it was dinnertime. As they walked into the mess hall, they were met by several other military units here for the same event—one of those learn-something-while-you-have-fun-getting-to-know-your-neighbor type of events. He was good with that. He'd yet to meet a Canadian he didn't like.

Just as they joined the chow line, somebody stepped right in between him and the next guy. He had to hit the brakes so as not to overrun her. Of course it was Summer once again.

She turned and beamed at him. "Hi. Nice to see you again."

Easton just glared at her. She seemed to be a person who would be in the wrong place at the wrong time on any given day. She reached for a plate and handed it to him.

Devlin leaned around Easton's back to say, "His name is Easton, and I'm Devlin. This is Ryder and Corey."

Summer's smile jacked up several more notches. "I'm the photographer for this event," she said. "At least the first part of it. I'm really looking forward to it."

Easton turned her gently so she could see the gap between her and the guy in front, seriously holding up the line.

"Oh, my goodness." She raced forward so fast she almost slammed into the man ahead of her. Easton stepped up behind her and pointed out several dishes she'd already missed. Using his long arms, he grabbed her plate and served her some vegetables and a big potato.

As he handed it to her, she looked at the food on her plate and then at him and asked, "How did you know I wanted this?"

He just stared at her.

She studied him for a long moment. "Thank you."

He rolled his eyes. "Do you ever say anything else?"

"Oh, you speak," she exclaimed. "I wondered for a moment if you were a deaf-mute."

Devlin snickered behind Easton.

He shook his head. "I'm definitely not deaf. I only speak when something needs to be said."

"Oh, me too," she said happily. "Could you reach a set of cutlery for me, please?"

Easton looked to where she pointed. Sure enough, on the far side of the double buffet line, somebody had placed the cutlery. He reached across and picked up a set for her and him, then snagged a bun from a large basket for himself.

"That looks delicious. I'm hungry. I missed lunch," she confessed, "and I really need to eat or my blood sugar drops.

Kind of like it has now."

He looked at her plate, already half-full.

She glanced at her food, but also stared at the bun in his hand, snatched it up and took a big bite.

Easton's gaze narrowed. "You okay?"

She nodded rapidly, her jaw busy chewing. When she could talk, she said, "Like I said, I haven't eaten for a while."

He noted a tremor sliding through her voice. "Is your blood sugar that low?"

She shrugged and took another bite. The color on her cheeks had bleached out.

He watched as she quickly ate as if she really needed it. He grabbed a second one for himself, wondering if she needed another too. He couldn't imagine her being that hungry, so it must be her blood sugar. He had several diabetic friends and understood white carbs surely weren't the best option. Still not a whole lot was available on base. With a couple hundred men in here, she'd have a hard time finding any other selections. Surely fruit or juice would be better, if available.

He searched down the line that had stopped just before the meat section and spied a juice bar in the center of the room. He turned and told Devlin to hold his plate and place and headed to the table. There he grabbed several juice bottles and came back, holding one out to her. She looked at him, her gaze getting wider and wider, and then awkwardly grabbed the bottle. He took her plate from her and, with his voice low, said, "Drink up."

She had already popped off the lid and took several swallows. By the time she was done, three-quarters of the bottle was empty.

She stood still for a moment, as if assessing how she felt,

then smiled at him. "Thank you. That was very smart."

She pocketed the bottle into one of the many pockets on her vest. Then she took her plate back and popped a piece of broccoli into her mouth. "Now I have to have something for the juice to slosh around in there with." She got another piece and surveyed the food to see what else she could snag.

"Here, have my other bun. You need it."

"I'll be fine. I'll grab more up ahead." She looked toward the meat with longing.

Easton dropped the roll on her plate and said, "Just take it."

She snatched it and took a big bite again.

He watched in amazement as she polished off the second. Orange juice and two buns were hardly a healthy dinner.

"I sure hope they leave me some," she muttered, seeing what the holdup was.

Behind him, Easton could hear Devlin snickering again. Easton shook his head at his friend. Slowly the line moved forward. Up ahead were more vegetables, salads, and finally proteins. He thought she wouldn't have any more room, that she'd be too full, but she loaded up her plate heavily with roast beef, a piece of chicken, then added salad with a slab of cheese on the side. There were more buns, and she grabbed yet another, then stepped out of the line and turned to look for a place to sit.

If she was alone, it would be a little hard to assimilate. It wasn't that military men weren't friendly, but they'd group up in a situation like this. Easton collected the rest of his dinner and waited for his friends. They turned and studied the room. An empty table was off on the far side. They slowly made their way in that direction, saying hi to a few friends as they kept going. They knew several of the Canadians and, of course, many from his own military branch. At the table, Ryder nudged him.

Easton glanced at him. "What?"

Ryder pointed. Up ahead Summer stood in the middle of the room, still looking for a place to sit. She wasn't very tall, and it had to be difficult to see far away.

"Really?"

"You know how it goes," Ryder said with a big smile. "Let's help her out."

"Damn it." Easton slammed his plate on the table, the sound loud enough to make several people turn in his direction, including Summer.

When she saw him, her gaze lit up. Seeing his group, her face fell. He motioned for her to come join him. She hesitated, looking around, making sure he had motioned to her.

"Oh, for God's sake." He walked toward her, took her by the elbow and ushered her to his table. "You hit me in the face," he muttered. "You ate the buns off my plate, and you drank the juice I gave you. You might as well sit at my table and finish eating your dinner."

She smiled. "Thank you so much," she said quietly. "I was a little intimidated, finding a place to sit."

He motioned at an empty seat on the far side, but, just as he pointed, Devlin dropped into it, leaving the seat beside Easton the only one open. He glared at his buddies; they all had big grins on their faces.

She turned to Easton. "I don't remember who your friends are." Instantly the men introduced themselves. As she sat down, she said, "Hi. Thank you so much for letting me join you."

The guys grinned, and Devlin said, "Any friend of Easton's is a friend of ours."

She beamed across the table. "That's a lovely thing to say."

SUMMER WAS DELIGHTED with Easton and his friends. They were dressed differently than the others here, but she didn't dare ask about it. Rank was a point of pride, and she didn't want to get it wrong and insult them. There was also an air—a commanding presence—surrounding the four of them that she hadn't seen around anyone else here.

She wondered at that. Hundreds of men and women were in this place. It wasn't that she had trouble making friends, but it was always awkward to acclimate at the beginning. She wasn't so sure Easton had been the first one to step forward, or if his friends had pushed him, but she was grateful and relieved nonetheless. The place was a busy hub. It had already been bad enough that she'd felt her energy drop. She didn't know if Easton had seen her swaying on her feet or not. It was a sure sign her blood sugar was low enough to cause trouble.

She'd been tested many times, but wasn't diabetic or even prediabetic. But she was given to severe blood sugar drops. She had to stabilize, eat regular meals, and avoid junk food or, in this case, simple carbs—because those helped in the short run but made it drop lower in the long run. Eating the buns would lead to trouble. But she hoped enough stabilizing food in the rest of her meal would counteract the side effects. Besides, she'd had to get her blood sugar back up, or she would've passed out in the lineup.

She couldn't believe she had hit this poor man. Her gaze

drifted over to the giant beside her, zooming in on the cut on his cheek. She gasped. "Oh, my God, did I do that you?" She gently stroked the dried blood.

He turned to look at her, his fingers checking out his injury himself. With his overlapping hers, he shrugged. "Maybe. Maybe not."

Her jaw dropped. "If that was my cheek, I would have known when and where."

He glanced at her. "With skin like yours, I wouldn't doubt it. But I'm tough and barely noticed."

She dropped her hand and picked up her fork. In a low voice she muttered, "I am so sorry."

"So you said," he replied in a laconic tone. "It doesn't matter. I'm not hurt."

She felt better. "Good. I wouldn't want to be responsible for having that."

She felt the others' interest in their conversation coming in waves. She gave them a bright smile and explained, "When I was getting off the plane, I had my bags and camera gear. Easton happened to be in the way. When I swung around, one of my cameras must've caught him as I came down the stairs."

The men's gazes turned to the cut on Easton's face.

He glared at them. "It's fine."

"Maybe she should take you to get that cleaned." Ryder smirked.

She stared at him suspiciously, but inside she wondered. "Maybe we should at that," she said hesitantly. "I wouldn't want it to get infected."

The other three men's heads bobbed up and down, but beside her Easton shook his head in a slow, bullish manner. She didn't understand the undercurrents going on here. She opened her mouth only to have a chunk of bun shoved in it. She glared at Easton as she chewed furiously to clear her mouth so she could speak.

"I'm fine. I'm not going to the first aid station. You have nothing to apologize for. Eat." He glared at her.

Still chewing furiously, she glared right back. "It could be worse than you think." But her words were hardly distinguishable around her food.

He studied her with a frown, then shook his head. "It doesn't matter what you just said. It's fine." He picked up his fork and stabbed in the direction of each of the three men, one at a time, and said, "Lay off."

But instead of being quiet, they had the most innocent of looks on their faces, and one even slapped a hand over his heart as if to say he'd never do anything to hurt his friend.

She stared at the three, then back at Easton and decided he was being too hard on them. "You should be nicer to your friends, Easton. You never know when you might need them."

A moment of shocked silence followed before the three men choked. She stared at them suspiciously, then turned to look at Easton. He gave a heavy sigh, and she realized they were just teasing him. She muttered in a low tone, "And again, I'm sorry."

But this time he grasped her hand in his and squeezed gently. "Don't be. They are my friends, my best friends. When I get a chance to beat the crap out of them for this, I will." He dropped her hand and resumed eating.

Only she couldn't take her gaze off her hand. His was so large it had completely smothered hers. And her hand—soft, almost fragile when compared to his—was such a contrast that she couldn't stop thinking about it. Amazing.

She wanted to see his hand over hers again. In her mind, her camera was already setting shutter speed and focus. She really wanted a picture of that, with just her hand peeking out beneath the shelter of his. She instinctively picked up her camera, still around her neck. With his friends at the table with them, she froze. No way would she ask him to cover her hand again. That could really alienate her. She was oddball enough for most people as she found it very difficult to separate herself from her passion.

Slowly she dropped her camera and forced herself to pick up the rest of her juice and finish the bottle.

Easton gave a simple nod as if happy with her.

And darn if it didn't make her feel better.

He cocked his head, talking to the other men.

His hand was in the same position it had been when it covered hers. She picked up her camera and studied it through the viewfinder. She loved everything about this man's hand—the angles of his knuckles, the strength of the muscles visible between the joints. The sheer size of it. She set her camera on the table, realizing all four men stared at her.

Color flashed up and down her cheeks. She could feel the heat rolling in waves. With a sheepish smile she said, "I'm a photographer, and the oddest things catch my attention."

Unfortunately, what also kept her attention right now appeared to be him.

CHAPTER 2

S UMMER POPPED OUT the SD card from the camera and slipped in another. She put the spare in her vest pocket and closed it securely, then went back to work. She was a freelance photographer under contract with a company hired by the military to take pictures for some of their new brochures. She'd worked for Ross for years now, and they had a great working relationship.

Not just in the States but also in Canada, as they were here doing training on outdoor survival. The Canadians had brought one of their new water container systems and some other new tech gadgets. She was to focus on pictures of the training camaraderie to have the images depict the atmosphere of the men working together with a purpose.

She understood that a lot of the brochures would end up concentrating on sales, while some encouraged more youths to join. She didn't care what they were for, her job was to get the right shot, and she knew she'd be lucky to get one in one hundred that met her standards. Thank heavens for the digital world. She'd shoot thousands of shots and delete over 90 percent of them. Right now she needed to catch as many as she could. She'd been at the water container system this morning; now a group of US and Canadian members were involved in a friendly game of tug-of-war.

She caught sight of her pilot on her last leg of this trip

and waved to him. She never forgot a face. He returned it with a nod and joined the other spectators.

The teams were lining up, ready to grab the rope to see who could pull whom across the line. The Canadians had dumped water all around, making sure nobody had a strong foothold. This would become mud wrestling with a rope. She was both grinning and swearing as she clicked as fast as she could. She set up another camera with video to take shots of the entire process. So much was going on that she was constantly on the move—so much to see, like this face, those hands, the white-knuckled grips on the rope, the mud across the knees, the grimace on the faces, the officers laughing while others cheered.

The cheerleaders stationed at either end of the teams rooted for their compatriots. She lifted her gaze and saw two men standing, talking on the far side of her, looking disinterested. She took the shot. Nothing like contrasts to make for a good subject.

She kept on shooting. The Canadians were winning; the Americans were swearing.

She was laughing so hard it was getting difficult to take the shots. Mud flew in all directions, and she was trying to stay out of range, but, with every step, struggle, and grunt, it seemed like more was flowing.

She knew, no matter who won, both teams would be in the mud. It was a beautiful day—sunshine, blue sky, lots of green trees, brown mud—and, of course, all the uniforms. Some men were dressed in deep blue on the US team, others in green for the Canadians. She didn't understand the significance of the uniforms or the contrast of colors, but it made the artist in her snap double fast.

As the flag slowly inched toward the Canadian side, the

groans were loud and long as were the cheers. Her fingers were so busy taking photos, she wasn't even sure where she started or stopped. The victor clear, the teams lunged at each other, knocking their opponents off their feet into the mud. The game continued. She straightened and did a complete panorama, showing the cries of dismay and joy, the agony of defeat, the cheers of success. Oddly, in the background, a small group of several men was completely disinterested.

She didn't understand. And, as such, had to capture the moment to consider later. Whatever they were talking about, their heads were bent; hands lifted so they could see something better. Phones were brought out; numbers probably exchanged.

There was no rest; no respite. She was thinking she could use that… When a hand landed on her shoulder, she cried out, jumping back several feet.

The tall blond male in a dark uniform stood in front of her. She did a double take. Easton. Damn he looked good. Instantly she lifted her camera.

Just as fast he lowered her arm.

She frowned at him only to realize he held out a cold beer for her.

"You've been working as hard as anybody else. Do you want one?"

"Still trying to feed me?" she teased.

He snorted. "Not likely. You don't need help in that area." He motioned toward the cameras around her neck and the canvas bag tucked between her feet. "What are you doing here?"

She shrugged, then took a long sip, catching Easton holding back a wince. Beer was meant to be drunk ice-cold for this kind of physical exertion. And, for her, that was the only time beer was palatable. It was awfully hard to get down the rest of it. She handed it back to him. "Here. You finish it."

He stared at the half-full bottle and then at her. "Why don't you?"

"For the same reason as before, blood sugar. More than half and I'll go down for sure." She fumbled for a different lens in her bag. After switching them out, she spun to see if the men standing in the background were still there. They'd be perfect to test out the new lens with this light.

She lifted and started clicking. One of the four men turned and saw the cameras around her neck, then motioned to the others. They turned their backs to her and walked away. Just as she was about to move to the other side, a huge chest stepped in front of her. Still looking from behind the camera, she raised her head to see the big biceps of the arms crossed over his chest. Higher and higher she raised the camera until it landed squarely on Easton's face. The angles, the square jaw, the chiseled lips … Her fingers clicked in panic, afraid of missing the moments the artist in her was enchanted by.

Until he closed his hand over her lens.

She dropped her camera, letting it hang around her neck, crying out, "Hey."

He shook his head. "I'm not modeling, and you're not printing any pictures of me for your brochures." He glared at her. "Make sure you understand that very clearly."

A gamine grin popped up. "How about for my private collection?" She waggled her eyebrows at him.

A reluctant grin formed on his lips. "No pictures, no-where, no how."

"Damn." She shot him a dirty look. "Party pooper."

"Is that so?" He opened his arms and said, "Of all the things you could say, you would choose that."

"I often say it. So what?" She turned her back on him, looking for more action to capture with her camera. When she turned again a good ten minutes later, she was alone. Good. She knew she had to have his permission to keep the pictures of him or to use them, but darn she really wanted a couple for herself. And she *really* wanted to get a photo of his hand over hers like he'd done at the table. There was something so caring, so protective about that image that it wouldn't leave her alone. It said so much about him.

The afternoon sped by. She worked, bent, clicked, crouched, clicked again, stood, shifted her position and clicked once more. When she finally stepped back, the late-afternoon sun shone through the trees, dust mites floating through the air illuminated by its beams. She went back into action again.

When she finally released her camera, turning around to find where she had left her bag, Easton held it in his hand, a frown on his face. His three friends stood beside him, sporting big grins. She beamed. "Thank you for finding that. But where did I leave it?"

"You mean, where did you leave it *this* time?"

She shot him a disgruntled look, snatching it from his hand. "So I might have a problem with leaving my bags behind."

He stared at her for a long moment, studying the bag and all the cameras around her neck, and laughed. "You look like ten crazy tourists in one."

She shoved her bag on the ground between her feet and put her hands on her hips. "We all have our weaknesses. I can be a tad bit forgetful when I get busy in my work."

Ryder chuckled. "*Can be?* Easton has moved that bag closer to you at least half a dozen times in the last several hours. Good thing this is orientation day so he had the time."

Her jaw dropped. "Really?" She winced. "I'm so sorry I was mean. You've been very kind to me. I really shouldn't be so forgetful, but it's hard," she said earnestly, formulating an explanation. "It's the light, the shadows. They capture my attention. I get sucked into my art and lost in the creativity of the moment. It's like being enchanted, and somebody has to break the spell before I step back into reality." She gave a small smile. "And I'm not always at the same place where I started."

This time the other men were openly laughing, but Easton still glared at her. "Maybe that's why you have low blood sugar. Did you eat lunch today?"

"Of course I did. I had lunch with you, silly."

He shook his head. "That was dinner last night."

She gave herself a shake. "Okay, so I missed breakfast. I did get up early because the light was so fascinating, so I went outside. I came running back to the mess tent, but it was too late. Thankfully, I still had some protein bars in my bags. Surely I didn't miss lunch too?" She checked her watch and gasped in shock. "I missed lunch," she wailed.

"Weren't you given a seating time to go in for your meals?"

She dove into her multipocketed vest and pulled out a piece of paper, holding it up for the men to inspect.

"You were in seating block A. That was the first group."

On cue her stomach rumbled, and she started to feel tired. "Oh, boy. When is dinnertime then?" she asked, scared to hear the answer. "It needs to be soon. Otherwise I'll probably end up in trouble again."

She was such a fool. She was so damn passionate about her work for the video and brochures that everything else slid into the dark recesses of her mind. Her parents often complained about it; her brother just laughed or made fun of her. Being self-employed gave her a lot of advantages. She didn't think that an employer would handle her foibles quite so easily. Still, it wasn't normally this bad. She'd put it down to exhaustion. She'd worked so hard to get her photos ready for each show that she'd burned a lot of midnight oil before she came on this assignment.

Ryder pointed at the piece of paper she'd lifted. "See the bottom line? Dinnertime. You're section A again."

She studied the paper for a long moment. Maybe it was because she was so tired, but it made no sense. She raised her gaze to him. "Translation?"

"Oh, for God's sake." Easton snagged her arm while she grabbed the bag at her feet. "We'll be eating in ten minutes. You're coming with us. It's the only way to make sure you eat. Otherwise I'll find you passed out in the dirt."

"That only happened once, and I'd been really sick. I should've eaten more then. I should have stayed home, but my friend was getting married so I had to go," she said as she was dragged along toward the mess tent. "Besides, you're probably at a different seating time."

He stopped to look at her and in a low, hard voice asked, "Where are your barracks?"

She frowned at him. She turned to the other men at her side. "Is he always this grumpy?"

Corey's eyebrows shot up. "Actually, he's probably the most patient of us all."

Her look of astonishment switched to joy. "Now I know

you're joking."

They all shook their heads.

She snorted. "Then I feel sorry for you because if your tempers and lack of patience are way worse than his…" She shook her head. "Wow."

"Enough." Easton followed her pointing finger to one of the barracks, taking the bag from her. "Of course it would be at the far end." He glanced at her gear. "Are you okay leaving all that in your barracks when you eat?"

She shook her head. "No way."

"How do you eat when you carry all that around your neck?"

She stepped forward and opened the one he held in his hands. She pulled out a second collapsible square bag and proceeded to very carefully pack all her camera gear from around her neck. When she was done, she connected some buckles and the two bags became one with shoulders straps. Then she grabbed those and flung them over her shoulder like a backpack. "Now let's go eat. This gear comes with me. Tens of thousands of dollars' worth of equipment is in here, plus the special photos I took earlier."

"The laptop?"

"That's in the barracks," she said, staring worriedly in the distance. "It should be safe, shouldn't it?"

The men exchanged glances as if knowing something she didn't. She turned her gaze from one to the other, walking up to Devlin. "What is he not telling me?"

He sighed. "A training camp was sabotaged a few months ago. Several drones, software, and a lot of research material was burned to the ground. A woman was killed at the same time."

"She was murdered?" she whispered in shock.

Devlin nodded.

"We can't give you all the details. Suffice it to say, things can happen on base as well as off."

She pushed out her chin and said, "Then I'm definitely not leaving my cameras there. Let's go eat, then I'll return to my quarters and work on the photos." She spun on her heels and raced off at top speed. A hand landed on her shoulder, dragging her to a stop before spinning her around.

"You're heading the wrong direction. Dinner is over there," Easton said without any humor.

As such, she accepted it with gratitude. She nodded meekly and said, "Thank you."

And this time she waited until he led, then she followed.

HE DIDN'T KNOW if she walked around like a child all the time, heedless of direction, just content to move forward. Did she have any navigational skills at all? He shook his head, knowing the rest of the men were chuckling inside. He wasn't. He was also quite perturbed at her photographing him like she had. He wasn't worried about her seeing anything he didn't want her to, but her comment about a private collection had him thinking a whole lot as to whether she did this all the time. Did she also take pictures when he wasn't looking, or of the other men as well? That he didn't like, making her actions all the more disturbing. He didn't want to care, but something about her got under his skin. He couldn't stop thinking about her.

He turned around several times to make sure she was still behind them. Each time he caught the men's grins. He glared at them, hoping it would make them shut up.

As they hadn't said anything, he was probably only making things worse.

In the mess tent, he directed her toward the line already formed for dinner. He kept her firmly in front of him, and all the other men fell into step behind him. He held her tray, and, as she was busy looking around, he was filling her plate.

When she turned to see what he was doing, already several buns were on her tray, along with butter and a big chunk of cheese. "Oh! I love cheese."

Several more slices landed on the small plate. He pointed to the vegetables up front. She ladled up her own and moved down the line, taking what she wanted. He was happy to see she was a big eater. With her focus and complete lack of awareness of what she was doing, how could she not burn through calories?

He'd met artists like that. Some painters, once they started, never stopped. He knew an author who would go for days getting the words down on paper before he stopped for a breath, rarely eating, living on caffeine as if that were the lifeblood of his muse.

By the time they reached the other end of the food aisle, her tray was full, but she still had no beverages. He took her by the shoulder, and, instead of talking, pointed toward the table in the center that held drinks. "Over there next."

She turned, and, with him making sure the path opened in front, they made their way to it. He placed an orange juice and bottled water on her tray and then doubled up on his. He glanced around to see the others were behind them. Of course they were, taking advantage of the pathway he had opened through the crowd.

Devlin pointed to the far side and said, "A free table is over there." He led the way, leaving the others to follow.

Easton did, taking Summer, and, behind them, Corey

and Ryder picked up the rear. Easton didn't know how it had happened, but she'd suddenly become a part of his group. As such, no way would he leave her—or anyone—behind.

At the table, they sat and unloaded their food. With the same focus and attention she put into her photography, she ate her food. She might be small and passionate about work, but she ate like a trucker. He watched as she completely inhaled everything on her plate, including the buns and extra cheese.

When she sat back, pushing the tray away, she said, "Oh, my God. Thank you for finding me."

"You'll pass out in the fields if you don't eat properly," Ryder said with a big grin.

She nodded. "I'll never let that happen again."

"You'll do it again—every time you get caught up in your work," Easton said drily.

"I love Canada," she said with a big smile, as if hoping to change the subject. "But I'm more used to the west coast than Ontario."

"Whereabouts on Canada's west coast?" Corey asked.

"Vancouver. There's something very magical about that city."

A discussion ensued about what the Coronado base and Vancouver had to offer. Having been both places many times, she had some insightful correlations between them. She was so passionate about Vancouver, Easton could feel a sense of wonder through her eyes. He wanted to see her artwork, how she viewed the world. Just listening to her gave such a different viewpoint that he couldn't imagine what she captured with her cameras.

"Do you do more than just brochures and still photography?" Easton was at a bit of a loss, not really understanding what her artwork entailed.

She nodded. "That's my bread and butter. I have showings in various galleries across the country as well. The one I call *Momentum* is in Washington state now, moving to Oregon next. I have to talk to my gallery manager to see where else it's traveling to."

"*Momentum?*" Corey asked.

She nodded. "Movement within the world and how it all comes together to create momentum," she explained. She gave a happy shrug. "If I could do that work all the time, I would love it. But I have to feed all my cats."

Easton frowned. "How many cats?"

She shot him a look. "Oh, don't tell me that you're a dog person?"

"I like cats too." He shrugged. "But no avoiding the question."

She grabbed her bottle of water, opened it and took a long sip.

He waited.

His buddies were right; he did have patience, in spades. She knew in some aspect her answer was important. With a heavy sigh she said, "You aren't going to let me off without answering, are you?"

"Nope."

"Well, right now I have six."

Corey whistled.

Ryder chuckled.

Devlin said in a low voice, "*Now?*"

With a wince she said, "One's pregnant."

Easton groaned. He was really in trouble. "Let me guess. They are all rescues?"

"Yes." She turned in delight. "How did you know?"

"Because it's just who you are." The trouble was, it was also who he was. All his growing up years, before he went off to training, he had animals at home. His mom had screamed, hollered, and stamped her feet, but eventually he wore her down, and she let him keep whatever animal he wanted. It could be anything from turtles to squirrels to dogs to mother cats with six kittens. His goal in life had always been to own a large property and take as many animals as was reasonable. He had a pretty good idea that the word *reasonable* would change on a day-to-day basis in his world. He glanced at her and wondered how she felt about taking pictures of animals. Especially in a few years when he got set up.

Something about her made him realize she'd be perfect for that role—that of standing right beside him.

CHAPTER 3

A S THE MEN finished eating, a soldier walked over and handed one of them a note. It was passed to all of them before they stood, nodded to her and walked away.

Easton called back, "We have to go."

She was still eating her dessert and sipping her coffee as she watched them. She was sad to see them go, although she often didn't mind being alone. They were friendly faces in a sea of strangers. Especially Easton, although he was more cranky than friendly.

Just as she decided to head to her quarters, two men came to her table and sat down across from her. They wore military fatigues. She glanced at their faces but didn't know them. "Hello," she said carefully.

The men nodded at her; one of them pointed at her bags and said, "You've been taking pictures all day."

She smiled. "Yes, I'm the photographer, doing a bunch of brochures and social media stuff on this camp. All goodwill."

"But you've been taking pictures of things other than just the activities, correct?"

She frowned. "Only scenery. Everything else has been about the men here."

Silence followed.

"The photographs need to be only what you're allowed

to take pictures of," the younger man said warily. "The superiors don't like to have any others taken."

"Oh, all the photos will be okayed before they are used," she assured them. "I've been doing this for a long time."

If she thought that would reassure them, she was wrong. They just stared at her with that bland, hard look. She didn't quite understand what the problem was, but something had obviously struck a nerve. Then again these men might have a darn good reason to be wary of a stranger, even if she had the right to be here. As she thought about the types of missions these men did, she understood their need to stay under the radar.

With a small smile, she excused herself. "I'll head back to my place now, thanks."

She got up and grabbed her bag, then slipped the straps over her shoulders. For some reason the conversation with Easton earlier, and now these men, made her a little more uneasy than she'd ever been on a base. It was unfortunate because she really loved being in Canada. She didn't want a negative overtone to her visit here.

From the mess tent, she found her way to hers without any trouble. It was spacious and empty. Inside, she sat on her bed and started her laptop. She had a lot of images to download. With her laptop beside her, she opened the first camera and looked at the screen on the back, quickly clicking through each picture, deleting the obviously bad shots. She'd make the decisions on the rest when she got home where she had a much bigger setup. But, for now, no point in transferring hundreds of images that were no good.

It took her a while, but it was work she loved. By the time she'd gotten to the second SD card, she realized she'd had quite a day. She kept looking, making instant decisions from long years of practice as to whether a shot was good or not worth keeping. She flicked, decided to keep, swiped again to the left. That next one was a keeper, followed by several that belonged in the garbage.

Dozens had the light completely wrong. She sent all those into the trash, wondering if everything from those hours of work would end up useless. She found several photographs of the uniformed men in the distance where she'd switched her lens. Those were okay but had zero value. Still, the background in the photos wouldn't be bad. She kept going until she came to the pictures of Easton and stopped, a smile on her face. Wow, those cheekbones sure came up nice. Not to mention that jaw.

He had a small dimple barely noticeable in his chin. Next came a shot with his arms crossed, glaring at her. He probably thought he was being scary, but, to her, he looked like a big protective teddy bear. He rocked that look. The shots were excellent. She took her time sorting through Easton's pictures and sent the next set of thirty to the garbage. She knew she had to get rid of them all but hoped to have a chance to talk with him about it.

By the time she finally reached the end, had them downloaded and filed away in the cloud storage, it was almost bedtime. She would be up early to do more and wanted to catch the teams as they headed out on their morning run. She answered a few emails, got ready for bed and turned out the lights. She'd assumed she'd be sharing a tent, as she often did in the past.

But this time she was alone. It didn't bother her, but it was a little unusual.

Just as she closed her eyes, she heard voices outside. Men would move through the camp all night. She had no idea what this training week would encompass. But surrounded by this many capable defenders of two nations, she was safe. Surely? Then she remembered the murdered woman Devlin had mentioned at another base. Summer closed her eyes again and tried to sleep, but the side of the tent rustled as if somebody gave it a small shake.

She rolled over to check it out, but it was so dark she could hardly see. It would be foolish for anybody to attack her here. Not that they would. She was in the middle of hundreds of military men. Still it took her a long time to fall sleep.

When she finally dropped off, it was an uneasy surface sleep. She could hear voices and movements all around her. She woke several times, rolling over, checking out the time on her cell phone. Each time she'd only sleep for another hour. "It's going to be a damn long night at this rate."

She rolled over, pulled the blanket against her cheek and closed her eyes, and that's when she heard…breathing. She froze, her eyes half open as she tried to identify where the person was. She was up against one side of the tent, so it was possible the breather was outside. She sure hoped so; otherwise it meant the person was inside.

When did he come in? Did he—she?—have a right to be here? Her tent had lots of empty beds, so maybe someone had been assigned to sleep here, yet no one had mentioned it to her? If it was a man she didn't know, she didn't care when he'd arrived. She wanted him to go the hell away.

She was here to work because she had a simple love of photography. In this case she was the right person for the job. Now she should probably get it done and leave.

As she lay there, she waited for the breather to leave. Instead it slowed down as if somebody had settled in for a long wait. Or had fallen asleep?

She rolled over casually, as if asleep herself. Then peered under her lashes, shifting just enough to look around. All the beds were empty.

She squeezed her eyes shut. Then, with a burst of energy, bounced to her feet and was outside the tent in seconds.

Only to run into a huge chest, then arms wrapped around her and lifted her off her feet.

She opened her mouth and screamed.

EASTON BARELY HAD time to react when he was body-slammed by someone small, moving at a very fast rate. He put his arms around her when she opened her mouth.

"Summer. Easy, Summer. It's me, Easton."

But he couldn't get through to her. She was shaking and screaming like crazy. People were yelling—coming to see what all the commotion was about. He couldn't calm her down. Finally he grabbed a handful of hair, gently pulled her head back and slammed his mouth over hers.

She quieted.

He cuddled her in his arms, slid his mouth to her ear and said, "It's okay now. I got you."

She buried her face against his chest, clinging to him for dear life. Taking a quick view of the area, seeing all the curious eyes, he stepped into her tent, carrying her. Devlin came in behind him. Ryder and Corey followed. They closed the flap as he sat down on the bed that looked to be where she'd been sleeping. He settled her into his arms. "Calm down, and tell me what's wrong."

She took several gasping sobs, scrubbed her face like a child and stared up at him, her eyes huge. Just when he thought she would speak, she threw her arms around his neck and held him tight. He rubbed her back gently and waited. The men spread out and checked to see if anything was wrong. Snakes weren't unheard of in Canada, and it was well-known for black widows but not this far north. Surely that wouldn't have been enough to have a photographer lose her cool like that, not one who'd spent months in the wilderness.

The other men stood together at one corner. He wanted to call out and ask what they'd found but didn't want to disturb Summer or set her off again.

Finally, she let go of a big shuddering breath and sank against him. "Thank you for coming," she said in such a formal voice that his lips quirked.

He didn't dare tell her it was an accident he was outside her tent at that time of night. He'd been part of a competition scouting out the opposite team hiding on the base. A no weapon game of skill for fun – and challenge. He hadn't even been aware which tent was hers. Still, he was glad it was him, not somebody else. He shifted her position ever-so-slightly, then tilted her chin so he could look in her eyes. "Are you ready to tell me what's going on?"

She glanced at the men behind him. "Somebody was inside my tent."

He straightened and studied her. She looked calm and rational, not still caught in the grips of a nightmare. "What do you mean, inside the tent?" He glanced at the other three. "Do you have a roommate?"

She shook her head. "Not that I know of. I haven't met anybody. And the person wasn't in bed nor did he say anything." She pointed to the far corner. "He was over there."

"It was a man? Did you see him?"

Again she shook her head.

"Are you sure you actually heard somebody in here?"

She grabbed his face, tilted it down so she could look him right in the eye. "Yes, because I could hear him breathing. I woke up when I heard a sound. While I lay here, figuring it out, I could hear heavy breathing—heavy male breathing—somewhere over there." She flung her arm up and toward that direction. "I rolled over and searched the beds, but no one was in them. Then the breathing got louder, as if he came closer." She took a deep inhale, shutting her eyes briefly, and continued. "I grabbed my courage, and I bolted, screaming for help."

The other three men walked toward Easton. He saw their frowns. "What did you find?"

"The corner of the tent at the floor level is cut. We can't prove it happened just now," Ryder cautioned, "but it is damaged. The opening is potentially big enough for someone to slide under without being easily seen. We can't be sure if someone was coming in or going out, but footsteps are on the outside at that corner, plus, we found a scuffed area as if someone slipped underneath."

"No footprints are inside though," Corey said with a gentle smile at Summer.

She shook her head. "I know somebody was here. I presume, as I ran out, he either came out behind me, or slipped back out the way he came in."

Easton shrugged. "It's possible."

"I was afraid you all thought I was crazy," she confessed. "I hate feeling this way, but I do need you to validate that my fear was logical and reasonable and wasn't acting like an idiot."

"Even if you ran from a nightmare," Easton said quietly, "it's valid for you. That's all anybody needs to know. No such thing as being foolish when you're as terrified as you were when racing out of your tent."

She took a heavy gulping sigh and nodded, then muttered, "Thank you."

In a surprise movement, she collapsed against his chest once more and snuggled in tight.

She yawned and said, "I should be able to sleep now."

Just like that, her breathing calmed down as if she were already asleep. He stared down at her, his eyebrows raised, and glanced at the others. They grinned. He frowned at them. Their grins widened. He shuffled her to lay her down on her bed, but she wrapped her arms around his neck and held him tight.

"You need to sleep."

"I do." She kept her grip around his neck.

He tried again. "I need to sleep."

"Got it" was her mumbled murmur.

He waited another few minutes for her to fall back asleep, hoping maybe he could disentangle her arms, get her to lie down again. But, every time he tried, she tightened her grip. Even in sleep she clung to him.

Corey said with a straight face, "You may as well lie down, Easton. You both need sleep."

Ryder chuckled softly.

"If I'm standing guard, then you guys are too," Easton snapped. "There are lots of spare beds—go for it."

They stared at him to see if he was serious, and, when they realized he was, groaned and said in unison, "Fine."

Each grabbed a bed, stretched out and closed his eyes. Easton shifted Summer in his arms, laying down sideways, then pulled her arms loose and tucked her against him. When she murmured and tried to twist around again, he whispered, "You're fine. Go to sleep. I'm here."

As if not quite believing him, she lay still for a long moment, then relaxed into sleep. Now that he was free, he wondered if he could leave, but, at the same time, he had promised to stay. Easton leaned back slightly to put some distance between them and closed his eyes. Almost instantly her body slammed against his. So that was how they slept. Spoon-fashion for the rest of the night.

"Easton?"

His gaze flew to Devlin, standing in the middle of the tent, his hands on his hips as he studied Easton. Ryder and Corey sat on the beds they had spent the night on, rubbing their faces, yawning.

"What happened?"

He was going to tell Devlin to keep his voice down, when he realized, while he had slept, Summer had disappeared. "What the hell?"

The other two men looked at him, and Ryder asked, "Where did she go?"

"I have no idea. I fell asleep," he admitted.

The three men looked at each other, then back at him. "The real question is, did she leave on her own, or was she kidnapped?"

They raced from the tent to find out.

CHAPTER 4

S UMMER STOPPED AND smiled. Not even daring to breathe, she watched as the small bird nested. She took a step closer. She wanted a picture of the nest and innocent baby birds inside. She wanted to get so close she could see all of them.

Switching her lens wasn't a good option. She was sure any movement would send the mother flying. She had to make sure the bird didn't abandon the babies. She took a photo, then, with a happy smile, slowly retreated.

It had been a beautiful morning when she woke up. Snuggled tight against Easton's chest, she'd felt so peaceful, rested. After all, she'd slept like a baby cradled in his arms. In the early morning light, it had been easy to consider the horrible event in the middle of the night as a bad dream. Except she still remembered being frozen in place, hearing the distinctive sound of a stranger breathing. And yet, when she'd been wrapped in Easton's arms, his breathing had been comforting.

Determined not to lose track of time again, she glanced at her watch. Breakfast was in the next twenty minutes. She carefully packed her bags, which were still clipped together. She threw them over her shoulder and made her way back to base. The sun shone brightly. She tilted her face to the warm rays and smiled. It was a gorgeous morning. She'd been very tempted to stay in Easton's arms but figured that would make it very awkward for him. Taking the opportunity, she had slipped out to get an hour or two of work done.

She tramped through the high grass as she glanced around, wondering at the natural beauty of the woods. Then she caught sight of something between the trees.

Stopping, she studied the area but couldn't see what had caught her eye. She kept walking, a creepy feeling of being watched nudging her. She picked up her pace slightly, glancing behind her every few steps. The feeling was getting stronger. She watched the wide-open field as she headed back, but the tree line ahead worried her because anybody could be hiding there. Last night she couldn't let go of the feeling that something lay in wait for her in her own tent, and now, with this scary creepy-crawly feeling all over her skin, it was a repeat of the same thing.

As she approached the trees, she studied the area, watching for anyone from the base out here. She'd like to be in the middle of a group right now, not coming in alone. Yet she had no way to get back except through that copse of trees. When she had headed out this morning, it seemed like a beautiful line of green, but now it was more a barrier, something she must cross to get to the safety on the other side.

She was still one hundred yards off as she looked for a pathway through. She didn't think the trees were very thick or deep. She remembered it only taking a couple minutes to get through the line originally.

As she approached, she picked out a pathway, took a deep breath and dashed forward. On the other side, she smiled in relief at the camp ahead. She slowed her pace slightly but kept going. As it was, she would likely be late for breakfast.

She burst into the camp fields and kept going right to her tent. As she walked in, she found her sleeping quarters empty. She frowned. She'd really hoped, for some reason, the men would still be here. They were the only friendly faces she had in camp.

Then, of course, they'd probably gone for breakfast. A meal she kept forgetting.

Still carrying her equipment like a backpack, she headed for the mess tent. Once there, she stood in line with all the others scheduled for seating block A, the first group. When she got to the food tables, she quickly filled a plate, grabbed a coffee and walked into the center of the room, looking for a place to sit. Inside she hoped Easton would find her. But no one called out her name. She caught sight of her pilot, Robbie, and gave him a wave. He returned it yet didn't ask her to join him. Neither did she get any friendly looks from those around the large tent.

Finding a table with an open spot at the far end, she sat down to consume her breakfast. Nobody said a word to her, but she never spoke to anyone either.

When she was done, she cleaned up her place and headed back to her tent. Feeling unnerved, not exactly sure what to do about it, she checked her schedule and remembered she had planned to take pictures of the morning workout but had missed it.

Under her breath she swore quietly. "That's not good." It was one of the things she was supposed to capture, something she'd have to do tomorrow morning; otherwise she'd be in trouble.

She checked to make sure all her gear was okay; yet again she packed up and headed outside. The day was chock full of training on signaling, navigation with and without evasion charts, route selection, and even shelters. She understood they'd be doing wilderness survival, traps and snares, food and water procurement, preservation and even improvised equipment. The classes sounded like a lot of fun actually. She'd do her best to make up for this morning. Her forgetfulness was legendary. Earlier she'd been alert and aware. She deliberately kept track of time for breakfast, but somehow she'd forgotten to account for the morning exercise.

Running back outside, she made her way to the artillery range where the military men were learning to create improvised weapons. The morning passed by quickly as she wandered from one activity to another, taking photos from every angle.

She really wanted to get photographs of the men in uniforms as they worked on the new water system on the far side. When she felt she had enough light moving high above, she moved to that part of the base where she'd get better photos this time of day. She set up a tripod and watched as the training session continued on the new water containers. They took creek and groundwater, processing them through the system—intended to handle anything, including saltwater, turning it into clean drinking water.

As she watched, the instructors broke down one of their large units and showed the trainees how to put it together again. When finished, they took it all apart again and stepped aside to let the teams learn to do it themselves. She stood then, picked up her cameras and moved closer. The looks on their faces, the discussions and the concentration of focus was phenomenal. She spent several hours here, then realized she was hungry. She glanced at her watch and swore softly.

Good thing she packed a lot of protein bars as she'd missed lunch again.

She lost herself for the next couple hours, interested in learning more about the water system. As the group of trainees switched to a new one, she returned to her bags, only to find they'd moved again. She glanced around, as panic set in. She had left the tripod only ten feet from the bench and was relieved it was still there.

Looking around, she saw a man carrying what looked like her bags. Leaving her tripod where it was, she raced after him. Just as he was about to go into one of the tents, she realized it was her bag. She snagged it off his shoulder, jerking hard.

The man spun around and glared at her. "Hey, what are you are doing?"

"Reclaiming my property, thank you," she snapped, glaring at him.

Confused, he looked at her, then the bags. "They're yours?"

She nodded. "Whose did you expect them to be? They were beside me when I was photographing the whole day."

"I just saw them, left in the middle of the field," he protested. "I was taking them to the lost and found."

She wasn't sure she believed him. She'd had some of her gear go missing before, so she had a hard time with that story. But that didn't mean he was lying either. "Well, it's not lost, and it's now been found, and this is my gear." She pointed to the tags at the bottom showing her name and a photo ID.

He held up his hands. "No worries. Sorry."

Giving him a muttered response, she quickly retraced her steps to her tripod, happy to see at least it still stood where she'd left it. Feeling a change in atmosphere during this visit, and not liking it one bit, she quickly stowed away her tripod and stepped off to the side.

Several logs were just outside the base compound. She sat down on one, out of the way from where everyone worked. She wanted this trip to get back onto a normal track. She'd been in several camps, and nobody had ever picked up her bags and took them to the lost and found. Why would there even be such a thing? The teams were only here for a few weeks. And surely she was the only freelance photographer on base.

She pulled a protein bar from her pocket and munched slowly. She had a bottle of water stashed in her bag somewhere. She dug into the bottom and pulled it out, popped the top and took a long drink. It was late already, almost four o'clock. She studied the angles of the sun and the shadows of the trees. She could get in one more shot today before she lost the good light.

She never had any guarantee of how long she'd be on-site. For all she knew, she'd get shipped out tonight. Her boss made those calls. With that thought in mind, she polished off her protein bar and water, then resumed taking photos. With a sense of impending change, she could spend the next several hours, right up until dinnertime, taking pictures of the crowds wandering in and out. The laughing, joking, and smiling, seeing the exhaustion, the pissed-off looks of those who hadn't done as well as they'd wanted to. Capturing it all was a challenge.

"Are you coming to dinner?"

She spun around, startled. For the first time since she woke up in his arms, she came face-to-face with Easton.

She smiled up him. "There you are. I haven't seen you

all day."

He raised one eyebrow. "Are you coming to dinner?"

She nodded. "I think I'm done here for now." She glanced around. "Where are your friends?"

"Heading for dinner."

She quickly packed up the last of her cameras. "Thank you for coming and finding me. I missed lunch again," she confessed.

He shook his head. "You need a keeper."

"Sounds like a good thing, but probably isn't." She stepped up to the chow line to find Ryder and Corey waiting for them.

"What was that about a keeper?" Corey asked. His voice was low, comfortable, relaxed.

She shrugged. "He thinks I need a keeper because I keep forgetting simple things, like lunch and dinnertimes," she said with a half-smile.

"Keeper…That word has a bit more meaning than you know," he said, nudging her slightly to take their place in the moving wave of people.

She never got a chance to ask what that meant. But she did notice her pilot in line before her. "Hi, Robbie."

He turned, nodded back to her, with a raised-chin greeting for the men with her.

By the time they made it to the food tables, she was more than happy to ride the wave. Easton's team made life here a lot easier for her; that was for sure.

She pulled out her phone just before she sat down. Still no text from her boss. Maybe that was a good thing. She had to admit she felt like her trip would end quickly. Or maybe she just wanted it to. Although, then she wouldn't see Easton anymore, and that would hurt. Putting away her phone, she glanced at the men. "I haven't seen any of you since I woke up this morning. So how was your day?"

There was silence at the table. She looked up from the bread she was buttering to see them all glancing at Easton. She looked at him and frowned. "What's the matter with you?"

"Nothing," he snapped.

"He's pissed off that you left the bed without him knowing. He prides himself on being a light sleeper."

She shook her head. "He was sleeping like a baby. I didn't want to disturb him," she explained gently. "It really was very nice of you to look after me last night. The least I could do was let him catch up on his rest."

The others nodded solemnly. But all she heard from Easton was a half-sigh, half-snort.

She rounded on him. "What was I supposed to do? Wait until you were awake? I couldn't do that to you."

He pointed at her plate. "Eat."

Considering it might be the best option, she turned her attention back to the food.

EASTON TRIED HARD not to keep a close eye on her as she ate. If he saw the motion of her fork out of the corner of his eye, he was content to ignore her as she seemed to be following his orders. When he chanced a glance at the other men, it was to find huge grins. He scowled at Corey especially. But it had the opposite effect than he wanted. Corey laughed.

Summer lifted her gaze to study him, paused for a long moment and then asked, "What's so funny?"

Corey was past the point of being able to answer her. He

shook his head and tried to control his chuckles. The trouble was, the others were in the same state.

"He has these fits every once in a while," Easton said. "Just try to be understanding."

Then the others got off on Corey's contagious laughter as well. She glared at them all suspiciously, then turned on Easton. "Are they making fun of me?"

His eyebrows rose. "No, they aren't."

"Seems like they're laughing at me."

She turned her glare at one of them. The men were beside themselves at this point.

Easton popped the last forkful into his mouth, waited until he was done chewing, threw down his fork and knife on the plate and pushed back. When she still hadn't resumed eating, he again pointed at her plate. "Eat."

She rounded on him. "Why are they laughing at me?"

"They aren't laughing at you. They're laughing at me," he snapped. He shoved his face into hers, making sure she turned and ate again.

Instead she picked up her fork and held it like a knife, threatening to stab his hand on her chair. "Why would they laugh at you?"

He stared at her fork in astonishment. "You're going to stab me?"

"To stop you from ordering me around, yes," she snapped back.

He glared. She glared back.

Finally he slumped in his chair and faced her. "You're hungry. You don't look after yourself. Someone has to make sure you keep food in your stomach."

"And who made you my guardian?"

"You did."

She reared back slightly, frowned at him in confusion and then settled in her chair. "They really are laughing at both of us, aren't they?" she asked glumly.

He nodded. "They are, indeed."

Together the two of them looked at the three men, who now had stopped laughing, but still had huge grins on their faces.

Devlin said, "Easton, I totally approve."

Easton shook his head in disgust. "You don't know what you're talking about."

"I probably know better than anybody here," Devlin said calmly. "And I've got to tell you, it's the real deal."

Instantly Easton froze. "Hell no."

"Hell yes," Ryder said. "Even I can see that much."

Easton shook his head rapidly, but it wasn't having any effect. He shoved his chair back and stood, gave them all a hard stare and snapped, "Hell no." He turned and walked from the tent.

"Easton?"

He ignored Summer's questioning voice. Outside, he stopped a few feet off to the side of the main entrance, hands on his hips, and glowered at the world around him. *No way in hell.* She was *not* the woman of his dreams. She was the exact opposite. He wanted somebody who could take care of herself. Somebody who wanted to be a part of his life but didn't need to be looked after. He wanted somebody who…

A small hand slipped around his forearm. He stared at the long slender fingers and knew it could be only one person. Summer. He groaned gently.

"Did I do something to upset you?" She stepped in front of him so he had no place to look but at her. She peered up at him earnestly. "I'd never want to hurt you. I do lose my temper occasionally though," she confessed. "But I don't think I'd really have stabbed you with my fork."

He stared at her, a reluctant grin tugging at his lips. "You probably shouldn't tell people you threaten with a fork that you're really not going to follow through. It kind of loses the impact the next time around."

She gave him a one-shoulder shrug. "The thing is, I'm really not very confrontational."

His eyebrows shot up. "Really?" he drawled. "I never noticed."

She shrugged and leaned forward to share a secret. "I'm too soft inside. Maybe, if I'd had military training, I'd be tougher. I did do karate. But I spent the class time apologizing, making sure my opponent was okay," she confessed. When he chuckled and then howled with laughter, she glared at him. "It's not *that* funny. I spent *a lot* of time apologizing."

He bent over, laughing. When he finally caught his breath, he said, "You could look at it the other way. How you finally got good enough to actually defend yourself."

She smirked. "I did get very good, but I stopped practicing because I was hurting people."

"Didn't they teach you how to fall?"

She nodded. "But it always seemed like the other person was hurt more than I was, so it made me feel really bad."

He rolled his eyes. "Then you know karate?"

She nodded. "I tried judo, but that didn't work out so well."

He winced, but instantly had to ask, "Why?"

She turned, catching the tone of his voice and glared at him. "Are you laughing at me?"

He shrugged. "You've got admit it's pretty funny. I've

done so much hand-to-hand combat training, martial arts training, weapons training, and to hear you are afraid of hurting your opponent, when that's the entire purpose of learning any of these skills, well…" He shook his head. "These are skills to defend yourself."

"But I didn't want to hurt them," she cried out. "They'd get mad at me, saying, if I didn't fight them, then they didn't get any practice either. So I'd get mad, defend myself, and they'd go down, and it would be all over. Whereas, if we play nice together, we could practice for a longer time."

He stared at her in astonishment. "Play nice together?"

She nodded her head earnestly. "Sure. If we could have gone through all those moves without hurting anybody, it would have been so much better."

He rubbed the side of his face. "Oh, boy."

"Now you sound like my master."

"Before or after he asked you to quit?" he asked, chuckling all over again.

She glared at him, refusing to answer.

He added, "I know—both." Easton wrapped an arm around her shoulders, tucking her close.

Instinctively her arms opened, and she wrapped them around his waist. She laid her head against his chest and cuddled in closer. "Most of the time you're a really nice man."

That started his chuckles all over again. "Most of the time?" he asked between his mirth, loving the natural open quirkiness of the woman in his arms.

"Yes. When you aren't laughing at me."

"I'd like to think I'm laughing *with* you. I'm not so heartless to laugh *at* you. Although some of the things you say are pretty funny."

She tilted her head back to give him a disgruntled look. And then she shrugged. "Maybe that's why I do better with pictures than people."

He hugged her gently. "You do just fine with people. Forget about the others."

"But your friends were laughing at me."

Ryder's voice came from behind them, interrupting. "No, Easton was correct earlier. We were laughing at *him*."

Easton turned to find all three of his buddies standing behind them, listening in. He rolled his eyes. "Don't you guys have something to do?"

Ryder tapped his watch. "Yes, so do you."

The reminder was so pointed that Easton checked his watch and groaned. "Right, we have a meeting tonight." He dropped his arms from her shoulders. "Try to stay out of trouble for the rest of the evening."

She stared at him in surprise, but he turned and walked away. Still he couldn't help glancing back to see if she had moved on. No, she stood there with such a forlorn look on her face that he wanted to pause and tell her it was okay.

Ryder and Corey grabbed each of Easton's arms and dragged him forward. Corey added, "Hey, she'll be there when we get back. We still have responsibilities."

This wasn't like him, and the revelation startled him. Nothing ever made him forget he had duties. Tonight they were doing an extra session on hostage negotiation in wilderness territory. It was a different issue dealing with a kidnapper in a high-rise of a major city versus a survivalist kidnapper in the wilderness. They were here to meet their counterparts and establish a network they could call on during strife. SEALs were known to be the best military force out there, but the Canadians were no slouches, even if they were more peacekeepers. The world needed more of those too. Easton was not here to be distracted. Especially not by a woman. He frowned, not liking this turn of events.

They entered one of the tents and saw the new water system he'd been hoping to get a closer look at. Four men stood as they walked inside. After a slight hesitation Ryder stepped in front and held out his hand, taking the lead.

Easton frowned; he should have been the first to shake hands. Not that he stood on protocol about rank with his own team, but he needed to get his head in the game. He was on duty. His personal life had to be kept separate. Not that he had one. At least not yet. Damn that woman …

In a low voice beside him, Devlin said, "Don't worry about it. You'll adjust—eventually."

CHAPTER 5

SUMMER WATCHED THE group of men drag Easton along. She wasn't sure what had happened, but knew something had. She'd finally met somebody who seemed to *get* her. Or maybe he was just a nursemaid kind of guy. She shook her head at that. Nobody in their right mind called Easton a nursemaid. The man was alpha all the way.

She wasn't a hugger by nature, but it seemed so natural to wrap her arms around his waist and snuggle closer when he tucked her against him. Dangerously natural. She didn't know him at all, though she wanted to. She wanted to look through her camera lens and learn everything about him.

But she knew he'd resist that idea. She had a little bit of time until Ross recalled her. She still had a lot of photos to go through tonight. With that thought uppermost in her mind, she headed toward her tent. She pulled back the flap and stood at the entrance. It didn't look like anything was different.

Not only were the spare beds pristinely made but somebody—Easton?—had made hers as well. And did a much nicer job than she would have.

She didn't see any sign of her laptop though, and that bothered her. She searched under the bed and pillow, then caught sight of it peeking out from underneath the bedding. He'd hidden the laptop. She lifted the covers, found her cord as well and set herself up for business. She went through all the photos, once again tossing and purging, then turned to her emails, finding one from her boss.

She read it quickly and dashed off an answer. "I have what I think I need outside of the morning exercises. I'll catch those tomorrow."

The response was almost immediate. "Good. Be aware there has been a complaint. We always get one or two, but this seems more pointed. Make sure you're only taking pictures you're allowed to."

She frowned and answered, "Sorry to hear that. I'll make sure I don't point my camera on anybody I shouldn't."

Which was stupid because how was she supposed to know who she was and wasn't allowed to show on camera? All the pictures would be vetted before they were used anyway. Sometimes the jobs were like that.

She pulled out a few she really liked and sent them to him. "Some came out great," she said in the email, then sent several more.

She had lot of work ahead of her, and preferred to do it when she got home. Right now it was all about collecting pictures. With that thought in mind, and knowing she may only have another day here, she put her laptop back underneath the covers and remade the bed. Easton really did a much better job. Then grabbing her other camera and backpack, she headed outside.

It was an unusually bright evening with the sun falling, sending dappled patches through the trees. She only planned to stay within a few hundred yards of her tent, as she left most of her equipment in there and it would get dark very quickly. She walked the perimeter, taking pictures outside the base and of the base from a distance.

She could see, for some people, having her always taking photographs might be irritating, but she really wasn't after anyone in particular. She was just getting the whole ambience of the group here. By the time she had walked all the way around and was back at her tent, she was proud of herself because she hadn't gotten lost. She'd been out for almost two hours. Surely that had to be enough. She checked her watch—it was going on ten o'clock.

With that thought she continued, intent on taking a shower before she went to bed. Her tent was empty still. That was good. She was kind of enjoying having the space to herself. Often when she went on assignments, she had to share with whomever was around. And sometimes, being female, she had the benefit of getting a space all to herself. She wasn't antisocial, but it was nice to be alone at times.

Back from the shower quarters, she sat on the bed in her pajamas with a towel wrapped around her hair. It would be another early morning again, but this time she was determined to get up and catch them for their dawn run. When she figured her hair was dry enough, she hung up the towel. Laying out her clothes for the morning, she curled up in bed and tried to sleep.

It was close to eleven o'clock. Curfew was somewhere around that time, she thought. But still a fair bit of noise was outside. She couldn't help but think maybe Easton might stop by. However, so far, she hadn't seen him this evening at all.

He was here for a purpose, a completely different one than her own. Apparently Easton and his group were SEALs, some of the most elite military-trained warriors in the world. And yet they were super-nice guys. She'd understood they were Navy but hadn't realized the type of fighters they were.

They'd never said, nor bragged in any way to show they were different.

But—as she'd observed before—they didn't have to. It was all in their bearing. Hell, there was a reason they didn't have to fight the crowds to maneuver in the mess tent. Like Gods, they parted the sea of people before them.

She snickered at the thought. Knowing them as she did, they were as real as anyone else. But it was lovely for them to have the respect of everyone.

As she lay in the bed, she studied the corner where Ryder and Corey said it looked like somebody had entered and maybe rolled out from underneath.

Where the wooden flooring lay near the side of the tent was a bit of a gap and the damage could be seen. It wasn't something likely to be fixed when she was only here for another night or two. Besides, she hadn't made a formal complaint so she doubted anyone other than Easton's group and herself knew about the intruder.

Unable to stop her curiosity, she grabbed her cell phone to light the way, walked to the corner and checked out the area closer. She heard voices on the other side. When she lifted the separated material, someone's hand grabbed it, pulling it down tight. She jumped back. Her heart slammed against her chest and her breath caught in her throat. Instantly she shut off her light. Then she heard Easton's voice. "Summer, I'm just checking the tent so nobody can come in, okay?"

She sighed with relief. "Thank you." She pulled on her long sweater to cover the camisole top and shorts she slept in, and, grabbing her slippers, walked around outside the tent to where the men were. It was dark but not pitch black. Just a half light that made it difficult to see. She almost tripped on one of the corners.

Easton grabbed her shoulder. "Easy. Use a light if you're coming out here."

"I just wanted to make sure nobody else could get in from the side either."

"It's secured now. No one will get in easily. You should hear the spikes being pulled out."

She nodded, studying their repair of the new opening. They'd used tent spikes to secure the material together.

"Don't worry about it. You should be safer now."

She sighed. "I hope so. How did your meeting go?"

He shrugged. "It was fine."

The atmosphere turned a little awkward when she realized he wouldn't or couldn't talk about it. Of course he couldn't. That whole honorable thing. She half turned to return to her tent, calling back, "Thank you for checking on me."

Inside she took off her sweater, kicked off her slippers and crawled back into bed. She wasn't normally nervous being alone, but last night's scenario had her on edge. She didn't think she'd be able to sleep very easily, but, as she lay there thinking about Easton, her body slowly relaxed. Just when she was ready to fall asleep, she heard him call out, "Summer, are you awake?"

She pushed herself up on one elbow and answered, "Well, I was almost asleep."

He stuck his head through the tent flap, saw her and smiled. "Okay." He walked inside, dropped his bag at the foot of the bed across from her. "I'm sleeping here tonight."

Inside, her heart jumped with joy. "Why?" she asked cautiously.

"Because, although you might be able to sleep, I can't,"

he confessed. "No doubt somebody was probably in your tent last night, and I don't want a repeat event." He waved at her. "Go back to sleep. I'll be fine."

While she watched, he took off his shirt, boots, socks, and pants, then crawled into the bed across from her. In the dim light, all she saw was shadows, but they hinted and teased. Her fingers inched to grab her camera. She desperately wanted to take pictures, but she doubted he would allow it. He had made it very clear he was off the menu. Forcing herself to lie back down and roll over, she whispered, "Thank you and good night."

His voice soft, gentle, he answered back, "You're welcome. Now sleep."

EASTON LAY QUIETLY on the bed, listening to Summer's breathing calming down. He could feel the stress drop off her shoulders as she succumbed to sleep. He shifted so his arms were under his head, staring at the tent ceiling above him. He'd been trying to sleep in his own room, in his own bed. All he could think of was her wide awake, afraid of somebody sneaking into her tent. Last night his first inclination had been that she'd had a bad nightmare when she'd come screaming into his arms, until they'd examined the tent from the outside and found the new opening.

Also scuff marks and footprints were right at the tear. Just enough for him to consider somebody had been inside. And that was very worrisome. He'd checked up the chain of command, but he was a guest on the Canadian base. The news had filtered through the ranks on both sides. No one was happy. He'd been a hair away from requesting guard duty, then realized he didn't need a formal process completed as he'd keep an unofficial eye on her himself. And keeping things low key right now in this small mixed group was paramount. Someone here was playing games.

That would never go over well. Not when the name of the game was *Torment Summer*.

The only reason to hassle her was if she took pictures someone didn't like. In which case confiscating the images would be one resolution, but not an easy one on her. She needed to complete her contract to get paid. Not to mention there was no guarantee the harassment would stop even then. Not if something else was going on…

She had gone crazy, taking pictures of everything and everyone in the camp. Of course, she had been hired to do so. And, so far, he hadn't heard anything more than a few disparaging remarks about her always being around. Nobody seemed to be pissed off enough to put in a formal complaint though. But he'd had enough experience and, as such, understood everything wasn't perfect in military base camps. And, if anybody was doing something wrong or illegal, having a photographer in their face, catching every moment, could get ugly. She was also small, pretty, and with a naivety that was very fresh. A lot of men were here. He'd seen and heard firsthand how devastating the out-of-control male libido could be. He didn't want that for her. He was quite astonished she'd been sent alone. He would've imagined at least a team of two.

He should ask her about that. Maybe the other one had to cancel at the last minute.

Using techniques he had learned years ago, he let himself drop into a light sleep. He would awaken instantly if anything wrong came about, but right now his instincts said everything was calm and quiet.

His phone buzzed against his chest. He lifted it to see Devlin's name.

"All okay?"

"Yes," Easton replied. "I'm sleeping here, just in case." There was no response after that. He closed his eyes and let himself drift to sleep.

Until something woke him.

He didn't know how long he had been out, but his instincts kicked in to full awareness. Something in his environment had shifted. He lay still in the bed, figuring out what bothered him. He didn't move but let his eyes search the small space. Outside of Summer's slow, steady breathing, no one else was in the tent. No shadows were cast along the three sides that he could see.

He heard a small scratching sound, like a peg being pulled, and sent a text to Devlin, warning him, then slipped off the bed on the other side. He hoped to stay out of sight long enough for the intruder to make it inside. Catching the bastard in the act was always the best, and riskiest, plan.

And then he heard the same thing Summer had earlier, breathing. Deep, heavy breathing. He frowned. The man's breath was uneven as he pulled the pins and lifted the tent edge. Easton watched carefully as the corner lifted. It didn't raise very high—about six inches. He was ready to pounce forward and catch the intruder as he tried to make his way underneath but heard another sound as well. A rattle. A sound recognizable enough to make anybody's blood run cold. And then footsteps quietly disappeared into the night.

Using the flashlight on his cell phone, he retreated, going to Summer's sleeping form, catching sight of the confused and angry snake on the inside of the tent. Its tail was upright and rattling. Some asshole put a pissed-off rattlesnake inside her tent. At the first movement Summer made, it would strike.

Jesus. He quickly took a picture and sent it to Devlin. He didn't want to hurt the reptile, but this was not a good place for it to be. He glanced at the blanket on the spare bed. It was his only option, short of killing the snake. However, the blanket was nowhere near as effective as the special tools they used to capture critters like this. He would have to subdue it, and that meant using the only option available, the blanket.

Killing the reptile was the last resort. It was a victim too. It had already suffered. It just wanted to be back in the wild, free to roam as it always had. He could wake Summer and they could both exit the tent, but that would just leave the rattler looking for another target.

No way in hell would he get it calmed down, and, if he missed on his first attempt, there would be chaos.

He snagged the blanket as the snake slowly approached Summer's bed, obviously attracted by her body heat. Using the blanket, he distracted it, hoping to send it in a different direction. It struck out, but missed. He didn't know how much poison the snake had. Could it strike multiple times? Or did it need hours to regenerate the venom? He figured there was way more than he could probably entice it to lose in this game of chance. Just as he contemplated wrapping up the snake, the tent flap behind him opened.

Devlin stepped in. "Holy shit."

In a low voice Easton said, "I know, right? Instead of coming in, the intruder actually left her a gift."

"He put the rattler inside the tent? What an asshole move." Devlin's voice was hushed, realizing the best thing they could do was to take care of this without waking her.

"Yeah, nice, huh?"

"Somebody has it in for her in a bad way." Devlin slipped to the far side near Summer and then stationed himself, knife in hand, at the end of her bed.

"I agree. First things first. We take care of this, and then we find out why." Easton studied the reptile, blanket in hand. He'd done intensive training for this. It was doable even without the proper tools. In his head he counted down. Three … two …

"Move back." Ryder stepped up behind them. "I got this."

He had a long pole in his hand with a wire around the end. He gently placed it over the snake's head and tightened it ever-so-slightly. He had a large heavy bag with him. Between the tool and the bag, he got the rattler cozied inside. As he lifted it high, the rattle slowed. He glanced at the other two guys. "Rattlers generally like small dark spaces. I don't know where this guy came from, but this was a pretty shitty deal for him too."

Ryder disappeared outside with the snake. Devlin and Easton looked at each other. Easton motioned to the entrance. They walked around to the back of Summer's tent, using their cell phones for flashlights. Once again at the rear wall, several pegs were pulled up and the corner loosened. Footsteps from dozens of men going in opposite directions were evident, but none seemed to belong to their intruder. Regardless of the crappy light, Easton took photos, hoping he might see something on his computer. Even if he couldn't, he had no qualms about sending this to a geek friend to see what she could find. Although he'd have to make sure Mason was good with Easton asking Tesla for assistance. Easton also had to report this up the chain of command. No way could Easton's unit overlook this second attack.

He checked his watch as he motioned his men back to the front of the tent. "Midnight," he said. "How did he know she'd be asleep?"

"Maybe he didn't care, or hoped she'd be awake, see the rattler and scream, and it would strike."

"As a lot of guys here would do," Easton said in a low voice. "But this was extremely targeted. She might've taken pictures of that rattlesnake, but I'm pretty damn sure that wouldn't have been her first thought."

Inside the open doorway, Easton could see Summer slept deeply.

Devlin looked at him. "I think we should all stay here tonight."

"No way in hell I'm leaving, but you don't have to stay." Easton glanced at Devlin, who made no move to leave. "I don't like anything about this. We need to find and follow the next lead."

Ryder returned then, dragging Corey with him. He nodded and said, "This guy was sleeping."

"What else am I supposed to do at this hour?" Corey protested. "Although I'm sorry I missed all the excitement."

Easton nodded. "We're set for a run at 5:00 a.m." He glanced at his watch. "That gives us just over four hours." On that note, the men split up and lay down in Summer's tent, Ryder and Corey taking the two nearest beds.

Easton returned to the bed he'd been in, Devlin snagging another on the far side.

With them all together she should be safe, pinned between them. As he closed his eyes, he whispered to Devlin, "Thanks."

And in a tone and words reminiscent of what he'd said to Summer himself, Devlin responded with, "You're welcome. Now sleep."

CHAPTER 6

SUMMER AWOKE THE next morning, her eyes opening to the sight of Easton lying on the bed across from her. Instantly her heart smiled. That was lovely. Then she recognized Devlin on another, as was Ryder.

The rest were empty, so either Corey was up already or hadn't stayed here. She grabbed her clothes and slipped out, walking to the showers. She changed and brushed her teeth. When she got back, she found the men still sleeping. The entire camp appeared to be too, but she promised herself she would be out for the run this morning. Maybe Easton's unit wasn't supposed to go.

She picked up her gear and, with one last look at the men, slipped back out again. She'd found a couple locations to take her pictures. She would need a few minutes to get out there. So, of course, she had to be early.

Moving as fast as she could around the base, she headed to the first location and checked the light before moving on to the second. There she set down her bags and set up her camera on the tripod. She checked her watch—still only four forty-five. But already the early morning sunlight broke through the trees.

With the second camera, she took pictures of the light. She was fascinated by the way it pulled through the branches, over the treetops, landing on the grass. The early morning sun just lit up a large corner of the world. At five o'clock she forced herself to put away that camera and awaited the uniformed men on their run. She had the video camera set up and switched to a second where she would continue to take still pictures.

The run should have started by now. Yet it was empty and dark, silent outside. She moved away from her tripod slightly so she could change the angle, then waited for the runners to arrive. The longer she did, the more an ominous feeling crept over her.

This didn't make any sense. She didn't like this creepy feeling of being watched. She hunkered down out of sight. The silence was nerve-wracking. As it went on, the more terrified she became. Finally, she couldn't stand it. She slowly peered above the grasses. No one was there. She laughed. "Idiot."

She plopped to the ground just as she heard an odd spitting sound come from her left. She turned, but couldn't see anyone. Now a headache was developing. That's what she got for not bringing water or coffee with her. She did have juice though.

Finally, she heard the rhythmic pulsing of a large group marching forward. Summer grabbed her camera and raced in their direction.

Sure enough, she could see them up ahead—well over one hundred runners. She started clicking as they approached. She quickly moved toward the video camera, making sure it was set up properly, and had it running as the men moved past. It was an intense ten minutes.

But, as the last man went by, she felt like she'd done okay. Good thing since she was getting tired. Still she wasn't done yet. When the runners were out of sight, she grabbed her gear and moved to where they would be coming back around again. They still had a good three miles to go. She had no more than ten minutes to get to where she wanted to be to set up again. Relief that she'd been here on time flowed through her. She slowly made her way to the far side with her back toward the base. There she set up all over again.

A few people stood around, watching, waiting. Summer checked the cameras a couple times, just aimlessly looking to see what the general atmosphere was like. Her head still throbbed. She hoped it went away before the heat of the day hit. She reached for a bottle of juice in her bag, twisted off the top and took a long drink. Putting the cap back on, she could see the men on the far side coming into view.

Immediately she went into action. By the time the last man crossed the line, she had hundreds, if not thousands, of pictures. Much happier with herself, she packed her gear. She had a bit of a walk to get back to her tent, but, by the time she entered, she was hot and tired, ready for coffee and food. More than ready, to be honest.

Sadly, the tent was empty. She'd tried to see if her four new friends had been in the sea of men. She thought she might have caught sight of Corey, but she hadn't had time to single him out.

Knowing she dared only give herself a few minutes, she sagged to the bed and flopped sideways for just a moment.

Her mind was spinning with wanting food and wishing she could leave her gear here. The bags and equipment were heavy, but too much unprocessed and unsaved work was in them.

She couldn't save it all right now either, and it wouldn't make her happy to lose her equipment regardless. No, she'd have to take it all with her to the mess tent. In a minute. Just a quick nap. That's all she needed.

And she closed her eyes.

She jerked awake moments later, bolting upright, spinning around in the small space. Her hand went to her head that was swimming at the sudden movement.

Unnerved, she sat back on the bed and checked her watch. Yes, she could still make breakfast.

She bolted to her feet again, quickly grabbed her huge backpack of equipment, and ran from the tent.

"NOW WHERE'S SHE going?" Easton asked.

He'd almost made it to her tent after his shower to check that she'd made it back. Waking up to find her walking out the first time while he'd been asleep was a fear-inducing experience. He could hardly order her to stay under his watch when she hadn't asked for anybody to watch over her, nor had she been ordered to stay with a bodyguard, but he contemplated asking for that just for his own peace of mind. But neither did she know about the rattlesnake during the night.

Corey, who was farther ahead of Easton, chuckled and pointed out the small running figure with her cameras and bag banging on her back as she ran.

At his side, Devlin asked, "What do you want to bet she just realized she almost missed breakfast?"

"We're in the same situation there."

The men picked up the pace and followed in her footsteps.

Easton was perturbed. He'd woken up just after she had bolted from the tent this morning. He'd followed her to see her setting up camera equipment, then had raced back to grab his gear to make the start of the run on time.

He'd passed her several times in the morning, each time a sigh of relief escaping him, knowing she was still here, still on point and safe. After the run, he had been caught by a couple men who'd wanted to talk about some of the plans for the day, which had delayed him getting back. He wasn't sure what happened to her in the meantime, but she was certainly scuttling toward food now.

The men caught up with her just as she walked to the food counter. Devlin stepped back and motioned Easton to go behind her. And, on cue, all the men lined up after him. It seemed to be a bloody habit at this point.

He grabbed a tray and large plate, scooping up sausages, bacon, and hash browns before grabbing pancakes, smothering them in butter. He looked at her plate to see yogurt and fresh fruit, and he sighed. "Remember that low blood sugar issue?"

Startled, she turned to look at him, recognized who he was, and a beaming smile broke across her face.

He almost groaned. Inside his heart melted—just a little bit. Damn, he'd do almost anything to see that expression of hers on a regular basis. He shook his head, his voice harder than intended when he pointed out the small amount of food on her plate. "Protein will help stabilize your blood sugar a whole lot better than the fresh fruits will."

She frowned. "I'm not that hungry."

He sighed, reached across and picked up a bowl of oatmeal. "You'll eat more now." And dropped it on her tray.

She stared down at it, then at his plate. "Oatmeal doesn't qualify as protein."

"It's a grain, and it's better than nothing. Add some nuts and cream, and you'll at least have something solid."

"I don't want a hot bowl of oatmeal."

The two of them argued back and forth until the cook on the other side of the counter banged a spoon and said, "Fight like an old married couple somewhere else. You're holding up the line."

Easton scowled at him and then turned his gaze back to Summer, who, by now, sported bright red flags of color on her cheeks as she hurried down the line with the bowl of oatmeal still on her tray. She stopped at one section, adding nuts and seeds. He grinned and followed behind her. When she came to the end of the counter, she turned her back on him. Because it was so late for breakfast, lots of empty tables were available. She headed to one in the rear of the room.

Devlin laughed. "She is really something."

"Yeah, she is." Easton walked over to the coffee area, picked up several juices and cups of coffee, and, with the rest of the men following him, tracked his way to her table, sat beside her, placing one of the juices and a cup of coffee in front of her.

She stared at him and sighed. "Why are you looking after me?"

"Because I don't seem to be able *not* to," he snapped, irritated because, of course, it had been a very valid question.

She was an adult. She was in the camp, and wouldn't be here if she couldn't take care of herself. The rest would just consider her an idiot for not looking after herself. He didn't know why he felt so protective, and now he was well past the point of changing it. The rattlesnake had secured that line of thought last night.

As the other men lined up around them and sat down, she smiled and said, "Good morning, Devlin. Did you sleep well? I did see you in the tent when I got up this morning. It was very nice of you to watch over me."

Devlin flashed her a wicked smile. "You're very welcome." He could barely hide his grin as Easton glared at him.

She turned to Easton. "I thanked your friends, but you don't deserve it."

His jaw dropped in astonishment, but the others laughed. He shook his head. "You're making me crazy."

"I thought you already were."

He sighed. "Just eat your damn breakfast."

There was an odd silence at his side. He ignored it for a long time. When he raised his head, he saw Ryder frowning at him. Easton glared back. Ryder nudged his head toward Summer. Easton rolled his eyes and turned to look at her, but her head was down, and she was eating very slowly. There was a suspicious sniffle occasionally. He froze and slammed down a spoon. "Oh, for God's sake."

Her head flipped up, and she glared at him. If her eyes were overly bright, he chose to ignore it. She continued to glare at him and snapped, "Now what the hell is your problem? If you weren't following me all over the place and sneaking into my tent to sleep with me at night, it would be a lot easier to get rid of you."

The men around the table froze. Several heads turned in their direction.

Easton pinched the bridge of his nose and sighed. "It's not like that, and you know it."

She gasped. "Does that mean you don't want to sleep with me?"

Across the table Corey could barely stop the food from exploding out of his mouth, and Devlin had a grin wide enough to drive a truck through. Easton glowered from one to the other in anticipation of more, then shook his head.

Summer said with a pitiful force, "Oh. Well, thank you for letting me know."

Easton turned to look at her and said, "Let you know what?"

"That you don't want to sleep with me."

He stared at the pixie at his side in complete shock. "I didn't say that. This is the most bizarre conversation I've ever had over breakfast."

She propped her chin on her palm, her elbow on the table and stared at him. "Do you talk about this stuff over lunch or dinner then?" she asked in interest.

He shoved his face in her direction. "No, I don't."

She nodded. "Figures. That's what I thought."

For whatever reason, she appeared to be much happier. She turned and started eating her oatmeal. With his shoulders up and his hands out in a questioning manner as to what just happened, he looked at his friends. But they were all keeping the humor off their faces, and failing miserably.

He groaned, leaned over and whispered in her ear. "I would have absolutely no problem sleeping with you."

Her head jerked up. She looked at him, their faces inches apart, and narrowed her gaze. "Too late. So don't get any ideas now, okay?" And damn if she didn't shove her face a little farther into his and say, "I am not crazy."

In a placating voice, he nodded as he said, "Good. Now can you please eat your breakfast without causing any more emotional displays? Everybody's been staring at us for the last ten minutes, since you yelled out the first time."

She glanced around at the tables beside them, sending several strong-enough frowns at various men that they turned back to their food instead of watching the entertainment. Then she spun around to hers, hunched over her bowl and ate quickly.

He gently patted her knee. "It'll be fine."

She gripped his fingers, smacked his hand onto the bench beside them and shot him a hard look. "Remember, you don't want to sleep with me."

Then she lifted her hand and went back to eating her oatmeal.

"Oh, dear God." He didn't know what the hell happened, but he felt like laughing and crying. She wasn't just crazy; she was making him crazy. Yet inside was a lightness he'd never experienced before. He couldn't explain it.

Still no way would he leave her with the wrong impression. He leaned forward and whispered, "I would love to, but it sure as hell wouldn't be here."

She smirked. "You should be so lucky."

"I need to tell you about last night," Easton said.

Before he realized, she had bolted to her feet and, with a small finger wave, dashed from the mess tent, leaving her empty dishes behind. He stared at the trail she'd trod and wondered why the tent suddenly seemed a whole lot dimmer. Shaking his head at his fanciful thoughts of the absolutely bizarre conversation he just had, he turned back to his breakfast and decided, if he was sane, he'd much rather spend time with his friends than take one crazy step in the direction of that chaos. But, even having made that determination, he couldn't stop his gaze from looking at the exit just in case she reappeared.

When Devlin kicked him under the table and glared at him, Easton realized just how bad he had it because all he'd been doing was staring like an idiot where she had stood. Determined to not let her get to him anymore, he turned his attention back to his own breakfast. He had a long day ahead of him, and he needed the sustenance, even if she didn't.

His gaze landed on the seat she'd vacated, catching flecks of blood on the back. All humor disappeared. He reached out a finger to touch one. Then slowly turned to look at the others.

CHAPTER 7

J UST AS SHE entered her tent, her phone rang. She sat on the bed, fishing it from one of her pockets. It was her boss. "Hey, Ross. How are you?"

"I'm fine. Why haven't you been answering?"

She frowned. "I had my phone off this morning while I was working. I just got back from breakfast." Inside she winced. "Why did you call?"

"Time to head home."

She nodded. "Okay. I'm good with that."

"Did you get everything you needed?"

She glanced around at the tent she'd been staying in and nodded. "Yes, I think I'm good."

"You've got six hours until you fly out so make sure. It's all arranged. They'll give you a copy of the itinerary when you leave."

She nodded as if her boss could see her. "I'll make good use of the six hours. Promise."

She hung up her phone and stared around the small room. For some reason she was delighted to leave. But, at the same time, the thought of not seeing Easton again was heartbreaking. She still hadn't gotten any more pictures of him. Her time was short, but she had to transfer all the material she'd taken this morning onto her laptop first.

She reached under the pillow for the computer only to

find it wasn't there. She quickly searched the blankets and looked under the bed. Nothing. With a sinking heart, she spun around the small room, hoping to find it on a different bed. But she found no sign of it anywhere.

She ran a shaky hand up and down her face, figuring out what she was supposed to do now. She didn't want to tell her boss just yet; that would be something he would blame her for as she had a history of forgetfulness. Another reason she supplied her own equipment as part of her contract. And, sure enough, to a certain extent, she was to blame, but she had to leave her personal possessions somewhere. Just in case she had it inside her bag, she opened the double bags and checked, but there was no sign of it. Making sure she had everything with her this time, she packed up all her gear, wincing at the weight, and headed out.

Could Easton help her sort this out? Maybe, but how was she supposed to find him?

She stopped before a group of men and asked where the US soldiers were. They pointed off to the far side. With a smile of thanks, she headed in that direction. A lot of men were there but not Easton. She turned and glanced around the corner. She had asked for US soldiers, not US Navy. Maybe she should have asked where the SEALs were? Still that could be a secret, and maybe not everyone knew. Heading to the administration office, she reported the loss of her laptop and asked where she might be able to find Easton, Devlin, Ryder and Corey. With a smile, the man in the office told her they were out back, in a meeting.

"How long will they be?" she asked trying to peek around behind him. She could see the backs of several men and they appeared to be leaning over something on a table. Like a map. But that's all she could catch a glimpse of. So not helpful.

The man shrugged. "Couple hours most likely."

She nodded her thanks. "Is there any way to get a message to them?"

He nodded. "I can take a message, but no guarantee I can get it to them very fast."

"I don't have his phone number, otherwise I could have texted him. And, of course, I can't get it from you, can I?"

He shook his head. "No, that's not allowed."

"Of course it isn't." She told him what the note should say and watched as he checked the lost and found to no avail.

With a smile of thanks, she turned and walked out of the small tent. She had little to no hope of getting her laptop back.

She also needed to take as many pictures as she still could of the camp. She set up to take a few of the administration office inside and outside, then several of the other tents, including the mess tent, while keeping an eye on the back area where she figured Easton might be.

An hour later, she was adjusting the shutter speed on her camera when a shadow fell across her face. She knew without looking it was Easton.

"So where can a girl find the laptop that went missing from her tent?" She turned to smile at him.

Easton stiffened. "Are you serious?"

"And, of course, perfect timing." She groaned. "I'm being sent back home." She checked her watch. "My plane leaves in four hours."

Easton studied her face for a long moment. "How are you feeling?"

She frowned up at him. "I'm fine. Why?"

"Your head is injured." He gently touched her hair.

She gasped at the stabbing pain.

"Hold still." He tried to separate the strands of hair. "Your hair is coated in dried blood. It's hard to see the wound under it." Reaching under her chin, he tilted her head so he could look her in the eye. "When did this happen?"

She straightened slowly. "I have no idea. Except I've had a hell of a headache all morning. But I've been so busy, I didn't worry about it. So it can't be a big deal. Can we get back to the problem of my missing laptop please?"

An odd look was on his face as he contemplated her head. She didn't know what that meant. She really wanted a photograph of his face. "You sure I can't take any pictures of you?"

"Hell no." He motioned at the bags by her feet. "You sure you don't have the laptop somewhere in all that gear?"

She nodded. "I left it under my pillow before I headed out this morning. I went back to download all my morning work, but it was gone."

Devlin, who stood beside Easton, asked, "Did you leave all the images on your laptop?"

She shook her head. "Everything is in cloud storage. It's a relatively new laptop though, and my insurance agent will not be happy it's missing."

"No reason for it to be missing unless somebody didn't like the pictures you were taking and thought, by taking the laptop, they'd remove them."

"At first I thought Easton had stolen it because he doesn't want me to have any pictures of him," she joked, but it fell on flat ears. "Look. I don't know what happened. I reported it missing at the lost and found, but nobody just *accidentally* finds my laptop under my pillow in my bed and takes it to the lost and found."

The men stared at each other. "It's a good thing you're going home," Easton said quietly.

She wilted a little inside but nodded. What else could she say? It was good she was getting out of here.

Devlin nodded. "I don't think it's safe for you here."

She spun on her heels to stare at him and winced as her head ached. Instinctively she touched her scalp and felt the dried blood. She frowned, trying to figure out what she might have done. "What do you mean, it may not be safe?"

"We didn't tell you what happened last night. Or the reason why we stayed in your tent." Devlin looked to Easton. "It'd be better if you explained."

He raised an eyebrow but readily told her about the rattlesnake let loose inside the tent. She listened in shock, her jaw dropping when she understood it had been a deliberate act. "Someone is trying to kill me?"

"Rattlesnakes don't necessarily kill, but it was a possible outcome. It was definitely intended to terrorize you." He picked up her bags and led her toward the main office. "And we're going this way."

"Why? I haven't done anything," she protested.

"And yet apparently somebody must not like you," Easton retorted.

"You mean, someone other than you." She came to a stop, her hands going to her hips as she tried to hide her fear. "Well, is anybody doing something about this?"

"The first thing they're doing is shipping you out of here."

Just the thought of a rattlesnake was enough to unnerve Summer. To think it was deliberately placed in her tent just blew her away. She glanced at Easton. "Did you tell anyone?"

He nodded. "Devlin and I reported it this morning. It's being processed quietly."

"Do you think it might have something to do with why I'm being moved out today?"

"When did you expect to leave?"

She shrugged, barely realizing she was once again moving forward. "Honestly I'm not sure. It could happen at any time. It just seems weird that right after the rattlesnake report, I get a phone call to go home. I still need to take some more photos, so if you'll excuse me."

Distracted, unnerved, already missing him, she scampered out of his reach, heading to another location she'd already picked out. She studied her surroundings with more awareness. Somebody had done something deliberately to freak her out, to hurt her.

Unbelievable. The sun had gone behind dark clouds. She thought that was about right. The approaching storm matched her mood exactly.

EASTON WATCHED SUMMER dart away. He hadn't told her that she shouldn't spend the afternoon on her own. He'd finally been given official instructions to keep an eye on her, to make sure nothing more happened. The last thing the base wanted was to have their photographer injured under suspicious circumstances. It was unusual to have someone like her come here, but the company she freelanced for had worked with the Canadians many times before, making it an easy choice apparently.

He followed to see her studying the clouds. "You okay?"

She gave him a sideways glance. "What do you think?

Someone's after me." She shook her head. "I know you might not believe this, but I'm actually a really nice person."

He gave her the sweetest smile. "I know exactly what kind of person you are. And nobody should be trying to kill you."

"So then why are they?" she cried out.

"The only reason any of us can think of"—and he nodded to the guys, now standing beside him—"is that you've taken pictures of something you shouldn't have."

She shook her head, wincing at the throbbing pain that resulted. "I take pictures of guys running in the morning, of a friendly tug-of-war between teams. I take pictures of sunshine and rain, storm clouds and flowers." She stared at him in bewilderment. "What I don't do is take pictures of drug transactions or car accidents or a murderer stalking his victims."

From behind her, Corey asked, "Can you think of any pictures you might have taken that involved people at places where they didn't belong?"

"How would I know?" she asked. "I'm taking pictures, not monitoring people."

The men exchanged glances. "Nothing else makes sense."

She snorted. "That doesn't make sense either. You're all here doing training and playing friendly war games. There's nothing to steal. Nothing to find. Nothing clandestine. If two people are involved in a relationship, then that's their business. I didn't take any sleazy pictures. I didn't see anything sleazy to take pictures of."

"Oh, it's all here, but good to know it wasn't on display," Ryder said quietly. "Lots of relationships form during these stays at camps."

Easton watched her facial expressions as she turned a blank face his way.

"I don't care about that. I came to take pictures for my boss. Not to be a private detective and dig into people's private lives."

"What is on the laptop?" Easton asked suddenly.

"Not much." She looked up at him. "I download my SD cards and then sort through the pictures quickly, save those I want to keep to my cloud storage."

"So, if you did take an image of something suspicious, you haven't seen the images close enough to know, correct?"

"Yes, exactly." She glared at him. "And I need to download my current set of images from this morning so they are safe."

"Therefore, outside of the inconvenience and cost …"

"I didn't lose much, I know. But that inconvenience and cost adds up," she grumbled, walking to the field on the left where several groups were working on hand-to-hand combat.

Easton watched as she grabbed her camera and was immediately lost to her work. Her focus instant. Her concentration complete. She crouched, twisted, shifted her stance, all in search for that perfect shot.

Beside him Ryder said, "Corey and I are going to her tent to take a look. Maybe something was left to find."

Easton nodded. "Good idea." With her head turned the opposite direction, he signaled to Ryder to check the surveillance cameras they'd set up on the fly. He knew the men would check the trip wire while there too. Ryder nodded and left with Corey.

The security measures had been an easy decision after he'd woken up to find her gone again this morning. She'd only be leaving and entering by the front door, so the other measures were for anyone else. Hopefully they were overreacting, but that head wound bothered him. He'd seen many like it, but, with all the dried blood, he couldn't be sure. She needed to get it cleaned up.

Watching two of his friends leave, Easton realized that, as much as he hated to see her leave, he wouldn't be happy until she got on the plane safely. Given what he knew now, that couldn't happen soon enough. "We should take her to medical to get her head looked at," Easton said to Devlin, who gave a quick nod.

She turned, narrowed her gaze and snapped. "Like hell. I'm fine."

"You're stubborn, not fine," Easton growled at her in irritation. "You need the head wound cleaned and checked over."

Her shoulders slumped. "Is arguing going to do me any good?"

"No."

"Well, it's been fine all day so let me finish my photos so I can keep my job. Then we'll go."

He looked at her for a long moment and realized nothing would change in the meantime. She could have her time. "You've got one hour. That's it."

"Make it three." She gave him a bright hopeful smile.

"One," he snapped. "And you're wasting time."

He heard Devlin's quick sucked-back chuckle at the look on her face, and Easton relented. "Okay, see what you can do in an hour, and we'll evaluate then."

CHAPTER 8

ALL SHE WANTED to do was focus on her photography, get the photos she needed and leave. It was one thing to imagine somebody in her tent one night, but a rattlesnake the next and the theft of her laptop was too much. Her entire trip had a taste of fear and ugliness she didn't want to deal with. She would be home safe and sound soon. That couldn't happen fast enough for her.

She took ten steps to the left, her camera clicking aimlessly. She had no intention of using any of these photos, which just sucked. But her focus was complete, the one thing that allowed all her confusion and pain to die back down.

For every step she took, she had two men in sync with her. She shook her head, lowered her camera and faced Easton and Devlin. "You don't need to babysit me. You know that, right?"

"Until you get on the plane, we will be babysitting you," Easton said. "I don't understand why you are alone here as it is. Doesn't your boss send you with someone else on these trips?"

"No, no need," she said blithely her eyes on the wind lifting a branch and giving it a nudge like pointing it in a specific direction.

"And yet look what happened this time."

"An anomaly," she said, turning to watch him. "It's the

first time in five years. I doubt it will happen again."

She didn't think he believed her. Hell, he was barely listening. His gaze never stopped searching the area around them. His tone was quiet, calm, controlled. It gave her absolutely no leeway to argue. His word was law, and she had just better accept it or else. At least when it came to keeping her safe. There was just something so very appealing about all that honor. Her heavy sigh slipped out as she tried to lose herself once again behind the camera. But this was no good. Her mind just kept circling.

She spun to ask, "Can you search for my laptop? I really hate to leave without it."

"The military is handling that right now," Devlin said. "The Canadians are quite pissed. They won't let something like this go."

She brightened. "That's good, right?"

Devlin's phone went off. He picked it up, stepping a couple feet away, and answered it. When he came back, he said, "Let's head to the office. They found the laptop."

"Yes!" That was perfect. Of course it also meant a side trip to get her head checked out.

The men on either side of her walked toward the office, keeping her between them. Sure enough, a laptop very like the one she had sat on the counter. The guy behind the counter asked, "Is this yours?"

She flipped it open and hit the Power button. As soon as it came up, she entered her log-in information. Within seconds, the desktop she knew and loved opened. She smiled, turned the laptop around and said, "Yes, this is mine."

She clicked the keys to search the control panel for the most recent things it registered. But her downloads and transfers last night appeared to be it. Everything was still here, although not much, as she only used it as a conduit to save her material to the cloud. She never kept any of her log-in information on the laptop either, nor did her email program automatically open. She brought up the browser, logging into her email. Everything appeared to be normal. She logged off, grinned at the man and said, "It's perfect. Thank you. Where did you find it?"

"At one of the places where you were taking pictures of the run this morning."

His tone was slightly disapproving, as if she'd accidentally dropped it, putting the camp through a lot of extra effort because of her accusation.

She stared at him for a long moment, then said, "Thank you for finding it. But I never take my laptop out when I'm in the field. I have enough to carry without packing extra things like that."

The slight accusatory look in his eyes fell away as his forehead creased in a frown. "When did you last see it?"

She quickly answered, "Under my pillow on my bed," as he wrote in a notebook. She had no hope of the men finding the culprit, but, as far as she was concerned, she would leave in a couple hours. Since she had all her equipment, she was good. She turned and exited the building, checking her watch as she did so.

"You're not leaving until after lunch, which is soon," Easton said. "So first your head, then lunch."

She pinched her mouth together and crinkled her nose. "I'm not very hungry. All I want to do is go home."

"Where is home?" Devlin asked.

"San Diego."

Devlin laughed.

She glanced at him and frowned. "Why is that funny?"

He shook his head. "It's just too serendipitous to ignore. I'm from there as well."

She studied him, not exactly sure what he was getting at. But no more explanation was forthcoming. She glanced at her watch again. "Maybe you can take me to wait for my flight."

Easton shook his head, grabbed her arm and started toward the mess tent. "We aren't leaving you, and, if you don't want to eat, that's fine, but we need to eat. And you're getting that head checked over."

"Oh, I'm so sorry. Just go and eat. I'll be fine here. Leave me in the administration office if you're so concerned."

"We're not leaving your side," he reiterated quietly but firmly. "If you want to stay here, we're staying here. And you won't get on that flight without getting your wound cleaned."

Disgruntled, she stared at him. "Fine. But there's no reason for you not to eat just because I'm not going to."

"What time are you landing tonight?"

She shrugged. "I don't know. Probably late afternoon."

"You're not eating the entire time?"

She thought about that and realized it was way too long to go without food. "It won't be a straight flight, and I'll take a trip to one of the stores and buy some nuts or something."

He rolled his eyes. "Come and eat, then we'll take you to the airport and wait with you until you're on the plane."

She glared at him. "Aren't you taking this protective duty a bit too far?"

"You've forgotten about the rattlesnake. Besides, we don't want anything to happen to you on our watch."

"Right. So, it's all about your watch, not my safety," she

said with a slight pout.

At that, he nudged her arm slightly as he led her toward the mess tent, where once again he would ensure she ate. Just before they got there, and just as she hoped he'd forgotten, he detoured to a small tent. Inside she found herself in a chair and her head being checked over.

Easton stood, arms across his chest, right in front of her the whole time. She glared at him. "You don't have to stay here, you know. I'm getting treatment."

He deliberately gave her a bland look.

"Are you always so damn honorable?"

His eyebrows shot up. "It's who I am."

She groaned. "Of course it is." Just then the medic hit a spot that burned, and she cried out.

Instantly Easton stepped forward.

"I'm okay," she whispered.

But he didn't step back. Instead he reached out a hand. She gripped it like a lifeline as the wound was washed, then some kind of ointment was gently placed on top. At this point her head was throbbing again. She could hear the conversation rumbling between Easton and the doctor, but the words were slipping in and out of her conscious mind.

"Bullet."

"Burn."

"Close."

She shuddered when someone poked the soft tissue on her head, and waves of greasy pain rose up. She gasped and bent forward, away from the prying fingers and to stop the dizziness.

Easton gripped her hand firmly. "Easy, Summer. Just keep taking deep breaths."

She closed her eyes and followed his instructions. Slowly

the nausea eased back. By the time she was on her feet and back outside, she felt better.

Until she remembered the earlier conversation. She turned toward Easton. "What was that about bullets?"

Devlin, who'd been waiting outside for them, looked at Easton.

His face hard, Easton said, "Her injury appears to be a graze by a bullet."

"What?" Devlin asked in a harsh whisper. "Are you sure?"

Easton nodded. "As sure as anyone can be without having been at the site at the time." He twisted slightly to look at Summer.

She stared at him in shock. In a small horrified voice, she asked, "Are you saying someone shot at me?"

He nodded. "And missed. Thank God. Are you sure you don't remember getting shot at?"

She closed her eyes, recalling what had happened. "I thought I was being watched. I was pretty unnerved for a time," she admitted. "So I hunkered down in the long grass. When I popped back up, I remember hearing something, but you guys were approaching then, and the runners made this heavy rumble. Although ..." She frowned. "My headache started around that same time."

"No wonder," Easton said quietly. "You were damn lucky." He wrapped an arm protectively around her and steered her toward the mess tent. "Now food. It will help settle the nausea in your stomach."

Once inside, still disquieted by the news, she made a sandwich from the sandwich bar, grabbed a cup of coffee and a bottle of juice, and motioned to the table in the far back as Easton navigated her through the crowd. Maybe it was her state of mind from the suspicious events, but people seemed to be watching her. Commenting, maybe gossiping about her. She hoped her laptop scenario hadn't impacted others. She knew it wouldn't take long for the bullet-graze news to travel through the ranks.

Then everyone would really be looking at her.

Their table was against the far corner beside the back entrance, set enough out of the way that they wouldn't be impacted by people coming and going. She carefully put down her tray, unloading the plate, juice and coffee onto the table. She stopped to stare at the sun. It was a beautiful afternoon.

Only it was hard to appreciate it at the moment.

She hadn't told her boss all that had gone on and knew she didn't dare mention her head injury. He'd never send her out in the field again. She hadn't had a problem before though, so she was determined to look upon this as an anomaly. Maybe she should have arranged to leave earlier. Then again, there were only so many flights out of the base. She wasn't sure what flight she was taking, and honestly she didn't care. She was a good traveler, and she should be fine. She just hated waiting.

She heard a funny sound like a cross between the crunch of dried leaves and a baseball hitting a bat. She turned in the direction it came from, bringing her to the back exit of the mess tent. She peered around the corner, her camera already in her hand, ready to take a picture.

"Hey," Easton said in a low tone. "Stay close."

She half-smiled, half-chuckled as she nodded at him. "Just a second."

He rolled his eyes making her laugh again. The one good thing about her life was she was following her passion.

Apparently she was in the right place for what was meant to be in her life. She had a lot of friends who did their jobs but didn't have the same love for it she did. She'd prefer to do just gallery showings, but the income from those sales was very unstable, so she still needed something a whole lot more secure. A day job. Her freelance assignments.

She didn't see anything outside, but, just for good measure, she quickly shot several photos in panoramic view from the tent opening. As she turned to step inside, returning to the table, she looked for Ryder, Devlin and Corey, but they were still at the food counter. Easton had his back to her as he snagged a few more chairs for their table.

At least they could all eat together now. She stepped toward her meal, and an arm came around her throat, a hand over her mouth, and her feet were kicked out from under her. She hit the ground hard, but the hand over her mouth stopped any sound from escaping. Just as quickly, she could feel her cameras banging against each other around her neck and her beaded necklace giving way as she struggled.

She couldn't see who had attacked her. When she realized they were after her equipment, her adrenaline kicked in—and her training. From a lying position, she kicked up full force and smacked her attacker in the head with a head butt. She continued all the way over into a backflip, turned around and lashed out with her right foot—caught him on the jaw. But she didn't stop there. She crouched down as she gave him a very hard punch to the throat.

By the time she straightened again, she was surrounded by uniformed men. Angry men. They glared at her. She put her arms across her chest and glared back. Almost instantly Easton and Devlin were at her side. The attitude around her rose perceptively. She continued to glare at the military men, pointed at the man on the floor and said, "He attacked me and tried to steal my cameras."

The atmosphere changed. Easton reached down, grabbed the man by his collar and whacked him hard across the face, waking him up.

She said, "You could let me do that."

When Devlin crouched to watch the attacker, Easton straightened. "I think he's had enough from you."

She spun on him but saw the humor on his face. She shrugged. "I told you that I knew self-defense."

"That's way more than 'knowing' self-defense," he said quietly.

She shrugged. "I was good at it."

The man on the floor groaned, opened his eyes, saw Devlin above him and cringed, his gaze darting from side to side, landing on Summer's face. He pointed at her. "She attacked me."

She snapped, "Not until you threw me to the ground with a choke hold and tried to steal my cameras."

He glared at her. "Like hell I did."

"Right, so you got beaten up by a woman for nothing?"

A twitter started at one end of the group gathered nearby and circled around the men. The attacker frowned at them, made his way to his feet. When he tried to disappear into the crowd, Devlin caught him and said, "Not so fast."

The man tried to shrug him off. "I didn't do anything."

Summer stepped forward. "So, when we take fingerprints off these cameras, we won't find yours at all, will we?"

He stared at her, a haunted look on his face.

She nodded. "That's what I thought. So maybe you'd like to explain why?"

The other men in the circle stepped forward too.

He held up his hands. "Look. I didn't mean to."

"Didn't mean to what?" Easton snapped. "Knock her to the ground? Try to steal her equipment?"

"Not to mention broke my necklace," she snarled. It wasn't the necklace that mattered as it was just a trinket. It was the fact that he'd attacked her in the first place.

"I had to," he cried out. "I didn't have any choice."

"So you admit to attacking me? And then trying to steal my stuff?" She wanted to make sure his confession was heard by everybody.

With a glare in her direction, and Devlin giving him a head shake, he nodded his head and said, "I thought it would be an easy snatch and grab."

"But you thought wrong, didn't you?" Easton said.

Sullen now the man nodded. "It should've been." He glared at Summer. "Bitch."

"Right. When a woman defends herself, she's a bitch." She snorted. "How typically male."

He rubbed his jaw. "What the hell did you hit me with anyway?"

"My foot. You can have the other one in your mouth if you keep it up."

"No, you don't," Easton said. "We'll see that he's disciplined. Let the military deal with this."

Her gaze slid from one to the other. "But will he get punished? Or will he get to walk free? You heard him. He tried to knock me out, steal my stuff, and all he'll get is a couple days latrine duty?"

A harsh voice behind him said, "No, it will be a lot more than that."

She turned to see one of the Canadian brass glaring at the man, who was now visibly wilting in front of them.

"He will be disciplined for this."

She wasn't sure exactly what that meant. From the look on the man's face, it would be enough. "Good. Hope he knows better than to attack a defenseless woman in the future."

"Defenseless," the man snorted. "You damn near broke my neck."

"Only after you wrapped your arm around my neck and threw me to the ground. If you hadn't attacked me, I wouldn't have had to defend myself." She glared at him. "A simple snatch and grab, you said."

"Bitch," he said.

"Soldier!" the Canadian officer interrupted. "One more time with the name-calling and I'll make sure you get your pay docked—twice."

"You attacked me first," he said to Summer, as if backtracking.

With her arms across her chest, hating his accusations, indignant that he did this in the first place, she fumed as she reined in her temper. Finally she snapped, "Listen, soldier, *if* I'd attacked you first, I would have had one hell of a good reason, and you would not be talking right now, because you'd be dead."

Silence filled the mess tent.

She didn't know who started the sniggering, but, within minutes, the place erupted in laughter, and then the clapping broke out. She didn't know who this soldier was, but his reputation would be in tatters now. She backed off, turned to look at the brass, nodded once and then said to Easton. "I told you how I could take care of myself." And she walked off.

WITH A SHARP hand motion at Devlin and Ryder to stay behind to watch what happened with the attacker, Easton grabbed Corey and bolted through the crowd after Summer. He took her arm. When she spun around and dropped into a crouch, he held up his hands. "It's just me."

She slowly straightened, but he could see she was still in combat mode right now. He didn't know where she had learned to fight like that, but he was damn glad for it. "I'm not going back in there," she snapped.

"And you don't have to. I'll grab our food, and we can sit out here." He motioned at a tree with some benches.

"Fine. Give me a minute or two to calm down. Do not haul me back into that place."

Easton turned to Corey standing nearby and motioned him to the bench.

Corey nodded.

Easton slipped back inside the mess tent, grabbed one of the trays and three plates, quickly piled up the food, grabbed some drinks and carefully walked back outside. Surely it was safer to eat directly from the buffet than from her unattended plate. Everyone in the entire mess tent watched him. He didn't give a damn. He just wanted to get her home, but, even then, he was afraid that wouldn't be the end of it. He didn't know what the hell she had caught with her camera, but it was something she shouldn't have. Therefore, his unit must look through the photos and figure this out.

Just because her attacker wore Canadian military garb didn't make him someone who belonged here. The nametag said Lemans. But was he wearing his own clothes or had he stolen it from someone else? With so many men around, it would be easy for somebody to slip in snag a uniform and wear it. Not a nice thought, but it was possible.

Back outside, his tray overladen, he slowly made his way to the bench. Corey had worked his way around behind the crowds and leaned against a tree on the far side. Summer sat in the middle of the bench, her legs crossed, her arms crossed, her knees bouncing restlessly. She still fumed. By the time he reached her, she didn't look to have calmed down at all.

She stared at the tray in front of her. "What did you do, take everybody else's plate too?"

"Enough for us three, right?"

She helped take the plates off the tray and laid them on the bench, then took a plate with a sandwich and dug in.

If nothing else, apparently that fight had given her an appetite. She polished off the sandwich without realizing it.

He handed her a second. He had just shorted his own lunch, but, if she kept eating, it was all good. The mess tent was still open, so he could get more food if necessary. But, with her current temperament after the scenario that just happened, her stress level was off the charts. He knew that would drop her blood sugar fast once the adrenaline rush was gone.

"I recognized him."

"Where?" He sat beside her, picking up his plate.

"He works in the kitchen."

He turned to look at her. "The man who attacked you?"

She nodded. "I never forget a face. I always forget the name that goes with a face but not the face."

He glanced where the culprit had been taken away. He tried to remember the man's face, but it hadn't been terribly distinguishable.

"He works in the back. Not in the front."

"How do you know?"

"He brought out several tubs of fresh food when we were in line."

"Interesting."

She shrugged. "I don't think he attacked me for himself. Somebody either paid him or forced him to take my cameras. But I doubt we'll get that information from him."

"Don't make excuses for him."

She shook her head. "I'm not," she snapped. "I just want to forget all this happened and go home."

"At least you get to go. You're alive, safe, and you're on your way home soon."

She stared at him for a long moment and then slowly sank back on the bench. "You're right. I have to remember the good things, not just the bad." She handed him her empty plate. "Do you know whose sandwich this was?"

He grinned. "Probably Corey's."

She groaned and stared down at the empty plate. "Now I have to apologize to him."

"You don't have to," Easton said cheerfully. "He'll get more."

She brightened. "Good thing," she said. "I might eat that next plate too."

A noise behind them had them turning toward Corey, walking around the tree to pick up his plate. "I'll grab my lunch before you empty the kitchen," he said with a grin. "By the way, nice display there."

"Display of what?"

"Self-defense moves. I watched you take him down, simple as pie."

She brightened. "Thanks."

He nodded. "You were doing a good job defending yourself. I didn't need to step in. I would have if need be."

She turned to Easton and snapped, "See? I told you how he attacked me first."

"And I believed you. I never said I didn't."

She glared at him, and he stared back.

"Why are you so lacking in self-confidence? You're good."

She frowned. "I just hate it when nobody believes me."

"Understandable," Corey said. "None of us likes it when our word is called into question."

She stared at her lap, picked up the coffee beside her and said, "I used to compete. I lost a bout once. But I knew my opponent had cheated. When we were rematched, and I won, she accused me of cheating. It was a controversy for quite a while. I ended up keeping the title, but it left a bad taste in my mouth."

"Something like that always does," Easton said. "Corey, she says the man who attacked her works in the kitchen."

Corey nodded. "I heard her. And she's right."

"We need to find out what he wanted with her equipment."

"And I won't know until I look at the pictures." She shrugged. "The trouble is, I have no idea what people did or were doing that was wrong. So they all will look fine to me."

They nodded. Easton checked his watch. "Finish your coffee. You leave in about ten minutes."

She nodded at his plate. "You better eat."

He rolled his eyes. Now she was looking after him. He settled back to finish his lunch. They were quite a pair. The thought made him freeze for a moment, then he relaxed. He'd be worried about anyone who'd gone through what she had. That she'd been shot at infuriated him. Then to be attacked here … in broad daylight. Nothing made sense. He didn't want to contemplate that whoever was behind this could then follow her home.

Ryder walked over and sat down beside him. "Negative on this morning's checks."

He studied his friend for a long moment, shifting from the thoughts in his head to Ryder's comment. Then it clicked. The trip wire in her tent hadn't been engaged, and their security showed nothing out of the ordinary.

"Good," he said quietly. "We'll keep it up until she's safely on the plane heading home." He had to hope she'd be safe there, but inside he didn't see it happening.

As he studied the food on his fork, he asked, *What would he do about it?*

CHAPTER 9

WITH THE MEN sticking so close, no way anybody would attack her again. She relaxed, watching and laughing as the men finished their lunches around her. She wasn't sure how she ended up being part of this group, but the thought of leaving them tugged at her heartstrings. Not fair. She barely knew them. Yet she wouldn't get a chance to know them any better. Especially Easton. And that really sucked.

She didn't know how his macho persona had such an effect on her. She'd never gone for big alpha males. She had always preferred smaller, less dominant, less aggressive, much-less-threatening boyfriends. Something about Easton didn't make him threatening. And it was lovely.

"What are you thinking about?" Easton asked with a frown.

She gave herself a mental shake, realizing she'd been staring at him like a schoolgirl. Feeling the heat climb her cheeks, she said lightly, "How to get pictures of you."

There was a moment of silence before the others chuckled.

"I don't mean naughty pictures," she explained. "I mean, pictures of your face, your giant hands."

He stared at her in disbelief and lifted his hand, looking at it. "What the hell are you talking about? Why would anybody want to take a picture of my hands?"

She smiled. "Because they're beautiful."

Dumbstruck, he stared at her.

She laughed out loud. "I'm an artist. I see things."

Corey stepped in front of her, his hands out. "I don't have a problem with you taking pictures of me," he said hopefully.

She chuckled. "I could take thousands of pictures between the four of you, but there is just something about Easton. He has all those hard angles and ridges. Clean shadows and highlights." She shrugged. "It's hard to explain."

"He doesn't mind. He's just shy," Devlin said gently.

She turned to Easton hopefully. "Is that true? May I take a few pictures?"

"Hell no." He glared at Devlin. "I do mind."

"You mind her taking a picture of your hands?" Devlin tilted his head to the side. "That seems fairly unassuming. Only she could identify it as your hand, and no name would be attached to it."

He glared at the whole group, hopped to his feet, loaded up all the dirty dishes and strode off to the kitchen area where he could dump them.

She watched him go with a smile. "He's really self-conscious, isn't he?"

"Oh, you noticed."

"Well, I don't want to make him feel bad, but I really would like to get a couple pictures of him."

"You always make sure you have their permission?"

"Yes. Always."

"Interesting," Devlin said. "Why do you carry so much equipment around?"

She winced and explained. "I may need something, a different lens, whatever. So I could hardly leave anything behind, could I?"

The men stared.

Easton strode back, looking at his watch in a pointed manner.

She hopped to her feet. "I got the message." She reached for her bags, lifting them to her shoulder. The laptop she had no choice but to carry in her arms. All the rest of her gear was on her back.

"Can you fit the laptop and gear in the bag?"

She nodded. "I'll do that when I get on the plane," she said. "I'll have time then."

All five walked to the side of the office building where a jeep waited. A man came out, spoke with Devlin and Easton and motioned at the jeep.

Easton said, "That's your ride to the plane."

She nodded, ran to the passenger side and set her gear on the back seat. She turned and walked toward the men. "I hate good-byes."

The men grinned. Devlin said, "Not much of a good-bye right now. Take care."

She gave them a wave and returned to the passenger side, hopping in. She really did hate good-byes.

The driver got in the jeep but didn't start the vehicle yet. She waved to the men behind her. A couple waved back but not Easton. Of course not Easton. Staring at the rearview mirror, she gave him a good frown, then turned in her seat to ask the driver, "How long is the drive?"

"Ten to fifteen minutes. Not too far. You ready to go now?"

She nodded and settled in her seat, forcing herself to not

look back at Easton. Just as the driver turned the key and put the jeep into gear, she was snatched off her seat, and hot lips covered hers. Easton's arms were hard but gentle as he held her close, kissing her as if branding her for the world to see.

And just as suddenly she was back in her seat, and the vehicle moved forward—away from him. Her fingers went to her lips in shock at the sudden shift from Easton. Her mind and emotions were in turmoil. And her heart? Yeah, it was in a serious meltdown.

Sighing heavily, she focused on the scenery speeding past.

Her fingers itched to grab a camera, but, at this speed, it'd be hard to get anything.

They weren't out more than ten minutes from camp when she caught sight of something in the bushes. She never saw what happened next. There was an odd sound, like a hard crack, followed by glass shattering in the jeep. She screamed as shards covered her. The vehicle came to a slow stop.

She turned to look at the driver, his head off to the side. Blood poured from his neck. "Oh, shit."

She slapped a hand over the blood pumping from his neck to stop the flow, realizing not only was he injured but she was a sitting duck. She didn't have any of the camp numbers to call for help. Why hadn't she asked Easton for his? She checked the driver's pockets for a phone. She found one and pulled it out, but it was locked, and she didn't know what his password was.

Pulling out her phone, she called her boss, screaming to call the camp, that her driver had been shot on the way to the airport. She reached into her bag, grabbed a spare T-shirt, folded it to press it, like a gauze pad, to his neck to stop the bleeding. "Hold on," she told her driver. "Just hold on. We'll get help."

She didn't know if he could hear her or not. She wasn't sure what else she could do. She didn't want him to bleed to death so couldn't leave him to run back to camp. At the same time she felt she should be doing more for him. The poor man. He'd been shot. A reminder of her own close call.

Was the shooter after her? If he was, he would be coming for a second shot. If so, she was exposed. She glanced around, looking for a place to hide. The trees were twenty feet away. She could run in a zigzag fashion and possibly reach the tree line, but that would mean leaving the driver, … and she had no weapon. Except … She reached around and checked the soldier's side, pulled out his handgun. Awkwardly holding her hand to his neck, she hefted the gun, checked to make sure it was loaded and set it across her lap. If nothing else, she wouldn't go down without a fight.

The soldier moaned.

"Help's coming. Stay quiet."

He moaned again when she pressed the cloth harder to his neck.

"Hold on. Just keep fighting. Don't you die on me."

She didn't know how long she waited. Frantic, she kept swiveling in her seat, looking for any dust plume to confirm help was on the way and alternatively to see if the gunman drew closer, or if he just waited to see what she would do. She wasn't worried about any animals in the bush. She'd learned a long time ago some of the worst predators were the ones who walked on two legs.

She crouched lower in the passenger seat, searching for their attacker. She'd called several minutes ago. Why wasn't anyone here?

Why the hell hadn't she gotten Easton's phone number? She'd wanted to. … Surely there had to be some way to get a hold of somebody in the camp. She tried getting into the driver's phone again, but nothing worked.

A crack sounded behind her. She slid lower.

She could hardly hear anything with her breathing so raspy. She didn't dare panic. The soldier's life depended on her. In the distance, she heard another vehicle. Summer sank lower in the seat just in case the shooter took another shot at her. Her imagination was in overdrive as she swore she heard sounds of someone running away. Either because they'd shot a soldier instead of her or were more worried about the approaching vehicle.

When she thought it was safe, she sat up slightly and peered through the back of the jeep. Several vehicles raced toward her. "Oh, thank God. Hold on. You're going to be safe. Just keep fighting."

Jeeps raced up on either side of her, covering them in a cloud of dust. Men swarmed around the vehicle. Her hand was removed from the soldier's neck.

She sat in shock, covered in blood, and watched as they quickly carried their fallen comrade on a stretcher. The vehicle left with the wounded man, racing back toward the camp.

"Shouldn't they be flying him out of here instead?" She was grabbed roughly and spun around, still in her seat. She stared into Easton's hard gaze.

"You're covered in blood. Are you hurt?"

She stared at him for a long moment, slowly shaking her head. "No. No, he shot the driver, not me."

"Good."

Easton reached for the gun in her hand. Her finger was still on the trigger. She let him remove the sidearm and said, "That was the soldier's. I didn't know if the gunman was coming after us again." She took a huge shaky breath and stared at Easton in shock. "Did someone really try to kill me—again?"

He stood still, glancing at the others. She presumed his friends were there, but her eyes were only locked on him. He gave a hard nod. She collapsed into his arms.

EASTON WRAPPED HIS arms around Summer and crushed her against his chest. He lowered his head, his chin resting on her hair, and held her close. Her whole body shook. The shock of what just happened was still something she would struggle to adjust to. Hell, he had trouble adjusting. He'd have nightmares over this for years to come.

He glanced at Devlin, and the two exchanged grim looks. They'd seen too much like this before. Obviously somebody had been watching her and had known when she was flying out, determined she wouldn't meet her destination as planned. Whatever the hell they did now, they'd have to come up with something fast.

He gently stroked her back. She was so very small. But she wasn't skinny. Decent muscle mass covered her bones, which he was grateful for. She ate well—sometimes— obviously had trained in martial arts but had no training that prepared her for shocks like this.

Finally she pulled back ever-so-slightly and wiped her eyes. She sniffled a couple times and then whispered, "I'm sorry."

He gently tilted her chin toward him and whispered

back, "Don't be. You've been through a rough experience."

"I'm so sorry for my driver." She pushed loose tendrils of hair from her face and looked at the bloodstained jeep. "Will he live?"

"We hope so. Everything's being done for him that can be."

"I didn't know how else to help him," she whispered tearfully. "It's not his fault. He was assigned to take me to the airport."

"Where were you sitting when he got shot?" Devlin asked. "Were you sitting straight up or were you bending over? Do you remember?"

She frowned as she stared at the passenger seat as if looking at the time gone by. "I was sitting up, staring out the window, thinking about taking pictures but decided not to as the road was so rough. Because of the bouncing I just tried to keep in my seat. Most of the time it was fine, but a couple places had rough spots, and that's all I remember before the first shot. But there was a second shot, once the jeep stopped moving."

"Right. Chances are you were the target. When the jeep bounced, the driver might've moved into the bullet's path, and you moved out of it, or maybe he just moved ahead of you. Once the shooter realized he hit the wrong target, he must have booked it. Or he ran not even knowing who he hit. Either way, it was a good thing for you." Easton gripped her shoulder, her tears washing down her cheeks. "It's not your fault," he said.

She glanced at him. "It's not my fault. But, if I wasn't trying to get to the airplane, then he wouldn't have been shot."

"Like you said, it could've been anybody."

"But it was supposed to be me." She looked in the direction of the base. "I don't want to go back there. Can I still leave?"

Easton glanced at Devlin, one eyebrow raised. "We'll call the base and see what they want to do with this."

Devlin pulled out his phone and walked a little bit away. Easton returned his attention to the waif in his midst. "We'll see if we can get you on a plane anyway."

"Just not fast enough." She wrapped her arms around her middle as if to ward off pain.

He knew how she felt. Sometimes the hits just kept coming, and all you could do was try to stay upright.

He knew where he wanted to go. Rage burned inside him; someone had tried to kill her.

That one of the soldiers had been shot was bad enough, but this was now yet another attempt to fire on her. By someone who knew she was leaving and was making sure she couldn't. If only she'd left yesterday. She wasn't safe here until they found out who had done this and why. If they couldn't fly her out tonight, she had to be in a secure location away from everybody, and they needed to go over her photos to see what they were missing. She didn't know what she was looking for, but the rest of them might.

Devlin came back, but his face was grim. Even as he opened his mouth, they heard a helicopter overhead.

Summer looked up and then realized. "That's the soldier, isn't it?"

"Yes. He's on his way to the hospital now."

"Good. And what about me?" she asked, biting her lip. "Can I still catch my plane?"

Easton glanced over at Devlin. "What's the verdict?"

"She's been redirected to leave in the morning."

He heard her gasp but ignored her. "And?"

"We're on assignment to keep her safe."

With a nod of satisfaction Easton said, "Good. I planned to anyway."

She stared at him as if processing what they just said, then immediately bolted backward. "Oh, no you don't."

He stared at her, patiently wondering what went on inside her head now. "*Oh, no I don't* what?"

"Oh, no, you cannot be looking after me. No way you're playing bodyguard."

He raised an eyebrow and in a low voice said, "Why not?" Of course he would. More men could be assigned as well, but no way in hell was he leaving her side until she was safe and sound at home again. He didn't know how to make that last part happen, but he would do his damnedest to have his supervisor send him home with her.

"Because someone will shoot you then," she cried out, lifting her hands for emphasis. "Can't you see that?"

He gave her a crooked grin. "So I can't be your bodyguard because I might get shot?"

"Of course."

Devlin chuckled. "What about me? Is it okay if I get shot being your bodyguard?"

She turned, and all the color drained from her face. "No, no, no. This can't happen. Nobody can be my bodyguard because that's exactly what'll happen. They will try to kill you." She shook her head, her hands resting on her head. "No, I need to go to the airport now, and I need to sit there and wait for the next plane to take me out of here."

Easton stared at her, wondering at what point she'd understand she wasn't safe no matter where she was. That it didn't matter if she was here, at the base or at the airport.

And he was afraid now she wouldn't be safe when she hit home either.

"We have weapons too, you know," Ryder said with a smile. "It's what we're trained to do, to look after people who are in trouble."

"Yes, I understand that. I can't have you getting hurt too," she said. "Enough blood is on my hands. I can't have more."

"It's not on your hands," Ryder said patiently. "You are not responsible for this."

Easton added, "And if any of us get shot while trying to keep you safe, that's not your fault either."

She glared at Easton, her temper rising to the front.

That was a damn good thing. He'd rather deal with an angry Summer than a weepy Summer.

Devlin's phone went off again. He answered it and, after a few minutes, looked back at her and said, "They want her at camp to answer questions."

Easton nodded. Of course. It was to be expected she'd be interviewed. Somebody wanted a full report about how their soldier got shot. In fact a lot of reports would be filled out. He just didn't know who would get stuck doing those. He knew one thing; it wouldn't be him. He'd asked to drive her to the airport and had been refused. No way would he ask again. He'd demand it. He didn't plan to leave her side until she was safely in the air—whether he was her next driver or not.

CHAPTER 10

B ACK AT CAMP, in the opposite direction she wanted to go, Summer was ushered into a small office. Easton and Devlin accompanied her.

Two men stood behind the man seated at a desk. He motioned at a chair in front of her to sit down. She took the seat and waited, Easton and Devlin standing right behind her. Fatigue hit her like she'd never seen or felt before. And she knew shock was leaving its mark. If that soldier died …

Before the seated man could speak, she leaned forward and asked, "Is my driver going to make it?"

The leader nodded. "We hope so. He's been stabilized and is on his way to the closest hospital."

Relieved, she sat back but only a little. "There was a lot of blood," she said softly.

"Can you tell us what happened?"

No way to avoid it. She took a deep breath and quietly, calmly—maybe too calmly, considering what she'd been through—related the turn of events.

When she fell silent, no one said a word for a long moment, then the questions started. She answered as best as she could. No, she didn't see the shooter. No, she couldn't tell if there was one or more than one. No, she never saw any of the weapons. No, she didn't think anybody approached the jeep. Yes, she did hear some branches crackling but didn't have any idea what caused that.

As she went through the last of the questions, she felt nauseated. Finally she shook her head and said, "I don't know if I'm staying here or if you're finding me another plane, but I need to lie down."

She looked at Easton and reached out a hand. He reached back. God, she loved that about him. Using his strength, she slowly got to her feet, feeling the room sway.

He wrapped his arm around her. "Easy."

She gave him a wan smile. "I'm fine. I just need to lie down for a bit."

The three men behind the desk discussed something to do with the room assignments, but she didn't care. As far as she was concerned, she hadn't left. Her same bed was still here.

With Devlin on one side, Easton on the other, they turned and led her back out. After taking a series of turns she didn't recognize and hoped she wouldn't have to repeat on her own, she entered the tent that appeared to be the same as the one she'd left. She walked over to the bed she'd slept in and sat down. She let herself fall sideways, her head hitting the pillow. Just before she let sleep claim her, she mumbled, "Where are my bags?"

There was a *thunk* as they landed beside her. She opened her eyes to find Easton standing there. Of course he carried her bags the whole time.

She smiled. "Thank you."

Her eyes drifted closed, and sleep followed. She desperately needed a rejuvenating rest, but instead nameless men chased her. Instead of bright blue skies in happy dreams, she had nightmares with nothing but terror and fear following her. She heard a soft whimper once or twice, and then a strong hand stroked her shoulder and squeezed gently.

"You're fine. Just go to sleep. You're safe here."

She recognized Easton's voice. So very comforting, his words even working their magic on her insides. Finally she relaxed and fell into a peaceful, healing sleep.

When she woke, she found herself alone. She propped herself up on one arm, looking around the tent. She had no idea if anybody was even close by, but she couldn't imagine them leaving her. Not after all that had happened so far. "Hello?"

A head popped through the tent flap. Easton.

She smiled at him and lay back down again. "So you didn't leave me," she teased.

"I won't be leaving you at all."

She bit her lip to hold back a retort. Because of course he would leave her at some point. She had to return to California, and he was stationed here for however long. Even if he went to California with her, he still had a life, and so did she.

He sat down beside her, and she let her eyes drift closed again. "I'm fine, you know."

"You're looking better than you did."

Her eyes popped open. "Any update on the soldier?"

He nodded. "He's in critical condition in the hospital, but they think he'll pull through."

She smiled. "Now that's good to hear."

"He owes you his life."

She shook her head. "That's a terrible thought. He wouldn't have been shot if it wasn't for me. I'm just glad the odds are that he'll survive." When he didn't say anything, she opened her eyes again to find him staring at her as if she was from Mars. "What's the matter?" She self-consciously brushed her hair off her face. "I must look a mess." She saw her hand and froze. A grimace whispered across her face. Because, of course, her hands were covered in blood and so was her shirt. "I need a shower."

"That you can have. We're still waiting for the brass to give us a time frame for when you leave."

She smiled. "Well, it wasn't exactly my plan, but, if I have to, I'll stay another day." Not that she had a choice. Her phone rang just then. Her boss. Shit, she hadn't called him back.

"Are you okay?" he asked, concerned.

"I am. Thanks for calling in the rescue."

"What the hell happened?"

Silently groaning, she went through the events for him. "I don't know when I'm leaving now. I'm back in my same quarters, only now with a couple bodyguards."

"Do you think the shooter was after you?"

And she realized he didn't know about the other incidences. She didn't want to tell him either. "No, not likely," she murmured. "Let me know if you hear an update on anything, will you?"

"I will," he promised.

When she rang off, Easton studied her carefully. "Why didn't you tell him the rest?"

She shrugged and sat up. "He can't help us here, so why worry him?" She glanced from one man to the other. "We should look at the images I took and figure out what is worth killing for."

The men nodded. "We were waiting for you to wake up, then to suggest that exact same thing."

She smiled. "Grab your laptops then, and let's do this. I have a few thousand to look at. And that's after I deleted a bunch."

IF EASTON HAD understood ahead of time how many photos they had to go through, he'd have asked for half a dozen friends to join them. He knew security and trust were an issue for her, particularly after the attacks, but she might've been willing to allow a few more men into their group. As it was, he wasn't even sure what he was looking for.

"I wonder if I saw something when I followed you guys in the race. I felt like somebody was watching me then."

Easton looked at her. "That was when you were shot at the first time."

She shrugged. "I never saw anyone. I did take pictures as I turned around in that area, just in case. So those are in here somewhere too. Maybe we'll get lucky."

Swearing to himself, Easton went backward to a couple dozen scenic photos and took a long moment studying each one. He couldn't see anything or anyone hiding in the bushes though. Although his laptop was a decent one, it didn't have the best graphics program to see details like that.

After a couple hours, all the pictures were starting to blur. She'd taken some of the strangest combinations of photos ever, and then he'd seen some that made complete sense, as if there was a theme to them. He didn't know from one picture to the next what he would be looking at. He knew the others felt the same way. They were all being as diligent as they could be, but this wasn't their wheelhouse. Yet it made sense that these photographs were the one thing she had that somebody wanted to get. Or at least to stop her from seeing or using them.

But, so far, he hadn't seen anything important.

He viewed several more photos of people standing in the distance, talking. He studied them but didn't recognize the people. He perused another and then another. People were in the foreground, with people in the background. But he didn't really see anything odd.

Just as he went to look at the next photo, he stopped to consider the people in the background and then moved a couple images earlier to the ones he'd just looked at. He studied the photos intently.

Devlin leaned over. "Find something?"

He tapped the screen gently and said, "Isn't that the man we have in custody who attacked Summer and tried to grab her cameras?"

Devlin leaned in, then nodded. "It is, indeed. But who's he talking to?"

"And look at their hands."

The image wasn't clear enough to see, but their hands were close together, as if handing something off.

Very quickly the rest of the group gathered around. Suggestions were tossed back and forth, but nobody had any answers, and nobody recognized any of the other faces on the screen.

"What's the number on that picture?" Summer asked. "Let's see if I can find out more about them. I have better programs on my laptop. But my lab at home is much better for processing, and my desktop there has several really good programs."

He stood and read off the number for her and watched as she made a search.

An image popped up, and she said, "Come here and see if this helps."

The four men formed a half circle around her as she made several adjustments to the image, sharpening its features. They all stared for a long moment, then Easton said, "I just might know who that is."

"Who?" Corey asked.

"He was here a couple days ago. Remember when we had the visiting brass? It was fairly quiet, but we had several people arrive that day. Then they left again."

"And what would the visiting brass have to do with a guy working the galley?" Ryder asked. "That makes no sense."

"And was it US brass or Canadian brass?" Summer asked. All the men turned to look at her. She shrugged. "It's kind of important to know. We're on Canadian soil, but this is a joint effort."

The men nodded, but Easton answered, "He's American."

With the picture number written down on a notepad beside her, she went to the series of photos she'd taken at that time. "I remember using the men as a point of reference to make some camera adjustments. I know I have several of those images."

Easton waited.

She found five. And then another set. When she brought those up, everybody leaned forward to see them.

The men in the photos had their faces turned ever-so-slightly away. Then she clicked on the last one. And the man who attacked her was glaring at her.

"Summer," Devlin said, "can you send that image to my phone? I need to talk to some people." He stood, nodding. "For safety sake, send it to all our phones and make sure you have it in storage somewhere safe."

"Good point," Easton said.

"It's hardly incriminating," she protested. "The men are just talking."

Easton continued. "We need all the pictures from this time frame, from the one before you started clicking on them right through to the images you took after this." He faced her. "Did you ever see these men again later?"

She tilted her head to the side, studying the image. "No. The man who attacked me was from the kitchen. But the other men, I don't know."

"Do you have any other photos of the man in the kitchen?"

She shrugged. "Potentially. I took pictures inside the mess hall, but I don't know for sure. I'll have to look through the rest."

Easton gave her shoulder a gentle squeeze. "Would you mind searching for those right now? Mark down the picture number where you are right now as well as the corresponding numbers from where we all were looking at these images, so we don't duplicate our efforts. Then let's check to make sure we don't have another photo of this guy."

Devlin looked at Easton. "I suggest we both speak to our commander."

Easton nodded. He glanced over at Ryder and Corey. He hated to leave her even for a moment.

Pointing to Corey, Ryder said, "We're staying here."

"Go. I'm fine here," she said, waving her hand at Easton to go away. "Do what you've got to do." As they turned to exit the tent, she called out, "Maybe double check to see when I'm actually flying out. Somebody should know something by now."

"Will do," Easton said, stepping out. He glanced at Devlin. "Isn't that General Morgan on the left in that photo?"

"I think so. I can't make out this other guy's features.

And someone is hidden behind him too. But why would the general have been here? And why would he have such a suspicious-looking conversation?"

"Then again it could be completely innocent. For all we know the kitchen guy could be the son of his best friend's daughter or something." Easton shrugged.

He hated to think something dark and wrong was going on here, but the events leading up to this point *were* suspicious. And anything suspicious needed to be checked out.

They were given admittance to the commander's office right away, but they had to wait another ten minutes to get into his private office. Once inside, Easton lost no time in explaining what they'd seen. Devlin and Easton brought up the images on their phones and handed them over for their commander to see. He steepled his fingers under his chin and stared at them. But the absolute absence of emotion on his face was telling.

Easton studied him, wondering what kind of position they'd put him in. Not that it mattered, because somebody had attacked a civilian. On a military base. The person had links to someone very high up.

"Send me a copy of these photos, please. I presume you have copies safely stored that can't be retrieved?"

"Absolutely."

He sighed and leaned back. "I'll see what I can find out. Are you sure it's related to his attack on her?"

"Nobody's talking yet, I presume," Easton said, "yet this shows a connection we hadn't seen before."

Their commander nodded. "But it's extremely circumstantial. And, for something like this," he cautioned, "we must be very sure of our facts, and we'll need proof to back them up."

"That goes without saying," Easton said, picking up his phone. "The photographer has a half dozen, maybe even eight, photos of the two of them together," Easton said.

"Of course she does." The commander sighed. "I'll make some inquiries."

"She's also asking when she can leave and if any plans have been made for her to fly her out of here."

"Not yet. She'll stay overnight. Maybe we'll put her in a different tent for the night. That way she won't be alone."

Easton and Devlin exchanged glances.

"What is it I don't know?" the commander barked.

"We've been assigned to watch over her. We've moved into her tent to stand guard."

The commander glared at Easton. "Is your interest personal or professional?"

Easton could feel the heat climbing up his face. "Both," he admitted. "I have been watching over her for the last few nights. It bothers me that anybody would target a woman alone. And then today they escalated, as if they were out of time, so she was attacked publicly."

"Good. Stay with her until she gets on the goddamn plane. If anything goes wrong, I'll be looking to you for answers."

"We must find out who is after her, or she won't be safe when she gets home again," Easton reminded the commander.

"It's not that bad, is it? What were the four attacks again?" he asked with a frown as if just seeing the problem was as big as it was.

The two men ran through what they knew had happened so far.

"Why is it I haven't heard about this before?"

Devlin said, "You weren't available yesterday when I came to speak with you, so I spoke with Halverson."

"Halverson." The commander grabbed his phone. "In my office now," he snapped.

Halverson arrived quickly. Easton didn't know the man very well himself but hadn't heard much that he liked.

Halverson took one look at the two men and rolled his eyes. "You two again?"

Easton stared at him. "I haven't met or spoken with you yet," he said calmly.

"Sure, but it's about your latest ladylove."

"Well, she isn't my ladylove, but she is a woman alone and in need of our protection," Easton snapped, his temper getting the better of him. "Yes, it is about Summer."

The commander turned to Halverson. "Devlin was here yesterday with information about attacks on her. He told you about them. Is that correct?"

Halverson shrugged. "He did also say it was Easton's friend. We don't deal with friends here."

"Of course we deal with friends here," the commander said with exaggerated calm. "What we also deal with is any attack against *anyone*. We are visitors on Canadian soil. Any undue action on the part of any of our men is unacceptable at any time. Now tell me exactly what it is that Easton and Devlin told you."

"I spoke with Devlin," Halverson said, losing some of this cocky tone. He relayed the information that he had been given.

The commander turned to look at Devlin. "Is that correct?"

"Yes, that's correct. Then today she was attacked at the mess tent during lunch and afterward shot at in the vehicle on the way to the airport."

Halverson's face turned to one of shock. "What? She was the one in the vehicle when our man got shot? How is it I didn't know about that part?" he demanded.

"Because you didn't want to know about the rest of it, I presumed," Devlin said with a hard edge. "It wasn't my job to keep you informed of Easton's friend, was it?"

Halverson had the grace to look ashamed. "I didn't realize it was serious."

"You think putting a rattlesnake in a woman's tent in the dark isn't serious?" Easton asked. "Or how about some stranger standing inside her tent, threatening her, or how about the bullet that grazed her head today? These are all escalations. It should take nothing more to understand that this woman is under attack. And from somebody on the base."

Halverson outranked him and was about to open his mouth and remind him of that fact when the commander spoke again. "Halverson, I need to speak with you."

At the rebuke, Halverson's mouth shut, and he nodded.

The commander waved to the door. "Give us five."

The men were alone again with the commander when he faced Devlin. "Stay with her at all times." He looked to the door, then back to the men, adding, "Is she alone right now?"

"Ryder and Corey are both with her, going through more photos, looking to see if they've seen the man we have in custody at any other point in time."

On that note, the commander nodded. He pointed at the images on the cell phone still on his desk and said, "Don't tell anyone about this and don't share the images with anyone else. Let me know if you see any other photos of General Morgan."

CHAPTER 11

SUMMER LIFTED A hand and rubbed her sore eyes. "I don't normally do this all day long. Usually I go through this much over a month or so. I'm sure we are missing something doing it this way," she fretted.

"Hopefully not. Three of us are making it easier."

"Sure, but because we all have to see each photo, we do a lot of duplicate searching."

"But it's the only way for us to make sure we don't miss anything," Corey reminded her. "Besides Devlin and Easton will be back soon."

Now for the first time she stared at the tent opening, wishing the men would arrive sooner rather than later. "I know that. I guess I'm just nervous."

"Good reason," Corey said. "But stay focused on the images, and we'll get through this."

She shot him a grateful smile. "You guys really are nice."

"*Nice?*" exclaimed Corey. "*Nice* is an insult. You know that, right?"

She chuckled. "No, it's not."

"Oh, yes, it is," Ryder said. "Men don't like to be called *nice*."

"If they don't, then that's foolish. Because all girls want nice men."

"No, women want dangerous. They want alpha males.

They want capable, powerful, strong males."

"And nice," she added.

"Who are you calling nice?" came a voice from the tent entrance. Devlin stepped inside, a grin on his face.

"I was just telling Ryder and Corey how nice they are."

Devlin nodded. "Yep, definitely nice men. Laid-back, quiet, peacemaker kind of men."

That set off a tirade from the other two.

When she could, Summer said, "Where's Easton?"

Devlin smiled. "He'll be here in a minute."

She frowned at him. "You two were supposed to stay together. What happens if somebody attacks him?"

Devlin's eyebrows shot up. "You really think somebody might hurt one of us?"

"Or all of you." She nodded. "You're hanging around with me. I put you all in danger. You should know better."

There was silence in the room as the men stared at her oddly.

"What did I say?"

"We're fairly elite soldiers," Corey said. "I understand you don't know us, and you don't know our training, but we're the ones who look after other people, like you." He smiled at her, adding humbly, "But thank you for being concerned about our welfare."

She glared at him. "Are you mocking me?"

"Of course not," he said with feigned innocence, his hand going across his chest to cover his heart. "It's just a unique experience for us. Most of the time we're sent into dangerous situations to help others out. Not having others be worried about our health."

At that point Easton walked in, and she brightened. "How did it go? Am I getting out of here anytime soon?" She rose from the chair.

He shook his head.

With a heavy sigh, she sank back down. "Really? Do I have to stay?"

"Is it such a hardship?" Corey said. "After all, we're nice guys."

She shot him a look. "I don't have a problem spending time with you guys but hate to stay in a place where I'm being attacked. That's not exactly comforting." She glanced over at Devlin and Easton. "What about the driver? Any update on him?"

"He's gone into surgery. That's all we know, but they are still hopeful."

"Right." She returned to her laptop. "I'll focus on going through these images then."

"You can also focus on this." Easton stepped out from behind Devlin with a tray in his hands. The other men grinned. She looked down at the coffee and plate full of fruit and muffins and smiled. "You must think I'll pass out at any point in time."

"Once was enough for me, thank you," he said firmly. He placed the food in front of her. "Eat."

She shook her head. "Only if you guys get some too."

Easton nodded at the tray. "There's coffee for me, and Devlin has his own. I figured Ryder and Corey could get something if they want to now that we're back."

Ryder stood. "Be back in ten." And he and Corey walked out of the tent.

Devlin said, "I'll take a look outside."

Easton nodded. He never took his gaze off Summer.

She watched as Devlin exited. "What is he looking for?"

"He's making sure nobody approaches and checking that

nobody's been here while we were gone."

She hated to think about somebody stalking her or watching her in the tent.

"Did you find any more photos?"

"No, not yet." She looked at him and reached for her coffee. "I did check through the photos I took in the mess tent but found no sign of the man who attacked me."

"Good. Let's work steadily through these so we can make sure we've seen them all at least once. The commander wants to know if we find more. We're also under orders not to show the images to anybody."

She frowned at him. "My boss has access to the online cloud server."

Easton raised his head. "How long have you worked for him? What's his name and the company's name? Is there any reason he would want to hurt you or any reason these photos would be of interest to him?"

She stared at Easton in shock, her jaw slowly dropping. "Hell no." She shook her head. "You're way off base there."

"I'm just checking all avenues, all possibilities. We can't afford to leave any option without checking it out first."

She sat back. "I've worked for Ross as a freelancer for five years now. We've never had a problem. We have a great working relationship, and we do these kinds of images all the time. The photos of the men can be just one of more than seven thousand photos, and he won't even bother to look at most of them. He wouldn't have a clue what I've taken pictures of and probably wouldn't recognize any of the men involved."

Easton nodded. "Good. But we must make sure. So don't get upset about questions you might consider personal or intrusive. I'm not trying to upset you. I'm trying to keep you alive."

"Thanks for coming and getting me, by the way."

"You've said that already." He glanced at her and smiled. "You're welcome."

She grinned. "So, when I'm gone, who are you going to feed and look after instead?"

"No one. Everyone here is top of their game and can look after themselves."

She chuckled. "Nice to be the best of the best."

"It is," he said without a hint of modesty. "A lot of good men and women are here."

"I noticed a lot of women too. More than I expected." She glanced down at the images. "I might not have enough photos of those brave women though." Instantly her mind went off into a bunch of different directions. "Normally we have directives in terms of what kind of pictures they want for this type of work. But, in this case, they were just looking for a general span of activities and team-related events."

"Do you have any photos of the women?"

"I have some, just not as many as I'd like." She checked her watch. "Any idea what might be going on right now?"

He shook his head. "Hell no. You're not going anywhere in public. You're a target already, but to be a target where anybody can get access to you, that's not happening."

"But you already got one guy in custody."

"But we don't have the sniper. We have no idea who he is."

She stared at him, debating whether she could change his mind.

He shook his head again and said, "Don't even think about it. You're staying here under lock and key until you leave."

She jutted out her chin. "Am I ordered to my barracks for the duration of my visit?" she challenged.

He hesitated.

"Right. I'm not. Therefore, it's just you keeping me in my tent."

"It's safer here for you."

She shook her head. "No, it isn't. Two of the attacks happened here."

"You were alone the first time, not the second time, and you didn't even know about it until we told you."

"But now that I do know," she snapped, "it's hard for me to let it go."

"Would anybody know you're scared of snakes?"

"No, but, along with spiders, it's pretty easy to say that at least 80 percent of the women in the world are terrified of both."

He nodded. "Good point but it's not just relegated to women. A lot of men I know are pretty scared of rattle-snakes."

"Not spiders. There is just something about spiders that you guys get."

He grinned. "They are great for the environment. We need them. They are kind of cute."

She stared at him in disgust. "*Cute* is not a term I would ever use for a spider."

"They've got beautiful hairy legs, interesting eyes and fascinating articulated body parts."

"It doesn't matter how articulated or well-designed they are. I'm not spending any time studying spiders."

He grinned. "Then let's keep going through these images to get to the bottom of this." He focused on the monitor in front of him and flipped through the images.

She should be doing that too, but it had been hours already, and she was bored of it.

She reached across the table to the tray that held the muffins. She snagged one, ripped it in half and put one half on each of the two plates. Then she did the same with a different kind of muffin. She handed him one plate and grabbed the other, sitting back to enjoy it.

"Why did you put half on each plate?"

She shrugged. "What if only one of them was really good? Then I could've been the one with a really good muffin, and you could have gotten a really bad one."

He stared at her in astonishment. "So you split them in half so we'd share the good one? Or you split them in half so you're sure you didn't get the bad one?"

"You are teasing me again."

"You're fun to tease. Plus you have these interesting little personality quirks that make it easy."

She shrugged. "When I was younger, it was almost standard for kids to grab the big luscious-looking cookie and leave the reject one for the other person. So I made a point of being the opposite. Instead of grabbing the good one myself or grabbing the worst one, I split them in half so everybody got some of the good and some of the bad."

"You really are trying to operate in a world where life is fair, aren't you?"

"Life is what we make it. I may not be able to influence the big picture stuff, but I can control the little stuff. In my world, if there are two kinds of muffins, and I don't know what either are, chances are I'd like one better than the other, but then so would you. So, if we split them both, we each get some of the good one."

He chuckled, picked up his plate and took a bite off the

first half. She took a bite off the matching half. She stared at the muffin. "It's okay, but it's awfully sweet."

"It's perfect," Easton said, his mouth full of muffin.

She chuckled. "Let's taste the next one and see which one we like better."

They did just that. She preferred the one that he didn't like as much. They switched halves so each got the muffin they wanted.

She said, "To be honest, which muffin, if you could pick first, would you have chosen?"

He stared at the plate and said sheepishly, "I would have picked the one I didn't like."

She nodded. "See? Now you get one you like, and I get one I like."

He shook his head and polished off his muffin. "It doesn't really matter. It's food. I need it for energy, and this way my body gets fed."

"But every day we should be enjoying ourselves," she said. "And that includes having a muffin you like." She knew her attitude was probably a little too Pollyanna for most people, but it made her happy to think she was being fair and enjoying what she had. She didn't have to have the best, the biggest or the fanciest, but it would be nice if, at least, she had something she wanted. She picked up her coffee and took a sip just when Devlin came back in.

He stopped inside the doorway.

Easton jumped to his feet and headed to Devlin. She followed and stood nearby, watching the two of them. Easton turned, pointed back at the table and said, "Stay there."

"I'm not a dog. I don't stay, and I don't beg," she snapped.

He glared at her. "You're under orders. My orders. Go back to that desk and sit down."

She crossed her arms over her chest and raised an eyebrow.

He raised his hands in the air in surrender and said, "Please?"

She gave him a short nod and returned to her desk, stating, "It's not so hard to be nice. You should try it more often. Ryder and Corey have it down pat."

Devlin burst out laughing.

Easton shot her a look and then pivoted to exit the tent, dragging Devlin with him.

She glared at their backs as they disappeared, muttering under her breath, "They should both try it."

ONCE OUTSIDE, EASTON stopped a few feet away from the front entrance of the tent. He glanced at Devlin.

"I found definite tracks around the tent," Devlin said, "but the trip wire is intact. The battery on the video ran out. I've replaced it and did a quick run through but didn't see anything suspicious on the film," he said. "Which makes it suspicious because of the current circumstances."

"Exactly." Easton considered all they knew. "They took a chance going after her in the jeep. I'm just sorry I didn't fight harder to drive her."

"Maybe, after the attack at the mess tent didn't work, they chose a sniper again. Figuring they almost made that one happen before."

Easton stood, considering how many witnesses had seen her go after her attacker. And yet she had no bruises. That show of her skills might well have stopped the sniper from attacking her with his own hands and doing it long distance. Or … "It could be somebody we all saw on a regular basis."

"As we know, a lot of battle gear is here too," Devlin added.

Angry at the circumstances, wishing he could do something to get her back home again, Easton muttered, "I hate waiting."

"We all know that. It's the same for any of us. She's in danger, and nobody can tell where another attack will come from. Obviously we'll be staying here overnight."

"That's fine, but it still doesn't solve the problem that she could be in danger when she gets home again. It's not like anybody here can't find out who she is, where she works and where she lives. If we don't resolve this before she's gone, he'll go after her."

"We do have one attacker in custody. Is he talking yet?"

Easton gave him a sideways glance. "We know all too well how that goes."

As they stood there talking, Ryder walked toward them, covering a lot of ground at a fast pace, trying not to look like he was racing.

Easton asked, "What's wrong?"

"Her attacker, Harry Lemans, killed himself, while under guard. When the guards checked, he was choking on some paper he had shoved down his throat. He'd done such a damn good job of it that they couldn't get the paper out, and he died right in front of them."

"Oh, shit."

Easton stepped back into the tent, instinctively checking on her after that news. His mind reeled at this sudden turn of events. To his relief, she was still munching away and going through images.

"I can be left alone for a few minutes. It's really not that big a deal," she said calmly.

"Your attacker just committed suicide. The only reason for him to do that is he's afraid of what staying alive will entail. When you choose death over life, life must be pretty bad."

She stared at him in shock. "You think he's the one who shot the driver? No, that can't be. He was under guard then so he must be working with someone else."

"But I think the person he was involved with on the base probably did."

She nodded quietly. "Poor man. To take such a drastic step …"

She was a mix of contrasts. Maybe his impression was contrary to reality. She was obviously very capable. She gave back at least as good as she got from Lemans in the mess tent. At the same time, she got so caught up in her art that she forgot to eat. Capable versus incapable—needing to be looked after. Still this new development was not good. No hope of getting answers from Lemans now. Easton sat down in front of his laptop, closed all the images and brought up the search engine. He'd checked out Lemans earlier, but, since she was flying out, it hadn't had the same urgency. Now things were spiraling out of control with no end in sight. He wouldn't get any sleep tonight while watching over her. He was a SEAL, and, damn it, although a heck of a bodyguard, he was a hell of a lot more.

But how did one fight an unseen enemy? He was used to missions where he went after designated targets. Often dealing with terrorists. Tangible enemies to hunt and destroy.

This was different.

Quickly Easton had Lemans's age, his relationship status and his family history pulled up on the computer screen. Lemans's brother had a business in California. His parents owned a shop in the same area. They were immigrants and had been in the country since Harry was less than one year old, his older brother four at the time. Harry was an average student, not award-winning, didn't lend himself to any kind of specialty, never finished high school. Easton sent off an email to Mason. When his phone rang a moment later, he said to Summer, "I need to take this call."

She raised an eyebrow when she looked at him. "You think I'm stopping you?"

He glared at her. "I have to step outside."

She shrugged. "Go ahead. I won't escape."

Outside, he motioned to Devlin, holding up his phone. "It's Mason."

Devlin nodded in understanding and went inside the tent, leaving Easton standing in the open doorway so he could still keep watch.

"Hey, I don't need to be watched every minute," Summer explained when she caught sight of Devlin.

"What if I just want to sit down and spend time with you?" he teased.

"Hell no you don't. You just want to go home to your love interest."

Easton glanced at her in surprise.

"What love interest?" Devlin asked suspiciously.

"You're already attached emotionally and mentally, even if you don't wear a ring. So trips out of town like this one are hard when you just want to be with her."

At that Easton had to turn away. Her insights were fascinating and very close to home.

"What the hell's going on?" Mason snapped in his ear.

Easton quickly filled him in. "Now with his suicide this morning, we're digging into his life."

"Why?" Mason's voice was curious but understanding.

"I'm not sure he committed suicide." In a hard voice, Easton continued. "The fact is, he could have been murdered."

Silence followed. "Where is Summer now?"

"Close by, being watched over by Devlin." He groaned. "I won't be letting her out of my sight until this is over."

"I understand."

Already knowing Mason and his partner, Tesla's, history, Easton knew Mason did understand. "Mason, I need someone with the right software to take a closer look at some of these images."

"Tesla has good software here."

"I'm not supposed to share these images."

More silence came. "Send me the images. I'll talk to the commander." Mason hung up.

Easton grinned. That was one of the great things about his buddies. They always had his back.

He also thought it was interesting Mason never once asked about Summer. As soon as Easton had said she was in danger, Mason had been there. Easton didn't know much about her yet either, but he understood how important it was that Summer stay safe. "But just how important isn't something I want to look at," he said out loud.

A few men walked past, staring at him strangely.

He shrugged and grinned. "Welcome to my world." Then resolute, he straightened his back, turned and headed back inside. He shared the information with Devlin. "He asked me to send the photos, so he'll call the commander."

Easton pulled out his phone and called Ryder. "We need more details to confirm this was a suicide. We also need permission to send some of these photographs to Mason. He'll contact the commander directly, but we need to do so as well."

"Done." Ryder hung up the phone.

"You have to like Ryder and his no-nonsense attitude," Easton said.

Devlin nodded. "He does that all the time."

"He's nice too," Summer muttered.

Devlin snickered.

"You should learn from Ryder," Summer said. "He is much nicer than you two."

At that Devlin laughed out loud. "I'm nice enough," he said. "Easton might be a little hard around the edges, but his heart's in the right place."

She sighed. "I'll give him that."

"Thank you," Easton said in an exaggerated manner and went back to his laptop. There had to be something he could find out. And fast. He'd yet to let an asshole get the better of him.

Devlin's phone rang a few minutes later. "Thank you, sir. Okay, I'll tell her." When he hung up, he said to Easton, "Mission approved to share photos with Mason. Summer's flight is leaving in two hours."

She brightened. "Awesome. As much as I love Canada, I can't wait to get home."

Easton held back the fact that she was likely safer here, but, at the same time, he didn't want her to panic. How could he give her a warning that was both cautionary and not reactive? Instead Devlin took the words from his mouth.

"I know you want to go home," Devlin said, "and I

know how that feels, but you need to be cautious when you get there."

She looked at him and raised an eyebrow. "Why?"

"Because one man committed suicide over this, and he wasn't working alone."

Easton added, "So, if you are going home, no way in hell are you are going alone."

She glared at Easton. "I live alone. I prefer it that way. The danger is here. When I get home, things will calm down."

"Do you really think so?" he asked quietly.

She slumped in place. "No."

CHAPTER 12

SUMMER STARED AT Easton without making it obvious she was watching him. But she couldn't stop. He was one of those born to be a guardian. She hadn't met too many of them. Sure, the military was full of alpha males, but he seemed to take it one step further, doing a little bit more every time.

She never watched her blood sugar, or when she'd eaten, but he did. For the first time since she'd been attacked, she had guards around her but with him at her side. And, when he couldn't stay next to her, he made sure somebody else was there with her. She didn't quite understand what drove him. Was it just his protective nature? Or the fact that she was a small defenseless female? As if … Would he do the same for anybody? Any other woman? She hoped not.

She wanted to think he was fond of her. Although he certainly didn't show it. Well, other than those two kisses, which he never acknowledged afterward. At the same time, she knew she had to leave, yet she didn't want to. At least she didn't want to leave him. Even now her heart ached for her driver who'd been an innocent victim in all this. She hadn't wanted anyone to get hurt. She hadn't thought something could happen here at a military base. *Was Easton correct? Would this follow her home?* That was the last thing she wanted.

"What are you staring at?"

"Your face," she said. "I still want to take some photos."

"No way in hell."

"I'll keep working on you," she promised.

He lifted his head and glared at her. "It won't make any difference."

She propped her chin on her hands, continuing to stare at him. She just loved that square chin, the high cheekbones, the deep-set eyes—such a beautiful blue. They were like lasers. She gave him a happy smile. "You should be a cover model." The look of shock on his face made her laugh out loud. "Okay, so not like a *GQ* model but an alpha-male-hero-of-the-world type of thing." She straightened. "Hey, that's not a bad idea. We need more heroes."

He snorted. "You got the wrong guy. You need Levi's company for that."

She stared at him in confusion. "Levi's company?"

"Never mind. Friends of mine, that's all."

"I'd be interested in meeting them." She didn't quite understand the twitch of his lips. She pressed further. "Are they working with you?"

He shook his head. "They all used to be military but now work for a private security company."

"How interesting. I could do a fabulous photo shoot with them," she said.

He shook his head.

She stared at him. "Does that mean they won't do photos either?" She smiled. "Maybe they could use the promotion."

He gave a harsh bark of laughter. "They don't need the advertising. They are overworked now."

"How come you don't have a partner?" The words just

flew from her mouth.

He raised his gaze to her again and said in a noncommittal tone, "What makes you think I don't have one?"

She grinned. "You are taking way too good care of me. If you had a partner of your own, you'd always be thinking that she'd be upset with you."

He glared at her. "I would not."

"You would."

"I would not because I wouldn't have a partner unless she trusted me."

She settled back and stared at him. "I'm really glad to hear that. Now that we know trust is important to you in a relationship, what else is important for you?"

He shook his head. "I'm not having this conversation."

"Why not?"

"Because I'm working."

"Fine then." Summer turned back to her screen, getting into her images, tossing the ugly and moving the good ones from folder to folder. "Still this is a conversation we should have."

"Why? We don't have a relationship."

"No, but I'd be open to one."

Silence filled her tent.

Inside she winced. That was so not her usual tactic. She was a lot subtler when she liked a guy. On the other hand, she didn't think that would work with Easton. She raised her gaze to find him staring at her, a look in his eyes that she couldn't even begin to understand. "Are you telling me that you're not interested?"

He opened his mouth and then closed it.

She grinned impudently. "See? You can't even say that. You don't like admitting it."

He sat back and crossed his arms over his chest.

She chuckled. "You don't like private relationship conversations either."

"This isn't the right time."

"Absolutely." She nodded. "It's a little hard to talk about relationships on base." She leaned forward. "Can you come with me?"

He shook his head.

"Ah, so you don't want to spend any more time with me?"

He frowned. "That's not what I said," he protested.

"Are you just saying that not to hurt my feelings?"

He shook his head.

She hurt inside. It was her own fault. She had no business bringing this up. She barely knew him. She should let him off the hook but didn't want to. She wanted to know if he was interested or if he was just pretending not to be. "I need to go home and forget about him."

"What does going home and forgetting about me do?" he asked.

She winced. "I didn't mean for you to hear that."

"Too late."

She glared at him. "Then forget you did."

Humor glinted in his gaze as he leaned forward. "This is a much better turn of events."

She glared at him. "Is not."

"Is so."

The two glared at each other until chuckles from the doorway had them both staring in the direction where Devlin stood, his arms over his chest, now openly laughing at them.

"What is your problem?" she demanded.

"No problem at all," Devlin said cheerfully. "But it's really nice to see this happening to someone else for a change."

"That makes zero sense." Easton glowered at his friend.

"Maybe it does, and maybe it doesn't," she said with a smile. At the same time, it was nice to see Easton was shaken up a little bit.

"You're good for him," Devlin said encouragingly.

"Except he doesn't like me," she said softly.

"I didn't say that," Easton snapped.

"But it feels like that," she snapped back, turning to glare at him. "You just want me back in California."

"I didn't say that either," he said, a haunted look in his eyes. "I just need you to be safe."

UGH. EASTON GLARED at her, feeling like a coward.

Of course he wanted to see her when he got back to California. But things were moving a little too fast. He wasn't sure he was ready. Hell, he knew he wasn't ready. He didn't want to get into the same scenario he'd been in before. Summer had no idea what it was like to be in a relationship with a military person. He got called out in the middle of the night, and sometimes it was days or weeks before he got home again. She wasn't ready for that.

Bristol was a whole different case with Devlin. She was so embroiled in her work all the time that Devlin had to drag her back to reality. The two of them were doing fabulously. But Easton didn't think it would be the same with Summer because she needed a keeper to make her eat before she passed out and to track and haul her equipment when she was on the job. Except she also got caught up with her work, and he would be pulling her back to reality, very much like Bristol and Devlin.

He frowned, not sure he liked that comparison. He was similar to Devlin in certain ways, but that voice inside said he was also very different.

Devlin chuckled. "Interesting times."

He glared at his friend. "Mind your own business."

"But it is my business," Summer said with a big grin.

"Glad you find this funny," Easton said. Then he growled, "Can't say it's all that funny from my side."

Her face switched from humor to regret. She leaned across, taking his hand with both of hers. "I'm sorry. I didn't mean to put you on the spot. I wouldn't ever want to hurt or embarrass you."

He stared at her, surprised to see her beautiful eyes shine like mercury. She was so generous in her honesty. She hadn't meant to embarrass him; she'd been teasing him, but he had taken it the wrong way because he felt cornered. He really did want to see her again; he had to let her know that. He shook his head, not sure what to say. "This isn't the time for such a discussion."

"I'm leaving in less than two hours. It's not like there's any other time for that kind of discussion."

He sighed.

Devlin laughed. "Keep pushing him. He had a bad experience. You have to help him get past that," he said encouragingly.

Easton glared at Devlin, promising retribution.

Devlin shook his head. "Easton, it's time something like this happened. It's so very rare that you have to make the most of it when it does happen."

"Not sure anything exactly is happening," he snapped.

"Oh, it is. You just can't see what we see."

Summer turned to him. "What is it you see?"

Devlin gave her a gentle smile. "He'll have to tell you that himself. But what we see is all good things in his future."

"My future too?" she asked with a hopeful smile.

He chuckled. "All good things for both of you."

Just then Ryder walked back in. Knowing he was off the hook, Easton settled back, but he couldn't stop studying Summer beside him. He'd never met anyone so giving and open. She watched Ryder while Easton was busy watching her. She was just so damn different from anything he'd ever experienced; he wasn't sure what to do with her.

"Easton?" Ryder called for his attention.

Easton glared at him. "What?"

"Oh, nothing. I was just talking to you for the last minute."

Easton sighed. He could feel the heat rising in his neck. "Now that you've all had a joke at my expense, please get back to the business at hand," he growled.

"She's leaving for the airport in just over an hour. Three vehicles will travel as a convoy by the commander's orders. He's checking into the death of her attacker. On the surface, it appears to be a suicide. There were two guards. Possibly a third."

"Why would there be three men?" Easton asked. "That's overkill."

"There appears to be some confusion as to how many were actually there as they shifted in and out."

"So was there an opportunity for somebody to have killed him?"

"Or did one of the guards kill him?" Summer asked.

"That makes the most sense."

The men turned to look at her. "Why would that make more sense?" Devlin asked.

"There was no time. So it depends on whether he was in full view of everyone, or if they were standing outside. Because, if one slipped in, then killed him, he could have slipped back outside. Nobody would know the difference. Or," she said, warming to her topic, "even better, two of them were involved. One to stand guard outside while the other does the job. Make it look like a suicide. They both could alibi each other."

Devlin nodded. "You're right. That would be the easiest and simplest method, but it's rare that it works out that way."

Easton stared at her. "You have a scary mind sometimes."

"I see things a lot of people don't see," she said quietly. "It would be very interesting to question the guards, watch the reaction on their faces. People lie all the time, but, when I have a picture of it, I can always tell."

"Do you have to have pictures?" Easton asked.

She shook her head. "No, I can read faces very well. I just prefer to see it through the camera lens."

The men looked at each other, and Devlin asked Easton, "What are the chances she could speak to the guards?"

She stood up. "If it's possible, let's do it now."

"We have to get clearance first," Easton told her.

"So let's get clearance." She raced to the door. "Since I have to leave soon, the quicker, the better."

It was all Easton could do to run behind her. "Do you even know where you're going?"

She tossed a glance his way and laughed. "No, but I can

count on you to correct me when I go off course."

He swore under his breath and raced to catch up.

The men laughed out loud behind him. "It's wonderful to see," Ryder called out. "She's a keeper, Easton."

Devlin chuckled. "Isn't that the truth."

Easton knew exactly what they meant. No way would he engage in a discussion on *keepers*. If they thought she was perfect for him or she was good for him, they were so wrong. The last thing he needed was to spend his life looking after somebody.

Not happening. His wife couldn't be like that, always wanting him to be her big protector. Protecting came naturally, that was true, but he wanted a partner to stand by his side. He didn't want to have to turn around and wonder if she could stand on her own two feet because he had to be out of the country for a few days.

He glared at the fleeting figure in front of him. She had picked up speed. "Wait up," he roared, power surging through his legs as he chased after her.

Her laughter sounded like that of a young child. It rippled toward him. He shook his head at her complete spontaneity and joy of living. Where was the bitterness, the subterfuge, the weariness or even the manipulation? He wasn't used to this spirit who just raced through life, one minute completely engaged in her art, and the next minute beating the crap out of a man twice her size. And he still hadn't reconciled that. He admitted quietly to himself how winning that fight meant she could handle herself. But …

He came around a tent to see she'd hit the brakes and stood in front of four men, one of them being his commander. He winced and pulled up right behind her, grabbed her hand and pulled her gently backward. "Sorry, sir."

The commander looked at him, at her and then back at him with a glimmer of a smile in the depths of his eyes. "From what I see, you can't do a whole lot to stop it."

"You are so correct there," he said with feeling.

She turned and looked at him, a beautiful sunny smile on her face. "See? I found him." She pivoted back to the commander. "Would it be possible to speak to the men who were guarding my assailant?"

The commander frowned. "That is not a good idea."

"But it is. You see, one of the things in my line of work is the study of people's faces. I understand a lot about how facial expressions change with questions and answers when they are covering up something," she carried on earnestly. "I don't need the camera in front of me, but I do need to see their faces when I ask them a couple questions."

The commander shook his head. "That would not be protocol."

She stuck out her chin ever-so-slightly and narrowed her gaze. "Was attacking a photographer protocol?"

"But the guards didn't attack you," the commander said gently.

She brightened. "Oh, did you catch the sniper then?"

Easton sucked his breath back and squeezed her hand in warning.

The commander studied her quietly for a long moment and then allowed her a small smile. "No, we have not yet caught the sniper. If there was a sniper."

"*If?*" She gasped. "You think I shot the driver?" Her shock was so real she almost wavered in place.

Easton gripped her shoulders as if to silently give her support.

"How could you say that?" she cried out.

The commander shook his head. "That's not what I meant. What I'm saying is, we're not sure the man who committed suicide wasn't the sniper."

"He couldn't have been the sniper unless he was freed after attacking me." She narrowed her gaze. "Did you let him go? Even after what he did?"

"He wasn't let go. But he was left alone for some time. And, of course, we can't prove he was the sniper. So most likely there is a second man," the commander conceded.

She crossed her arms over her chest. "Considering I'm the one who was shot at on two different occasions plus physically attacked, I would very much like to speak with the three men guarding the suspect."

The commander opened his mouth.

Summer rolled right over his next objection. "I do believe I have that right."

He shook his head.

She ignored him. "I'm the one who has to live with the nightmares. I'm the one who needs to know if he said anything, did anything or in any way gave any indication as to why he did what he did."

"I can assure you that we will get to the bottom of this."

"But *you* cannot take away my nightmares. I need to see his body, and I would like to speak with the three men who were standing guard when my attacker died."

The commander opened his mouth and then closed it, his gaze going to Easton.

Easton shrugged as if to say, *What can I do?* He glanced at the other men standing here, all with matching looks on their faces.

"Seeing the body is out of the question."

"In that case, I'll accept that if I can speak with the three guards instead."

She had said it so smoothly that it was hard to believe it was on purpose. But, from that firm square jaw of hers, Easton had no doubt that somehow she had just outmaneuvered their commander into giving her the one concession she wanted, because the other one was too off the wall for him to allow.

The commander glared at her. And then turned to Easton.

Easton smiled. "Yes, welcome to my world, sir."

The commander gave him a half eye roll and said, his gaze returning to Summer, "You can have five minutes with them. Easton stays with you."

"Actually I'd like Devlin to be inside as well, and the other two can stay close by."

"Are you afraid of my men?" the commander countered. "They were standing guard over the prisoner."

She gave a shuttered look. "Yes, they were." And she dropped it.

She turned and walked to the right. Instinctively Easton tapped her shoulder, motioning to the left. She gave him a sunny smile, nodded to the men and turned, walking away in the other direction.

Corey stepped up to walk beside her.

Easton turned to look at the commander and said, "Thank you, sir."

"You watch her. She's dangerous."

But, from his commander's tone, Easton could tell it wasn't that the commander thought Summer was dangerous in terms of Easton's life, but that, as a female, she was very good at getting her own way.

"I understand, sir."

The commander laughed. "Oh, I don't think you do. Not yet anyway. Devlin, keep an eye on them both."

Devlin chuckled, patted Easton on his back and said, "We better get there before she starts questioning the men, and we don't have a chance to even hear the answers."

"Shit."

The two of them ran, catching up with Summer, Corey and Ryder with her as they reached the guards. Devlin quickly explained why they were here.

The two guards on duty looked at her in surprise. "I'm sorry you were attacked," said the first man, who identified himself as Paul.

"Thanks, Paul. How long were you looking after him?"

Paul shook his head. "A couple hours, that's all." He glanced down at his watch. "Since he attacked you, it's been—what? Five hours?"

"And in all the time he was with you, did you ever leave him alone? Did he ever have a chance to be unsupervised?" she quickly rephrased.

Paul shook his head. "No, of course not."

She smiled at him. "Thank you for making sure he couldn't come after me."

The man visibly relaxed. "No problem."

"Could you show me where he was kept?"

There was surprise in Paul's eyes, but he was willing to open the tent. "Sure. He stayed in here."

She walked in and saw a simple barracks setup. "So he wasn't in a jail or anything?"

"No, he was just confined to these quarters."

She nodded. "Did he die in here?"

Paul nodded. "Yes, this is where we found him."

She turned to look at him. "So how long was he alone?"

"He wasn't alone at all. We were here the whole time."

Easton got into the conversation. "You said this is where you *found* him. Meaning that you weren't here at the time he tried to kill himself."

Paul turned to his partner as if looking for help. "Sometimes we stepped outside for a bit of fresh air," he said quietly. "We weren't allowed to converse in front of the prisoner."

She nodded as if to say she understood. "Did he have any visitors?"

Paul shook his head, but his cooperation was wearing thin. "No, it was just the two of us the whole time."

She switched her gaze over to the second man who was smaller, wiry, with a swarthy complexion. But Easton didn't like the look in his eyes. Obviously she didn't either.

She nodded to him. "Were you ever alone with my assailant?"

He shook his head. "Neither of us were ever alone with him."

The man spoke smoothly enough, but there was just that odd tone. Easton was suspicious. He knew she would say that he was the guilty one. But he had to have more than just a suspicion.

"Did either of you search the man's pockets?" Summer asked.

Paul raised his eyebrows and said, "No, of course not. That would be unethical."

The other man stayed quiet. Easton had been watching his face and saw the look that whispered across it with her question. Easton wouldn't have thought to ask these men these questions. It was interesting to see their responses. And he realized just how correct she was. If she'd had a camera to capture these images, it would be so easy later to pinpoint what kind of reaction they had. Right now, he was going on gut instinct, and he knew both guards were lying.

It was also interesting to see her technique. A natural one at that. He'd done weeks to months of intensive interrogation training, but he didn't have the same simplistic trickery skills she did.

"Please tell me what you did when you found him," Summer asked Paul.

Paul shrugged. "I ran over to him and tried to help him. I thought he was choking, so I did the approved first-aid procedure for a choking victim, and then I realized, from checking his mouth, paper had been stuffed down his throat. I tried to pull it free, but it was way too deep. I couldn't get a good grasp of it."

"Oh, dear. That must have been terrible. He died right in front of you then."

Paul nodded, a shadow crossing his eyes for a fleeting moment. The second man remained silent.

"Hello. What's your name?"

The second man narrowed his gaze but answered readily enough. "Nick." Then as if having said all he was going to he shifted his position to cross his arms over his chest to support his tough-guy image.

She smiled at him. "What did you do to help?"

He raised his eyes to her. "I was trying to help Paul here."

She nodded but didn't say anything. "How well did you know Harry Lemans?"

Both shook their heads. Nick answered, "We didn't know him at all."

Paul looked from her to the four men who had arrived

with her and asked, "Are we under any kind of suspicion here?"

Devlin answered, "Is there any reason you should be concerned?"

The man shifted back slightly. "You need to call my commander."

"Who is your commander?"

He named a person Easton didn't know. He filed the name away for later. This guard was from the American military; Nick with the attitude was Canadian. Then that made sense as the prisoner had been American as well.

Summer turned to Paul. "When you searched his pockets, you didn't happen to see my necklace, did you?

It was all Easton could do to hide his own stare of surprise. What necklace?

Paul didn't manage to hide his. He started to say he hadn't searched the pockets when she ran right over him and said, "I lost it when he attacked me. I was pretty sure he grabbed it from my neck, possibly accidentally," she conceded, "and I just wanted to see if I could get it back."

But Paul was edgier and on to her. "I said I didn't search his pockets."

She turned back to Nick. "Did you see my necklace?"

He shook his head. "No, I never saw him with it, and I never saw the contents of his pockets either. Maybe check with the commander."

"I'll do that, thanks."

She turned to face Easton and Devlin and said, "We can go now."

Easton stared at her in surprise. "If you're ready? I know you really wanted to see his body."

"I didn't want to see his body," she said quietly. "All I

really wanted to know was if my necklace was in his pocket."

"I'm sure somebody would've already searched his pockets," Devlin said.

She smiled. "Maybe. But I'd also like to hear Paul's explanation as to why my beads are tucked into his pant legs."

All eyes turned to Paul's boots. And sure enough a couple small beads were in the creases of his pant legs, tucked into his boots.

"My necklace was beaded," she said. "So I already know you're a liar," she snapped at Paul. "The real question is, why you killed my assailant. Not that I'm upset he is dead, you understand. But I'm upset because we didn't get any answers from him."

Easton stared at Paul and saw the guilt on the man's face. What the hell?

"It wasn't me," Paul protested. Then pinched his lips together to stop more words from flying out.

"If it wasn't you, then there is another man involved…" Easton narrowed his gaze. "Which of you was the heavy breather in her tent – and which one of you assholes pissed off a snake?"

Paul stayed quiet, but Easton saw the almost imperceptible shake of his head before he could stop it. "Not you? Then we need to find the last asshole – and fast."

CHAPTER 13

NOW THAT IT was time to go, she didn't want to leave.

Chaos had ensued after she'd exposed the beads from her necklace caught in the rolls of Paul's pant legs. Ryder had grabbed him; the commander had been called in, and Nick had been nabbed at the same time. They were on the lookout for the last man involved – if there was still one. The trouble was, after all that, when she was so close to getting answers, she'd been ushered out to a jeep.

Now she sat in the passenger seat, hating the memories flying at her from the last time she'd been in a jeep. A man had been badly injured while driving her. Now two other men had been detained and were to be questioned. And that still didn't mean their actions made them the sniper.

But now she would be driven to the airport to board a plane. Since she hated to say good-bye, she wanted to stay and see this thing through. Easton stood beside her. "I don't want to leave now," she said in a mutinous tone of voice. "But yet I do."

"How did you know? How did you even think to look for the beads in his clothing?"

"Because beads were on the floor where he'd been standing and where the assailant had been kept in that tent. Which meant he had my necklace."

"But it could've been accidental that the beads caught in

his clothing."

She shot him a look. "Accidental when? When he was eating? Sleeping? Training? Or when he went to empty Harry's pocket in a hurry, and the beads went flying?" She settled back in her seat. "It was a matter of getting the right poke to make him show himself."

Easton nodded. "You're good at that."

She sank back into her seat. "Okay, so maybe I'm not a nice person all the time. But I try to come from the heart." She closed her eyes and sighed. "I still want to leave now, but I need answers to so many questions."

"You'll get as many as we can get," Easton said. "Just because you're leaving doesn't mean we'll cut you out of the loop."

She shot him a look and then turned and closed her eyes again. "Of course it does. It will be handled internally, and that'll be the end of it."

"I will follow up with you."

She turned to him. "Promise?" His fathomless gaze held a warm glint that set her heart pounding.

"Absolutely."

She snorted. "You're just saying that."

"Hey, I always follow through on my promises."

"I hope so. And you can spend a few days with me when you're back in town."

He went silent.

"You do that a lot."

"I do what?"

"Go very quiet when you're not sure what to say."

"Well, I haven't been propositioned by a woman very many times in my life," he admitted.

She snickered. "But how else are we to carry on a relationship if we don't get to see each other? So, when you get some days off, you can visit and spend some time with me."

He stared at her. "Maybe you should be the one coming to spend time with me," he snapped.

"Accepted."

He turned and glared at her. "Did you do that on purpose?"

She shrugged. "Sometimes I have to do a little bit more poking than I would normally do to get what I want." She smiled. "It's who I am. I go after what I want."

He stared at her.

Her smiled widened. "Yes, I want you."

A red color washed all over his face.

She watched in fascination, her hand diving in her pocket to pull out a small camera. Before he had a chance to argue, she took several photographs. He grabbed her hand, but she snatched away the camera so he ended up just holding hers.

"Perfect." She took a picture of his hands. "I promise I won't sell it or do anything with these images. They're for my own personal collection.

"A picture of my hands?"

She gave him a smile. "I'll send this one to you if it turns out good. Then you'll see what I mean."

He shook his head. "You are something."

"I am, indeed."

When he released her hand, she turned the camera around backward so she could see the pictures she had just taken. One with his face was decent, not perfect, but it was okay. She got rid of the other one. And then she looked at the one with him holding her hand. She stared at it for a long moment, and then she smiled.

Quietly she said, "When you look at that, what do you see?"

He frowned at her, picked up the camera and looked at it. "I see my hand holding your hand," he said briskly. "Nothing special."

He went to delete it, but she snatched the camera out of his hand. "No! You can't do that. This picture is special."

He stared at her in surprise. "It's nothing."

"It's so much more than nothing. It's perfect." She was so happy with the image that she just stared at it, seeing the same strength and caring she'd seen that first day.

Just then the driver came back out. She realized it was Devlin. "Oh, no. You can't drive," she exclaimed.

Puzzled, Devlin turned to look at her. "Why is that?"

"What if you get shot?"

Devlin smiled. "Would you rather Easton drove?"

She frowned. "That's not fair."

He grinned. "Sure, it is. It'll be the four of us. So who is it you want to risk his life?" He got out and said, "Easton, you drive."

Before Easton had a chance to get behind the wheel, she scrambled to the driver's seat, sat down and turned on the engine. "There. Now if anybody shoots at the driver I will be the one who gets shot."

The men stared at her, turned to look at each other, and Easton frowned. "I'm driving."

She shook her head. "Can't have that. You might get hurt."

He pulled his hands into fists and put them on his hips. "So, what if, this time, they don't get the range right and shoot the passenger instead of the driver?"

She bounced up so she stood on the open jeep front step

and stared at him. "Then you might get shot."

He raised his hands. "Exactly."

She shook her head, bounced back down onto the seat. "Then I'll take myself." At that she hit the gas, driving away as fast as she could from the men, leaving them standing in the dust.

She drove straight out of the camp, remembering the way from the last time. She could see the men shouting at her from behind. But she was too busy laughing at herself. No way would she let anyone else get hurt. As soon as she was on the main road heading toward the airstrip, she checked the jeep for any music, but, of course, there wasn't any.

It wasn't a long drive. She settled back, loving the feel of the fresh air and the sunshine. It was late in the day, and the sun was setting. There was something magical about it.

There was also something very freeing about having left the four men in the dust. They probably wouldn't appreciate it, but she thought it was pretty damn funny. She'd pay for that one in time, she knew. No way Easton wouldn't get back at her for this. But she really couldn't stand to let the men get hurt.

The dry roads kicked up a cloud of dust behind her. Nothing to worry about though because at least it would stop anybody from following her too closely. She stared at the trees, watching the tree line as it approached. Close to here was where she'd been shot at the last time.

She couldn't see anything suspicious, but subconsciously she hit the gas and drove faster. She stared at the road ahead, then glanced at the trees one last time and caught a glint of something shiny.

Hearing something hit the vehicle, instinctively she

ducked down. She was barely above the steering wheel, so she could see just over the hood of the jeep through the windshield. She flattened the gas pedal and drove as fast as she could. She had no idea how much farther it was, but she couldn't get there fast enough.

Without any more shots fired, she figured the sniper had missed his opportunity. She thought she heard something else in the background, like backfiring from a vehicle, but it wasn't hers. Just as the new thought threw ice through her veins, she realized he was probably giving chase. But she couldn't push the gas pedal any harder. The engine was going flat-out.

The airstrip was up ahead. She pulled in amid a cloud of dust, raced past the couple men standing around, waiting at the plane, and tried to dart inside the aircraft. She was shaking so hard. One of the men inside stopped her. With her teeth chattering, she said, "Sniper."

The men pulled their weapons and nudged her inside.

"Be careful," she cried out peering around the corner. "He shot my driver last time."

The men nodded. "Any idea where?"

"Five minutes down the road where I was shot at the first time." She could barely keep her mind still. She walked deeper into the plane barely noting the seats as she paced.

She pivoted. And came up against a hard chest. She was grabbed and lifted.

Instinctively she opened her mouth to scream.

Only to find a hot passionate mouth sealing the scream inside. Easton. Somehow. But she wouldn't argue with the fates. She threw her arms around him and kissed him back.

When he finally withdrew, she whimpered and tried to remember … "Another sniper. Another sniper shot at me," she babbled.

"We heard. Are you hurt?"

She shook her head. "He hit the jeep." She turned to Devlin. "Will they get mad at me for the bullet wound in the jeep?"

Devlin never cracked a smile. "No, they won't be upset at a bullet wound in the jeep." Then he gave her a gentle smile. "They are practically used to it."

She turned back to Easton, her hands on the side of his face and shook his head. "I thought you were looking after me."

He stared at her. "I would have if you hadn't raced off, trying to protect me."

She gave him a smug smile. "But it worked. You realize, if you'd been driving, you would've been hit," she exclaimed. "How absolutely horrible." She wrapped her arms tight around his neck again and held him close.

EASTON CLUTCHED HER to him. "I could smack you for racing off like that," he murmured against her hair.

In response, her arms just closed tighter around his neck. He shot a gaze at Devlin who had retreated to speak with a man standing by the plane.

"Thank God you're safe," she whispered.

He shook his head. "You got that backward. Thank God you're safe."

He had to admit she might've been right. If he'd been driving, it was quite possible he'd have been shot. He picked her up in his arms and turned and sat down in the airplane seat with her tucked in his lap. He held her close against him. He was shaking inside, and she was shaking all over.

"It's okay. You're safe now."

She shook her head, her face buried against his neck. He smiled and tucked her closer.

After a few minutes, Devlin sat down beside him. "Summer, can you tell us what happened?"

She raised her head, leaned over and poked him in the chest. "I just saved you. That's what happened."

Devlin gave her a look of astonishment. "What?"

"If you had been driving, you could be dead right now." She gave him a nod. "So, with me driving and being much smaller than you guys, I saved your life." She turned on Easton and poked his chest. "Yours too."

The two men looked at each other and then at her. Easton said, "It's possible we might've been shot at, but that's no guarantee we would have been injured."

"I suppose you're just so good you can dodge a bullet too, right?" She rolled her eyes and curled up against Easton. "Give it up, Easton. You owe me one."

He chuckled. "Okay, fine. I owe you one. At least maybe that's the easiest answer here."

She snorted. "You can't just hand over wins like that. You have to fight for what you want." She nestled in deeper. "And right now I don't want to move. I'm so tired."

Easton stared at Devlin.

Devlin said to him, "Bet you don't even know what hit you."

"No, I don't," she whispered, mistakenly answering the question directed at Easton.

Easton glanced down, and, in just seconds, her breathing had deepened, going from bright and lively to exhausted and asleep like a two-year-old. "I've never seen anything like her." He waited for her to say something, but she was out already.

"And maybe that's not a bad thing. Everything else you've seen out there wasn't right for you. Maybe this is."

"This is chaos," Easton protested. "I like peace and quiet and calm and serenity."

"This is excitement and passion," Devlin corrected. "This is life. This package comes with so much exuberance. Even the way she talks trips you up. She makes you stop and think. Her whole view on life is completely upside down."

"You mean completely backward," Easton corrected. But he was smiling. And he was smiling inside because of all the things Devlin had said. That spark, that passion inside her was something that really intrigued Easton. Most people were polite and calm; they laughed at jokes but didn't get exuberant, over the top, like she did. He didn't know if it would be wearing over the long-term. But it wasn't fake. It was just a huge part of who she was. He didn't think it could wear off.

He lived a quiet life. The guys had been talking to him, telling him to get out, get a girlfriend and live it up a little bit. But he wasn't sure that living it up would be a good thing.

"When you find her, you really find her," Devlin said with a smile.

"Hell, I didn't find anything. She pretty well just passed out right in front of me." Then remembered their first meeting where her camera had smacked him across his face.

"She's such a mix," Devlin said. "Fascinating woman."

"She is. I just don't know what I've got here."

Devlin looked down at the armload sitting in his friend's lap beside him and said, "What you've got is an armful. A very special package."

Beside them Corey stepped up and said, "You better

look after her."

Ryder chuckled. "Isn't that the truth? And if you're not keeping her, we wouldn't mind a shot."

"Don't even use that word around me," Easton warned.

Corey glanced at Devlin who was grinning wildly. "I'd be happy to keep her, if you don't want her," Corey said in a serious tone.

Easton planned to tell them to go ahead; they could have her. That was fine with him. But the words that came out of his mouth shocked him. "Like hell you will."

He really didn't understand what he said until the plane erupted in laughter.

CHAPTER 14

S HE'D BARELY SLEPT. Surely she'd only closed her eyes for five—maybe ten—minutes. She preferred to sleep sprawled on her bed on her belly, arms and legs akimbo, but today she was uncomfortable as hell. She stretched an arm to reclaim some space and hit something solid. She mumbled and tried to roll over. But she couldn't move.

Arms tightened around her back and chest. She was shifted and flipped, as if in somebody's arms.

Her eyes flew open. She bolted upright, banging into Easton's chin. She stared around the plane as memories came sliding back. She tried to get up and run, but his arms clamped like steel bands around her.

"You're fine. Take it easy. Just relax."

She took a shuddering breath and turned to face him. "Did you get him? Did you get the shooter?" she demanded.

He shook his head. "I don't know. I haven't had an update. You're on the plane, and you're safe."

"But you're not," she snapped, trying to get out of his arms. "Don't you realize, if the shooter comes after me, he'll find you? We need to take off now," she cried.

His arms tightened around her, slamming her tight against his chest again. "Good," he growled. "Then he'll actually have to face a man for a change. And I don't go down easy."

She stared at him, her brain still grasping the new circumstances around her.

He gave her a small shake. "You are not alone. And, if he tries to get you again, he'll come up against something he hadn't planned on."

She studied him, as if deciding she believed him, then sagged against him in relief. "Thank God. But I really don't want you to get hurt."

"And I won't. We have a lot of men out looking for the sniper right now."

"Good. I would really like to go home now."

"By the time you arrive, it'll be late."

"I don't care," she snapped. "I want an end to this."

He nodded and settled back. "Get buckled in because you are leaving soon."

Eagerly she hopped off his lap and took the seat next to him. She buckled up and relaxed, closing her eyes again. "I had no idea I was so tired."

"It's the shock. Many people react to it that way."

"If you say so," she murmured, yawning. She quickly covered her mouth with her hand. "Sorry."

"I never understood why people apologize for a yawn," he said.

"I guess it's for opening your mouth so everyone can see inside."

He shrugged. "Why? It's not like you can avoid yawning."

She yawned again and laughed. "No, I sure can't."

An odd sharp whistle sounded outside. Easton bolted to his feet, raced to the side of the plane and peered out. He slapped against the side wall and then raced to check what he could see from another window near the entrance to the plane.

She realized she wasn't out of danger yet. She unbuckled her seat belt, ready to find a hiding place, but, as before, there sure as hell wasn't much selection here.

She stood behind Easton, figuring that to be the best place for her. He turned and glared at her, pointing at the seat on the far side. She shook her head, not saying a word.

Another whistle came from outside, but it was a different tone. He relaxed slightly.

Devlin came up the stairs, a hard look on his face. "Someone sighted the sniper on the other side of the woods. They have search teams out now. The pilot is getting ready to fly us out."

"Good," Easton said. "Let's get her home. Enough people are here to go after the asshole."

"You're not kidding."

She froze. "What do you mean, fly *us* out?"

He turned to look at her but stayed silent.

She shook her head. "No way you're coming home with me."

In a dead, flat voice, without expression on his face, he said, "You said it was okay for me to visit, to spend some time with you." He raised an eyebrow ever-so-slightly. "What's the matter? You scared?"

She fisted her hands on her hips and glared at him. "Oh, no you don't. You're not sidetracking me right now. You're not coming for a visit. You're coming as a bodyguard."

"The bottom line is, I'm coming. Whatever role you choose to assign as the reason behind my trip has nothing to do with what I'm doing."

She glared at him and turned to Devlin. "You're coming too?"

"I'm always happy to return home," he said sincerely.

"That's because you'll be with your lady friend."

Devlin's grin flashed. "I'm always happy to go to Bristol. But she'll be so involved in her work, she might not have noticed I even left."

Summer snickered. "I doubt that."

"Besides, home is my favorite place to be," Devlin added.

She glared at him. "What about the other two? You can't just leave them here to get into trouble."

Just then Ryder and Corey stomped into the plane. Two more after them. The last two headed to the cockpit. She watched as Ryder and Corey secured the doors.

Easton walked her back to where she'd been sitting and pushed her into the seat and then buckled her in.

She glared at Easton. "See? Once again you take care of me."

"Once again you need taking care of."

"I'm not a helpless female."

"Nope, but you are forgetful, sometimes absentminded."

She frowned, thinking about that and gave a decisive nod. "Okay, you might have me there."

He took a seat beside her and buckled up. "We'll be in the air in a few minutes."

From the window, she could see several vehicles full of military men spreading out around the plane. They must have been worried somebody would make another attempt.

"It makes no sense he would still be trying to get me. As far as I'm concerned, you guys can have all those photos. And if we make a public announcement throughout the camp, letting everyone else know, maybe they'll stop coming after me." She groaned. "You guys have way too much drama in your world."

The two men exchanged a glance, turned and looked at her, and Easton said, "How did this become about our lives? *Your* life is full of drama."

She shook her head. "That's not my fault. That's your fault."

Easton's jaw dropped. "Our fault?"

She gave him an innocent look. "Of course. My world was completely normal until you arrived."

He shook his head and turned to sit forward. "You're not making sense."

"Nope," she said. "I'm creative."

He snorted. "That's the truth."

She snickered.

Easton groaned. "How about you just go back to sleep? There must be an off button to you somewhere."

She shot him a wicked look. "You could kiss me. For the fourth time. That might do it." At the sudden silence, she turned and glanced at the others. "Guess not, huh?"

They all stared at her in complete fascination.

She shrugged. "Okay, so he brings out the worst in me. That's all I can say."

"How about you don't say anything," Easton said quietly. "You've caused enough trouble already."

"I haven't caused any trouble," she cried out.

He shot her a hard look.

She crossed her arms over her chest. "Okay, I won't speak to you for the rest of the flight."

He snorted. "You won't be able to keep quiet for one minute."

"I can. Well, maybe not the whole flight but at least for an hour."

"Can't. See? You already failed."

She glared at him, turned, dropped her head against the back of the headrest and closed her eyes. She could do it. It might kill her, but she could do it.

"THAT'S ENOUGH OUT of the rest of you too."

Corey chuckled. "This is fascinating, considering your image of the perfect woman. Summer certainly has a lot of interesting aspects to her that I hadn't quite seen before."

Easton watched her stiffen beside him. But her lips pressed tight together. She was bound and determined to not speak. For some contrary reason, he wouldn't let her keep that promise. "She does, but she also has some very perverse characteristics."

Ryder chuckled. "And you love it. Admit it."

"Hell no."

At that he glared at his friends, and, unconsciously imitating her, he crossed his arms, leaned back and closed his eyes. He'd be damned if he would go through all this shit with his buddies watching.

Forty minutes later they landed in Toronto, only to find their flight plans had been changed. She was booked on a commercial flight from Seattle to San Diego. Quietly knowing they had to go one step at a time to get her home, he hooked his arm with hers as he led her through customs and to the adjoining gate to catch their connecting flight.

Through it all, she answered only questions the official asked her; she never said another word to him.

By the time they made it to the boarding gate, he started to miss their banter. "You don't have to keep silent, you know."

No response.

He shrugged. Well, he had tried. He was handed the boarding passes, and he led her through the door, down the tunnel, to the plane and found their seats. He knew the men would follow behind them, and they'd be scattered throughout the plane. He got her settled, tossed their bags up top and sat down beside her. He gave her the window seat.

She buckled up, leaned back, closed her eyes, and that was it.

He groaned. "Really?"

No answer.

He opened his mouth and said the words, surprising them both. "I'm sorry." He froze. He didn't know the last time he'd apologized to anybody. Still, he had really angered her into this, so it was only fair that he apologize.

She leaned forward so she could see him and then grinned. "Gotcha."

He turned and looked at her, a frown on his face. "What?"

"I had to make up for the minutes when I was questioned at customs. But other than that, one hour." She held up a watch so he could see. "And you bet me."

"We weren't betting for any prize."

"Nope, so I get to choose that."

He stared at her in surprise, but laughter bubbled up inside. "You can't just create new rules as you go through the game," he protested.

She shot him a cheeky look. "But, if I don't ask, who's to know I'll get anything?"

He sighed. "What do you want?"

She leaned forward and said, her voice soft and gentle, "A kiss."

He reared back in surprise.

She snickered. "You don't have the guts."

The words were barely out of her mouth before his lips slanted down over hers. But was that kiss meant to be short and sweet, or was that kiss meant to teach her a lesson?

It failed on both counts. Instead, heat spread through his veins and flashed up to his lips as she wrapped her arms around his neck and held him close.

The laughter going on around them had her pulling back first. She snuggled up against his chest and buried her face, hiding. "Don't look now," she said, "but people are laughing at us."

"Don't look now," he whispered, "but they've been laughing at us since we first met."

She chuckled. "Not my fault. You're so cute."

He sighed and wrapped an arm around her shoulder, tucking her close. "What am I going to do with you?"

She opened her mouth to say something naughty, but his finger slammed down over her lips as if reading her mind.

"Not in public, sweetie."

At the endearment, her heart swelled happily. And she snuggled in closer. "Plane seats are not the most comfortable for two, are they?"

"Especially not commercial flights."

"Oh, well," she said, settling back into her own seat. "We're not far from my place."

What was he supposed to make of that comment? He knew what the hell he wanted to make of it. Besides, he wanted her back in his arms, and he wanted her in his arms now. He couldn't believe he'd just kissed her like that in public. He knew the guys were having a field day with this. They were probably texting the rest of the unit, but there was no help for him. He'd met a sprite who had bounced into his heart and was in the process of bouncing around inside his rib cage, making herself right at home.

He just didn't get it. If this was fate's idea of a slap up the side of his head, she couldn't have been any more opposite to what he thought he needed. He couldn't see that this was a good thing. But he was pretty sure he was past the point of even understanding he had a choice.

He had always been very reserved, never one to push a relationship faster than it needed to go, and he'd lost several because of it. He'd loved deeply once, and, after losing that, it took him a long time to open up his heart. Summer didn't appear to have any problem with ripping open a window for herself and jumping inside. It was his response he didn't understand. He was normally the kind of person who would not let that happen. But, with her, it seemed like he had no control, like he had no wish to even change it. As if he were already under her spell.

And how the hell could that be? What could he do about it?

Was it already too late to do anything?

CHAPTER 15

B Y THE TIME she unlocked her front door and stepped inside, she was so tired and so damn happy to be home. She dropped all her bags, kicked off her shoes, tossed her coat on top of them, walked into her living room and collapsed on the couch. Easton, Corey, Devlin and Ryder stood in the small space, and she called out, "It's not much, but it's home."

Instantly a huge Siamese cat waddled toward her. "Hey, Baby," Summer cooed and picked up the obviously pregnant mother and cuddled her close.

"My place is not much bigger," Easton said. "But it doesn't have any animals."

She chuckled. "One day I hope to have a big house and fill it with kids and spend my days photographing every moment, every mood they have. In the meantime I have cats."

"Do you have somebody with a lot of money who'll pay for that?" Easton bent down to stroke the back of a small ginger-colored cat.

"That's Tammy you're stroking." Summer put Tammy on the couch, adding, "Maybe I'll make it big one day. I'm allowed to dream, aren't I?"

He leaned against the living room wall and nodded. "You're allowed to dream. And, speaking of, are you going to bed?" Then to the others he said, "Who's sleeping on the couch?"

She glanced at the others. "I only have one bedroom. You guys are welcome to sleep on the floor."

Devlin shook his head, a black cat in his arms obviously enjoying the under-the-chin scratch it was receiving.

Summer smiled. They were all good men.

"We're dropping Easton here with you. We're heading back to the base."

Midnight was now lying in Ryder's arms. She walked straight up to Devlin, threw her arms around him and gave him a big hug. He hugged her back. She stepped up to Ryder, then Corey, repeating the motions. Backing up several paces, she said, "Thank you so much for looking after me and Easton."

"They looked after you. They weren't looking after me," Easton said with a sigh.

She shot him a bright grin. "But, if you get into trouble, they would help you, right?"

He nodded. "Yes, of course they would." He opened his mouth and then thought better of it. He shook his head and muttered, "Damn."

"Have fun," Corey said with a bright grin, heading toward the door.

Easton glared at them.

She patted his arm and said, "He'll be much better in the morning. He gets cranky when he's tired."

The men laughed out loud.

Devlin nodded. "It's good you know him so well, because he does get cranky when he's tired."

"Or maybe I'm just hungry," Easton said in exasperation. "None of us got to eat much today, remember?"

She turned to look at him. "I was gone for days. I don't have food in the house. My neighbor looks after my cats for me when I'm gone. I'll let her know I'm back in the morning."

He nodded in resignation. "I guess it's pizza?"

"Pepperoni with anchovies," she cried out, walking toward her bedroom. She wanted a shower and now.

"Hell no."

She turned and glared at him. "You won't know until you try it."

The other guys hovered by the door, watching the new couple interact.

"I like my pepperoni plain."

"You like your life plain. You like your women plain. You like your pizza plain. Well, guess what? I'm not eating my pizza plain, and I'm about to make your life anything but plain."

With barely controlled mirth, Devlin said, "We'll see you in the morning." And he closed the door on the two of them.

Easton glared at her. "Are you always this public?"

She looked at him in surprise. "Am I being public?"

He shrugged and said uncomfortably, "I usually don't show how I feel."

"They're your friends. They already know how you feel."

She walked to a kitchen drawer, pulled out menu with a pizza store number from around the corner and said, "These guys have awesome pizzas and deliver."

He snatched the menu from her hand as if eager to have something else to look at. "Would one be enough?"

She stopped, looked at him—as if to say, *Duh?*—and shook her head. "Two."

He nodded with satisfaction. "Two it is."

With a laugh, she walked into her bedroom and headed for the shower. It had been a crappy day, but it was almost over, and she couldn't wait for tonight. Easton didn't have a clue what was coming, but she did. And she wanted nothing more right now than to sleep in his arms. This time in a bed.

EASTON LEANED AGAINST the bedroom doorway, studying her room. Like her, it was a bit chaotic, a study of contrasts. Fluffy white curtains hung from her bedroom window almost to the floor, but her bed was covered with a duvet in a rich deep chocolate color on what had to be a king-size bed. Not only was she a romantic, but she liked her comfort. She couldn't possibly take up more than sixteen inches of that bed.

For the first time, he wondered if she had been in a recent relationship. Had a man lived here with her? Was Easton presuming when he shouldn't be? Just because women teased, made it sound like it was an invitation, didn't mean it always was. But, for the life of him, he didn't think that was the case here. No way could he have mistaken her words, her actions or the sparkle in her eyes whenever she looked at him.

He heard the water in her shower stop.

Her voice called out from behind the bathroom door. "If you're standing there staring in my room, you might as well come in and take a shower."

He straightened. "How can you know what I'm doing?"

"Because the bathroom door is open, and I can see you in the mirror." She laughed. "I was kind of hoping you'd hop in anyway but too early for you, huh?"

He sucked in his breath. So not a good idea with her still in danger. Then the thought disappeared and was at her bathroom doorway in an instant. "And I was kind of half hoping I could too," he said, "But I figured we weren't there yet."

She opened the shower door, reached for a towel at the side.

He could see her creamy flesh as she slid the shower door open a little farther and popped her face out. He smiled. "You look like a drowned rat."

She batted her eyelashes at him. "How sexy is that?"

"Incredibly sexy."

He shook his head, leaned forward and kissed her. Not hard but not light, a promising kiss. He still wasn't sure what the hell was going on here. He knew what he wanted, but it was so damn fast. He was a steady kind of guy. He wanted to take his time.

When her arms clasped behind his neck and yanked him forward into the shower, he figured he'd been moving a little too slowly for her liking. He wrapped her up, her nude body slick and hot as warm steam rose around them. Blood burned and boiled as her hands busied themselves undoing the buttons on his shirt, pulling the shirttail from his jeans and undoing his belt buckle, seemingly all at once.

He grabbed her roaming fingers and pulled them back, but she wouldn't have anything to do with it. She let her arms slip out of his grasp to reach up around his neck with his shirt open. She pressed her bare plump breasts against his hot skin, sliding slick skin against hot skin.

And he was lost. His hands slid down, unable to do anything but caress the warm silky skin, the lush curves as he devoured her hot mouth with a sizzling kiss. She pressed herself against him, one hand sliding to the opening of his jeans. He gave a strangled yell and found himself pinned against the shower door, her hands frantic as they opened the zipper of his jeans and one hand slid inside. He sucked in his breath, pulled his head back and groaned, the sound echoing in the small bathroom.

"You have way too many clothes on," she whispered as she found him. She dropped a kiss on his nipples, then gently scraped her teeth across the tender skin. Her other hand stroked his shoulder, trying to pull the shirt off his back. He shook his head. "Let me get the clothes off."

But his hips had a mind of their own, lifting into her hand. She stroked his length with her thumb, caressing the tip of his erection.

But it wasn't enough. This would never be enough. He finally managed to get the soaking-wet shirt off his back, his hands dropping his jeans to the shower floor. He kicked them into the corner, only to have her hands now inside his jockey shorts, pulling them right to the floor. Only she went with them exploring the path of skin that was suddenly available.

He could barely see with the shower water falling between them and more steam forming, but it was one of the most erotic experiences he had ever had. Her tongue, her lips, her body sliding, slipping wet skin to wet skin, and her damn hands that just wouldn't quit stroking, seeking, exploring. He wanted to do the same, but he was rooted to the spot. Afraid to do too much and interrupt the magic of this experience.

She nudged him back to lean against the hard shower wall, then wrapped her arms around his neck and tugged him down, kissing him with a hunger that surprised him.

And then she slid one leg over his hips as if crawling up his frame.

He groaned, lifted her higher, spun and pinned her against the shower wall. He growled, "Now it's my turn."

Positioned just as he was, he could tease the heart of her without giving her any satisfaction until he was damn good and ready. Seeing she had done nothing but evoke a frantic heat in him, he could do no less for her. With her pinned, yet struggling to place herself where she wanted to be, crying out, he lowered his head and took one plump nipple into his mouth and suckled hard.

She plunged her hips up and down, still crying out for him, but he wouldn't let her take him in. Not yet. His mouth went from one secret place to the next, caressing, suckling, biting, nipping. "Jesus, woman, you're going to kill me."

She groaned. "You're killing me. I want you inside me now," she demanded.

"I don't want this over too fast," he whispered, trailing kisses up her neck, across her chin, breathing deep against her ear, feeling her body melt deeper into his arms. Lowering his hands along her back to her cheeks, he shifted her position and drove deep inside.

She cried out and wiggled against his hips, her body rocking in place, as if trying, searching, reaching for the satisfaction she knew he could give her. Wondering at the wild woman in his arms, he drove inside her again and again, his lips suckling her lower lip, plunging his tongue deep in her mouth, caressing, squeezing as he drove deeper, longer, harder.

She wrapped her arms around him tightly and kissed him back, giving him ounce for ounce more pleasure than he thought he could handle. And still it wasn't enough. She wrapped her thighs tight around him and ground herself against his hips. Pelvis to pelvis they were melded together as one.

He stroked between her cheeks, caressing the soft skin. She shuddered and reared back. He lowered his head and suckled at her neck and her collarbone, pushing her higher and higher against him.

She kissed his bottom lip and sucked hard. At the same time, her inner muscles clamped and released, clamped and released, and he thought he'd died and gone to heaven. He gripped her hard and slammed into her again and again and again. She urged him on with her cries until finally she screamed his name and shattered all over him.

With one last ounce of strength he drove once more and exploded inside. His last pleading thought was where the hell had this woman come from? And how the hell did he keep her?

WELL OVER AN hour later she lifted her head off her damp bedding and smiled at him. His arms were thrown across his forehead, his heart just starting to calm as his breathing slowed. She leaned over and kissed his chin gently. He dropped his arm to wrap around her, pulling her close. Against her ear he whispered, "Where have you been all my life?"

She snuggled in closer and replied, "Waiting for you to show up. How silly that we had to go to Canada first to meet."

She loved the low rumble as his chuckle worked its way out of his chest. Such a lovely sound. She laid her head against his shoulder and smiled. "Now, if all that shit around us wasn't happening, this would be perfect."

He squeezed her gently. "It's perfect regardless."

She grinned. "Okay, I'll give you that. I still would like to know they caught the asshole up north."

"We'll get an update when there's one to give."

"You're more trusting than I am."

"Nope," he said casually. "But I have a long reach, and I'll get some information soon."

She nodded. "I'm so tired, but, at the same time, my mind is spinning."

"That's lack of food."

"Did you ever order that pizza?" She pushed herself upright and stared into his face. When she realized he hadn't yet, she groaned. "We'll die of starvation. You know that, don't you?"

He grinned, his gaze lowering to the lush breasts against his chest. "I can't think of a better way to die."

She spun, swatted his hand as it slid down to her cheek. "Oh, no you don't. Get up and order pizza. I'll get some clothes on, then I should take care of my camera equipment. Considering the problems I've had, I'd like to go through my gear to make sure it's all here and that all my photos have been sent to cloud storage."

"All that before bed?"

She nodded. "It won't take long. By the time we're eating our pizza, I should have it all done." She bent down and gave him a long, slow kiss. "Besides, I'll need the energy before I go to bed."

He raised one eyebrow. "You need energy to sleep?" But his voice was teasing and warm.

She chuckled and slid off the side of the bed, her hands stroking down Easton's massive chest to his flat hips, sliding across the inside of his thigh, teasing gently through his curly hair as she worked her way to an upright position.

Instantly his body responded.

"You might not need energy," she said wryly, "but I got that blood sugar issue, remember?"

"Absolutely I remember." He hopped off the bed beside her and walked into the bathroom. "You realize you completely soaked all my clothes."

"You're the idiot who got into the running shower fully dressed," she called back.

She walked to her dresser and pulled out a pair of yoga

pants and a camisole. She didn't want to get dressed in anything more confining than that at this point. Besides she was hoping to be in bed right after they'd eaten. She intended to make the most of every minute she had with him. And all that time she would let him know where he belonged— with her.

She pulled her hair into a braid that draped around her shoulder and reached for a band. Secured, she took one look at him standing there, holding his soaked clothes, and the look of dismay on his face. She burst out laughing.

"I'll put them in the dryer," she said. "Or do you want them washed first?"

She pointed to the laundry utilities inside the closet, and he stuffed his clothes into the washing machine and turned it on. Still nude, he grabbed his bag from the front of the hall, carried it into the bedroom, where he pulled out fresh clothing.

As soon as he put on jockey shorts, she sighed sadly, turned and said, "I'll be set up in the kitchen."

In the living room, she went to her bags. Moving the one packed with clothing into her bedroom, she grabbed her camera gear and took it to the kitchen.

She scrounged in the cupboard to see if she had a bottle of wine. Finding one on the top shelf, she pulled it out in case he wanted some. She thought about coffee, but it was pretty late, and she didn't want anything to keep her up. Then she realized, by staying awake, she could enjoy him more. She put on coffee.

He wandered into the kitchen, looking at all her gear. "Wow. There's a lot of stuff here." He picked up a camera, looking through the viewfinder. "I didn't see these before."

"Nope. You wouldn't have. I keep them in the bag. It's

mostly lenses. I have one main SLR camera and a couple snap-and-shoots just for when the occasion demands a quick response. That's my old favorite in the bag, but it's not in the same shape anymore, not anything like the others. Once I upgrade to a new one, it's hard to let go of an old friend, so I just pack it with me anyway." She grinned at the look on his face. "They're friends. You don't just let friends go."

A look of understanding whispered across his face, and he smiled at her gently. "I'm sure you have other friends."

"Of course I do."

He reached inside and pulled out a film case. "Surely you are not still using these?"

She chuckled. "No, not at all. That went out years ago."

He popped open the lid and pulled out a USB key, holding it up. "What's this for?"

She turned after pulling two cups from the cupboard. "That's not mine."

He froze. "Are you sure?"

She put the cups on the counter, walked over and picked up the USB, turned it around and looked toward the film case. "I have one like this, but I keep batteries in it." She placed the USB key on the table and dove into her bag. Sure enough, on the bottom, she found another film case, the same as the one he'd dug out. She popped off the top and showed him the batteries she always kept as spares. "This one's mine. I don't know about that one."

The two of them stared at each other, then Easton said, "I'll grab my laptop, and we'll see what this is."

She stared at the duplicate film case, wondering when she could have picked it up. When he returned with the laptop, he turned it on, waiting for it to boot up.

"You know, when I first arrived on base, the pilot escorted me into one of the offices with all the military's computer equipment. As per Canada's standard security check protocol, I took out the equipment I brought with me. To make sure there was no problem with any of the gear I use and to claim it as all my equipment," she said quietly. "But a lot of equipment was already on the table. When I put everything down, it's possible that, when I collected it all again, I thought that second film case was mine and put it into the bag."

"And it's quite possible that everybody who's been after you has actually been after this." He held it up in front of her, popped it into his laptop. But it was password protected. "I have a solution for that."

She watched as he clicked away on his keyboard, then a program opened and raced through password combinations. "You're trying to break the password?"

"I *will* break the password," he said with a smile. "The question is, just how long will it take? Do you remember what was in that room or who was in that room when you took out your gear?"

She shook her head. "No, because I had just arrived. I was tired from all the traveling. I was excited to be there and wasn't thinking about who else was around. When I picked up one of my cameras, I did take a couple photos, just randomly clicking, and somebody yelled at me. But I told him how I was just adjusting my camera and stuffed it away again. I wasn't taking actual photos as they wouldn't be any good."

He looked at her. "Can you find them? Maybe we'll see something of interest on those earliest photos."

She nodded and sat down to go through her cameras. She loved the snap-and-point cameras. She picked up the first one, not knowing which one she had accidentally taken those initial pictures with. But getting back by date, she swiped through several of the photos, clicking until she found the right time frame.

Easton picked up his phone. "Hey, Devlin. We got two interesting developments here."

She listened to him explain what they'd just found and how Easton was running a password detection packet on the USB key.

"I'm on my way over," Devlin said. "Did you guys ever order that pizza?"

Easton chuckled. "Two large pizzas are on the way."

"Awesome. I'll be there in a few minutes."

He placed his phone on the table beside him. "Devlin's coming over. He wants to see what's on the USB key too."

"HOW LONG WILL it take to crack the password?" she asked, standing at his side.

The warm scent of her propelled his thoughts right back to the bedroom. "Hopefully not long."

She placed two cups of coffee on the table beside them as the doorbell rang. They walked to the door and paid the pizza delivery driver.

In the kitchen, they grabbed pieces of the hot food and ate as the program worked. An hour into the search, the program stopped, giving a check mark of success. Easton quickly opened the program to see several folders. Clicking the first folder, he opened it and saw all kinds of diagrams. Not only the design of the water system the Canadian military had but also a list of all the names of those attending the camp. "Interesting." He leaned in to study the plans.

"That looks very similar. Similar but not the same. This is the next-generation water system development. *Very* interesting." He quickly scrolled down farther to find blueprints and yet another list of names and ranks. And what appeared to be contact information. He stared at the last part, seeing many international addresses. This part was seriously bad news.

"How did they get this?" She studied the information. "This is espionage stuff."

He nodded. "When you grabbed this other film case, the owner was in that room at the same time you were." He turned to look at her. "Did you find any of the photos you were looking for?"

"Not yet. I'll check further when I'm done eating."

"Good. Maybe we'll finally catch a break."

Easton went to the other folders, realized this information was too important to keep. He sent Mason a quick text and copied the material to his own personal cyberspace storage. Mason responded while he removed the key from the laptop. Unfortunately Tesla hadn't found any useable information in the images Easton had sent. Figures. They had to catch a break somewhere. Someone had been stealing information from the Canadians and the American military. He didn't want to admit it, but, chances were, it was one of his own countrymen.

"I think I might've found something." She frowned and leaned closer. "It should be one of these."

He waited for her to explain when the doorbell rang. "That will be Devlin."

He hopped up and walked to the front door, checked through the peephole and saw Devlin, then unlocked the door. Devlin stumbled inside as if pushed. Easton went to slam the door closed, but he was too late. The gunman was already inside.

Dressed all in black, the long lean male was impossible to identify as his outfit included a black mask.

"Sorry, Easton. He caught me as I exited the car," Devlin snapped in a hard voice, glaring at the gunman.

Easton nodded. "No problem. We were just figuring out who this is. About time we got to the bottom of this mess."

The gunman snorted. "You have no fucking clue who I am."

Just then from the kitchen he heard Summer call out, "Found it." And then she gasped again. "Oh, my God, I know this man. We all know this man."

The gunman motioned at the two men to walk into the kitchen. "Join her."

Easton and Devlin exchanged glances, but both turned obediently and walked into the kitchen.

Summer smiled at Devlin. "I found it." She held the camera up to show him. "See?"

He didn't need to see the image she had in her hand—he'd already recognized the voice of the gunman. He nodded at Summer and said gently, "Yeah, it's the pilot."

SUMMER STARED AT the man standing behind Devlin and Easton. She couldn't believe the asshole was the same man she'd seen off and on throughout the days she'd been up there, even since he'd led her to the office where she'd unloaded her gear in the first place.

She stared at the pilot. "Is that really you, Robbie?"

"Don't use my name," he roared.

She frowned and stood from the table. "Why wouldn't I? It is your name. But what the hell are you doing? Are you involved in this?" She shook her head and approached. "That's really not very smart. No good can come from this, you know," she added gently.

He waved the gun at her. "Stay back."

She stopped, frowning at him. "You're not afraid of me, are you?"

He snorted. "Hell no. But I don't trust these two with you."

"That's probably a good idea." She gave him a bright smile. "They are pretty sneaky men."

Easton slid her a sideways glance. She hooked her arm through his. "You know, you can walk away from all this, right?"

"Like hell, bitch."

She frowned at him. "There is no point in getting nasty."

She motioned to the computer on the table. "I presume you're after that USB key." She watched as his gaze darted to the table and then back at her again.

"You can't get into it so no point in trying," he said as he motioned at the laptop. "Get me the key."

She shrugged, walked over, ejected it. "Here it is."

He snatched the USB key from her hand and shoved it into his pants pocket. "Finally," he snarled. "You've been a pain in the ass since you picked that up."

"What do you mean, I picked it up? It was an accident."

"I know that now, but, at the time, when you did it so casually, I figured you were the drop. I was supposed to hand it off to somebody, and I didn't know when, until the next day, after I was told where the drop would happen and realized you'd snagged that thing for yourself."

Her jaw dropped. "You thought I was part of this?" She looked at him in horror. "I would never do such a thing."

"At the time I wondered. It seemed like a masterful plan." He shook his head. "Imagine my shock when I found out how wrong I was."

She glared at him. "Did you have to shoot the driver?"

"It was supposed to be you."

"Oh, that's why they couldn't find the sniper," she cried out. "Because they thought he headed back to camp to disappear into all the people, but instead you were on the plane. You just had to sneak back to where you belonged." She glowered at him. "But really, shooting the driver is unforgivable. And shooting at me too. I had a really bad headache for the rest of the day." Instinctively she reached up to check her head, but, as she'd barely noticed it all day, she presumed it had healed just fine.

He glared at her. "After all this, it won't make any difference."

"You really think anybody can pay you enough to run for the rest your life? Always looking over your shoulder?" She shook her head. "You're not thinking straight."

"You don't know anything about it, and it's none of your goddamn business."

"What?" she cried out. "None of my business? After all you put me through?"

"That wasn't me. That was Harry."

"Well, he's dead, so he isn't talking anymore." She stared at the pilot, her mind thinking about the chain of events. "One of the guards killed Harry, right? And you were the sniper both times. Instead of making your way back to camp you returned to the airfield. What about the heavy breather and the damn snake? Henry again? Is that why he was killed?"

"Yes. Failure was not an option. He died because he failed."

"That's why you're so desperate to make sure you don't fail, because you will be next on the chopping block."

He nodded. "Once I deliver this to him, I'm off the hook, and I'm out of here."

"There is nothing important on that thing," she snapped. Beside her she felt Easton stiffen, and she realized she probably shouldn't have said anything about it.

The gunman stared at her. "You don't have a clue what's on this."

She shrugged. "No, but I can guess. Somehow it must have something to do with the water program the Canadians are working on. It's hardly important stuff."

It was almost funny to see Robbie relax his shoulders,

calming down right away. "You don't know anything about it."

She slipped closer in front of Easton. She wasn't quite within range, but somebody had to make a move soon. Robbie couldn't afford to let any of them live. She'd already identified him.

She snuggled back against Easton's chest, hoping he would put his arms around her. Of course he did. He was that kind of a guy. She could feel the tense muscles against her back, his grip on her arms. Chances were he really wanted to move her out of the way so he could jump Robbie. But she wasn't having anything to do with that. As soon as his arms came around her, she grabbed him by the wrists and lifted herself ever-so-slightly. She placed one foot on his foot, and, while the gunman looked around, figuring out his next move, she whipped out a leg and kicked Robbie's gun hand. Then, using Easton's arms for support, she twisted, slashed a hard kick to Robbie's head. Her foot connected with his jaw. She landed and cried out, "Goddammit, that hurt."

Devlin was already on Robbie, tackling him to the ground. Easton picked up the gun and emptied the clip, putting the gun on the table. She jumped up and down on the floor, holding her foot. "That was your fault."

"None of this was my fault," Easton said with a sigh. "What the hell were you doing, kicking a gunman in the head with a bare foot?"

"Somebody had to do something."

Devlin chuckled. "Well, I am glad you do what you need to do when you have to."

She glared at him. "Of course you're just trying to be nice."

He laughed. "And you were being very much you."

She looked at him in confusion and shrugged. "That's all I know how to be."

"Exactly," Easton said. He wrapped an arm around her shoulders and tucked her close.

She glanced at the gunman. "Are we done now? Can I get on with the rest of my life? That should be the end of it?"

"Not quite," Devlin said from the floor. He rolled Robbie to his back. "Who is your contact?"

Robbie just glared at him.

Easton walked over, bent toward Robbie and said, "General Morgan by any chance?"

Robbie's gaze widened, and he stared at the group of them. "How did you know?"

Both men pointed at Summer.

She grinned. "I caught him on camera."

Robbie was still swearing when the cops and Mason arrived twenty minutes later. She stared at the distinguished-looking man as he walked into the room. She could sense the leadership in his stance, the sense of absolute control of a situation at a glance. She gave him a winsome smile. "May I take your picture?"

His eyebrows rose, and he studied her as if she were a creature he'd never seen before.

Easton sighed. "Forget about it, Mason. She does this to everyone."

"I want to take pictures of all your friends. You won't let me take pictures of you," she told Easton in a cajoling voice.

Devlin smirked. "I'd give that some serious thought," he said to Easton. "Imagine if she starts taking pictures of Saul and Dakota. Or Ryder and Corey. They're all single."

Easton shot Devlin a hard glance, looked at Summer and

asked, "If I agree, will you leave my friends alone?"

She beamed at him. "Of course," she said. "I can have a lifetime of fun taking pictures of you." She cupped his chin and stroked his cheek. "And I don't care if they're good or bad, I'm keeping every one of them."

Mason said, his voice interested, "Keep the images? Not keeping the man?"

She grinned at him. "I'm going to keep them all. He doesn't have any say in the matter. He might think he does, but he really doesn't."

Devlin chuckled. "Easton, what do you think about that?"

Easton rolled his eyes. "Like I have a choice."

She rounded on him. "You do have a choice, you know. I would never do anything you don't want me to do. If you don't want me to keep you, that's okay."

He stared at her, then laughed. "And how is it okay?"

She smiled. "Well, it's okay for the moment. After all, I'll keep badgering you—until you see it my way and change your mind."

He shook his head and wrapped his arms around her. "This isn't quite over yet. The general must be picked up for questioning. Their fate won't be resolved any time soon."

"That's okay. I trust you," she said. "Whatever you do sounds perfect to me."

He shook his head. "You're perfect."

She chuckled. "Yep. But you love me, so that's perfect too."

He stared at her for a long moment as if the truth just now dawned on him. She watched his gaze widen, the look of shock in his eyes and finally the understanding. She knew he hadn't quite accepted it yet. But she'd known days ago.

She hoped he'd get there soon.

"How did you know?"

She wrinkled her nose at him. "It couldn't be any other way," she said. "Because I love you. And you're a keeper. That means, I'm never letting you go."

He held her close. Just before he kissed her, he whispered, "You better be sure because I won't let anybody else get near you."

She was still chuckling when his lips closed over hers. When she could raise her head again, she smiled at him. "That's all I ever wanted."

EPILOGUE

R YDER LEWIS SETTLED back in his folding chair, beer in hand, and watched as Summer completely won over the large gathering around her in Markus's backyard. Markus was another SEAL and a member of Mason's unit. He and his partner were celebrating the end of some serious renovations on their house and celebrating with all their friends.

Summer didn't seem fazed at all by the crowd.

That she was busy taking photographs of couples didn't hurt.

The laughter was contagious. Even he was smiling. Normally he was not an upbeat personality but lately …

"Hey, you still nursing that same beer?" Corey sprawled in the folding chair next to him. "Personally I'm thinking I might need something harder."

Ryder glanced at him. "Why's that?"

"A little too much lovey-dovey stuff here. I never expected to feel so lost by being alone."

"You brought a girlfriend," Ryder pointed out. "You aren't alone."

"A friend, yes. A girlfriend, no." Corey slid Ryder a sideways look. "No way would I come alone. You're braver than I am."

"Damn, I didn't think of that."

Corey chuckled. "You need to plan ahead. If you had the

sisters I do, you'd come up with that camouflage in an instant."

"Ha, if I had that many sisters, I'd have left town." Ryder shook his head. "I also don't think I know a woman I could have called to step in and help me out in a situation like this."

"Sure you do. What about Caitlyn?"

Ryder's heart hiccupped. "Hell no."

"And why is that?"

Corey's curious tone said he didn't understand anything about Ryder's long history with Caitlyn.

"You took her to prom. You were there for her when she graduated from nursing, … gave her away at her wedding and got her drunk to celebrate her divorce. Dude, that's a major friendship. She'd have been delighted to show up here today."

Ryder shook his head, but he didn't say a word. He couldn't.

"Unless something's changed?" Corey asked, leaning forward suddenly. "As in, you had a fight?"

"No fight," he said, trying to keep his voice neutral, but his voice dropped. He took a deep breath; Corey was no fool.

"If no fight, then it's the opposite."

Silence was Ryder's only response.

"Ah, hell."

More silence followed.

Corey took a deep breath. "Don't tell me. When the two of you got drunk, you slept with her."

Ryder lifted his beer and poured the cool liquid down his throat, anything to shove the hot painful memories to the back. The hurt. The loss.

"And it didn't work out?" Corey pushed cautiously.

"Work out? She got up the next morning and walked away. I haven't heard a word since. It's been fourteen goddamn months. I'd say that fits the definition of *it didn't work out*."

Corey reached into the cooler at his side and pulled out two more beers. He handed one to Ryder. "Sorry, Ryder. Here's to staying single."

The two men clinked cans, and a commotion at the corner of the house caught their attention. Another arrival. The party had already swelled to close to sixty people. What were a few more?

"Isn't that Mac and Quinn?"

"Looks like it." Ryder settled back at the sight of more men he knew. A break in the crowd showed they'd arrived with dates. "Figures. I think I'm the only one who came alone."

"And you might want to prepare yourself. I could be wrong, but I think that's Caitlyn on Mac's arm."

Ryder's heart froze, then shattered. He shoved his beer can into Corey's hand. "Here. I'm done." He got up and walked down the opposite side of the house. He could handle a lot of things in life. But seeing the only woman he'd ever loved with another man—again—was not one of them.

This concludes Books 11–13 of SEALs of Honor.

Read the first Chapter of Ryder: SEALs of Honor, Book 14

SEALS OF HONOR: RYDER
BOOK 14
CHAPTER 1

THE SILENCE WAS deafening.

Ryder shifted his gaze across the deserted buildings on his left. The intel was good. That just made this Iraq mission all the worse. This bomb maker had gone to ground now, pinned inside the dilapidated structure in front of Ryder. He wanted to make sure the bomb maker didn't set booby traps to allow him to escape. The US military wanted him for questioning regarding the two bombs that blew up a stadium in Baghdad. Twenty-two people had died with another seventy-plus severely injured.

Devlin and Easton were on the far side of the building, tracking enemy movement. Corey watched Ryder's back. Another four-man team checked out other buildings. Ryder's headset crackled. "Beta team moving in."

Ryder swept forward, silent and deadly. Nothing in front or to the side. He dropped low and did a fast sweep inside from the doorway. No trip wires. Good.

In sync, Ryder and Corey went through all the ground-level rooms while Easton and Devlin maintained surveillance of the perimeter. Ryder and his partner found ... nothing. Ever aware, Ryder kept moving. This was not the time to drop his guard. Too much at stake.

Gunfire sounded in the distance. *The other SEAL team.* Devlin's voice crackled in Ryder's headset. "Watch your back. Bullies coming up on the outside."

Instantly Ryder and Corey faded into the shadows. If somebody was coming, Ryder wanted to see them first. Anybody who knew the bomb maker was of interest to them. More wild gunfire sounded. Ryder exchanged a look with Corey. Ryder knew exactly what that meant. *The other SEAL team taking more fire.* But they couldn't help. Not just yet. He and Corey had done a full sweep of the downstairs, but they had the rest of the building to check.

"Sweep completed," Easton whispered in Ryder's headpiece. "I'm on the other side of the front entrance. We have company."

Silently Ryder signaled to Corey before slipping around the outside of the building, following the wall toward the front. He peered around the corner. One man stood guard, his back to the entryway. A second man crouched against the front door and placed something on the step. *A bomb.*

Ryder warned the others with the appropriate *click*s of his comm.

Of course it would be a bomb. As a weapon they were so damn unforgiving. Ryder had no way to calculate the devastation this one could bring, and he had no plans to find out. At the single tap on his comm, he lifted his semiautomatic rifle and waited.

From the far side he heard, "Step back away from the bomb. Hands in the air."

The crouched man spun, lifting a rifle.

A single shot clipped the air. Ryder sprang from his hiding spot, his weapon on the man still standing. The other man had collapsed on top of whatever he'd placed on the front step. From his position, Ryder could see the wires connecting to the doorknob. It was crude but effective. The questions of the moment were, did the bomber die with the trigger in his hand and was the bomb ready to go off?

Ryder returned his gaze to the other man. The guard inched backward as he stared at his fallen comrade.

"Everyone take cover," Ryder yelled into his comm before diving to the ground. Seconds later the bomb exploded, sending clay and body parts flying. Ryder rose immediately, his weapon once again on his prisoner who'd been thrown down by the blast.

With Ryder's alpha team now at the designated rendezvous spot, but earlier than expected, Devlin and Easton pushed forward to the far side of the town where the earlier gunfire came from. The beta unit hadn't checked in on the comm. Ryder had to assume they were in trouble, and he wasn't taking any chances. Shoving his weapon into his prisoner's neck while backing him against a wall, Ryder asked, "Where's the bomb maker?"

Black eyes flashed his way as the man stayed silent.

Ryder shrugged. "We'll get the answers one way or another."

He didn't for a moment believe the man who had died in the doorway was the bomb maker. Men like him had a dozen faithful helpers who'd die to protect him. So many young men had died for nothing.

Devlin reported in for him and his partner, Easton. "Alpha team still in search of beta team."

Ryder wanted to leave too but with another mission in mind. He studied the prisoner, wishing for an easy way to get him to talk. But men like this would take a bullet rather that give away their secrets.

Ryder glanced at Corey and said, "Keep him here. I'll be back in five."

Corey protested. But Ryder wanted to check the bomb maker's house. Now that they'd left the bomb maker's building, Ryder wanted to know who had showed up. The bomb blast would have alerted the rebels. Ryder raced back to where the remains of the dead man lay. Ryder kicked open the door, sending a hail of gunfire inside. Cries ripped through the house. He didn't go inside but slipped around to the back and sent a message to Easton and Devlin.

Gunfire shot out from the floor-to-ceiling windows. The men were disorganized. As far as Ryder could tell, only two gunmen were inside. Ryder took a quick look through a broken window, popped off a shot, and one gunman dropped. Now that was more like it. The second gunman stood in front of an older man who cowered behind him. This then was the bomb maker. As soon as Ryder had a shot, he took out the final gunman and stepped through the window, holding his weapon on the bomb maker. "Ahmed Amin?"

Book 14 is available now!
To find out more visit Dale Mayer's website.
https://geni.us/DMryderUniversal

Author's Note

Thank you for reading SEALs of Honor, Books 11–13! If you enjoyed the book, please take a moment and leave a short review.

Dear reader,

I love to hear from readers, and you can contact me at my website: www.dalemayer.com or at my Facebook author page. To be informed of new releases and special offers, sign up for my newsletter or follow me on BookBub. And if you are interested in joining Dale Mayer's Reader Group, here is the Facebook sign up page.
http://geni.us/DaleMayerFBGroup

Cheers,
Dale Mayer

About the Author

Dale Mayer is a *USA Today* best-selling author, best known for her SEALs military romances, her Psychic Visions series, and her Lovely Lethal Garden cozy series. Her contemporary romances are raw and full of passion and emotion (Broken But … Mending, Hathaway House series). Her thrillers will keep you guessing (Kate Morgan, By Death series), and her romantic comedies will keep you giggling (*It's a Dog's Life*, a stand-alone novella; and the Broken Protocols series, starring Charming Marvin, the cat).

Dale honors the stories that come to her—and some of them are crazy, break all the rules and cross multiple genres!

To go with her fiction, she also writes nonfiction in many different fields, with books available on résumé writing, companion gardening, and the US mortgage system. All her books are available in print and ebook format.

Connect with Dale Mayer Online

Dale's Website – www.dalemayer.com
Twitter – @DaleMayer
Facebook Page – geni.us/DaleMayerFBFanPage
Facebook Group – geni.us/DaleMayerFBGroup
BookBub – geni.us/DaleMayerBookbub
Instagram – geni.us/DaleMayerInstagram
Goodreads – geni.us/DaleMayerGoodreads
Newsletter – geni.us/DaleNews

Also by Dale Mayer

Published Adult Books:

Psychic Vision Series

Tuesday's Child

Hide'n Go Seek

Maddy's Floor

Garden of Sorrow

Knock, Knock…

Rare Find

Eyes to the Soul

Now You See Her

Shattered

Into the Abyss

Seeds of Malice

Eye of the Falcon

Psychic Visions Books 1–3

Psychic Visions Books 4–6

Psychic Visions Books 7–9

By Death Series

Touched by Death – Part 1

Touched by Death – Part 2

Touched by Death – Parts 1&2

Haunted by Death

Chilled by Death

By Death Books 1–3

Second Chances...at Love Series

Second Chances – Part 1

Second Chances – Part 2

Second Chances – complete book (Parts 1 & 2)

Charmin Marvin Romantic Comedy Series

Broken Protocols

Broken Protocols 2

Broken Protocols 3

Broken Protocols 3.5

Broken Protocols 1-3

Broken and... Mending

Skin

Scars

Scales (of Justice)

Broken but... Mending 1-3

Glory

Genesis

Tori

Celeste

Glory Trilogy

Biker Blues

Biker Blues: Morgan, Part 1

Biker Blues: Morgan, Part 2

Biker Blues: Morgan, Part 3

Biker Baby Blues: Morgan, Part 4

Biker Blues: Morgan, Full Set

Biker Blues: Salvation, Part 1

Biker Blues: Salvation, Part 2

Biker Blues: Salvation, Part 3

Biker Blues: Salvation, Full Set

SEALs of Honor

Mason: SEALs of Honor, Book 1

Hawk: SEALs of Honor, Book 2

Dane: SEALs of Honor, Book 3

Swede: SEALs of Honor, Book 4

Shadow: SEALs of Honor, Book 5

Cooper: SEALs of Honor, Book 6

Markus: SEALs of Honor, Book 7

Evan: SEALs of Honor, Book 8

Mason's Wish: SEALs of Honor, Book 9

Chase: SEALs of Honor, Book 10

Brett: SEALs of Honor, Book 11

Devlin: SEALs of Honor, Book 12

Easton: SEALs of Honor, Book 13

Ryder: SEALs of Honor, Book 14

Macklin: SEALs of Honor, Book 15

SEALs of Honor, Books 1–3

SEALs of Honor, Books 4–6

SEALs of Honor, Books 7–10

SEALs of Honor, Books 11–13

Heroes for Hire

Levi's Legend: Heroes for Hire, Book 1

Stone's Surrender: Heroes for Hire, Book 2

Merk's Mistake: Heroes for Hire, Book 3

Rhodes's Reward: Heroes for Hire, Book 4

Flynn's Firecracker: Heroes for Hire, Book 5

Logan's Light: Heroes for Hire, Book 6

Harrison's Heart: Heroes for Hire, Book 7

Saul's Sweetheart: Heroes for Hire, Book 8

Dakota's Delight: Heroes for Hire, Book 9

Michael's Mercy: Heroes for Hire, Book 10

Tyson's Treasure: Heroes for Hire, Book 11

Jace's Jewel: Heroes for Hire, Book 12

Heroes for Hire, Books 1–3

Heroes for Hire, Books 4–6

Heroes for Hire, Books 7–9

Collections

Dare to Be You…

Dare to Love…

Dare to be Strong…

RomanceX3

Standalone Novellas

It's a Dog's Life

Riana's Revenge

Published Young Adult Books:

Family Blood Ties Series

Vampire in Denial

Vampire in Distress

Vampire in Design

Vampire in Deceit

Vampire in Defiance

Vampire in Conflict

Vampire in Chaos

Vampire in Crisis

Vampire in Control

Vampire in Charge

Family Blood Ties Set 1–3

Family Blood Ties Set 1–5

Family Blood Ties Set 4–6

Family Blood Ties Set 7–9

Sian's Solution – A Family Blood Ties Short Story

Design series

Dangerous Designs

Deadly Designs

Darkest Designs

Design Series Trilogy

Standalone

In Cassie's Corner

Gem Stone (a Gemma Stone Mystery)

Time Thieves

Published Non-Fiction Books:

Career Essentials

Career Essentials: The Résumé

Career Essentials: The Cover Letter

Career Essentials: The Interview

Career Essentials: 3 in 1